Blood Cove

R.J. Belcourt

Ignatius Fay

Blood Cove is a work of fiction. Characters whose names resemble those of historical figures are used in a strictly fictional sense for entertainment value only and bear no relationship, real or implied, to their historical counterparts.

Belcourt, Ray, 1960-, author, and
Fay, Ignatius, 1950-, author

Blood Cove, RJ Belcourt & Ignatius Fay

ISBN 978-0-9809572-9-7 (pbk.)

Design: Ray Belcourt & Ignatius Fay

Layout by: Ignatius Fay

Published by: Ignatius Fay, PhD and IngramSpark

Copies of this work may be purchased online at any reputable online book seller, such as amazon.com, barnesandnoble.com or chapters.indigo.ca

To Luc Houle (1956–2012), our dear friend,
who brightened our lives with kindness, laughter and adventure

Origins

In the beginning, the Raven flew over the water
After many days, he grew weary, in need of rest
Ahead a large reef jutted from the water
There he chose to perch and regain his strength

A giant clamshell lay out of the water
There on the edge of the reef
Next to the clamshell rested a smaller mussel shell
From it he heard a strange scratching sound

The Raven was suspicious of the mussel shell
Soon he heard faint voices coming from the great clamshell
Curious, he pried it open with his powerful beak

The first of the Haida people huddled inside
They were naked, cold and scared

The Raven said, 'Don't be frightened
If you help me open this mussel shell,
I will take care of you'

The Haida people agreed and climbed upon the mussel shell
They pulled and pulled until finally they forced the shell open

A dark mist rose from the mussel shell
A mist that smelled of death and decay

The Haida people jumped off the open shell
Sadly, one man lost his footing and fell inside
The Raven told the Haida people to go in and rescue the man
But they were afraid and refused

A black form, half man–half winged creature,
Crawled from the slimy mussel shell
Its wings were broad and its teeth long and sharp

Terrified, the Haida hid behind the Raven

The creature was hungry and lusted for Haida blood
But the Raven would not allow the creature near his people

The Raven said, 'I created you, so I will not kill you

Fly west to the horizon, and there you will find food
Never return to hurt my people
If you do, I **will** destroy you.'

The creature, angry, growled and snarled
Still it stretched its wings and flew west over the great water

#
1980

I'm cold, and my neck hurts! Why does he have to lock the door? Nobody comes near this old war camp anyway. The big shot army guys don't let anybody in here. They got Keep Out signs everywhere. He must be somebody special. I miss Chance. I hope Ma remembers to feed him, give him his favorite treats.

Miss White is gonna be so mad at me for missing school. I'm in so much trouble. He promised it'd be okay. He'd talk to her and tell her I had to go out of town for a few weeks on a family trip. I know it's wrong to lie, but he said it was only a white lie. He said it was a secret. Only Ma, Pa and me know about it. A top secret 'speriment to give me super powers. Ma and Pa will be so proud of me. Wonder what super powers I'm gonna get. Maybe I'll shoot fire from my fingers like the Human Torch from Fantastic Four or maybe have razor claws like Wolverine—Awesome!

When he drove up to the school and asked me to get in the car, it was sorta weird. Ma and Pa warned me not to get rides from strangers. He told me Ma said it was okay. Besides, he's not a stranger. He drove me up to Look-Out Point and shared his treats with me. Sour Gummies—how'd he know I like them best? He was real nice. He told me all about the secret mission and why the scientists picked me. They needed someone with my kinda blood, and got good marks in school. I didn't really understand a lot of it. Sounded important, though. He said I couldn't tell anybody or the bosses would be real mad. Said I was lucky they were giving me this chance. Pa always told me if I worked hard something good would come to me one day. Guess he was right. But I didn't think I'd be the only kid here.

Anyway. I been here a long time, and still don't feel any special powers. I just feel sad and tired. I'm tired all the time. I feel icky all over when he gives me the medicine in that 'special way.' The scientists told him he can't use a needle. The metal would make the serum bad and it wouldn't work. I don't care. I don't think I want to get the medicine anymore. It hurts too much and his breath smells real bad.

I hate being alone. It's so quiet. I'm scared! Why can't Ma and Pa come visit? I don't like the way he touches me. It hurts and it's yucky. I want to go home now. I want Chance! I don't like secrets. Ma? Pa? Where are you? I don't believe I'm gonna get super powers. I don't want them anymore, either. I wanna go home!

That noise! The lock?

'You're back! Please, mister, can I go home? Mister? No! Please mister, not again! It hurts! It burns!

Please don't! Please…'

Matt & Jesse
1980

'How many times have I told you to close the goddam window? You sure as shit don't pay the bills around here, do you?'

'Sorry, Dad. It was warm earlier, and I needed some fresh air,' says Matt.

'And that makes it alright, then, does it? I'm going to bed. Don't be waking me up with that damn trashy noise.'

'C'mon, Dad. It ain't trash, it's Hard Rock! Mötley Crüe, AC/DC—they're the best.'

'Bull! It's all crap. They don't make real music any more.' Making a dismissive gesture, he turns toward his bedroom.

Frustrated, Matt runs out of the house, the screen door slapping the frame behind him. 'Have another drink, old man,' he says under his breath. 'Can't wait till I'm old enough to get out of this fucking hell hole!' He heads across the backyard to Jesse's. She is the only other person his age he knows that is allowed up at this hour. They meet at the tree house most evenings after supper, light a candle and share their dreams of a life away from Blood Cove. Their favorite fantasy is that one day they will tour together in a band, traveling from city to city, happy and carefree. And making lots of money!

Climbing the old wooden fence with ease, he drops into the Fairchilds' muddy garden. He slogs through the mud, trying not to step on anything that looks like it was intentionally planted. He leaves a trail of muddy prints in the dew-covered grass as he crosses the lawn. Feet cold and wet, he searches the ground around the old weathered porch for a pebble to toss at Jesse's bedroom window. He finds one just the right size and shape. He must be careful not to break the window. He tosses the pebble and hears the tink as it bounces off the glass. He is about to toss another when the window slides up and Jesse peers out into the night.

'Matt, that you?' she calls softly.

'Jesse, bring a flashlight an' meet me at the tree house.'

'Okay. Be right down.'

Jesse's mother, Big Mama, has treated Matt as if he were her own son ever since the death of his mother twelve years ago. The youngsters quickly became inseparable, and with time, have become the closest of friends. Frank, Matt's father, fell into a depression and began drinking heavily after the death of the woman he considered his soul mate. When he isn't ignoring Matt, he is criticizing him.

Matt exits the yard through the back gate and stumbles along the pathway to the edge of the forest. Amidst a grove of younger cedars stands a giant, at least four times the size of the others. Somehow this one cedar managed to survive the inferno that destroyed the rest of the trees along this valley many years ago. New seedlings eventually grew, surrounding the giant like supplicants at a king's court.

Matt grabs the rope ladder hanging from the majestic old trunk and climbs with practiced ease; opening the latch, he pushes up on the trap door and pulls himself into the tree house. Groping along the shelf just inside the trapdoor, he finds a box of wooden matches, strikes one along the wall, and lights a candle. Candlelight fills the room with a soft golden glow. Matt sits on the floor and slides into a corner leaning back against the weathered wall. He takes a deep breath and closes his eyes.

He has spent many hours over the years, playing, relaxing and crying in this tree house. It has been his sanctuary, his place of refuge from the abuse, neglect and despair that make life at home miserable and, often, overwhelming. Matt built the tree house himself using wooden planks from discarded pallets that the owner of the hardware store allowed him to take free of charge. For weeks he dragged a single wooden skid home every day on the way back from school. He stacked them in the forest just far enough inside the tree line to be out of sight. He had asked his father many times to build the tree house, but his dad had always been too tired from long days working at the mill and long evenings working at getting drunk.

Jesse often helped Matt with the construction and, despite many failed attempts, they eventually completed the project. The tree house was rickety, but sound enough to support the two of them, a table, two chairs and a shelf of their favorite books.

Startled by the sound of the latch opening, Matt snaps out of his thoughts. A second later, the trapdoor swings up, and Jesse climbs in. 'Hey, Matt.'

'Hey, Jesse. Sorry if I woke you up.'

'It's okay. I was just reading.' Jesse crawls over, sits next to Matt, and shoulder checks him so that he rocks a little off balance. 'What's up?'

'The old man—you know.'

'He hit you again?' asks Jesse.

'Naw. I'm just tired of his shit.'

'Yeah, I imagine you would be.'

Matt slides his left arm around Jesse's shoulder. The awkward silence of the next few moments is broken by Matt.

'You know, I envy you a little, not having a father around to make your life hell. Your dad was murdered, right? What happened?'

'Ah, come on. You know what happened. I told you about him a long time ago.'

'Yeah, but I only vaguely remember. I was pretty young. Besides, the way my dad treats me, I was jealous that your father was a good guy. His name was Stanley, right?'

'Yeah. He was born in White Slope on the north end of Graham Island. He was a well-known fisherman in the area. But that's a hard life and he eventually moved to Skidegate to open a fish cannery. He met mom there, they got married pretty quickly.'

'So who murdered him?'

'Dad was a conservationist and an expert on medicinal herbs and plants. He spent a lot of time trying to protect the old growth Red Cedar forest from the forestry companies.'

'Oh, yeah. More of it is coming back to me. He was able to stop them from cutting down the trees, right? How'd he do that?'

'He organized protest groups to block the roads into the logging areas. They'd hammer nails into the trees to break the chainsaw blades of any lumberjack who tried to cut the big trees down.'

'That's pretty clever.'

'Yeah, but after a few lumberjacks were seriously injured from flying nails or pieces flying off the broken chains, things turned ugly; fights broke out and the RCMP had to be called in to stop the violence. Dad didn't want any more workers injured, so he talked the government into agreeing to give the area's aboriginal rights, including control over the land and trees, to the Haida tribes. He also was a respected totem sculptor and used his art to try to spark pride and unity among the Haida. He was surprisingly successful, too, which just made the whites angrier.'

'That's pretty cool. I don't remember you telling me he was a sculptor.'

'Well, I did. Dad became leader of the new council, and after that the lumber companies had to get approval for the number of trees they could cut, and negotiate deals with him before cutting any trees down. They were pissed. Mom says that's when he started to get harassed by the lumberjacks traveling through town. Many threatened to kill him.'

'Holy shit! That's right. You said he died in a fire.'

'His workshop burned down. The police said it was done on purpose.'

'Did they catch the guy who set the fire?'

'They found the body of a lumberjack nearby, his head crushed and mangled. Many people assumed that he was the arsonist.'

'Who killed him?'

'Mom never told me. She said it wasn't important for me to know the details.'

'Why do parents always say things like that when they don't want to tell you something? Anyhow, were they able to pin it on the dead lumberjack?'

'They could never prove that the lumberjack killed my dad, but mom says it was karma. I was born later that year, so she named me after my dad.'

'Wait a minute! You said his name was Stanley.'

'My father's middle name was Jesse.'

'Aww! That explains Jesse with an 'e'!'

'Yes. It was also my grandfather's first name. Mom didn't bother spelling my name any different. I like it just the way it is!'

'Me, too,' says Matt with a smile. 'So. You still coming with me to Vancouver next summer? You know, like we talked about? We need to get out of this shit hole. With your sweet vocals and my new guitar licks, we can make enough money to take a bus to L.A. an' make it big.'

'You're a nut bar,' replies Jesse with a laugh. 'But yeah, I'm in. Vancouver, Los Angeles—wow! Mom will be worried to death. I hope she doesn't get too awful mad at me.'

'You can leave her a note explaining everything and call her when we get to Vancouver. She'll get over it,' says Matt. 'Besides, once we cut our first album, you'll have enough cash to buy her a big house in Victoria, overlooking the ocean. Your mom'll be thrilled.'

'That'll be so freakin' awesome,' exclaims Jesse. 'I guess she'll have to forgive me for leaving, once she sees her new mansion. Hey, did you hear about Donni?'

'Yeah. I saw the RCMP in town with dogs, searching the beach,' says Matt soberly.

'D'ya think somebody kidnapped him?' asks Jesse.

'I don't think so. Not for ransom, anyway. His parents have no money to pay a ransom. Some pervert, maybe. You know, like you hear about on the news in Vancouver.'

'Sickos,' agrees Jesse.

'I heard a story on the news just last week,' Matt offers. 'A perv dragged a girl off the trail in Stanley Park in Vancouver. Her body was found by an old man walking his dog. The dog must have smelled the blood and followed the scent into the forest. Anyway, the girl was found dead, lying naked on the ground, her ribs and pelvis broken. The freak choked her with her own panties, then smashed her head in with a branch. Blood everywhere!'

'Christ, Matt. D'you think this nut case is here in Blood Cove?' Jesse is almost shouting. 'God, he could be stalking us right now, looking for another victim.'

'Jesse, no! Calm down!' shouts Matt.

'What if he raped…'

'Easy, Jesse!'

'…and killed little Donni, cut him up…'

'Take a deep breath.'

'…in pieces and threw his…'

'You didn't let me finish!'

'…remains in the bay?' cries Jesse, almost hysterical now.

'Calm down, damn it! It's okay. They caught the guy yesterday.'

'Oh! They caught him?' asks Jesse, losing momentum.

'Yes. A neighbor complained about a bad smell coming from his apartment. The landlord banged on the door, and when no one answered, he used the master key. The perp was hanging by his neck in the closet, dead as a door nail. The TV in front of him was on, porn still playing from the VCR. They figure he was playing some sick sex game and something went wrong.'

'What does sex have to do with hanging yourself in a closet?' asks Jesse.

'He was jerking off while choking himself with the rope—supposed to give you a rush or something,' explains Matt.

'What the hell! Sicko—serves him right, justice served. Amen!' proclaims Jesse. 'That's enough. This is giving me the heebie jeebies, Matt.'

'I'm sorry, Jesse. Anyway, we have to find Donni before, well, before it's too late.'

'Let's ask my Uncle Bill for help,' replies Jesse.

'Who the heck is he?' asks Matt. 'You've never mentioned him before.'

'My uncle is an old trapper, and he knows this forest like the back of his hand. He told me he has lived in the rain forest for a coon's age. I'm not sure how long that is, exactly, but by the wrinkles in his face, I think it's a long time. If anybody is lost or wandering around those woods, Uncle Bill will find them.'

'Wow. Sounds awesome, like Grizzly Adams or Daniel Boone.'

'Ha, ha. He's more like Indian Joe from the Forest Rangers, just a lot older and hairier.'

Matt and Jesse laugh out loud. 'Okay, Jess! I'll meet you back here at 7:30 tomorrow morning.'

'You mean this morning. We better get home and hit the sack if we want to get going so early. 'Night, Matt,' says Jesse as she leans over and kisses his cheek.

'G'night, Jess.'

Celreau

1721

A chilly autumn wind sweeps down the cobblestone streets in the Romanian town of Buftea, blowing dead, dry leaves along the gutter and fine dust into his face. Thick, gray, ominous clouds race overhead, streaking ghostlike shadows across his path. He turns down a long, dingy alley startling a pair of mangy ravens feeding on a heap of rotten garbage outside a locked door. Several homeless people lay, misshapen and starving, on the ground, their backs against the moldy walls. Wrapped in dirty rags, shivering and moaning, they extend their hands toward this stranger, begging for money. He grunts as he rushes past.

He steps out of the drafty alley onto the dirt road leading east, out of town. Turning left, he sets a steady pace and is soon surrounded by the pastures and grain fields of the Tamasi farming district. After several leagues of slogging through mud and puddles, he turns off the road, effortlessly hurdles a flooded ditch, and heads towards an old barn.

Everyone in the community considers twenty-two-year-old Angela Florescu to be an old maid, and she is becoming a source of embarrassment and worry to her family. Many local businessmen have tried to woo her with their charms and their money, but she has rejected them all—much to her parents' dismay. Her father cannot fathom why his beautiful daughter rejects the thought of marriage to one of these pillars of the community; after all, they are well-bred, wealthy and charming. Marriage to one of them would mean a step up in class for Angela, and she is fortunate, at her age, that they come courting at all.

The subject comes up repeatedly at home, usually in the evening after supper. The discussion always develops along the same lines. This evening her tată starts by saying, 'If only you weren't so damned smart. Your beauty attracts men like flies to manure. Just pick a suitor and keep your mouth shut—at least till after your damned wedding.'

Angela just laughs and quickly answers, 'Tată! I swear you're trying to get rid of me. If I leave, won't you miss all my hugs and kisses? Besides, this is the eighteenth century, and I should have the right to choose my own husband. These men are not for me. I don't love them, and they can't buy my love with their money. Tell me, Tată, did mother marry you for your money?'

'Well, aw...but I, aww...,' her father mutters.

'She has a fine point there, Nico,' her mother interjects from the kitchen.

'Darn it, Angela! You got me again. You are too clever for your own good, girl,' her father replies.

Angela ends the discussion by saying, 'Tată, I'm going out for a walk to Willow Creek. I need some fresh air.'

Kissing her father's cheek, she walks to the door and lifts her hooded cloak from its peg.

'Angela,' her mother says. 'It's getting late; I worry about you walking out on the farm alone at this hour. There's talk in town of a vampire in the area. A hunter stumbled upon Elena Stancu's dead body in the meadows last week just outside of Buftea.'

'Her body was pale as snow,' adds Nicolai. 'The coroner said her body was completely drained of blood, and tooth marks were found on her neck.'

'Mamă, Buftea is more than two leagues from here. Nobody in his right mind, not even a vampire, would know where it is, let alone want to visit Tamasi. I'll be fine. You and Tată worry too much. Besides, everybody in the county knows Elena was a fallen woman and a slave to laudanum. The teeth marks on her neck are likely from one of her gentleman callers. She probably took too much of the drug, got lost and passed out.'

'My God, Angela,' says her mother. 'I swear you know more than the police! Where do you get this knowledge?'

'She must have got the brains from me, sweetheart,' says Nicolai.

'Why do you say that?' asks his wife.

'Because she obviously got her beauty from you, my love,' replies Nicolai, smiling.

'Aw, Nico, you are so sweet,' says his wife, as she kisses him.

'Okay, you two love birds,' says Angela. 'I am off for my walk. Don't worry. I'll be back shortly.'

But Angela doesn't walk very far. In minutes she is sitting in the hay loft of the old barn, waiting patiently for her lover. She nervously brushes back her long dark hair. Her hand moves to her throat and descends to the delicate golden heart hanging just above her cleavage. Grasping the pendant in her palm, she coils the filigreed chain around one finger and blushes at thoughts of her last romantic encounter with her tall handsome lover. He gave her the pendant when he told her that she was his true love, and that his heart would forever belong to her. The gift is Angela's most valued possession. Some nights, lying perfectly still in her bed, she can almost convince herself that she feels it pulsing at her breast.

The sharp squeal of the rusty hinge on the old barn door startles

Angela, even though she is expecting him. He is always so quiet. Her heart races with anticipation as she strains to hear her lover crossing the barn floor; the straw makes the softest rustle under each footstep as he approaches.

The weathered barn is dark and drafty. He frowns at the pungent smell of the cow patties strewn everywhere. His nostrils flare abruptly as he catches the sweet fragrance of lavender and lemon drifting from above, leading him to the tall wooden ladder to the hayloft. He climbs.

Angela feels the loft floor shudder as he approaches. Her senses kindle as she anxiously slides back against the wall. She gasps as he appears, rising over the lip of the loft. Before she can speak, he pounces. In a single leap, he straddles her, stares deep into her dark blue eyes and kisses her. Trapped by his body weight, vulnerable, powerless, she surrenders to him. Her body trembling with excitement, she lays dazed and breathless.

'Shh, my lamb,' he whispers in her ear.

He kisses her long slender neck, nibbling her sweet pale skin, sending shivers up her spine. He slips her bodice down exposing her beautiful firm breasts. She moans as he teases her, gently circling a hard pink nipple with his fingers. She grasps his broad shoulders and feels his muscles ripple under his shirt. He slides down, caressing her tender young breasts with his mouth, gently licking and sucking her erect nipples. He reaches under her dress with his other hand. Angela quivers as he slides his hand along her thigh and up to her mound, gently running his fingers along her moist skin and into her wet gash. Her back arches as he gently pleasures her. Her breathing becomes shallower, and her moans increase in rhythmic ecstasy. She screams as she reaches orgasm.

He rolls away from Angela and lies next to her. He hugs her, gently kissing her long neck as she regains her breath. 'Gabriel, you're amazing. You take my breath away. You're not like any man I have ever known. I feel so safe and free when you make love to me.'

Gabriel toys with the heart pendant at her throat. Leaning closer, his breath soft and warm on her ear, he whispers, 'You make loving easy, Angel. Your beauty, your passion, your total abandon are irresistible to me. I desire you more than you know, my love. Your young body, so firm, so soft, tastes as sweet as red wine. It fuels my appetite; I cannot have enough of you.'

'Gabriel, you are so sweet. I swear you would eat me like a wolf does a lamb if you could,' says Angela, laughing. 'Now relax, my prince. It's your turn.'

Angela runs her hand up Gabriel's leg and feels his long swollen member under his trousers. She unbuttons him and slips his hard penis into the cool night air, then squeezes her hands around his pulsing shaft. Gabriel moans in ecstasy as Angela wraps her soft red lips around his cock and pleasures him. Angela feels her lover begin to tremble and his cock pulse as he is about to cum. She abruptly stops and rolls onto her back with her long black hair strewn against the golden straw. She looks up at Gabriel with her big blue submissive eyes and says, 'Take me, my wolf. Satisfy your hunger, for tonight I am your lamb.'

Gabriel stands above her and takes off his shirt. Angela watches in excitement as he exposes his large muscular shoulders and chest. Gabriel's biceps and forearm muscles ripple as he climbs over his prey. Angela, already wet in anticipation, spreads her long slender legs. Gabriel lifts Angela's legs over his shoulders and pins her hands down behind her head. 'You are mine, Angel. Surrender.'

Angela screams in pleasure as Gabriel slides deep into her. He slowly thrusts his cock, steadily increasing his pace as her body responds, trembling and pulsing with every stroke.

Angela moans in delight as she feels a wave of ecstasy building deep within her. Mind and body she is engulfed, consumed with a joy beyond anything she has ever experienced. Suddenly, as her lust and desire are about to peak, she cries out, 'Now, Gabriel! Oh Lord, now!'

Suddenly, Gabriel screams, a terrifying bestial sound, and pulls out of her. He rises and turns in one motion, then rushes down the stairs. Angela, startled, sits up and yells, 'No! Wait! What's wrong? What happened? Gabriel, don't go!'

He shouts back, 'I'm sorry, Angel, I'm sorry!' Without another word, he runs out of the barn, into the night. Angela, upset and confused, grabs a handful of straw and angrily throws it in the direction Gabriel has gone. The action gives her no satisfaction because the nearly weightless stalks, rather than flying across the barn, just waft a few feet then drift to the hayloft floor.

Gabriel, equally frustrated from the aborted encounter, leaves the farmyard, heading back toward Buftea. The weather has worsened to match his angry mood; dark, heavy thunderclouds hang overhead as a strong wind pelts his pale face with sharp hail and ice. The muddy roadway constantly threatens to slip from beneath his feet.

Matt & Jesse
1980

Jesse wakes before sunrise, rolls out of bed, stretches and puts on her faded blue jeans and favorite wool sweater. In early September, the mornings in Blood Cove are damp and cool, a chill mist usually flooding the forest along the coast. She stumbles down to the kitchen, still groggy from the late night chatting with Matt. She sits down to a bowl of Rice Krispies. Hoping to replace some of her dissipated energy, she spoons in two big scoops of sugar. The familiar sound of the rice snapping is comforting and warms her soul. Finishing the cereal, she drinks the rest of the milk straight from the bowl, then clears and wipes the table. She makes a quick lunch of peanut butter and jelly sandwiches—one for Matt and one for her. She packs the sandwiches, along with two chocolate Wagon Wheels, wooden matches and a couple of cans of Coca-Cola, in her backpack.

'You're up early, sweetheart. Big plans for today?' asks Betty, as she steps into the kitchen. She pads over to the coffee maker to begin her own morning ritual.

'Morning, Mom,' answers Jesse. 'Matt and me are gonna hike down to Kettle Creek and help search for Donni…'

'That poor boy,' says Betty. 'If the cold night didn't get him, the wolves probably did. Why do you think he would be in that area? And by the way, it's Matt and I are gonna.'

'Yeah, of course. Sorry. Anyway, we think Donni may have skipped school yesterday and snuck down to the fishing hole. He loves to fish just downstream from where the river trail ends. Maybe he strayed off the path and got lost. That'd be unusual for someone who's been down there so many times, but I guess it could happen. Matt and me—uh, I mean Matt and I—know the trails inside out, so we figure it's worth a look.'

'Pastor Dewar's housekeeper, Sarah, called me last night,' said Betty, as she poured the first of her several daily cups of coffee. 'She said Darlene Cardinal, Donni's mom, is beside herself with worry. Sarah overheard Pastor Dewar trying to console her, to no avail. That old Scottish meddler! Just trying to make himself look like the saint he isn't. Anyway, Sarah's afraid Donni's mom will have a total breakdown, so she asked me to go to Darlene's house and comfort her. Dewar would never stoop to asking a good-for-nothing Indian for help, that's for sure.

'I can manage just fine without his two cents, myself. When your father passed away and I moved us from Haida Guaii to Blood Cove, all we had were a couple of bags and a few hundred bucks. It was tough, but we didn't need his nor anyone's help. Not that the good Christian offered any help. We managed. I cleaned houses for enough money to pay the rent. Our clothes were mostly things from the Salvation Army that I mended and altered. Some times late in the evening, when I was exhausted and discouraged, your dad would appear to comfort me. He told me that everything happened for a reason and that things would get better. And they did, eventually.'

'I wish I'd have met Dad. He sounds like a wonderful man.'

'I miss him so much, but I see him every time I look at you.'

'Aww, Mom. That's so sweet. Thanks. Anyway, I've been meaning to ask you something, Mom. Was Matt's dad always an alcoholic?'

'No. Actually he was once a wonderful man.'

'So, what made him start drinking?'

'Frank Taylor moved here from Vancouver when he was a young man. He confided in me once that his father was a mean drunk who routinely abused both him and his mother. When he got old enough, Frank worked at the local cannery for a while, living at the church hostel till he had enough money to buy a house. He got a new job at the Kodiak lumber mill, where he met Doris Grandmaison. He fell head over heels for the young receptionist. And she for him, apparently.'

'I can't imagine anybody falling for that miserable man,' says Jesse.

'Frank was handsome back in the day, quite the charmer. Doris and Frank were inseparable; they would walk hand-in-hand for hours along the beach. Before long he proposed and they were married.'

'What made him change into a drunk, a jerk who treats his kid like dirt? Was he, after all, just following his own father's example?' asks Jesse.

'No, no. Nothing of the sort,' her mother went on, 'When Matt was born, everything was fine for a while. They were such a happy young family. Frank doted on Matt. Then Doris was diagnosed with cancer.'

'What kind of cancer?'

'Lung cancer. Frank and Doris were both heavy smokers. Doris tried chemotherapy and radiation, but once the cancer metastasized to her liver, she stopped treatment.'

'That's awful!'

'Frank was furious. He could not understand why she gave up the fight. When Doris passed away, he was devastated. He fell into a deep depression and turned to the bottle.'

'Who took care of Matt?'

'I did. He was barely three when his mother died. I suspected the boy was being left home alone while Frank was at work or passed out drunk. I feared social services would find out and place Matt in foster care, so I offered to look after him.'

'Mr. Taylor agreed to that?' The surprise was, once again, evident in Jesse's voice.

'Frank hated me, as he hated all the other natives in town. He was a bigot, still is I guess, but he couldn't muster enough energy to give a damn. Having no other options, really, he accepted my offer. It worked out well, actually. You and Matt became playmates, and that kept you busy and out of my hair while I did my housework.'

'Matt hates his dad. I don't blame him, though. The way he treats him,' explains Jesse. 'He's always putting Matt down and swearing at him. Matt can't seem to do anything to please him.'

'Hate is a terrible thing, sweetheart. Hate-filled people become like wolves, licking their wounds, savoring morsels of pain both given and received. They smack their lips, gnash their teeth and worry at past issues that they can't resolve. The real problem, and what that sort of person doesn't realize, is that the morsels they are wolfing down are actually pieces of themselves.'

'Hmm. I don't understand. Isn't Frank the one with the problem?'

'Alcoholism is a disease, dear, and unfortunately it often has greater affects on others than on the drunk.'

'But that doesn't make it right or excusable, Mom.'

'No, it doesn't. But if Matt wants peace of mind, he must find it within himself to forgive his dad and hate the disease.'

'I can see that would help Matt deal with the situation, but that won't fix Frank's problem.'

'Frank is the only one who can fix his problem. The change must come from inside. Matt has been affected by his dad's disease, so he needs to heal himself. Otherwise he will likely pass it on to his children. He needs to heal and break the cycle that his grandfather passed to his son and, through him, to his grandson.'

'Wow, that's messed up. I hope Matt forgives his dad, then, but I really don't think it'll happen anytime soon.'

'It's never easy, Jesse, but I hope so too.'

'I have to run, Mom. Matt's probably already waiting for me by now.'

'Okay, honey. Be careful and be back before dark. We don't need another search party out in the woods looking for you two bandits.'

'Don't worry, Mom. You know Matt and I couldn't get lost in that area. Besides, the rain-forest is the Haida's home, so technically I'm never in dangerous territory.'

'Okay, my little Indian princess,' answers Betty. 'It's good to know you've listened to some of my lessons.'

'Thanks, Ma. Love ya. Don't worry,' says Jesse as she scampers out the front door. She hops down the rickety steps of the old wooden porch and into the empty street. Badger Avenue is flanked by military-style houses and a few apartment buildings dating back to the '40s, built to accommodate the families of soldiers stationed in Blood Cove for training. The houses are now mostly run-down, long past easy repair; walls faded and flaking, weathered shingles badly twisted, the remaining eaves troughs filled with pine needles and covered with moss. Old cars in various stages of disassembly are parked in some of the front yards, picked over for parts or vandalized after they were abandoned. Jesse turns onto Main Street and spots a group of adults gathered in front of the general store. Pastor Andrew Dewar, Mayor Cliff Brady and RCMP Sergeant Tom Kirkpatrick are taking turns talking to the crowd. Jesse moves closer to hear the conversation.

'Okay, listen up! Everybody in the search party that combed the beach front yesterday, please continue from where you left off,' orders Sergeant Kirkpatrick. 'Look for Donni's footprints in the sand. His mother says he wears size one youth shoes, and he was wearing sneakers when he left the house. About half of you should be scanning the tree line as you go. And remember to call out Donni's name. Stop every now and then to listen carefully for a response from the boy. Keep in mind that he is likely tired and weak from spending the night in the cold.

'Be aware that the Canadian Coast Guard has been alerted, and they are searching the bay for the boy. If you spot the boy or a body floating in the bay, fire the flare gun we supplied the team leaders. The Coast Guard will respond at once. Do not search past Eagle's Point. The cliff wall is nearly impassable, and rogue waves could easily wash away the unwary. We don't need anyone getting hurt. Everybody report back here at the General Store at noon sharp. High tide is expected just after two this afternoon, and we don't want to have more people who need rescuing. Am I clear?'

'What about the rumor that Donni was kidnapped?' calls out one of the men from the crowd.

'There's no reason to suspect a kidnapping,' answers Mayor Brady. 'The head office of the RCMP in Vancouver has been notified of the boy's disappearance. They informed me that, as a precaution, a roadblock has been set up on the Yellowhead Highway outside the city limits. All vehicles leaving Blood Cove are being stopped, drivers are being questioned, and in some cases, the vehicles are being searched. I stress that this is simply a precautionary step and that a kidnapping is not our main focus at this time. No need to be spreading rumors or talking to the media in this regard. Stay calm and concentrate on the search.'

'Constable Kennedy and I will search the town site and surrounding area,' interjects Sergeant Kirkpatrick. 'We will meet everybody back at this location at noon. At that time, we will coordinate a grid search of the valley, starting from Longboat Inlet, along the valley north to Frenchman Mountain. Any more questions? Alright. Pastor Dewar has asked to lead us in a prayer for Donni. Father?'

'Please bow your heads,' says the minister. 'Dear God, our Father in Heaven, please keep Donni safe from the wildlife and the cold. We pray that you guide our search group to Donni so that he can be returned safely to his family and community. Amen.'

'Amen,' murmurs through the crowd. They turn and head down Muskrat Street to the beach front.

Turning to the sergeant, Mayor Brady says, 'Tom, we have to find this kid quick. The Fall Fair and the lumberjack competitions are only a week away. If that boy isn't found soon and rumors of a kidnapping get out to the press, people could stay away in droves. The impact would be the last nail in the financial coffin for our dying town.'

'I understand your concern for the town, Cliff, I do,' Sergeant Kirkpatrick responds, 'But my main concern right now is finding Donni Cardinal before he dies of exposure. His parents are worried sick about the child, and we need to get him home.'

'If only these people would keep an eye on their children like the rest of us, this would not happen,' offers Pastor Dewar condescendingly.

Tom looks at the minister sharply. 'Father, I really don't think the color of the Cardinals' skin has anything to do with how they raise their children. Levi and Darlene Cardinal are responsible, god-fearing, hard-working members of our community.'

'Just a minute, Tom,' says Brady. 'Between you, me and a fencepost, Pastor Dewar is right. You know as well as I do that these Haida let their kids run around wild. We are just lucky it wasn't a white kid lost out there in the woods.'

'That's quite enough of this nonsense,' replies Sergeant Kirkpatrick. 'That kind of attitude could bring this town a lot more negative publicity than a kidnapping rumor. Anyway, I have work to do, and I would guess you have, as well.'

'Tom, there is no need to get upset. I was simply making an observation,' says Pastor Dewar.

'Have a good morning, gentlemen.' Sergeant Kirkpatrick turns to his constable, and the pair walk away from the general store.

Jesse, having heard the gist of the conversation, leaves in disgust and heads up Muskrat Street towards the Kettle Creek trail head to meet Matt. This was not the first time Jesse had heard such nonsense about the Haida. In school they taught her to cherish her traditions, culture and religion, but out in the real world, she was just another Indian looking for hand-outs and welfare, destined to be a burden on society.

She had been born in a small town named Place of Stones (Skidegate) situated on the southeast coast of Graham Island. When her father was killed in that mysterious house fire, she and her mother moved to Blood Cove on the British Columbia mainland. As a single mom, Betty needed steady employment and Blood Cove provided the opportunity to raise Jesse in a relatively stable environment. Betty was a member of the Raven Clan, and like her father before her, she was known to interact with the supernatural world; this, combined with her wisdom and knowledge of traditional aboriginal methods of healing, gained her the respect of the local Haida. Soon she had assumed the role of Shaman for the group. Whenever anyone fell ill or needed help in childbirth, Big Mama would be called to help.

Betty taught her daughter all the Haida stories and folklore that were passed down from her own parents. Jesse learned to be proud of her Haida lineage and ignore the racism and prejudice common around town.

Arriving at the tree house, Jesse finds Matt leaning against the tree. He is wearing a tuque, a black Pink Floyd sweatshirt, a baggy pair of Levis and an old pair of rubber boots.

'Hey, Jess,' says Matt. 'Man, am I bushed!'

'No guff, eh?' replies Jesse, as she leans to kiss him. 'We definitely should have caught some Zs much earlier last night. You want a Wagon Wheel?'

'No, I'm good. I had toast. Let's go find the little shit-head before he gets eaten by a cougar or something.'

Matt takes Jesse's hand as they walk into the forest and down the trail towards the creek. A tangle of moss-covered trees and tall ferns line the muddy trail. Matt snags a giant banana slug from the leaf-littered ground and threatens to throw the slimy critter at his companion. Laughing, Jesse says, 'Don't you dare, Matt. I swear I'll pin you to the ground and shove that thing down your throat.'

'Aw, Haida-girl, you sooo tough and yet afraid of this poor little creature? Look,' threatens Matt as he holds out the slug and moves towards Jesse. 'I think he likes you. C'mon, give him a kiss.'

'Matt, I swear, I'm warning you, boy.'

Matt takes a step towards Jesse. With one quick kick to the back of his legs, Jesse flips Matt onto his back in the muddy trail. Matt drops the slug and lies there, half-winded and stunned by the sudden assault. Jesse picks up the slug, quickly straddles Matt's chest and suspends the slimy mollusk over his face.

'I warned you, Whitey! Bon appétit!'

Matt laughs and screams, 'No Jesse! No. I give! I give!'

Giggling, Jesse says, 'Who's your Mama?'

'You know you are, Jess. Now please, throw it away!'

'Right answer, Whitey,' says Jesse as she tosses the slug into the trees. They both get up from the wet ground. Laughing hysterically, they try to brush most of the pine needles and muck from their clothes.

'Look at the color of those trees. I love the forest this time of year,' Jesse says wistfully. Then, energy building in her voice, she shouts at the top of her lungs, 'Makes me feel like singing!'

'Oh, it does, does it? Are you sure?' teases Matt, laughing at the crazy dance Jesse is doing, head back and arms spread wide. Matt is reminded of his favorite image of Snoopy from the comic strip Peanuts. 'Hey, by the way, been meanin' to tell you. I think I got the chorus for our road song.' He reaches into his jacket pocket, pulls out his shiny Hohner harmonica and begins to blow a rock riff. Jesse runs ahead, smiling and dancing as Matt sings.

'gotta leave this backwoods town behind
get out while we still can
just you an' me together girl
an' this guitar in my hand'

Jesse turns excitedly to Matt. 'That's it! You're brilliant. Play it again and we'll sing it together.' They continue down the trail, trying to get the harmony right.

When they reach the creek, they take the trail that leads east past their favorite fishing hole towards Frenchman's Mountain. Stashing the harmonica, Matt tells his friend, 'When we get to the fishing hole, keep your eyes peeled for signs like chocolate bar or gum wrappers that he may have tossed; surprisingly, for a Métis, he's a bit of a litterbug. Broken branches and running shoe prints are not as obvious, but we might get lucky.'

'Okie dokie, Scout Master Taylor. Question? Who died and made you head tracker?' teases Jesse.

'C'mon, Jess. Cut me some slack,' answers Matt, more than a little perturbed that Jess would challenge him, even in jest. 'I'm just tryin' to find Donni. You know I don't really mean to boss you around.'

'Oh, is that why we're here? I thought we were looking for a McDonald's.'

'Shut up, you meatball, and start looking,' orders Matt. The pair hike well past the fishing hole with no sign of Donni. After following the trail for several more minutes with the same lack of results, Matt suggests, 'We're quite a ways from the trail head, Jesse. Do you think he'd have wandered this far out?'

'Anything's possible,' answers Jesse. 'If he wondered off the trail for some reason, he might've gotten lost and walked for miles. Uncle Bill's cabin is just a few kilometres ahead; let's drop in and check on the old guy. Maybe Uncle Bill found Donni already, or maybe he isn't even home and Donni took shelter from the rain last night inside the old log cabin.'

'Sounds like a plan,' says Matt. 'Let's go.'

Donni

1980

Cold and pale, the boy sits in the cellar, alone with his thoughts. Shivering, he huddles under his damp woolen blanket. He rubs his red swollen neck, and nervously picks at the scab that has formed over the bruised puncture wounds. Tired and confused, he runs his sleeve under his runny nose, then wipes the tears from his dark sunken eyes.

What was that? Footsteps. Someone's up there!

The heavy trap door shrieks open.

'Ma? Pa? Is that you?'

'Hi, Donni. It's me,' says Celreau, smiling and descending the stairs.

'Can I go home, please?' begs Donni. This has become a litany he repeats every time Celreau arrives. He tightens his grip on his blanket.

'Soon, Donni. Look, I brought you pizza.'

Ravenous, Donni grabs the box from Celreau's hand and wrenches the top open. With no thought to manners, he stuffs a slice into his mouth.

'It's pepperoni and cheese. Your favorite. Here, son, have a cola to wash it down. And slow down. Eating too quickly is not good for you.'

Donni takes the drink from Celreau and backs into the corner on the bed before gulping it down.

'You were hungry. I brought you some more comics. Look. Even the new issue of Superman.'

'I wanna go home,' answers the child, beginning to cry.

'You have to be patient. The serum is starting to work. You will be discovering your new powers very soon.'

'Please, mister. I just wanna go home,' pleads Donni. 'I miss Ma and Pa, and I really miss Chance. Please, can we just go now? Please?'

Celreau sits down next to Donni and speaks to him in a calm soothing tone. 'I understand that you're tired and that you miss your family, but you've started your mission, and it's important that you complete it. I talked to your mom and dad, and your teacher, about how brave and strong you are. They're all so proud of you.'

'I want to go, please. Let me go home.'

'Donni, you don't want to disappoint everyone, do you?'

'No, I guess not.'

'Listen. I have a great idea.'

'What?' asks Donni, hesitantly.

'Write your mom and dad a letter, and I'll take it to them right away.'

'I guess,' answers Donni, tired and disappointed. He walks over to the table, takes a pencil and a sheet of paper from the drawer and begins to write.

Behind the boy, Celreau's insincere smile becomes a glare as his hunger for blood arouses the feral fever. With effort, he controls the urge to feed, trying to be patient. Finally, Donni puts down his pencil, turns and hands the paper to Celreau.

'Very good, Donni. I'll get this to them straight away.' Celreau slides the letter into his jean pocket before returning his attention to the boy. Recognizing that now too-familiar look on Celreau's face, Donni grimaces in fear.

'No, please, not again. Please, no. My neck hurts so bad.'

'It's just a little sting. When you wake up, you'll have your powers, I promise.'

'There are no powers. You're a bad man,' shouts Donni. 'Let me go or I'll scream.'

'Now, now. Calm down, boy. There's no need to get upset.'

The sound of barking dogs interrupts them, and they both look toward the trapdoor. Donni leaps out of the chair and runs to the stairs.

'Help! Help!' screams Donni. 'I'm here. Help!'

'Damn you, boy!' hisses the vampire. He rushes Donni, grabbing him by the back of the shirt and dragging him back down the stairs. 'Be quiet, damn you.'

Donni looks up terrified at the sight of huge fangs and bloody eyes staring down at him. The sounds of barking, now accompanied by human voices, are heard overhead, approaching quickly. Donni summons up his courage and yells, 'Help! Help! Down here. Help!'

The vampire, now enraged, slaps the boy across the face, launching him across the room. Donni falls to the floor limp and silent. The vampire hurries over and removes the boy's shirt. He tucks it into his belt, runs up the steps and closes the trap door behind him.

Quickly composing himself, Celreau exits the building, locking the barracks door behind him. Reaching into his pocket, he throws Donni's letter into the burn barrel just outside the door. Taking the boy's shirt from his belt, he soaks it in a muddy puddle by the entrance, then wrings some of the water from it. Peeking around the corner of the building, he spies hounds running towards him quickly, the search party following at a run.

Celreau calmly steps away from the building and walks towards the group. The hounds catch the scent of Donni's shirt and surround Celreau, barking and jumping, excited by the find. Yelling at the hounds, the handler leashes the dogs and pulls them away from Celreau. The dogs settle down when the handler feeds them well-earned treats for their efforts.

'Mr. Celreau, good morning,' says Kirkpatrick, looking puzzled.

Celreau
1721

For him, the squall is much more annoyance than impediment. He treks into the wind until he is within a few leagues of the city limits. A long gravel driveway leads him to a carriage house that, according to the sign swinging above the entrance, is called Journey's End Inn. Hanging below the name is the exhortation, Travelers Welcome. And below that, a removable plaque announces Vacancy. The two-storrey colonial building, with its gable roof of moldy twisted shingles, stands solitary in an open field. The weathered window shutters hang crooked, and the stone façade is overrun by climbing vines, giving the old structure a cold, eerie look.

Crossing the yard, Gabriel stops by the tall oak tree that stands alone only a few yards from the inn. He examines the trunk of the old tree closely and finds the initials T&G carved into the bark. Sliding his fingers across the initials, he smiles at the sweet childhood memories of his friend, Tatiana. Tati was a beautiful girl, the same age as he, with long brown hair and hazel eyes. She would visit every year with her parents, as they traveled from Hungary to visit friends and family near Bucharest. Both parents were vampires, but her mother protected Tati from other bloodsuckers, adamant that her daughter would not be cursed to share their eternity of hell on earth. Tati and Gabriel would spend the days together, laughing and playing in the yard. Tati's mother forbade her to wonder away, but Tati could always persuade Gabi to run through the forest with her. Tati loved to explore the forest, climb trees and sing at the top of her lungs. She was the only one at the inn that ever made Gabi laugh. His rare moments of true happiness always occurred when she was around. Every summer Gabi was excited to spend that one special week with Tatiana.

The year they turned sixteen was the last summer they spent time together. Tatiana's parents had decided to move to Paris because the local community was becoming suspicious of them. Some people began to suspect they were vampires based on their unchanging youthful features, strange behavior and odd nocturnal schedules. As a consequence, the yearly pilgrimage to Romania would no longer be an option. Gabriel was heartbroken when Tati gave him the news. That was the day they carved their initials in the old oak tree, and the day Gabriel got his first kiss. Gabriel and Tati swore that they would one day, somehow, be together again.

Gabriel snaps back to reality, looks around nervously, then approaches the inn's side entry. He knocks on the door three times, then twice more, and waits anxiously. The heavy oak door creaks open slowly, and standing in the doorway is a thin, pale, white-haired lady.

'Gabriel, what a surprise! Quick. Come in, son.' She gives the young man a warm hug and steps back with a smile. 'Let me have a look at you. You've grown so strong and handsome. How are you?'

'I'm okay, Mom. What about you? You look a little paler than when I last saw you.'

'Well, you know, Gabi. Sometimes his needs can be a bit much. Sit down, Gabi. Sit—sit. Let me make you a nice cup of peppermint tea, perfect to warm you on a night such as this.'

Gabriel pulls a chair and sits at the kitchen table. Hanging his head, he says, 'Damn it, Mother! You know I don't drink tea.'

With a sigh of resignation, she sits opposite her son at the table and returns to his earlier question. 'He is hungry lately; as he gets older, he becomes lazy. He desires more frequent feeding, but he is loath to go out to get it. So, because it's easier, he takes more from me, Gabi; more than we bargained.'

'That bastard!' exclaims Gabriel in disgust. He looks closely at his mother, tracing her features with his eyes. 'What gives him the right to take advantage of you like that? You're not young anymore; he could kill you—or worse! Where is he? Is he home? It's time I had a chat with that lazy leech.'

'Please don't, Gabi,' his mother pleads. She reaches across the table and clasps Gabriel's hands in her own. 'You'll only upset him, and he'll take it out on me. I understand your hatred of him after what happened to you, but it really wasn't his fault.'

'Yeah, right, Mom. He's a real sweetheart,' Gabriel spits out bitterly. Sliding his hands from his mother's grasp, he stands and nervously walks about the room.

'Gabi, the innkeeper put a roof over our heads and fed us through all those hard years. Because of him, I was able to keep you near me and raise you. Don't you remember how destitute we were after the plague took your father? I couldn't afford to feed us. We were dying and not very slowly. When he approached me with his offer, I had little choice. I could either accept the role of host for Leopold or watch you die of starvation like a dog in the street. Sure, he got the best of the deal, but Leo made it possible to raise you in a healthy, safe environment, not having to worry about where I would find our next meal. I know it wasn't easy, son, but...'

'How can you paint him as our benefactor? Look at me, Mother. Just look at me! Because of that...I was going to say man, but he hasn't been a man for hundreds of years. Because of that unholy beast, your son has become a monster.'

His mother, sobbing speechlessly, stares at her son.

'I envy you, Mother. I really do.'

'But why, Gabi? Why would you say that?' Tears are now streaming down her pale wrinkled face.

'Because you're going to die, Mother.'

His mother gasps at Gabriel's remark and lowers her head to her arm on the table, sobbing loudly. Gabi walks over to her and lays a powerful hand on her thin shoulder. 'You will die and rest in peace, Mother dear, while I'm cursed to stay, to feed on poor, innocent people. Some of those people will die, and others will turn into blood sucking animals like me. And now? Now I am in love, Mother, in love with a beautiful young maiden. I love her with my whole being, and I can't even make love to her without wanting to drain her dry of blood. I am cursed. I can't live like this. You should've let me die all those years ago. We'd all be better off. After all, I am not really alive anyway.'

'I don't understand. I did what I thought was best, Gabi. I knew Leo and his friend Petru were lovers, but I never thought Petru would take an interest in you, try to seduce you.'

'Well, Mom, that's the problem, isn't it? You never thought.' interrupts Gabriel with dismay. 'And what he did was abuse, not seduction.'

'How was I to know, Gabi? Sure, Petru was eccentric and flamboyant, his gestures and statements a little overblown, but he never gave me any indication that he harbored any inappropriate intentions toward you. When you were young, he always brought toys for you, and he never treated you with anything but kindness. That was part of my initial agreement with Leopold. He warned Petru from the beginning to keep his hands off us, Gabi; he assured me that Petru understood and could be trusted to leave us alone.

'Whenever Petru came to stay, they enjoyed each other's company and spent most nights gallivanting the streets of Buftea, gorging themselves on prostitutes and the homeless. Leo's hunger, his need for blood, was always sated during these periods, so he would leave me alone, allowing me much-needed time to rest, recuperate and regain energy.'

'Well, wasn't that considerate?' Gabriel's sarcasm hangs heavily on the air. 'Poor Petru must've run out of luck the night he decided to visit me in my bedroom. He probably couldn't find enough male prostitutes. He figured I was the next best thing.'

'I didn't see him enter the house, Gabi. I had no idea you would become attractive to him in that way, you know, when you grew up! And if you hated him so much, why didn't you leave?'

'I stayed for you, Mother, to protect you. I never trusted him.'

'I didn't need protecting. Leo promised that Petru would not...'

'Where do you get off calling that bastard Leo?' shouts Gabriel in tones of outrage. 'Since when has your relationship become so informal? Really! Have you become attached to this monster and his abuse after so many years of submissiveness? And spare me the excuses. Petru asked me for sex that night, Mother! And he was used to getting what he wanted. When I refused, he was more than insulted; he was enraged. He yelled, 'I don't need your consent. Don't you know I can just take what I want from you, and you are powerless to stop me?' I began to laugh in his face. Imagine—that little pipsqueak of a faggot trying to force me to do anything. You know, since my teens, I've been in pretty damned good shape.

'When I started to laugh, he lost his senses and attacked me. Imagine my surprise when I tried to stop him and he tossed me around like a scarecrow with too little straw. That vampire had the strength of five men. He held me down and raped me, Mother! And when he was done with me, he bit my neck and fed on my blood till I passed out and died.

'And I awoke to find I would never have to fear death again. I was already dead! My God, Mother. You're not blind. You must know that the monster I've become was created by Petru that night.

'And what has Leopold done to you? Sure, he hasn't turned you into a vampire. Small mercy. That vampire has kept you as a blood slave for over twenty-five damnable years, leeching the very life and soul from you!'

'Gabriel, that's not true!'

'Mother, how can you be so blind? Surely you see the truth. I was brought up watching my mother being preyed upon by a vampire. Most nights I cried myself to sleep listening to you screaming in pain, either in his room or in yours. Many weekend evenings, when you thought I was asleep, I'd sneak down to the big hall and watch Leopold's orgy of blood frenzied vampires fucking prostitutes and then sucking their arteries dry. During the daytime, I kept myself entertained by playing football alone. None of the other parents in the village would let their kids anywhere near Leopold's manor. And my football pitch? It was a yard peppered with shallow graves; every week a few more appeared with freshly disturbed soil.

'If that sick and twisted life is part of the safe and healthy environment you mentioned, Mother, I guess I truly am blessed. Alleluia! Thank you, dear sweet Leo!'

'Gabi, how can you talk to me this way?' His mother is crying again.

'Mother, I love you, but you're in denial.'

'Why do you say this, Gabi? What am I doing that torments you so?'

'Mother, you've been in this hellhole so long that you believe this life is normal. You can't imagine anything else. For goodness sakes, you have become emotionally attached to a vampire!'

'No, Gabi, that's not true. Please don't say that.'

'Mother, answer me one question and I'll leave you in peace.'

'Of course, Gabi. Anything,' sniffles his mother.

'I left the inn two years ago. You no longer have anyone to protect, no reason to stay. Why are you still living here?'

His mother stands silent, trembling. Staring into Gabriel's dark eyes, she searches for an answer. 'Well, I, I…' She falls into Gabriel's arms and says, 'I'm sorry, Gabi, I am so very sorry.'

'Mother, leave this place. Come with me to Bucharest. We can travel tonight. He won't find us there; you'll be safe and free from this monster's grip.'

Gabriel's mother pulls away from her son and stands at the kitchen table with her back to him.

'We're expecting a group of tourists tomorrow evening. I have so much food to prepare, and then I have all the linen to wash and rooms to clean.'

A heavy silence hangs in the air as she turns to see Gabriel staring at her in disbelief. 'Have a good life, Mother. I will always love you.' Gabriel steps through the kitchen door and disappears into the night.

The rain has stopped while Gabriel has been with his mother. Now, as the rays of pre-dawn slowly crest the Romanian horizon, the dark storm clouds are dissipating. Feeling weak from the oncoming sunlight and anemic from the lack of fresh blood, Gabriel rushes in near panic to the city and his lair. His encounter with Angela and the time spent visiting his mother have eaten away the night hours. And now the darkness is fleeing with each passing moment. He will not be able to seek a victim, a source for his nightly sustenance. The vampire almost literally drags himself to the safety of his lair just as the sunrise fills the sky with myriad pastel colors. Shielding himself from the sunlight with his black cape, he staggers around to the back of the house and down the concrete stairs to the cellar. He opens the heavy oak door at the bottom of the stairwell. Feeling a little of his tension lifting as he steps into the room, he turns to lock the door. Gabriel fumbles in his vest pocket for a wooden match, strikes the head along the stone wall, and lights a single candle among the five in the candelabra next to the door. An old mattress lying in the middle of the damp windowless room becomes visible in the faint glow. Exhausted and miserable, Gabriel shuffles to his bed, where he collapses onto his back, exhausted and miserable. Twisting and turning, unable to relax, his troubled mind wonders, tormented by the evil existence to which fate has condemned him.

Matt & Jesse

1980

When the kids finally enter the small clearing, they approach the log cabin from the west side and are greeted by a whiff of something sweet on the air. They round the corner toward the south-facing front of the cabin to discover a steaming pot of tea brewing over an open fire. A Winchester 30-30 rifle leans against a stump next to the fire pit, and metal leg-hold traps of all sizes hang on the cabin wall. A red cedar-strip canoe is overturned at the water's edge, its wooden paddles lying next to it on the pebbled shore.

'We're in luck, Jesse. Looks like Grizzly Adams is home,' chuckles Matt, as he surveys the scene. 'Will you look at the spit shine on that rifle? He must spend all day rubbing it with a diaper.'

'Shut up, you knucklehead. He'll hear you,' whispers Jesse. She knocks on the door and listens for a response. Nothing.

'Knock louder,' urges Matt, nudging Jesse in the back. 'The old codger's probably a bit hard of hearing, or maybe having his afternoon nap.' That comment earns him an elbow in the ribs.

'Ow! Dammit!' yelps Matt.

Jesse knocks much louder this time, but again gets no response. A sudden 'Caww! Caww!' startles the pair.

'Holy Shit!' says Matt. A large raven is perched on the barrel of the rifle, neither of them having noticed its arrival. 'I think I just had a heart attack!'

'I think I just peed my pants,' says Jesse. Visibly shaken, she tries to gather her senses.

'Get! Go! Get out of here,' yells Matt, waving both arms in what he hopes is a threatening manner. The bird cocks its head at him almost quizzically. Apparently neither afraid nor hurried, the Raven spreads its broad wings and launches into the air to glide across the creek. It caws again as it lands on an upper branch of a pine tree on the far side.

'Scuse me,' says Matt as he slips past Jesse to squeeze the latch and open the door.

'Matt! What the H?' questions Jesse.

Ignoring Jesse, Matt opens the door and calls out, 'Anybody home?' Receiving no answer, he steps through the doorway into the dimly lit cabin, Jesse on his heels.

Jesse looks around the room. 'Uncle Bill must be out checking his trap line.'

'Not likely, Sherlock,' quips Matt. 'Grizzly can't have gone very far. The teapot is still steaming over the fire, and I doubt he would've left for any length of time and forgotten his rifle leaning against the stump.' Gazing around the room with widening eyes, Matt says, 'Look at all this cool stuff.'

A pair of rawhide-webbed snowshoes, and various sizes of steel traps and wooden pelt stretchers adorn the log walls. A cast iron potbellied stove, still warm from a morning fire, rests on a jumble of washed rocks, its long stove pipe extending straight up through the ceiling. A red kerosene lantern and a large silver box sits on a wooden table next to the solitary willow branch chair. Thick wool blankets cover a log-framed bed. Above what obviously served as the kitchen counter, a double-doored cupboard of rough-hewn cedar planks hangs on the wall, flanked by pots and cooking utensils hanging from hooks. Tin cans of condiments and large burlap sacks of flour, sugar and rice are stored under the counter.

Matt walks up to the small table, picks up the silver box and opens the lid. 'Nice stash! Jess, come check this out. Look at all this stuff. Wonder if any of it's real.'

Jesse rushes over and stares down at the rat's nest of silver and gold necklaces, rings and bracelets tangled with knitting thimbles, silver coins, paper clips, keys and bottle caps. 'What an odd mix,' says Jesse, bewildered. 'Quick. Put it back before he shows up.'

'What a nut bar!' laughs Matt. He closes the lid and sets the treasure box back in its place.

'Can I help you?' resonates a deep voice from the doorway.

'Shit!' exclaims Matt, startled. Neither of them had heard sounds of someone approaching.

'Uncle Bill! Oh, hi,' says Jesse, her voice tense and anxious. 'You startled us. We came to visit you.'

The large man standing in silence in the doorway frowns, staring with black narrowed eyes at the young couple.

'Shit, Jess,' whispers Matt. 'I think I really did pee my pants!'

Jesse elbows Matt in the ribs and continues. 'The door was open, so we thought we'd come in and surprise you.'

The burly man steps into the room. Still staring, he walks slowly towards them, seemingly reluctant to say another word. Matt and Jesse, quite shaken from being caught essentially trespassing, take a few steps back. Gathering her courage in the face of the big man's silence, Jesse offers, 'We're searching for Donni Cardinal, the kid who's gone missing.'

Ignoring the kids, the man approaches the table, picks up the silver box and tucks it under his arm. He glares at Matt, then turns and carries the treasure box to the kitchen area. 'What made you think he'd be here?' asks Bill as he places the box in the cupboard and closes the door.

'We didn't, really. We wondered if you might've seen a boy in the area.'

'And who's he?' he asks, nodding in Matt's direction with a frown.

'Matt, my best friend.'

Bill humphs. He points at the table and tells them to sit down. Without waiting to see that they do, he limps across the cabin to the door, favoring his left leg, and goes outside. The two kids look at each other quizzically.

'What the hell...?' starts Matt, but the shh shape on Jesse's lips brings him up short. The pair do as they were told and go to sit at the table.

The door swings open and the trapper comes back into the cabin, the steaming teapot in his right hand. He shuffles across the floor, noticeably rocking side to side as he shifts his weight from one leg to the other. Leaving a trail of spilt tea, he crosses to the cupboard. Stains on the floor, both old and not-so-old, hint that this is not unusual. He draws a couple of tin cups from the cupboard and pours the hot, black tea. Matt nudges Jesse and whispers, 'D'you see that? He must have asbestos hands. That teapot is burning hot!'

The trapper sets the tin cups on the table in front of the children and sits down awkwardly. Maintaining his balance and coordination seems to take an odd concentration.

'Thank you,' says Matt politely. The trapper nods noncommittally at Matt and grunts.

'Did you hurt yourself, Uncle Bill?' inquires Jesse.

'Huh? Hurt myself?' questions the trapper.

'Yes. You seem to be having trouble walking, like you have to focus on each step. What's the matter with your leg?'

The trapper nervously reaches for the silver chain around his neck. He feels along the chain for the gold pendant and, seemingly in a trance, stares at the shiny nugget, anxiously rubbing it between his fingers. An uncomfortable silence occupies the room. Matt and Jesse look at each other, puzzled by the trapper's reaction.

'Uncle Bill?' prompts Jesse.

'What? What're you talking about?' The trapper releases the pendant as he snaps out of his stare. 'I walk just like everyone else. 'sides, what's it to you?'

'Well, the way you walk looks funny to me,' says Matt.

'Matt! Don't be rude!'

'Sorry, Jess. I didn't mean nothin' by it, Bill. I was just making conversation is all.'

The trapper glares at the boy, then turns to Jess. 'My time is precious. What do you want, child?'

'Well, we were just wondering if you could help us track down Donni Cardinal. He's a seven-year-old boy who went missing from his home sometime on Friday. Matt and I think he may have skipped school that day to go fishing along the river and, maybe, got lost in these woods.'

'Sorry,' answers the trapper. 'You kids are the first people I've seen in these parts in weeks.'

'Well, d'you think you could help us look for him? You know these woods better than anyone around.' Jesse decides to lay it on just a little thicker. 'If anyone can find him, you can.'

'I got many traps that need tending. No time for a wild goose chase lookin' for some delinquent kid.'

'Donni's no delinquent. He's a good kid and a close friend of mine. I'd hate to think what could happen to the little guy if he spends another night lost in the wilderness. We would really appreciate your help,' pleads Jesse.

'The harp,' blurts the trapper.

'Excuse me?'

'The harp,' repeats her uncle. He turns to look directly at Matt. 'Give me the harp and I'll help you find the Métis boy.'

Matt looks over at Jesse clearly puzzled.

'Matt, he wants your harmonica.'

'What? My harmonica! No way,' protests Matt. 'D'you know how long

I had to save to get that harmonica?'

'Matt, give it to him,' repeats Jesse, her tone demanding.

'But…but I special ordered it from Vancouver. It's a freakin' Hohner Meisterklasse!'

Jesse just glares at Matt, her right hand on her hip.

'Fine. Fine!' He reaches into his pocket and surrenders his prized possession to the trapper. Uncle Bill smiles mischievously at Matt as he takes the silver harp.

The old trapper rotates the harmonica lovingly in his hands, starring at the gleaming chrome instrument. Almost mesmerized, he fixates on the harp, his teeth chattering. Matt turns to Jesse, crosses his eyes and rotates his finger at his temple in a sign of craziness. 'Well, would you look at the time, Jesse. I think we should run,' says Matt.

'Thank you for the tea, Uncle Bill, and for agreeing to search for Donni,' adds Jesse. The trapper, still absorbed by the glossy harp, doesn't respond.

'Uncle Bill,' says Jesse, a little more sharply.

'Huh? What?' her uncle responds as he snaps out of his daze.

'We're leaving now. We need to get back to town before my mother gets to worrying about us. If you find Donni, just bring him to my house. Mom would love to see you, I'm sure.'

'See me? Yes, of course. I'm sure she'd be surprised. Okay. I have errands to run now myself. Goodbye.'

'Goodbye. We'll visit again soon,' answers Jesse as she rises to leave.

'Maybe when hell freezes over,' mumbles Matt under his breath. Jesse pushes Matt through the open doorway and kicks him in the butt.

'Ow,' complains Matt.

'Why can't you behave?' barks Jesse.

'Shit! Your Uncle is crazier than a loon! Did you see how he stared at my harmonica?'

'I guess that was a bit awkward,' concedes Jesse.

'Awkward my butt. He's a freak! I don't want my harp back now. God knows what he's going to do with it.'

The kids head back towards town along the trail paralleling the river. 'Jesse, how'd he know Donni was Métis?'

'What do you mean?'

'We never mentioned it, yet he knew. Don't you find that a bit weird?'

'Well, Donni's last name is Cardinal. Maybe he assumed he was Métis from his handle.'

'I suppose that's possible,' says Matt. 'Okay, Sherlock, explain this one to me. How'd he carry that burning hot teapot in his bare hands, huh? He never even winced once in pain. It was scalding hot.'

'I really don't know. Some people have been known to walk on red hot coals on their bare feet. Called 'Firewalkers,' they do it all the time. I saw it on TV.'

'Oh, well, if you saw it on TV, I guess it's gotta be true!'

'Shut up, Matt!'

'No, you shut up!'

'No, you shut up!'

Matt and Jesse turn to each other and laugh hysterically. When he catches his breath, Matt says, 'I'm starving.'

'Me, too. If we hurry back to my house, momma will make us our fave—Klik sandwiches.'

'Yum! I'm in. Last one there is the rotten egg!' says Matt.

'Grow up,' answers Jesse as she turns and bolts up the trail ahead of Matt. She's quicker than he is and Matt only catches up to Jesse when she lets him. The two continue along the trail in silence. After a few minutes, Matt takes Jesse's hand and squeezes it lightly.

'Matt, do you think Donni is okay?'

'I really don't know, Jess, but my gut feeling is that it's not going to be a happy ending.'

'I can't help thinking the same thing, and I feel sick about it.'

'Let's try to stay positive, Jess. A lot of people have gone missing in these forests over the years, some in pretty weird circumstances. Most have been found alive.'

'I know you're right,' answers Jesse. 'Donni is a tough kid. He'll be okay.'

'Damn straight, he will,' agrees Matt.

Celreau
1721

Gabriel is startled by a loud commotion from outside accompanied by menacing shouts, the only word he can make out is the repeated kill. He sits up in a panic, trying to collect his senses, still drowsy from his disturbed rest. The angry, chanting voices grow louder as what sounds like a good-sized crowd approaches the dwelling. Trapped within his own cell, he curses the lack of foresight that allowed him to choose to occupy a cellar with but a single door as his only exit. Rushing to unlock the door, he lifts the latch and steps out just in time to meet the furious mob. A screaming swarm of men and women carrying pitchforks, scythes and axes advances towards him with only one intention—kill the vampire!

Gabriel doesn't have time to wonder how they found him. He retreats into the cellar, locking the door behind him. The door shakes and rattles as the crowd beats against it with their weapons. Gabriel knows he is safe for now as the large door is solid oak, strong enough to keep any intruders out. The vampire smirks in relief as the crowd soon comes to the same conclusion, and he hears them leaving the entrance. An eerie silence follows. Then suddenly, an ear-splitting crash rattles the entire structure, jolting the door from its steel hinges. A battering ram explodes through the entrance sending the big door and the startled vampire crashing against the far wall. Gabriel, stunned by the destruction of a door he'd thought impenetrable, lies on the floor covered in stone dust from the shattered wall and wood fragments from the door. He has been impaled by one of the large wooden splinters, which now protrudes grotesquely from his side.

The mob, cheering now, surrounds the wounded vampire. Delighted by the sorry state of the beast, they prepare their weapons for a final assault. To their horror, the vampire stands, grasps the splinter with one hand and slides it red and dripping out of his abdomen. Holding it out in front of them like a bloody sword, he screams, a terrifying sound. The crowd stands in shock as they witness a sudden transformation; His eyes turn charcoal black and sink deep into their sockets. His brow furrows and widens, and his ears seem to pull back. His lips recede and two large sharp canines, dripping of saliva, extend from his gums. His forearm muscles swell to twice the size ripping through his shirt, exposing large veins like swollen dew worms burrowing under his thin skin. They watch as the wound heals in seconds.

The enraged vampire uses the bloody wood splinter to spear one of the attackers through the heart, then drags it downward opening a long gash. The victim's chest explodes in blood and guts, and he falls backwards to the floor. The crowd screams and rushes the vampire in retaliation. Gabriel throws his attackers around the room like so many matchsticks. The gashes and cuts from their forks and axes heal as quickly as they are inflicted. The crowd regroups and charges together again and again, relentlessly stabbing and cutting into the vampire.

Gabriel suddenly feels light headed and stumbles under the crowd's continued onslaught. The bright afternoon sunlight spilling in through the open doorway and a whole day without feeding on fresh blood is now taking its toll and making him vulnerable.

Sensing the vampire's weakness, the mob is revitalized and charges the beast from all sides. Gabriel, overwhelmed by the force of the group, loses his footing and falls backwards to the stone floor. Momentarily disoriented by a blow to his head, Gabriel is pinned down by eight strong men. He opens his eyes to the sight of the sharpened end of a wooden stake against his chest. Gabriel desperately attempts to free himself from the mob's grip as he watches a mallet descend and drive the stake through his chest and into his heart. The vampire looses a terrifying scream as the stinging pain engulfs his being and his body, turning to ash, caves in upon itself.

Gabriel jerks to a sitting position on his mattress, clutching his chest. His eyes search every corner of the room for the killer mob. His gaze encounters only the weak glow of the candle in the candelabra near the big oak door; a door that remains locked and secure. He curses the vivid nightmare as he falls back onto his mattress, frustrated yet much relieved.

Thoughts of Angela begin to invade Gabriel's tired mind. Lacking the will to organize them, memories of shared passion and quiet contentment intertwine inseparably in his mind. He conjures the image of her young, lean, naked body under him, quivering and responding to every stroke of his manhood, satisfying her need with every powerful thrust. Her tender pink nipples are hard and pointed against his hairy chest, and the sweet smell of her sweat mingles with her perfume to permeate his senses. He can almost feel the softness of her warm breath against his cheek as she pants and moans and begs for more. Her finger nails bite into his back, ripping thin scratches as the young lass reaches each powerful orgasm.

The remembered passion begins to shift subtly. Slowly the focus turns from Angela's nubile and nearly insatiable body to the hot fluid of life pumping through her veins. Gabriel's hunger for blood combines with his carnal need for flesh, overwhelming his senses. The lust is upon him and it will not be denied. Without conscious volition, he rises and crosses the cellar. Unlocking the door, he peers into the shallow stairwell; he is pleasantly surprised that darkness has already descended upon the city. While he has been near delirium, contending with murderous intentions of avenging mobs and fantasizing lustfully about Angela, the daylight hours have slipped quietly into night. Gabriel carefully checks that nobody is near. Then he is up the steps and running along the street towards Tamasi.

When Gabriel arrives at the Florescu farm, he cautiously follows the trees that define the property line to the side of the old log house. He hurdles the front porch railing and lands gently next to a rocking chair. Standing at the edge of the large single pane window, he peers inside and inspects the scene. The Florescu family has just finished their supper. Angela's mother is tidying the kitchen; her father, having gone to sit in the living room, lights his corn pipe from the candle on the table beside him. Gabriel catches sight of Angela as she passes the kitchen and goes into her bedroom, closing the door behind her. His heart quickens.

Angela removes her outer clothing, down to her chemise. She lies down on her soft feather bed, weary after a long day of house cleaning. She rolls onto her tummy and fondles her necklace as she daydreams of her tall handsome lover. Why did he run off like that? she wonders silently. Was I too aggressive? Should I have taken Mamă's advice for when I get married? She told me to just lay back and pretend that I enjoy it, that this is how a woman should please a man. I don't understand. How can lovemaking be a burden? I don't need to pretend!

Grasping the locket in her fist, she draws both hands to her chest just above her breasts. Gabriel has taken me to heaven and back; how can this be painful? He makes me feel so wonderful, so free. Perhaps it's me. Could

I be intimidating him? If only Gabi were here so I could make things better for him.

The bed bounces suddenly, making Angela gasp in fright. Her shriek of surprise is muffled by Gabriel's large hand. She stares in disbelief into his dark eyes. 'Shhh, my lamb, it's only me. Be still. We don't want to alert your parents, now do we? going to remove my hand now.'

'Gabi!' whispers Angela, visibly trying to restrain her emotions. 'I can't believe my eyes. You startled me! I was just wishing you were here. How did you get into my room without Tată noticing?'

Ignoring her question, Gabriel says, 'I came to apologize, sweetheart, for my rudeness last night. I don't know what came over me. One moment I was in the thralls of ecstasy and the next I had...'

'It's okay, my dearest,' interrupts Angela. 'You don't need to explain. I understand.'

'You do?'

'Gabi, when you make love to me, you bring the animal out in me. I become aggressive and wild.'

'You have the same effect on me, my lamb' answers Gabriel, smiling.

'That's wonderful, Gabi, but you're wrong about that,' says Angela giggling.

'Wrong about what?' asks Gabriel.

'True, we are both animals,' explains the girl. 'You are the fierce hungry beast, but I am not your helpless lamb. I am, in fact, your playful sly fox. I submit to your desires, but not without a fight.'

'You are indeed a sly fox, always one step ahead of the hunt. But I am wiser and just as sly. Your scent always gives you away, my dear.'

'Ah, but your vanity misleads you, my love,' laughs Angela. 'What you perceive as a weakness is nothing less than my lure, drawing you right to where I want you—in my arms.'

'The hunter has become the hunted, trapped by his cunning prey. What am I to do?' asks Gabriel.

'You will submit to my needs and obey my wishes. I am now your mistress.'

'And if I refuse?' asks Gabriel, amused by the exchange.

'This fox will rip your clothing off, bit by bit, tearing at their threads, till your body lies vulnerable and naked, ready for my sexual pleasure.'

'Tell me, my fierce little fox, what assurance do you have that I'll not turn on you, as all wild things inevitably do, and fulfill my appetite?'

'You're so naive, sweetheart. You would only be unleashing your lust on me and satisfying my desires, as I have planned all along. So, now that we both know who is truly in control, shut up and kiss me, you beast.'

Gabriel kisses Angela passionately. He slips her chemise down from her shoulders exposing her beautiful white breasts. Angela unbuttons his shirt. Slipping her hands under the loosened fabric, she caresses his chest, then runs her hands over his powerful shoulders. Pushing Gabriel back onto the mattress, she slides down and unbuttons his pants. She reaches in and grabs his large penis in both hands. Already rising, it is immediately hard and strong in her grip. She slides her tongue along his shaft, caressing his balls with her fingers. He moans and strokes her hair as she gently pleasures him.

After a few moments, she sits up in the bed and finishes removing her chemise, exposing the rest of her tight voluptuous body. Gabriel, kneeling, stares in wonder at the beautiful creature before him; his mind fills with lust and fantasy as he anticipates the moment. Angela, naked and wet, kneels on the bed and bends forward, coming to rest on her elbows. She looks back at her lover and whispers, 'Ravish me, my wolf. I am your prey for the taking.'

Gabriel grins at Angela, enjoying the rising passion in her expression as she watches her lover slide his pants down completely exposing his hard, swollen member. Angela's heart races and her body trembles as Gabriel kneels on the bed and crawls slowly up behind her. She shrieks as she unexpectedly feels his warm tongue slide along her thighs and into her wet vagina. His tongue skillfully explores all of her; licking and sucking her sweet nectar, his fingers simultaneously sliding inside her.

'Oh, Gabriel! You drive me insane. Take me, take me now!' With no hesitation, Gabriel straightens and quickly thrusts the full length of his manhood into the young lustful maiden. 'Ravage me, you beast,' shouts Angela. Gabriel, fully aroused by her command, grips the young woman by her hips and pounds his throbbing cock into her. 'You're such an animal. Yes! Yes!'

Completely enraptured by love and fantasy, the vampire gives himself to the consuming pleasure. Without discernible transition, thoughts of tenderness and sexual pleasure morph into images of flesh and blood. Angela screeches in pain as the beast suddenly drives his shaft harder and deeper; wedged between her alabaster thighs, he viciously hammers his penis into her repeatedly.

'Gabriel, you're hurting me. Gabriel, I said you're hurting me. Gabriel stop!'

The beast is unresponsive to Angela's insistent plea. The pungent smell of sex and fear permeates his olfactory senses and ignites his primal hunger. His powerful hands turn her head to expose her long slender neck. Instinctively, he lunges, sinking his canines deep into her tender neck, puncturing her blood rich carotid artery. Angela's struggles beneath him quickly subside. She loses consciousness, the loss of blood depriving her brain of vital oxygen.

The vampire savagely continues to thrusts his phallus into his lover-turned-victim, the rhythm perversely matching the blood surge that fills his mouth with every beat of her failing heart. In an erotic trance, his eyes roll back and his body tightens in ecstasy. He reaches orgasm and explodes within her as she surrenders her last spray of blood and gasps her last living breath.

A deafening shotgun blast shatters the room. The vampire's shoulder erupts in a spray of flesh bits, bone fragments and blood. The impact propels the screaming vampire off Angela and over the side of the bed. Slimy, blood-soaked particles cover the headboard and Angela's pretty face. Angela's father, Nico, stands shaking in the doorway, reloading in preparation for his next shot. Gabriel, still caught up in the blood lust and infuriated by the surprise assault, leaps over the bed, landing next to the big farmer. Terrified, Nico freezes, staring at what should be a critical shoulder wound as it heals before his very eyes. The vampire wraps his arms around the farmer's head, and with one quick movement, he snaps the thick weathered neck. Nico crumbles in a heap to the bedroom floor, dead. At that moment, Angela's mother steps through the doorway behind the vampire and sinks a sharp carving knife deep between the vampire's shoulder blades. Agony grips Gabriel. He screams. While the woman stares, he reaches back and pulls the knife from his back. Turning, he grasps her throat in one hand, raises her into the air and squeezes, watching her face turn blue. With his other hand, he sinks the knife into the woman's convulsing body. He brings her in close and sinks his teeth into the big woman's neck, drinking her blood until she goes limp. Still holding fast to the carving knife, he slices down, opening her from breasts to waist. Her innards spill wetly out of her body cavity, landing in a slippery pile at the vampire's feet. He drops his victim on top of the steaming heap like so much butchered offal. He turns and kneels next to Nico to complete his blood feast.

Invigorated by the meal and sexually fulfilled, he stands at the doorway, overlooking the scene. He looks at Angela's pale naked body lying dead on the bed. An intense pang of grief engulfs his empty soul. And abrupt embarrassment, realizing he is still exposed; he rearranges and buttons his trousers.

Walking to the blood-stained bed, he picks Angela up in his arms and desperately laments, 'Why? Why?' He lays her limp and bloodied body back on the bed. Crying, he gently brushes her hair to the side with his fingers, then removes the heart-shaped pendant from her punctured throat. The vampire squeezes the pendant tightly in the palm of his hand and screams with all the anguish in his soul. Infuriated by his folly and the evil fate to which he is condemned, he rushes out of the farmhouse onto the muddy road towards Bucharest. His cloak flapping in the cool night air, he runs like a wild animal along the mucky path. Unhindered by slippery rocks and deep puddles, he sprints, desperate to rid himself of the sorrow and pain that torment his conflicted mind. The taste of Angela's blood lingers in his mouth and on his tongue, infusing his body with strength and vigor, while thoughts of passion and lust torture him. Feelings of regret and remorse threaten to unhinge him.

Approaching the river, he jogs up the slope of the wide arched bridge, stopping at the center. The torrential current crashes against jagged black boulders as the river narrows under the bridge, funneling steeply towards the precipice where the rushing water cascades hundreds of meters to the valley below. Arms extended in front of him, he grips the stone wall tightly, staring at the falls and the raging river. With little effort, the vampire pulls himself onto the wall, continuing to stare at the muddy flow. He screams in desperation and dives into the roiling waters. His shoulder and ribs shatter against a boulder, the loud snap echoing through his head. He cries out in agony as the sharp broken bones of his rib cage tear through his skin to protrude from his chest. His head slams against a large rock, splitting his forehead open. The force of the blow spins his body wildly into the raging swells and down river. His broken body bobs uncontrollably in and out of the water as he is carried toward the waterfall. Abruptly he jolts to a stop, impaled through the stomach on the broken branch of a fallen pine tree.

But much as he wishes to die, he doesn't. Even as he hangs on the piercing tree limb, he feels his head and ribs repairing themselves. After a few minutes, still despondent, he faces the reality and, one-handed, pulls himself off the impaling branch. By the time he pulls himself ashore, using the tree for stability, the stomach wound is almost completely eradicated.

He lies for a time face-down on the riverbank, grieving. Rising, he works his way back to the road.

Just before daybreak, the drizzle finally lets up. The cobblestone streets of Budapest are empty and quiet, except for the barking of the few stray dogs roaming in the distance. Coming upon a coach house on the outskirts of the city, he takes cover by the side of the horse stable and strips out of his wet clothes. He hangs them to dry on the lower branches of an old oak tree. Naked, he lowers himself to his belly and crawls under the front porch of the building. Huddling in a dark corner, he contemplates his plight.

Later, during the daylight hours, he hears voices and the stomping of feet above his head, as passengers arrive and depart the station. Some children, sent off to play by impatient parents, discover the vampire's clothes where he left them to dry. They giggle and laugh, taking turns trying them on before strewing them all over the yard. Sometime after they tire of this game and move on, a farm dog discovers the clothes and worries at them until they are in shreds. The dog picks up the scent of the vampire from his clothing and follows the trail to the front porch. Sticking his head under deck for a better look, the hound receives a slap on the snout causing the animal to retreat with a whimper.

The day seems to last forever, but the sun finally sets over Bucharest. The vampire crawls out from under the deck. Still naked, he hides in the shadows against the station wall, biding his time, watching and listening intently. Finally one last passenger prepares to board an otherwise empty coach. The coachman steps down and opens the carriage door.

'Good evening, Dr. Palka,' says the coachman. 'Looks like clear weather for your journey to Slovenia.'

'Wonderful! I am looking forward to getting some rest along the way,' answers the traveler.

'Well, you'll have no other passengers to disturb you, sir, and I will do my best to keep the ride smooth and steady.'

'That would be much appreciated,' answers Palka, as he boards the coach. He is barely seated when he hears the crack of the whip. The carriage lurches as it pulls away and heads out of town. The vampire, sprints from the shadows and jogs down the road, overtaking the carriage. He leaps onto the luggage hold on the back of the coach, clinging to the leather straps. Once the coach passes the town limits and turns onto the country road, he pounces to the right rear corner of the carriage. Gripping the steel roof rack with his hands, he raises his legs just enough to miss the spinning wheels, shuffles precariously along the side of the carriage, trying to maintain a small profile, until he is close enough to kick the door handle open. The door swings wide, and the vampire drops inside, startling Palka. The sight of the naked intruder evokes a sharp gasp of surprise from the lips of the lone passenger.

'What is the meaning of this? Who are you, sir? And, more to the point, why are you naked?'

'So many questions! Perhaps a simple 'How do you do?' is in order.'

'What do you want?'

'Want? I'll tell you what I want. I want to die.'

'What? That's absurd! No one wants to die.'

'Well, I do. Is that too much to ask?'

'I am a physician, sir, devoted to the preservation of life and the enhancement of health. I am quite sure I can help you. Whatever troubles you. You don't have to die.'

'You're a fool. You know nothing about me.'

'I am quite confused. You are the intruder, sir, so kindly explain yourself. What do you want from me?'

'Blood.'

'Blood? Why, whatever for? How much do you need, and how do you propose to extract it?'

'My, you are innocent, aren't you? I need to feed, so I am going to take all your blood.' Celreau smiles, his canines visibly lengthening.

'Oh my. You're a vampire! I have always thought vampires were not real, fictional beings invented to scare children into obedience. I have never seen any scientific evidence of their existence.'

'I assure you, I am quite real, as you are about to learn.'

'But you can't. I have a wife and children who depend on me. Please. I…I am a man of medicine. People depend on me. Listen, I am not a poor man. How much do you want to spare my life?'

'Your money is of no value to me.'

'You're—you're mad.'

'Do I look mad to you?'

'Only a madman would kill a stranger for no reason.'

'You're right, but you see I have a reason, one that I would not expect the likes of you to understand. My thirst, my need, for blood was never reasoned into me, so alas it can't be reasoned out.'

'Dear God, help me.'

'Ha! Your dear God never helped me, so why do you think he will help you?'

'Please, I beg you. Please don't hurt me?' begs the traveler, now openly crying.

The vampire climbs onto the man and whispers in his ear. 'Listen. I'm sure you're a fine, respectable man. I don't hate you nor have I any grievances with you. In fact, I am beginning to like you. But unfortunately, as fate has it, I must kill you.' Gabriel's face is grim as he moves his head towards the victim's neck.

'No, no! Stop! Listen to me. You just said you like me. We are becoming friends. Surely you wouldn't harm a friend,' pleads the doctor in desperation.

Enraged, the vampire grabs Palka's head between his powerful hands. He stares into his eyes. 'I killed the most precious, beautiful creature on earth—the love of my life. How dare you suggest that you are worth more than my Angela.'

In one smooth motion, the vampire snaps his riding companion's neck. Biting into Palka's pale throat, the vampire revels in the rhythmic pulse of the dying man gushing into his mouth. Palka's heartbeat slows... abruptly stops. Gabriel lets the doctor's body slip to the floor of the carriage. Fed and content, for the time being, he relaxes and slides back into the leather upholstery. He wonders how Palka's wife and children will survive now that the good doctor is dead. Considering Palka's profession, Gabriel assumes that they are financially stable and will somehow manage without him. The widow will likely sell the house and move to a small apartment. He pictures her spending her days caring for the children and the evenings knitting by the fireplace. He feels no guilt at these thoughts; after all, his torment is forever, while Palka suffers pain no longer. If Gabriel feels anything at all, it is envy of the mortals around him. For them eventually comes a time of rest and peace, a time that he knows will never arrive for him.

Abruptly, Gabriel's contentment turns to anger and a desire for revenge. He damns the man who inflicted him with this curse. The only potential consolation, the only possible satisfaction, is to find Petru and exact sweet revenge. He realizes that the coach's next stop, its final destination, is Budapest, Hungary, coincidently the home of that homosexual vampire. Gabriel smiles. He has reason to go on a little longer.

Stan

1965

The sweet smell of red cedar fills the tradesman's senses. His feet shuffle through the layers of wood chips that litter the floor as he moves around the totem he is carving. Skillfully his chisel etches the outside ovoid of the Raven's eye deep into the trunk of the ancient tree. The rhythmic tap-tap-tap of his hammer striking the chisel handle echoes from the walls of the longhouse, reminiscent of the ancient drums of his Haida ancestors.

In his youth, Stan spent years developing the skills of his art. He learned from the best. His Uncle Walter was watghadagaang, a master carver. Endless days were devoted to observing his uncle chop and carve the huge trunks into magnificent totem poles. At first Stan simply helped by handing tools to the artist and sweeping up wood chips, but after a few years he gained his uncle's respect and was taken under the older man's tutelage.

Abruptly his uncle is there, in the longhouse, reminding him in his patient voice, 'Concentrate Stanley. Let the blade do the work.

'Easy now. Widen the outer ovoid,' the old artisan goes on. 'Remember the basics I taught you; thick on top, thin on sides, and bottom symmetrical. That's it. Now, compress the edges on the eyelid lines. Yes, yes.'

Under his uncle's eye, Stan had learned to chisel and paint, but had been limited to the top character of the pole. The carving of the 'bottom man on the totem pole,' despite the saying, is reserved for the master craftsman, being the most highly viewed character of the structure.

'Stanley! Balance your fine lines.'

'Uncle Walter! Enough already. I have this.'

'Careful, son. I may have taught you everything you know, but I did not teach you everything I know.'

'Sorry, Uncle. I appreciate your advice, but I do remember everything you taught me before you passed away.'

'Very well, Stanley, understood. I will go now and leave you in peace. I look forward to the raising ceremony.'

'Thank you, Uncle. I will make you proud.'

'Goodnight, Stanley,' answers the ghost as he walks away and dissipates through the wall.

Today, Stan Fairchild is one of only a handful of Haida artists left on the island who practice this art and are interested in preserving the native traditions and culture in any form. Growing up deep in the rain forest of Masset, Stan learned to fish the coastal waters with his father, while his mother taught him the medicinal value of native plants found hidden on the lush carpet of the forest floor. Stan was prone to visions when he roamed the forest alone. Quite commonly he would see ghostly shapes and forms in the forest, and not knowing what they were, he was afraid of them. Eventually he confided in his mother and she explained that he was special—that he was touched. She told him that the presence of his ancestors' spirits was nothing to fear; rather, she taught Stan to train his mind to communicate with them. He soon learned they were not only a source of support and encouragement, but they were willing to share a trove of knowledge and folklore long lost to living band members.

Stan eventually moved south to Skidegate to open a successful cannery business. He became proud of his heritage and somewhat of a self-proclaimed ambassador of Haida Guaii. Stan enjoyed sharing his fishing stories with the fishermen at the local watering hole. He loved teaching the mothers and caregivers about the herbs and plants with secret medicinal properties that could be used to heal patients of ailments that modern medicine failed to cure.

His enthusiasm was contagious, and soon the band began to experience a rejuvenation of Haida pride and confidence. Stan spearheaded the development of the Haida Council and was elected president. The protection of the Western red cedar forest was his main priority, which put him at odds with the big forestry companies seeking huge profits by harvesting the massive trees found throughout the area they egotistically called Queen Charlotte Island.

The crowd huddles together on the beach, wrapped in tightly held blankets to shield themselves from the cold wind blowing off the ocean. They watch in silence as a Haida canoe approaches, propelled by ten strong men chanting and rowing in unison to the rhythm of the drummer seated at the center. The steersman stands at the rear and guides the formidable canoe towards the beach. Carved from a single sixteen-meter Red Cedar log and capable of holding up to five tonnes of cargo, the Lootaas, or Wave-eater, meets little resistance as it breasts the ocean waves.

The group onshore erupts in applause and joins the paddlers in chanting and drumming, as the men step from the canoe into the icy water and drag the dugout onto the beach. Forming a loose procession, they move up the beach towards the totem pole lying on the sand. When they and members of the crowd have taken their positions along both sides of the pole, Stan shouts directions through a megaphone. On his count, the crowd hoists the totem pole and carefully carries the heavy trunk towards a deep hole that has been dug near the tree line. The elders, wearing ornate white ermine hats and chilkate blankets, sit proudly in chairs to observe the celebration. With its bottom end overhanging the hole, the totem pole is lain back down and heavy ropes are attached to its upper portions. These ropes are linked to a series of poles and levers.

Stan separates the excited crowd into four groups that, at his command, tug the ropes to raise the pole. As the pole nears vertical, the bottom drops into the hole. The jubilant crowd cheers and yelps at the sight of their marvelous totem pole standing tall and magnificent. Once it is in position, everybody participates in filling the hole at the base with large rocks and sand. A ceremonial dance ensues; warriors with raddles pursue masked children covered in cedar bows.

Stan is overwhelmed by emotion. The project over which he has toiled for more than a year has come to fruition. He holds back tears as the ceremonial dance ends and the local Shaman blesses the great totem pole.

'You've accomplished a wonderful thing here, Stan,' says Big Mama, wrapping her arms around her husband.

'Thank you, dear, for your patience and support.'

'Look at the pride in their faces. It's been years since we've experienced such fellowship in the band.'

'We must take responsibility for helping our young people to discover their Haida roots. We need to educate them, to lead by example.'

Big Mama looks up at Stan's weathered face and smiles. 'This is why I married you.'

'And here I thought it was because of my boyish good looks.'

'Love you, baby.'

'Love you, too, honey'

'Let's go home now, you silly old fool,' she says playfully. 'You need your rest.'

'Just a moment, hon. I have one more thing I must do.'

Stan walks over to the carving, closes his eyes and presses his right hand against the pole. When he opens his eyes after a moment, he sees his Uncle Walter sitting cross-legged in the sand nearby. His uncle smiles, nods his head in agreement and puts his hand on his heart. Stan puts his hand on his heart and smiles back at his uncle.

'Stan, is everything okay?' asks Big Mama.

'Yes, honey,' answers Stan, turning and walking to her.

'Walter just appeared to you, didn't he, sweetheart?'

'Yes, he sure did.'

'And he approved?'

'Yes, he sure did,' repeats Stan with a wide grin.

As the celebration ends, the beach empties. Soon the only things moving are a pair of lumberjacks stumbling along the water's edge towards the area just vacated by the band members. Stan and Big Mama are among the last to leave.

'Hank, give me another swig of that poison you call whiskey.'

''kay, Jed, but no backwash this time, you drunken fool.'

'Hey, look! What's that?'

'It's the totem pole that asshole Fairchild's been workin' on.'

'That dirty injun and his council put me out of a job.'

'Yeah. They won't let me cut down trees to feed my family, but somehow seems he's got the right.'

'I know. It just ain't right.'

'Fuckin' bullshit's what it is.'

'I'm cold to the bone. What say we find us some firewood and start us a fire?'

'Great idea! An' I got us just the right piece of dry kindling for the job.'

Jed gathers several armloads of dry beach grass and lays it thickly around the base of the totem pole. 'Hey, I don't like the way that stupid bird is lookin' down at me from the top of the pole.'

'Now, now, Jed. That ain't no way to talk. That there stupid bird happens to be the natives' creator and supreme shithawk. I do believe you owe it an apology.'

'Aw, shucks. Your shithawk holiness, I am so fuckin' sorry,' laughs Jed. Taking a wooden match out of the box pulled from his pocket, he strikes it on the zipper of his pants and lights the beach grass. 'Sorry, but you're about to become the largest Haida birthday candle on this miserable island.'

The pair of drunken fools lie down on the beach and watch the flames slowly climb to the top of the tall totem pole.

'Serves him an' the rest of those wagon burners right. Las' month my son lost his right eye when the chain on his chainsaw blew apart. He hit one of the nails those savages hammered into the big cedars hereabouts. My boy was just tryin' ta make a livin' doin' a little loggin'. He hadda do somethin' after Mr. High-n-Mighty Stan decided my son weren't good enuff ta work at the Fairchild cann'ry.'

'I hear ya. And then half our paycheck goes to taxes to support them lazy redskins. D'you know they don' pay no damn taxes, not even on smokes? How the hell'd they swing that? Better yet, why'd we agree ta such a thing?'

'You said it, man. And then they got the balls ta drive on our highways an' get free Medicare. Fuck Stan Fairchild an' the wagon he rode in on,' adds Hank, his face distorted in anger.

'Damn straight! Somebody gotta stand up to them stinkin' injuns and teach 'em some respect. How long did that dirty redskin take whittlin' this stump?'

'Over a year,' answers Hank.

'Aww, ain't that a shame,' says Jed sarcastically.

'Damn shame, but ain't it purdy all lit up though?'

'It's a beaut, alright,' answers Jed.

'Enjoy the moment fools,' says a voice in the dark.

'What'd you say?'

'I said Ain't it pretty all lit up.'

'No, no. After that.'

'I didn't say nuthin' after that. Go to sleep. Yer drunk.'

'Aww, shit. I'm sure I heard somebody say somethin'.'

'Yeah, sure. Maybe the shithawk is talkin' to you.'

'Fuck you!'

'Fuck you, too, Jed. G'night. I'm hittin' the sack.'

In the early dawn, Hank shivers awake on the cold ground. 'Jesus, it's colder than a witch's tit out here.' As he tries to sit up, the throbbing in his head is magnified tenfold and dizziness overwhelms his senses. 'Ow. I think I'm going to throw up! Jed, you 'wake? Jed?' Fighting back the nausea, Hank glances around the beach and finds no sign of Jed.

'Where'd that pinhead go?' he mumbles to himself rising to his feet. He looks at the smoldering totem pole and takes a step back in horror. He rubs his eyes, tentatively moving closer to the charred pole for a better look, his mind unwilling to accept the evidence of his eyes. 'What the hell? This some sorta fuckin' joke?'

Caricatures of the two lumberjacks, their tongues hanging down from their mouths, have been carved into the bottom half of the charred totem pole. Looking down the beach, he waves his arms and yells to attract the attention of a young man jogging along the water's edge.

When the jogger approaches, he asks, 'What happened to the totem pole?'

'You got me. I jus' spotted the smoke and come over ta have a look myself,' answers Hank.

'Yeah, right,' the young man comments skeptically. The inebriated antics of Hank and his cohort are well known in the community.

'Anyways. I's wonderin' if you happened ta see a tall, lanky guy somewheres along the beach.'

'No. The beach is pretty much deserted this time of the morning. In fact, I was quite surprised to run into you. This guy you're looking for, is he missing?'

'Naw, we just sorta got separated somehow. You know what, don't worry about it. Forget I asked.'

'Suit yourself. Hey, that's you,' exclaims the jogger, pointing at the totem pole. 'That face is your spitting image.'

'Yeah, someone's idea of a joke. Very funny!'

'That's no joke, mister. You better update your will.'

'What's that s'pposed ta mean? You bes' not be threatenin' me, boy.'

'Relax, mister. It's not me you need to worry about.'

'Who, then?'

'You see how the long tongue is sticking out of your mouth on that carving?'

'Yeah—very funny, eh?'

'Well, no, actually. Not the least bit funny. The message it sends is very serious indeed.'

'So, what's it mean then?'

'The Haida carve a long tongue like that on dead characters.'

'What?'

'Yep. And if the subject is still alive when the carving is made, they always turn up dead in short order. Man, sucks to be you. Listen, I gotta run. Literally.'

'Why you…'

'And good luck. You're gonna need it, mister!' Hank turns and again looks at the figures of Jed and himself carved into the burnt totem. What a bunch of injun BS. Jed must've woken up and headed back to town is all, he thinks to himself. Stepping back, he stumbles. Looking down, he sees he has stepped into a groove in the sand about four inches deep. The groove, evidently made by something heavy being dragged, extends down the beach to the water's edge, where Hank can make out something partially buried in the wet sand. Even at this distance he can see that it is Jed's wool tuque. Walking over to pick it up, he sees that the tuque, and now his hands, are covered in blood.

'What the hell?' He drops the tuque to the ground and wipes his hands on his jeans. 'Shit. Somethin's happened to Jed. Somethin' real bad.'

Hank, now more than a little shaken, starts jogging along the beach, eyes scanning everywhere for a sign of his injured friend.

'Jed! Jed! Where the hell you at? Can you hear me? Jed!' yells Hank repeatedly. After only a few minutes of this exertion, he drops to his knees to catch his breath, cold and exhausted. He sits back, gazing out over the ocean, trying to relax. The gentle, repeated motion of the waves has begun to lull his senses when he sees something dark rolling back and forth with the surf a short distance up the beach. Getting to his feet, he runs splashing into the cold water for a closer look. His worst fears are realized.

'Oh, my God! Jed! What've they done to ya?' He grabs the dead man by the collar of his jacket and drags the swollen body out of the water onto the beach. Hank moves close to Jed's head to check for signs of breathing. He gasps and sits back on his haunches in disgust. The side of his friend's head has been caved in; brain matter is strung through his hair like jelly.

'Jesus!' Hank, nauseated by the scene, throws up. 'Fairchild, you son of a bitch!' swears Hank, wiping vomit from his lips. You'll pay for this, ya fuckin' tree hugger.'

Stanley wakes early. He slowly sits up in bed, careful not to wake Betty. The open window admits the early hints of a colorful sunrise. A warm feeling of contentment from the raising of the Totem Pole last evening still lingers. He smiles.

'Honey, you're up early.' Betty's voice is soft with sleep.

'Sorry I woke you, sweetheart. Go back to sleep.'

'Is everything okay, dear?'

'Things couldn't be better. I'm still excited about last night.'

'You did a beautiful thing, Stan. I'm so proud of you.'

'Honey, go back to sleep. There's a bit of cleaning up to do around the longhouse, then I'll come home and join you for breakfast.'

'Okay, hon. I'll have the coffee on,' answers Big Mama, giving her husband a kiss.

The forest trail leading to the longhouse is off the main road to town. The walk takes Stan less than ten minutes. He, along with the band council, built the traditional six-beam house in an effort to inspire a resurgence of Haida culture in the area. The magnificent structure, entirely constructed of Red Cedar, measures sixty feet long by thirty feet wide. All who come and go must pass through the shadow of the tall, carved memorial pole freestanding at the entrance. A magnificent carving of the Raven, with large eyes and a strong beak, adorns the top of the pole, seemingly guarding the house.

Entering the building, Stan begins the task of sweeping up the thick layer of cedar shavings that has accumulated on the floor during almost a year of carving the totem pole. He spends over an hour shoveling the mess into a pile at the center of the room, then goes over the floor again with a push-broom to clear the thick red dust from the floor boards. Sweaty and exhausted, from the hard labor and the late evening of festivities, he sits down to take a breather in one of the wooden chairs along the wall and is soon asleep.

Hank, still rattled by the sight of his drowned friend, arrives at the longhouse with one thing on his mind—revenge. Light escaping from the crack at the top of the front door alerts him that there's someone inside. Sliding his long buck knife from its belt holster, he quietly opens the big solid door. He peers inside. Happily surprised to see Stan fast asleep in a chair, he walks around a giant pile of cedar chips in the middle of the floor and slowly crosses the great hall, careful not to disturb his unsuspecting victim. Scanning the big room, he soon finds what he wants—a tin can full of long wooden matches standing next to the central fire pit. He grins, picks a match, and walks back towards the entrance. Striking the match, he flips it onto the pile of dry red cedar chips.

André

1980

Dawn Brady, the mayor's daughter, and her best friend, Christine Henderson, are headed home after spending the early afternoon at the beach. Not much of anything was happening, so they have decided to look elsewhere for amusement. Although it is a little out of their way, they walk past the town fairgrounds, hoping to run into someone interesting.

Big André Robillard is standing in one of the fairground's open fields chopping at a block of wood with an ax. He is wearing heavy caulk boots, tight faded blue jeans and bright red suspenders over his sweat-soaked T-shirt. The over-sized, double-bladed ax looks almost small in his huge hands. Great chips of wood fly off the aspen log as he strikes the wooden trunk repeatedly with powerful blows.

'Mmm, look at those sweet biceps, Dawn. André is so dreamy.'

'Yeah, he sure is a hunk,' answers Dawn. 'Too bad he's a stuttering retard.'

'Dawn, you're terrible. André is twenty-five years old, Métis, and has a learning disability. He has the mentality of a twelve-year-old. He's not a retard. They wouldn't trust a retard anywhere near such a dangerous tool, especially unsupervised. As a matter of fact, he's practicing for the Lumberjack Competition next weekend.'

'Thanks for the profile, Dr. Henderson, but he's still a stuttering retard as far as I'm concerned,' laughs Dawn. 'Now, c'mon. Follow me. Let's get a closer look at the stud muffin.'

André puts down his ax when he notices the girls approaching. 'Hi, Paul Bunyan,' says Dawn, chuckling. 'Where is 'Babe'?'

'Allo, Dawn. M-m-my name is not P-P-Paul, it is André. Who is 'B-B-Babe'?' asks André. His brow furrows in bewilderment.

'Never mind, big boy. We just came by to watch you work out. That okay?'

'Yeah, sure, I g-g-guess,' stutters an embarrassed André.

'You have such big muscles, André, I bet you could pick me up with one arm, eh?' teases Dawn coyly.

'Well, m-m-maybe. I d-d-don't know,' André replies, his stuttering getting worse, shy to be the focus of their attention.

Christine is uncomfortable watching Dawn tease the gentle simpleton. She turns to her companion and says, 'Well, Dawn, on that note, I'd better be heading home. I'm starved. Call you after lunch, 'kay?'

'Okay, girlfriend. Later.' answers Dawn, making no move to do the same.

'Behave yourself, girl,' says her friend. She winks and walks away.

As Christine moves out of earshot, Dawn steps a little closer to André, making him even more uncomfortable.

'So, André. Looks like it's just you and me now. Would you be a sweetie and escort me down to the beach? I forgot my sunglasses on the pier and I don't want to walk there alone. It isn't safe.'

'I dunno. I'm supposed to be p-p-practicin' my chopping,' answers André anxiously.

Dawn wraps both hands around André's sizable forearm and tugs. 'It's only fifteen minutes to the beach and back. C'mon, you big lug. Don't be such a stick-in-the-mud. Live a little. It'll be fun.'

'Okay, Dawn, as long as we c-c-come right b-b-back.' With one swift motion, André drives his ax deep into the log and follows Dawn out of the fairground and onto the beach trail. The narrow path steepens and widens as the ocean comes into view. They descend along the sandy bank. About to step out on the rocky shore, Dawn turns right, away from the pier. 'This way!'

André stops. 'B-b-but the pier is over there?'

'I know, André,' pleads Dawn, 'but my feet hurt from the walk and I wanna rest on the bank for just a minute. You don't want me to be in pain, do you?'

'N-n-no, 'course not,' answers André, following her into the tall beach grass. She sits down in the soft sand and, looking up at André, pats the sand next to her. André sits down next to her in awkward silence and nervously stares out at the bay.

'So-o, André. Do you have a girlfriend?' Dawn asks, setting her hand on André's lap.

'N-n-no, I don't,' answers André. Uncomfortable, he slides his leg away from her hand. Dawn, undeterred, takes one of André's big hands in hers. 'Do you think I'm pretty, André?'

'You're b-b-beautiful, Dawn. You're the m-m-most beautiful g-g-girl in town.'

'Aww! You're so sweet,' replies Dawn. She leans over and kisses him on the cheek. André wipes his cheek with his other hand and stares at Dawn, speechless. 'You ever kissed a girl, André? Bet you haven't. Would you like to kiss me?'

'I have to g-g-get back to m-m-my ch-ch-chopping,' answers André.

'Really André? Is that what you really want to do?' taunts Dawn.

'I-I-I got t-t-to g-g-go.'

Before the big fellow can move to stand, Dawn rolls onto his lap and pushes hard on his chest, sending him flat on his back.

'Not so quick, big boy.' She leans over and kisses him hard on the lips. Dawn pulls back to look down at André's half-stunned look. 'Feels good, huh? Congratulations, André. You got to first base.'

'B-b-but I g-g-got t-t-to...'

'Shhhh. Relax, André,' whispers Dawn. 'Everything's okay. We're just having a little fun. Pay attention now.'

She slowly unbuttons her shirt and exposes her firm young breasts. She isn't wearing a bra. André stares at her exposed chest in shock. He is captivated by the visual stimulation, yet ashamed to be seeing something he knows he is not supposed to see. Dawn takes André's hands and places them on her breasts. 'Mmmm. I can tell by that manly bulge against my butt that you enjoy second base.'

André smiles uncomfortably and says, 'F-f-feels n-n-nice b-b-but...'

'Get ready for third base, André,' interrupts Dawn. She slides her hands down André's muscular chest and unfastens his belt buckle. She unbuttons his Levis and slides his zipper down. André arches back as Dawn slides his erection from his underwear and grasps his hard shaft in her hand. Dawn looks up at André with a mischievous grin and says, 'Third base!'

André pulls back in surprise and horror. He jumps to his feet, bumping Dawn in the process, catapulting her down the sandy embankment. André turns and runs back up the trail toward the fairgrounds, zipping his pants as he runs. He mumbles to himself, 'M-M-Mama said n-n-nobody can touch my p-p-privates. M-M-Mama said n-n-nobody can t-t-touch my p-p-private parts. Dawn is a b-b-bad girl, a b-b-bad girl.'

Dawn, a little dazed from a knock she took to the back of her head, is covered in grass and sand, lying at the bottom of the slope. She gets to her feet, a bit dizzy, and wipes the dirt from her dress. Her hand comes away bloody when she feels for the bump on the back of her head. 'Freakin' retard! I'll get him for this. What the hell? Does he think I'm not pretty enough for him? I'll fix him. Wait till my dad finds out how he tried to rape me! Freakin' retard!'

Matt & Jesse
1980

Making their way down Muskrat Street to Main, Matt and Jesse arrive just in time to find Sergeant Kirkpatrick, Mayor Brady and some unknown man in an RCMP uniform addressing the morning's search party, which is assembled in the front parking lot of the general store.

'First and foremost, I want to thank you all for your time and effort in searching for Donni Cardinal,' says Kirkpatrick. 'I know some of you are feeling discouraged because you failed to find the boy along the shoreline, but in fact you have helped us eliminate the waterfront as a possible whereabouts for the boy. We can now focus our search efforts in other areas.

'And we'll have a little additional help. I decided to swallow my pride and request some assistance from the regional RCMP office.' Pointing to the new officer, he continues, 'I'd like you all to meet Corporal Fontaine. Please give him your full cooperation.

'This afternoon we will concentrate on the area along Kettle Creek down towards Frenchmen Mountain. I know it's getting a little late, but we have a few hours before sunset this time of year. Now, Donni's parents informed me that their son spent a lot of time fishing in that area. He may have gotten disoriented and lost his way, or perhaps even injured himself. We'll search the trail and the woods on either side. Stay about five meters apart and in sight of the searchers on either side of you at all times. We will all meet back here at 4:00 pm, just before dark. Stay safe and good luck. Are there any questions or concerns?'

'We already searched the Kettle Creek trail, Officer Kirkpatrick,' Matt calls from the edge of the group.

'What is your name, young man?' asks Kirkpatrick.

'Matt, sir, and this is my friend, Jesse.'

'He is Frank Taylor's boy, and the little Indian is Betty Fairchild's girl,' adds Mayor Brady.

'What were you two children doing down by the creek alone? Do your parents know where you've been?'

'Well, sir, my dad, well he is…'

'My mom said we could go,' interrupts Jesse. Turning to face the mayor, she adds, 'And for your information, Mr. Brady, I am 15 years old and I am Haida. Indians live in India. Anyway, Officer Kirkpatrick, we searched the Kettle Creek trail clean to my uncle's cabin. We didn't see any trace of Donni, but we convinced my Uncle Bill to search the valley ASAP and let us know if Donni was in the area.'

'Well, young lady, thank you for the report, but if it's okay with you and your mom, I will take over the investigation from here.' Giggles and outright laughter move among the adults around Matt and Jesse. 'That trapper's cabin has been abandoned for over ten years, young lady, and I don't appreciate your lies. Frankly I don't understand why you would tell a story like that. I would advise you and your friend to head home now before I have my constables arrest you both for impeding this search. Am I clear?'

'But my uncle said—' begins Jesse.

'I said, am I clear?' demands Kirkpatrick in a commanding tone.

'Crystal,' answers Matt. He takes Jesse by the arm and pulls her away.

Suddenly, Dawn bursts into the parking lot, beginning to cry when she sees her father, the Mayor. By the time she reaches him, she is crying hysterically as he takes her into his arms. Her summer dress is ripped and covered in seaweed and sand. Dried blood is evident on her forehead and cheek.

'My sweet angel, please don't cry. You're alright now. What happened? Are you okay?' asks her father.

'He attacked me. He tried to rape me, Daddy! I tried to fight him, but he is a monster,' sobs Dawn.

'Who, Dawn? Who did this to you?'

'André Robillard,' answers Dawn. A gasp passes through the crowd. 'He followed me down to the beach from the fairground. I told him to go away, but he wouldn't listen. He wouldn't listen, Daddy! He said he wanted to…to…'

'He wanted to what?' asks her father.

'Oh, Daddy. He said he wanted to have sex with me. When I said no, he grabbed me and…and…' Dawn collapses into her father's arms.

'Back up, give her some breathing room, please,' Kirkpatrick orders. Approaching the girl, he stoops close to her and asks, 'Dawn, are you alright?'

'Uh, yes sir, I think so. But please stop Robillard before he attacks someone else, if it's not already too late.'

Jesse turns to Matt and rolls her eyes in disbelief. Loud enough for the crowd to overhear, she says, 'Oh, pulease! The poor virgin child!'

'Shut up, you little savage,' yells Dawn's father. 'Go home to your tipi, and take your sidekick with you.'

'Fuck you!' Matt shouts. 'You go home and take your sleazy actress daughter with you!'

'Why you little shit,' answers the Mayor, and he lunges at the boy. 'You are as useless as your drunken father.'

Corporal Fontaine holds the mayor away from the boy. 'Alright, that's enough! Settle down. Tend to your daughter, Mayor Brady; she needs you right now. Matt and Jesse, you heard the Sergeant. Go home. If we have to tell you again, you will be spending your weekends doing community work. If you don't want to start picking up bottles and trash, I advise you to leave. Now!'

'C'mon, Jess. Let's blow this Popsicle stand.'

The two kids turn and run down Main Street towards Jesse's house. The Mayor, turning to Kirkpatrick, says 'What are you waiting for, Tom? Send your new help to arrest that pervert retard, Robillard. You can bet your bottom dollar he is also responsible for Donni Cardinal's disappearance. I won't be surprised when you locate young Cardinal that you find he has been sexually abused, then murdered by that retarded degenerate.'

The crowd gasps in horror at the accusation, and before Kirkpatrick can respond, one of the search members says, 'You heard the mayor—Robillard is responsible for Donni's disappearance. Let's find the pervert, and I'll personally make sure he tells us where he stashed the body.'

'Yeah, let's get the retard before he abuses another child,' yells another hothead in the crowd. Mutters of agreement pass through the frenzied crowd.

A gunshot startles the near-rioting crowd into silence. All heads turn to Sergeant Kirkpatrick standing with his smoking pistol pointed skyward. 'Stay where you are! There'll be no vigilante actions in Blood Cove while I'm in charge. Now listen up. Constable Fontaine?'

'Yes sir.'

'Pick up Mr. Robillard and take him to the station for questioning. Mayor Brady, take your daughter to the medical clinic for first aid and examination. I'll want a report from them as to the extent of her injuries ASAP. The rest of you will follow through with the search plan. Head immediately down to Kettle Creek and search the valley towards Frenchman Mountain. This is still a search and rescue operation; we have no evidence as yet to indicate anything different.'

'But what about André's attack on Dawn?' shouts a group member.

'Yeah. Yeah, that's right. What about it?' yells the crowd.

'I will deal with Mr. Robillard. Until I have questioned the suspect and discovered otherwise, this incident is considered isolated and unrelated to Donni. Anybody caught anywhere near André Robillard or his home will be arrested and charged with public mischief. Now! Am I clear?'

The crowd mumbles and chatters incoherently.

'Am I clear?'

Several voices respond in unison, 'Yes sir,' and the crowd exits the General Store parking lot muttering amongst themselves.

Matt and Jesse are already more than halfway to Jesse's house. 'Dawn is such a ho,' says Jesse. 'Imagine the kind of nonsense she would've had to pull in trying to seduce poor André. He wouldn't understand the first thing about sex, and he hasn't got a hurtful bone in his body.'

'Thank God for that, Jess. He is built like a brick shithouse. I pity the fool who ever pisses him off. He is a shoo-in for first place in the lumberjack competition next week.'

'I hope Kirkpatrick isn't too hard on him. André doesn't have the smarts to defend himself,' Jesse continues. 'He will be devastated by this.'

'Kirkpatrick isn't fooled by Dawn's fake drama one bit,' answers Matt. 'At least, I don't think he is. Everybody in town knows her reputation as a flirt. I'm sure he is only doing his job strictly by the rules to keep her daddy, the Mayor, off his back. It's Fontaine I'm worried about. He's new in town and doesn't know Dawn or André.'

'Fontaine may be a tough cop, but he is Métis.'

'So, what's that supposed to mean?'

'Relax. Fontaine is Métis. Likely he had to take more than his share of crap when he joined the mostly-white RCMP. And he's rising in the ranks, yes, but only slowly, I'd bet. He has to be fighting prejudice from nearly all sides. He wouldn't rough André up.'

'You're prob'ly right. Don't worry, Jess. Kirkpatrick will get to the bottom of this. André will be fine.'

The kids skip up the steps and into Jesse's house. 'I sure hope you're right, Matt.' Then raising her voice, she cries, 'Mom, we're home!'

'I'm in the kitchen, sweetheart,' answers Big Mama. 'Take your shoes off and c'mon in.'

'Matt is with me, Ma. We just got back from searching Kettle Creek.'

'I'm just making lunch. You two Coureurs des bois must be famished. How about fried Klik on toast and a big bowl of hot Habitant pea soup?'

'You read our minds, Mrs. Fairchild,' enthuses Matt. 'We're starved and that sounds delicious!'

'Any luck finding Donni?' asks Betty, as she opens the big can of soup.

'Nothing, Ma, but we stopped at the trapper's cabin and convinced Uncle Bill to help us in the search.'

'Yeah, right! Only after he got his hands on my prized harmonica,' interjects Matt.

'Relax. He will give it back,' soothes Jesse.

'Like I want it back after he sets his blistered old lips on it.'

'You both want mustard on your sandwiches?' asks Jesse's mom.

'Yes please,' came the chorus.

'Uncle Bill is not going to find Donni, sweetheart, unless Donni happens to be wandering around the cemetery.'

'Huh? What cemetery?' asks a confused Jesse.

'St-Jude's cemetery. That's where your Uncle Bill is buried. He died in a hunting accident ten years ago, honey. He was setting his traps along Spirit River when an inexperienced member of a hunting party from Vancouver mistook him for a bear. The dumb-ass shot him from two hundred yards straight through the temple. He pretty much blew Bill's head off.' Betty pauses a moment, then sighs and continues. 'I had to identify the body. The killer whale tattoo on his wrist was the only way I was sure it was my brother.'

Jesse and Matt look at each other in silence, confusion written all over their faces.

'Okay, Jess,' says Matt. 'I am really confused and a little creeped out right now. Your mom is kidding, right?' Turning to Big Mama, Matt laughs nervously. 'Ha ha, good one, Mrs. Fairchild. You had me going for a bit there.'

'I wish I were kidding, Matt. I loved my little brother. We were very close.'

'Ma, how can he be dead? Matt and I talked with Uncle Bill at the cabin this afternoon. He gave us tea.'

'He took my harmonica!' exclaims Matt.

'Enough with the damned harmonica already,' snaps Jesse. Turning to her mother, she accuses, 'You never told me about the hunting accident. I just assumed he was like the black sheep of the family, a loner, and just kept to himself in the woods.'

'When Bill was shot, you were too young to understand, Jesse, and I didn't want to upset you. I guess I should've told you when you got older. I'm sorry, dear. Bill was very special to me, and I suppose I was in denial. I didn't want to dredge up the memories of that awful incident again.'

'Mom, I've been to Uncle Bill's cabin before today. I stopped by a few times this summer after swimming at the creek with my friends. I chatted with him. Seriously, he is real. I mean, I'm not dreaming this up. He was there then and he was there today, in the flesh.'

'Children, I know for a fact you did not visit Uncle Bill. If my intuition is right, however, you are now two of the very few who have met Ne-kilst-lass. You are very fortunate to have spent time with the Raven. Most Haida only know of him through stories passed down by the elders.'

'Okay, you lost me again. Ne-kilst-a who, and what raven?' questions Matt.

'My mom is referring to Ne-kilst-lass, the Great Spirit who, according to the Haida, created the world. He is a mythical black Raven that is renowned as a greedy trickster.'

'He is no myth, young lady. Ne-Kilst-lass is very real. He may be mischievous, but he has helped humans with many issues. He has even interceded in our encounters with other supernatural beings.'

'Wow! He sounds like Batman,' says Matt, laughing. 'No, wait. On second thought, he's a bird so he could replace Robin. Cool! The new adventures of Batman and Raven.'

'Okay, that settles it,' says big Mama, as she takes Matt firmly by his thin upper arm and pulls him to his feet. 'It's about time you two smart asses learned a thing or two about respect.'

'Yeow!' yelps Matt, over-reacting to the moderate discomfort inflicted by Big Mama as she leads him to the spare room.

'Ma, you're hurting him,' says Jesse.

'You, too, Jess. Come with us,' answers Big Mama ignoring her daughter's lament.

'Ma, please let Matt go. He's not 5 years old.'

'Well, maybe he should act his age, then. I was going to wait till your sixteenth birthday, but I think today is as good as any to show the pair of you the transformation ritual.' Big Mama releases her grip on Matt's arm and says, 'Young man, before I start, do you have something to say to me?'

'Yes, Ma'am,' answers Matt sheepishly as he rubs the pink finger marks she left on his upper arm. 'I'm sorry I made fun of the Raven, Mrs. Fairchild.'

'Accepted. Now sit down on the carpet next to Jesse and pay attention.

'Your encounter with Yáahl is not to be taken lightly. He is a powerful supernatural spirit with knowledge and wisdom beyond our understanding. He created the earth and stole the sun, moon and stars for us. He freed the Haida from a giant clamshell, then provided us with fresh water, salmon and fire. I assure you, Ne-kilst-lass appeared to you for a very specific reason.'

'Ma, I know you believe in the Haida folklore and myths, and I respect that, but I'm telling you, we were talking to Uncle Bill and not some spirit or bird.'

'Jesse, sweetheart, listen to me. Uncle Bill is dead and has been buried at the old church for many years.'

Jesse, now noticeably upset, stands up and strides to the wall where she takes down a picture of her Uncle Bill. 'Ma, this is who I talked to. I know what I saw.'

'I understand that you think you met Bill, but remember what I told you. Yáahl is a master trickster and deceiver.'

'But, Ma, I…'

'Come, Jesse. Sit down.'

Jesse walks back and sits next to Matt; he puts his arm around her. Big Mama opens a large cedar chest and pulls out an oversized wool blanket.

'Wow! That's an awesome blanket,' says Matt.

'It's a Chilkat blanket, handed down to me from my father. He received it at a potlatch ceremony in Shoeakawoo, along with other treasures. It is mountain goat wool, dog fur and yellow cedar bark woven together. Our Raven Clan crest is woven into the fabric.'

Big Mama reaches into the chest again to retrieve an ermine headdress, a decorative wooden rattle, a necklace and a Raven mask. Matt glances at Jesse, a puzzled look on his face.

'Potlatch is a huge party put on by the rich nobles,' Jesse explains. 'They show off their wealth by giving away everything they own.'

'That's insane,' says Matt. 'Where is my invite? I'm in! Where is this Shoeca—what is it?'

'Oh, that's just the Haida word for Haida Quaii. It means land of the Haida.' Betty's voice becomes more somber. 'You're about to bear witness to a transformation ritual, a unique experience. I perform this dance only on very special occasions, but I think it's time to put an end to the doubt and confusion you have about the Haida culture. Do not be frightened by what you are about to see, as the spirit I beckon is not evil and will not harm you. Spirits do demand respect, so mind your manners. Remember: all that happens here must stay within the confines of this room. They must never be shared with others.'

Big Mama puts on her costume and faces the kids. Sliding the large mask over her face, she begins to chant in a steady monotone. She prances about the room, her neck jerking from side to side, shaking the rattle in rhythm with her song. Jesse slides close to Matt and squeezes his hand tight as she watches in amazement. The chanting and dancing gets louder and faster, then suddenly stops. An eerie silence fills the room as the kids wait in anticipation. The shaman stands frozen on the spot.

Abruptly, large wing–like flaps on the raven mask slowly open to reveal a tattooed face. A deep, low voice emerges from the mask startling the two youngsters.

'Speak to me, Haida child. Tell me now what troubles you so?'

Jesse and Matt stare in disbelief at the mask. This is definitely not Big Mama's voice.

'Don't fret, Jesse. I am your Uncle Bill. I have been summoned to help you.'

'Shit! This is B.S.,' says Matt. 'It's just a trick, Jesse. I call bullshit.'

The Shaman points at Matt and yells, 'Quiet! You will be quiet!'

Matt's eyes grow big as he turns to Jesse in a panic. Unable to open his mouth, he mumbles unintelligibly through closed lips. Jesse turns to the shaman and asks in a demanding tone, 'How can you be my Uncle Bill? We talked with him in person today at his log cabin.'

'The Raven appears in many shapes and forms, dear. He is a trickster and you were deceived.'

'But how can I be sure you're not the trickster? After all, you're nothing but a voice behind a mask.'

'I will ignore your insolence, Jesse, since your question has some merit. If it's proof you need, so be it. You visited my trapper's cabin, you say?' asks the mask.

'Yes, we did,' answers Jesse. 'It's just downstream from Frenchman Mountain, where Kettle Creek meets Spirit River.'

'Tell me, Jesse, how many furs did I have stretched and hanging around the cabin?'

'Well...none, I guess. That doesn't mean anything. Maybe Uncle Bill didn't have any luck lately.'

'A seasoned outfitter with the only trap line in one of the most productive wildlife corridors of the Canadian North and you seriously believe he didn't get even a single muskrat?'

'Well, when you put it that way, I guess it's a bit odd.'

'Indeed, my child,' answers the mask. 'There were no furs because the Raven would never kill nor harm a living creature. They are his own creations. He also has an obsession for all that glitters. Did you notice any shinny knickknacks around the cabin?'

Matt mumbles loudly at Jesse. Holding his hands to his lips, he gestures in a side-to-side motion.

'He took Matt's stupid harmonica in exchange for searching for Donni Cardinal.'

'Anything else?' urges the mask.

'Yeah,' surrenders Jesse. 'He also had a curio box full of all kinds of odd jewelry and shiny odds and ends. Now that you mention it, he was really weird about us touching his trinkets.'

'Indeed,' says the mask.

'I don't get it, though. Why would this powerful spirit bother fooling us? Why waste his time on a couple of kids like us?'

'The Raven enjoys being mischievous, but not without a purpose. He often helps humans solve serious problems, but he always benefits in some manner from the exchange. I don't have knowledge of his intentions with you. Perhaps he will help you find the missing boy, or perhaps the benefit he seeks is unrelated to the search. But he will not harm you. I can also assure you that he is not me. Just as you and your mother do, I also carry our family crest, the killer whale, tattooed on my right wrist. When next you encounter the Raven, check his right wrist. I am confident that he will have missed this small detail during his transformation. He may not even know the tattoo exists.

'Furthermore, Jesse, as a token of my love for my favorite niece, I have a very special gift for you. Go back to my cabin and look along the north wall. It's the only wall with a window in it. Pull up the third floorboard from the wall, and under it you will find a gold nugget. I panned it from Spirit River many years ago and stashed it there for good keeping. I died in a hunting accident before I could cash it in. I want you to have it. I am the only one who knows about that nugget, so finding it should remove any doubt in your mind that the being you saw was not your favorite uncle.'

'Wow, a gold nugget! Are you serious? I don't know what to say?'

'Say thank you, Jesse. Use the money wisely, and it will help you achieve your dreams.'

'Thank you, Uncle Bill, I will.'

'Remember to listen to your mother. She is wise and knows the ways of the Haida and the supernatural. As for you, young man, learn to mind your tongue and respect your elders.'

Matt mumbles, 'Yes sir.'

'I must go now, child. Dámaan agang hl kínggang (take good care of yourself).'

The wings of the ceremonial mask slowly close and Big Mama collapses like a marionette whose strings have been cut.

'Ma!' cries Jesse, rushing to her mother now lying on her right side on the floor. 'Ma, are you okay?'

Matt opens and rubs his clenched jaw, then joins Jesse at her mother's side. He removes the mask from Big Mama's head. 'She's breathing, Jesse. I think she just passed out.'

Big Mama opens her eyes and looks up at her worried children. 'I'm getting too old for this transformation business. I'm fine. Really. Help this old Shaman woman up, will you?'

'Wow! Mrs. Fairchild, I would never have believed any of this hockus pokus if I hadn't seen it with my own eyes,' exclaims Matt with enthusiasm.

'Did Bill help you kids understand what you've gotten yourselves involved in?' asks Big Mama. She leans on Matt as she stands up.

'Yes, Ma, and a whole lot more. But why do you ask? Don't you know what he said?'

'No, dear. When I am in the transformation trance, I am not conscious of anything. The spirit possesses my body and I become a portal from the supernatural world to our realm. It does tire me, though. I am exhausted. Help me to the kitchen and make me a cup of wild blueberry tea, please.'

'Okay, Ma, but we have to head back down to Kettle Creek right away.'

As Jesse puts the kettle on, Big Mama settles in a chair at the kitchen table and asks, 'What's so urgent?'

'We have some unfinished business to tend to, and I have a wonderful gift to collect.'

'Oh? What gift is that, sweetheart?'

'It's a surprise, Ma. I'll show it to you when I get back.'

The whistling kettle interrupts the conversation. Matt drops a tea bag into Big Mama's cup and pours the steaming water.

'Ma, I'm really sorry for having doubted you about Haida beliefs,' says Jesse, stirring a teaspoonful of honey into Big Mama's cup.

'I didn't raise you to accept things without question, dear. I hope that you now understand a little bit more about our culture and continue to live your life with pride and respect for your ancestry.'

'I sure will, Ma. We have to go before it gets too late. Enjoy your tea. C'mon, Matt. Let's go on a treasure hunt.'

Stan

1965

'Stanley.'

'Huh? What?'

'Stanley, wake up.'

'Wha? Yeah. Who is it?' answers Stan, slowly waking and opening his eyes.

'It's me, Stanley. Uncle Walt.'

'Hey! Holy shit! I'm on fire!' screams Stan, beating at his burning clothes as he gets to his feet.

'The whole building's on fire, son.'

'Help me! Don't just stand there. Help me.'

'Stanley, I can't help you. It's already too late.'

'What are you talking about?'

'You're dead son. You suffocated in the smoke minutes ago.'

'You're crazy! Shit, I'm burning up!'

'Really? Do you feel pain?'

Sudden realization stops Stan in mid-swat. He stares down at his burning open hand, then looks at his uncle with no comprehension on his face.

'I feel no pain. I feel absolutely no pain.'

'Be at peace, Stan. You're safe. You are qqatxhana, a spirit hovering near your dead body, free of all the woes of the mortal world, free to join me and the others on your new journey.'

'But…but I don't want to die.'

'Sqaatsi—be brave. They are not dead who live in the hearts they leave behind.'

'Don't give me any of that crap. Who did this to me? I don't understand.'

'You have rejuvenated the Haida pride in our community. Because of you, our people once again walk with their heads held high. You, more than anyone, know it was a long, difficult road, and along the way, you have stepped on many toes. Some people harbor a lot of resentment toward you.'

'None of that matters now. I need to know who did this to me? Look at our beautiful longhouse—destroyed! I'll kill the bastard who did this.'

'Calm yourself.'

'But we can't let him get away with this, Uncle Walt.'

'Forgive the fool. There is no place in your heart for anger and revenge.'

'So we just let him get away with this?'

'Let Ne-Kilst-lass serve him the justice he deserves.'

'I wish it were that easy, Uncle.'

'Have faith in the Raven, Stan. He has given us life and he can take it away.'

'I guess you're right, but I still would love to get my hands on whoever did this.'

'Enough said. Step away from your body and follow me out.'

As he steps forward, he sees that his body, engulfed in flames, is still sitting in the chair where he fell asleep. He takes a long look at his dead flaming body, then follows his uncle through the flames and smoke, and out the front door.

Bill stands on the entrance walkway and smiles in satisfaction as the flames begin to rise from the longhouse rooftop. He pulls the pack of smokes from his shirt pocket and calmly lights up. Flames shoot out from the spaces above and below the front door, out and around the gayang, the dry red cedar totem pole that adorns the entrance. In seconds, it is burning nicely as well. Bill smirks at the sound of the emergency sirens approaching in the distance. He knows too well that the firemen's attempts to extinguish this fire will be too late and in vain.

'Look. That must be the bastard who burned the place down,' says Stan, pointing at Bill.

'Yes, it certainly is,' agrees Walt.

'Let's get him,' urges Stan.

'Wait. Remember what I said, Stanley. Trust in the Raven.'

'But he will get away,' exclaims Stan.

'Look,' answers Walt, pointing up at the Raven carved at the top of the burning totem pole.

'Trust the Raven,' he repeats.

Bill's expression abruptly freezes as a rush of terror envelopes his consciousness. He cannot believe his eyes. He is watching two men standing in the inferno, apparently unharmed, watching him.

The cigarette falls from his lips, his mouth gaping. He recognizes Stan, surrounded by flames, the man beside him pointing at the carved Raven atop the totem pole. Uncomprehending, he looks up in time to watch in horror as the burning totem pole falls, the Raven bearing down on him. Before he can react, the Raven's large wooden beak splits the lumberjack's head open like an over-ripe cantaloupe. The fiery pole crashes down on top of him crushing his body into the walkway.

'You see?' asks Walt, pointing at the lumberjack lying dead under the fallen pole. 'That idiot thought he could break the spirit and pride of our people by killing you tonight. What he actually accomplished was to make a martyr of you. Now your memory will not only inspire the Haida to rebuild, but to become united in the fight to keep our culture alive.'

'So, you're saying I'm worth more dead than alive?'

'Well, not exactly. Think of it this way. Most men only accomplish things while they are alive. You, my son, will help accomplish many wonderful things long after your passing.'

'I guess when you put it that way, it's not all bad, then.'

'Not at all bad, Stanley. And, in any case, nothing you can do to change it.'

'I will miss Betty, though, and my friends.'

'Yes, and they will miss you. On the other hand, you now have many new friends.'

'Huh?'

'Here. Let me reintroduce you to some old friends and family,' says Walt, pointing towards the tree-line. Stan follows the gesture, seeing only flashes of light from the burning building illuminating the pines.

'I don't see anything but trees.'

'Wait for it', cautions his uncle with a smile.

Staring into the shifting shadows, Stan thinks he can make out a faint form and movement. At first he is more than half convinced that the wavering light is playing tricks on his sight. Squinting, he tries to focus. Gradually, one of the darker areas coalesces into a person slowly stepping away from the dense shadows.

'Who is that?' asks Stan.

Before Walt can respond, another person, then a couple more emerge from the mass of trees. The few soon become several, and in no time, fifty or more of these shadow people are walking slowly toward the burning building.

'Where are all these people coming from?'

A look of wonder transforms Stan's face. His childhood friend, Ray, is at the front of the group, grinning ear to ear. Ray died of Leukemia when he was twelve years old. Next to Ray are Stan's Grandpa Jesse and Grandma Tata, both of whom died just a few years ago.

Stan, overcome with emotion and speechless, recognizes many others: the mailman, Jake Sabourin, who died in a car crash; Linda Belanger, who drowned when she fell through the ice on Silver Creek. In fact, everybody in the group is deceased. Facing the fire now, the newcomers stand holding their right hands over their hearts. A feeling of peace and understanding consumes Stan. He surrenders to his destiny and, with pride, covers his heart.

'Thank you, Uncle Walt,' says Stan.

'No. Thank you, Stanley.'

Cathy & Devon
1980

In response to the final buzzer, Matt and Jesse hasten from their classrooms and meet in the crowded hallway. Weaving through the throng of students, they are soon outside in the parking lot, headed for the football field.

Cathy Webster, Jesse's cousin, rides up on her CCM bicycle and stops to chat.

'Hey, Jesse. Hey, Matt.'

'Hey, Cathy,' answer Matt and Jesse as one.

'You guys going to the Lumberjack Fair this year?' asks Cathy.

'Yeah, for sure,' answers Jesse.

'We're performing on the main stage on Saturday,' adds Matt.

'What time?'

'1:30-ish.'

'Cool, I'll be there. Can't wait to hear you guys again.'

Cathy's younger brother, Devon, has joined the trio.

'Cathy, you coming? We can't be late for supper again.'

'I love your music. You guys sound so great together,' adds Cathy, ignoring her annoying sibling.

'Cathy, Mom said we had to stay together. She'll be mad if we're not on time.'

'Just go, Devon. I'll catch up to you,' insists Cathy impatiently.

'Fine! No skin off my butt,' answers Devon, walking away.

'Yeah, so anyway, did you guys hear what Dawn Brady is up to now?'

'I can only imagine,' answers Jesse.

'Anita Langdon told Susan Menard who told me that Dawn and her dad plan to sue André for pain and suffering caused by the assault.'

'That bitch! I wouldn't put it passed her,' says Matt.

'Like, ten thousand dollars!' adds Cathy.

'As if the Robillards can afford to fork out that kind of money, anyway,' says Jesse.

'Things could get a lot worse for André if they don't find little Donni soon,' says Cathy.

'Don't worry. Donni will turn up. I'm sure he's okay,' says Jesse reassuringly.

'And Karma will take care of that Brady bitch,' adds Matt. 'Just wait and see.'

'What the hell is happening to Blood Cove lately? It's so bizarre, eh? Anyway, I'm headed to the store for a soda. You guys coming?'

'Naw, we got some stuff to do, but thanks. Catch you later, cuz.'

'Okay. Later, guys.'

—❦❧—

'Devon, please take your muddy shoes off in the porch. I just cleaned the floors.'

'Oops, sorry, Ma. It's raining again and there's mud everywhere. I need new shoes — these have holes in 'em and my socks're soaked.'

'I know. We'll go buy you a new pair next week. I promise. Your dad is back from trawling Monday, and as soon as he gets paid, we'll go shopping. Okay?'

'Swell!'

'Where's Cathy? Didn't she come home with you?'

'No. She took her bike to school this morning, remember? My chain's busted, so I walked.'

'She should've gotten here before you, then, if she's riding her bike.'

'She was chatting with Jesse and Matt in the school parking lot when I left.'

'Didn't I tell you two to travel back and forth to school together?'

'Aww, Ma. Do I have to? The guys'll think I'm a sissy, that I can't go anywhere without my sister. Besides, she's always stopping to yap with her friends.'

'The streets aren't safe, honey. Donni Fairchild is still missing, and God knows what happened to him. Till he's found, you two will go to school together—understand?'

'I thought they said he got lost in the woods?'

'I have my doubts about that. He pretty much spends most of his spare time playing in that forest. He knows the trails better than the streets in town.'

'So wadda you think happened to him?'

'I don't know, Devon? Do you have any homework to do before supper?'

'Not much. Some kids at school said a weirdo might have took Donni and done some bad things to him. The things they said were pretty stupid, though.'

'Never mind that nonsense. Now, go get your homework done. Supper will be ready soon.'

'But the things they said…'

'Enough—homework please!' Under her breath, she mutters, 'Where is that child?'

'What's for supper?' asks Devon, pulling his books from his school bag and setting them on the kitchen table.

'Mac and cheese.'

'Ugh, again?'

'Times are tough, sweetheart. I'm sorry. I tried to get some hamburger from the grocery store, but our tab is maxed out for this month,' explains his mother.

'It's okay, Ma. Mac and cheese is fine,' says Devon, despite still feeling disappointed.

'Your Dad'll be back soon and things'll be better. I promise.'

Mrs. Webster looks out the kitchen window and frowns at the sight of the dimming light. As she focuses on how worn her reflection looks in the window, the pot of noodles overflows on the stove top.

'Oh, damn it!' Moving quickly to the stove, she turns off the heat and uses the dish cloth to wipe up the starchy spill. 'Did Cathy say she was coming straight home after school?'

'She didn't say anything to me. She was too busy yapping with Matt and Jesse—silly girl stuff prob'ly, as usual. Maybe she stopped at one of her friends' places or something.'

Mom carefully takes the pot from the stove and pours the boiling water into the sink.

'Even so, she would have called home by now. It's almost 6:00 o'clock.'

'Oh. Maybe she took the park trail.'

'But that would take her down along the beach and back up through the forest to town.'

She mixes a pat of butter and the powdered cheese into the noodles with her wooden spoon.

'Yeah. It's a bit longer, but sometimes we go that way and stop at the grocery store for chips and a pop,' explains Devon.

'So that's why you guys aren't always hungry for supper!'

'I'm just tryin' to help, Ma. It might be why she's late. We only go that way sometimes,' explains Devon.

She scoops the gooey blend onto three plates, puts one on the counter, and takes the others to the table.

'I'm sure she's fine, Ma.'

'Well, supper's ready. No point in letting it get cold. Move your books and let's eat. Cathy will be going straight to bed without her supper tonight—worrying me like that!

Devon pours himself a glass of milk and digs into his mac and cheese. He looks up and notices his worried mom staring at the kitchen clock.

'Mom, you're not eating?'

'I'm not really hungry.'

'She'll be home soon. Don't worry.'

'I heard they released André Robillard from jail today. I sure hope they know what they're doing.'

'He didn't hurt Dawn,' assures Devon.

'How can you be so sure,' questions his mother.

'André wouldn't ever do that.'

"Oh, really? Well, straight from the lips of Dr. Webster, the world-famous psychologist. Don't I feel relieved now,' answers his mom sarcastically.

'Aah, Mom, c'mon! André has never hurt anyone, and he wouldn't hurt Cathy either. Certainly not Cathy. He wouldn't even hurt a fly.'

'That boy is strong! He could out-wrestle a grizzly bear, if he set his mind to it. I know he seems innocent enough, but sometimes we don't always know what's going on in people's heads—especially people like André.'

'Whatever, Mom. André is a bit slow, but it doesn't seem like somethin' he'd do, is all,' answers Devon, flustered.

'There is only one way to find out.'

Devon's mom gets up from the dinner table, walks to the kitchen counter and picks up the phone. She dials quickly and waits a few seconds.

'Mrs. Robillard? It's Emma Webster. Can I speak to André, please?'

'Mom, really?' asks Devon, embarrassed.

Ignoring her son, she asks, 'Why? Well, Cathy hasn't showed up from school yet. I want to ask André if he saw her on the way home from school this afternoon. Oh, André didn't go to school today. Oh, okay. Sooo, André is home with you right now? Hello. Hello. Shit! She hung up on me!'

'Mom, is Cathy going to be okay?' asks Devon, his mother's fear obviously starting to rattle him.

'I sure hope so 'cause I'm gonna kill her when I find her.'

Emma re-dials and taps nervously at the receiver with her index finger.

'Betty, this is Emma. Hi. Yes, I'm fine, but I'm getting a bit worried about Cathy. She hasn't showed up from school yet. Is she with Jesse at your place? No? Hmm. Devon said she was with Matt and Jesse after school. What? Are you serious? Jesse and Matt came home, and you allowed them to go out searching for Donni—at this hour? Betty, I swear, ever since Stan passed away, you have lost all sense of reason. Yes, Yes. Sorry. I didn't mean to upset you. I miss my brother, too. I'm just worried about Cathy. Anyway, if Cathy shows up, please have her call me right away. Please. Okay, thanks, Betty. Bye.

'Jesus Christ, what is that woman thinking, letting kids scurry around after dark with a madman on the loose. Grab your coat. I'll get the flashlight. I'm not going to just sit around and wait.'

Moments later, buttoning her jacket, she opens the door to be startled by Cathy reaching for the door knob.

'Hi, Mom. Sorry I'm late. First I got a stupid flat on the bike, and then I had to wait at the grocery store for the rain to let up a bit. Where are you guys going?'

'Um, nowhere. Just for a walk while we waited for you.'

'Well, I'm here and I am starved.' Cathy kicks off her shoes and moves past Devon and her mother to the kitchen. 'What's for supper? Ooh, mac and cheese. My favorite!'

Matt & Jesse
1980

Matt and Jesse run across town. When they reach Kettle Creek trail, Jesse is still well ahead of Matt, who is struggling to catch up. 'Wait up, Jesse' he yells. 'Let's take a break. I'm beat.'

'Okay, but only for a few minutes.'

They sit down on a moss-covered rock along the trail. 'I'm so excited. I can't wait to collect my gold nugget. Waddaya think its worth?'

'A big nugget is prob'ly worth a couple thousand dollars, maybe more.'

'Wow, really?'

'I think so. I heard on the CBC that gold is around $800 an ounce, and I think a big nugget would be pretty heavy. What are you planning to spend it on, Jesse?'

'Well, what do you think, silly? It's our ticket out of Blood Cove, Matt. It's everything we talked about the last couple of years. We can move to Vancouver and make the Big Time in the music industry.'

'Are you nuts, Jess? Big Mama will never let you waste your money on that. She'll expect you to deposit it in the bank and save it for your education.'

'She doesn't have to know, does she? Besides, you heard Uncle Bill.

He said that I should use the money to pursue my dreams. So, are you in, Whitey, or are you in the way?'

'You're nuts, Haida girl, but you know I'm with you all the way.' He tries to reassure her with a hug.

'Alrighty then.' She stands and wipes the moss and grass from her pants. 'Let's go! Last one to the trapper's cabin is a rotten egg.'

'Grow up!' answers Matt, but he springs to his feet and speeds past Jesse, laughing as he tears down the trail. In short order he meets a few of the members returning from the search for Donni. He stops and Jesse catches up in time to overhear the conversation.

'Where are you two troublemakers heading to, now?' asks John Graham, owner of the General Store. 'Didn't you hear what officer Kirkpatrick said to you about going home and not impeding the search?'

'For your information, we did go home, and now we're heading to Jesse's uncle's cabin on personal business.'

'Yeah. And besides, this is Haida land. We got more right to be here than you,' adds Jesse.

'This happens to be Crown land, young lady. What the hell do you expect to find at that trapper's place, anyway? There is nothing left of that cabin but a heap of rotting, moss-covered beams. You had a lot of gall telling the officer your uncle was getting involved in the search. Everybody in town knows your mad old uncle died in a hunting accident over ten years ago. I suggest you go home to your crazy shaman mother, and take your loser boyfriend with you.'

'Oh, yeah?' Jesse says, hands on her hips. 'Well, I suggest you go to hell, and take your friends with you! If you can find any!' She tugs on Matt's sleeve and they turn to run off down the trail.

Overhead, a raven caws and circles before banking suddenly and flying swiftly ahead of the pair. Matt and Jesse pass the remaining members of the search party along the path and, after a few minutes, arrive at the trapper's cabin.

They examine the site while they catch their breath; the cabin stands erect and strong, just as they had seen it earlier in the day.

'The canoe isn't here and the fire's out, Jess. I think we're in luck. Doesn't look like the Raven is around. Let's go in.'

'Wait, Matt. Think about it. The searcher said the house was a wreck, basically a heap of rotting timber. The Raven must have seen us approach and transformed the cabin back to its original state. Let's be careful. He must be nearby, maybe even watching.'

'Maybe he…it is sleeping' answers Matt.

'I don't think spirits sleep. Do they?' answers Jesse.

'Well shit, Jess. This is freakin' spooky. Maybe we should head back.'

'You kidding? Not without my nugget, we're not!'

Before she can lose her nerve, Jesse hurries to the cabin and presses her ear to the door. 'I don't hear a thing. He must not be here.'

'Maybe he's perched in the rafters inside waiting to swoop down and peck the eyes out of our heads. Thought of that?'

'Don't be silly. You heard Uncle Bill say the Raven won't hurt us.' Jesse opens the unlocked door and peers in. 'C'mon, the coast is clear.'

Entering the cabin, she runs straight across the room to the North wall.

'Over by the window,' says Matt, following her inside.

'I'm way ahead of you, buddy,' quips Jesse. 'Let's see—third floorboard from the wall, third floorboard from the wall.'

Jesse squats and grips the end of the floor board with her fingertips. She pulls with all her might and lets out a screech, as her fingers slip from the plank. 'Ow! Damn, I just ripped my nail.'

'Suck it up, buttercup,' teases Matt. 'Move over and let a man take care of business.'

Jesse comes right back with, 'Did you happen to bring a man with you?'

Ignoring the comment, Matt grips the edge of the stubborn old floor board and pries. He yelps as he loses his grip. 'Damn! This thing is full of splinters. It's nailed tight and won't budge. We need something to use as a pry bar to lift the sucker.'

Jesse crawls over to the old stove and brings back a wrought iron poker. 'How about this, Suzy?'

'Ha ha. Touché,' laughs Matt. 'Yep, I think that'll do the trick.' He drives the end of the poker down into the seam at the edge of the plank and pries hard on the bar. The nails squeal and rip from the joist below as the old plank lifts. Jesse reaches over and helps pull the board up. Throwing the board aside, Matt quickly reaches into the hole, pulling out a small burlap sack. 'Look what I found,' he taunts.

'Hand it over, Matt. You know it's mine.'

'Ha, I don't think so, Haida girl—finders keepers. So, waddaya think it is?' asks Matt in a teasing tone. 'I know! A bag of shinny marbles, or maybe...'

Jesse gives Matt a sharp kick in the shin.

'Ow!' yelps Matt. Dropping the sack to the floor, he grabs his leg. 'Damn, Jesse. Really?'

'Serves you right, Whitey. Now let's have a look at my prize!' Jesse carefully unravels the twine knotted around the neck of the sack.

'How dare you enter my home without permission!'

Jesse and Matt freeze in place. Their attention focused on the sack, they have not heard the old trapper approach. The infuriated trapper is standing in the cabin's entrance, his glare fixed on Matt. Raising his arm, he makes a fist and hobbles across the room towards the terrified boy. Before Matt can move, the trapper latches onto the boy's arm, tightening his grip like a vice. 'Why are you here? You have come back to rob me! What have you done with my treasures, you little brat?'

Matt winces in pain. Struggling desperately to escape the madman's hold, he says in a defiant tone, 'Let go, you crazy old codger. I didn't touch any of your crap.'

'Well, you lying little thief. Tell me why I should not wring your neck and toss you in the river like a stray cat. Quick, tell me now. I am a man of little patience.'

'Stop! You're hurting him! Let him go!' demands Jesse loudly, pulling on the arm holding Matt.

The trapper, without loosening his grip, turns to Jesse, his face only inches from hers. Staring deeply into her eyes, he asks, 'Give me one good reason why I should spare you and your boyfriend?'

Trying not to allow the foul odor of the old man's breath make her vomit, Jesse stares right back at the mad trapper and says, 'I have the best reason. I know who you are—Ne-kilst-lass.'

The trapper releases his grip on Matt and takes a few steps back from Jesse. 'Stupid girl! What do you know of Ne-kilst-lass? I am your Uncle Bill, and this is my cabin. I ought to call Kirkpatrick and have you two misfits arrested for trespassing.'

'Okay, Ne-kilst-lass. Two can play that game. C'mon, Matt. Let's go to the police station and turn ourselves in. I'm sure Kirkpatrick will be thrilled to come down to the cabin to get a written report from Uncle Bill about our unwelcome visit.'

'D'you mean the same police officer who laughed at us when we mentioned meeting your Uncle Bill here this morning?' asks Matt, a smile creeping across his lips. 'Oh, and let's stop by your house on the way to the station and invite Big Mama to come back here with us. I'm sure she would be thrilled to see her brother again.'

'Great idea.' Jesse turns and steps towards the trapper. 'Especially since the last time she visited her brother Bill was ten years ago at his funeral!'

'Oh, and hey, Uncle Bill! What happened to the Killer Whale tattoo on your right wrist? Did it wash off?' prods Matt sarcastically.

'What tatt…' slips from the Raven's lips before he can stop himself.

'Yeah, exactly,' says Matt. 'Didn't even know he had one, did you?'

The Raven glares at Matt and takes a couple of awkward steps back, then turns to stare at the young girl, speechless for a moment. He stares deeply into Jesse's eyes, as if to read her mind; finally he speaks. 'The Shaman woman has taught you well. Through the centuries, the Shamans have passed to the people the knowledge and stories of the spiritual world, but only a few have met Ne-kilst-lass. With this knowledge comes great responsibility.'

'Yeah, yeah. Whatever. Tell us where Donni is,' demands Matt.

'Quiet, you impertinent child! You have no idea the forces that oppose you.'

'Ne-kilst-lass, please help us find him,' begs Jesse. 'Matt doesn't mean to be disrespectful. We just want our friend back before it's too late.'

'Very well. Admittedly your intentions are noble, but my time is valuable. Give me the gold and I will help you.'

'What gold?' asks Jesse, reflexively tightening her grip on the bag.

'I have wasted enough time with you both,' says the Raven, as he turns towards the door.

'Wait,' shouts Jesse, holding the bag out in front of her. 'Here. Take it. It's yours.'

'Jesse, no! That's our—uh, your—future, our ticket out of Blood Cove. Uncle Bill gave you that to invest in a new life.'

Smiling, the Raven takes the bag from Jesse and loosens the string to open it.

'It's okay, Matt. We will find another way out of Blood Cove. We have a lifetime ahead of us to get our shit together and make it to the big city. Donni's life is at stake here. He's running out of time. Soon he'll have no future. We need the Raven's help or Donni will die!'

'Holy shit!' interrupts Matt, pointing to the gold lying in the Raven's palm. 'Look at the size of that nugget'

'Quite impressive indeed' says the Raven staring down at the precious hunk of rock. Closing his hand tightly around the gold, he turns and glares at the kids. 'Listen closely and listen well, for I will not repeat myself, and your inattention will put your lives at risk.'

Insatiable fangs ravage the one whom you seek
The captor grows strong as the child grows weak
Extending the Dark One's desperate hours
This vessel entombed in structures of power
Cursed by the dark and blood he desires
Save for the oak tree, he cannot expire

'Ne-kilst-lass has spoken. The spirit of the Raven is now with you. Dámaan agang hl kíngwang (take good care of yourselves).'

An ear-splitting blast startles the young couple, sending them to their knees, then prone to the cabin floor. The room goes dark. Flying debris and dust fill the air, borne by a wind from nowhere spinning about the room. Matt hunches over Jesse to protect her as shrapnel of boards and splintered wood bounce off his back.

'Stay down.'

The whirlwind subsides as quickly as it arose, and they slowly get to their feet. They look about the cabin as they dust themselves off.

'You okay?' asks Jesse. 'Your shirt's all ripped and blood stained.'

'I'm fine, just a few scratches. But look at the cabin. What a shambles! It's covered with dust, spider webs, moss—as if it's been abandoned for years. I wouldn't believe it if I hadn't seen it with my own eyes. Man, your mom was right, though. This Haida shit is wicked.'

'You know, Matt, my mom always told me the legends and stories of the Raven were true. I never really believed her, though. I figured the Raven was just another made-up character, like Santa Claus or the tooth fairy. After the transformation ceremony, and now this, I have a new respect for my mom.'

'Your mom is awesome. Anybody who can chat with dead dudes and spirits has gotta be pretty special.'

Jess gives Matt a weird look and says, 'Anyway, did you make any sense out of that riddle the Raven dropped on us before the roof fell in?'

'Heck no. I was hoping you did.'

'No, not really, but we better write it down before we forget it. Obviously it contains clues to Donni's whereabouts.'

'All we get for my Hohner Meisterklasse and your gold nugget is a lousy riddle? Man, did he see us coming!'

Dawn

1980

The grade ten teacher, Mr. Celreau, steps into his Monday morning French Immersion class. Unlike in the other classrooms at Oceanview Junior High School, the lighting is subdued in this room and heavy curtains are drawn across the windows, the room dimly lit by a single fluorescent light fixture. Mr. Celreau has Cutaneous Porphyria, a rare and incurable skin disorder. At his job interview, he explained that he had been diagnosed as a child, and that symptoms include burning blisters and swelling of the skin when exposed to the sun, along with severe cramping, paralysis, and, sometimes, psychosis. Without these lighting arrangements, the teacher would have had to turn down the position.

Attracting teachers to the small northern communities is always a challenge at best. Most experienced educators prefer to move south, to the comfort and amenities of Vancouver. The northern school district usually has to make do with young, first year graduates looking for teaching experience, only to eventually lose them to the lure and security of the big city. The Education Board considered it a bit of a coup to have hired Mr. Celreau, an experienced young foreign teacher accredited by the University of Toronto, for their little school. When made aware of his health issues and special needs, the board was only too pleased to accommodate his request.

Mr. Celreau's class is different from the rest of the school in other ways, as well. The atmosphere is less rigid, less formal. In his class, when the bell rings, the kids continue to chatter and laugh among themselves without reproach.

'Good morning, class. Please stack your chairs and tables neatly at the back of the class. If you work together, that should only take a minute or two. When you're done, come and sit in a half circle at the front of the room.'

A few moments later, his students are ranked in four semi-circles on the floor. He lowers himself to sit cross-legged in front of them.

'By now you probably are aware that one of our students, Donni Cardinal, has gone missing. No one has seen him since Friday morning. Over the weekend, a search party combed much of the town, the forest and the shoreline, to no avail. The search resumed this morning and, with luck, he will be found. I know some of you are Donni's friends and may be quite upset. That is perfectly natural and understandable. Does anybody have anything to share with the class about the situation?'

'I think Donni probably wondered off into the forest to go fishing or to play, and got lost,' Jesse volunteers. 'I just pray he's alright because the nights have been chilly lately, and combined with that cool drizzle, he's probably getting weak.'

'Man! You're dreaming,' says the mayor's son, Jack, voice dripping sarcasm. 'That's a load of bull! My dad told me the little savage spends all his time in the bush and knows his way around the sticks better than he knows the town. There's no way he got lost. Everybody knows André the retard got his hands on the boy. The perv prob'ly dragged Donni off into the woods, did some sick thing to him, strangled him with his gorilla hands, then tossed him in the river.'

'Shut up, Jack. You and your Dad are the retards! André wouldn't hurt a fly and you know it.'

'Really? So how do you explain what that retard did to my sister?'

'Your sister's a slut and I'm sure she asked for it!' yells Matt from the back of the group.

'Okay, okay. That's quite enough,' intervenes the teacher. 'Everybody is upset over this, but that's no reason to insult each other in this way. Matt, you know better than to use such language in our classroom.' Turning to Jesse, he adds, 'Jesse, I for one also hope that Donni will be found alive soon, but Jack has a right to his opinion. He could have been much more diplomatic in his argument, but nonetheless, he made a valid point. André is under investigation for the rape of Jack's sister, Dawn. That being said, he has not been convicted or even charged for the assault yet. He is only being held for questioning, so let's not jump to conclusions.

'That being said, I don't think any of us are in the right frame of mind this morning to concentrate on school work.'

Celreau rises and walks over to the corner of the room. He opens a leather case leaning against the wall and pulls out a strange looking musical instrument.

'That's one crazy looking guitar,' says Matt.

'Actually, Matt, this is a French lyre.'

'It looks ancient, Mr. Celreau. Where did you pick that up?'

'Well, you're right, it is quite old. I bought it at an estate sale in France. The owner claimed it once belonged to Marie Antoinette. Most of her belongings were either burned or sold after she was guillotined.'

'Wow! That's morbid, but really cool,' says Matt. 'What's that writing on the side?'

'The lyre is inscribed with the French words 'liberté, égalité, fraternité.'

'Very cool, I think. What's it mean?' asks Matt.

'I believe it's from the lyrics of an old French revolution chant. Anyway, sit back and relax, close your eyes and enjoy.'

Playing a melody on the lyre, the teacher begins to sing in French…

Quelle est cette lenteur barbare?
Hâte-toi peuple souverain,
De rendre aux monstres du Ténare
Tous ces buveurs de sang humaine.
Guerre à tous les agents du crime!
Poursuivons-les jusqu'au trépas;
Partage l'horreur qui m'anime,
Il ne nous échapperont pas.

What is this barbaric languor?
Sovereign people, hurry
To return to the monsters of Tenairon
All these drinkers of human blood.
War against all those who practice this crime!
Hound them to the death;
Share the horror that impels me,
They shall not escape us.

The ballad ends to the applause of the students.

'Thank you,' says the teacher. 'Glad you enjoyed it. That song means a lot to me.'

The buzzer indicating a class change blares. Celreau gets up to put the instrument away. As one, his students rise and rush for the exit.

'Okay, everyone,' the teacher shouts above the ruckus of exiting students. 'Be ready to get back at it tomorrow. We have some catching up to do!'

A collective moan passes through the group funneling through into the hallway. Matt and Jesse stay behind and approach the teacher.

'Mr. Celreau, may we ask you for some advice?' asks Jesse.

'Of course, Jesse. You know my door is always open. I will give you any help I can.'

'Thanks, Mr. Celreau. We wanted to ask you some questions because, well, me and Matt know we can trust you. Right?'

'Matt and I,' corrects their teacher, 'and, yes, you can be assured our conversation will remain confidential.' Celreau steps to the door and closes it. 'What did you want to ask me?'

'Do you believe in the spiritual world, Mr. Celreau?' asks Jesse.

'Well, that depends on your definition of a spirit, Jesse. I don't believe in ghosts or demons, if that's what you mean.'

'What about vampires, werewolves and zombies?' suggests Matt.

'That is a very unusual question, but now you are not talking about a spirit world. These are preternatural creatures, beings that, if they exist, were once human, and have abilities that cannot be explained by science. What has spurred your interest in regards to such dark and sinister characters?'

Jesse hands her teacher a piece of paper. 'What do you make of this riddle?'

Celreau reads the page intently. Raising an eyebrow, he side-steps her question by asking one of his own. 'Where did you get such a conundrum?'

Jesse recounts the extraordinary encounter with the Raven and the events that had taken place at the trapper's cabin. Without interrupting, Celreau listens intently to the bizarre story. He runs his fingers through his pitch black hair and takes a seat at his desk. 'You realize, of course, that's a pretty tall tale for anyone to accept at face value, even someone with an open mind. Do you really expect me to believe this story, Jesse?'

'She's telling the truth, Mr. Celreau,' says Matt. 'Honest. I was there and witnessed it all myself.'

Rubbing his forehead, Celreau shifts his gaze back and forth from one child to the other. 'Remarkable. Well, I see three possibilities here. The first is that you're straight out telling me a lie.'

'Why would we lie to you. We have nothing to gain from lying,' says Jesse.

'Indeed. You would certainly leave yourself open to ridicule and embarrassment. The second possibility is you stopped along the river path while searching for Donni, chewed some magic mushrooms and hallucinated this whole outlandish experience.'

'We're not into 'shrooms, Mr. Celreau. Too many kids we know have gotten really messed up trying that crap. And Matt frowns on alcohol on account of, you know, his dad. The only thing I've ever inhaled is the smoke from the burning of my mom's herbal sage and sweet grass during our smudging ceremonies.'

'I can accept that. I know a 'shroomhead when I see one, and you two display far too much upstairs to have been effected by even mild drugs. The third and final possibility, inconceivable as it may sound, is that the Haida Raven has in fact contacted you. If that's true, he has cleverly deceived you into surrendering your prized possessions in return for the promise of his help in the search for Donni, while in fact he has involved you in a deliberate plan to solve his own conflict with the spiritual powers of the underworld.'

'Spiritual powers of the underworld? You mean, like, a vampire?' questions Matt. Without waiting for a reply, he continues, 'Wait a minute; look at the lines from the riddle again. Extending the Dark One's desperate hours—he's referring to a vampire! Makes perfect sense. This vessel entombed in structures of power—vampires have tombs! Or, at least, they sleep in caskets. Cursed by the dark and blood he desires—it all fits. It's gotta be a vampire.' The excitement in Matt's voice is now more than a little tinged with fear.

'Save for the oak tree, he cannot expire?' the two young people say together in confused tones.

'According to legend, vampires can only be killed by a wooden stake through the heart,' clarifies Celreau, scoffing. 'Evidently, the use of the word 'oak' was meant as a reference to wood in general.'

'Holy cow, Jesse. What kind of black magic shit are we getting involved in? And what does any of this have to do with helping us find Donni?'

'I'm not sure I get it either, Matt. What do you make of it, Mr. Celreau?' asks Jesse.

Celreau leans back in his chair, his hands clasped behind his head, and closes his eyes, thinking. He breathes a heavy sigh, then inhales slowly through his nose, sits up in his chair and gently slaps his thighs. He looks from Jesse to Matt.

'Vampires, tombs, blood and stakes all make for a very interesting story, but as romantically attractive as they might seem, their origins are rooted in folklore. They are just medieval stories created in an effort to explain events and phenomena not understood by the uneducated and ignorant. All of which, by the way, have sound medical and scientific explanations today. In the drab modern world of human reality, we use these nonsense tales to spice up otherwise unexciting lives. I recommend that you avoid giving this thieving Raven any more of your prized possessions or precious time. Cut your losses. Forget this silly riddle and concentrate on finding young Donni Cardinal.

'Now, if you don't mind, I have a stack of tests to grade before my next lesson, and you two young detectives are late for your history class with Ms. Villeneuve. If you don't want the old bird handing you detentions, I suggest you hightail it to class.'

'I guess so,' answers a reluctant Jesse.

Frowning, Matt and Jesse turn and leave the classroom.

'There are no vampires? Yeah, right! Just like there's no Haida Raven,' says Matt sarcastically.

'Exactly!' says Jesse. 'We freakin' know better. Meet you at the track bleachers after school. We got ourselves a riddle to solve.'

'I'll be there,' answers Matt laughing. 'That vampire's ass is grass.'

—⟨⟩⟨⟩—

Now alone in his classroom, Celreau also has ravens and vampires on his mind. Ne-kilst-lass! Damn that filthy Raven! The first day I set foot in Blood Cove and caught him peering at me from the top of the pines, I sensed that he was going to be trouble. I could sense the power. He knew me and everything about me at once, including why I'm here. He didn't speak, but he communicated his thoughts to me very clearly. How'd he do that?

I almost got back on the bus, but we came to what seemed a simple understanding—I would be allowed to stay in town and feed as I pleased, as long as I left the Haida alone. Should I harm one of his, I would face the wrath of the Raven. Damn it! I should have known better. Where was my head? With three thousand Caucasian candidates in town, I had to pick a blood native child as host for my cursed lust. Brilliant! Just fucking brilliant! Damned fool!

Now that blasted Raven has Matt and Jesse all riled up, poking around, asking questions. As that joker in my grade nine class would probably say, the Raven's gonna be on me like a fat kid on a Smartie. Damn you, Ne-kilst-lass!

Celreau's focus returns to the classroom to find the silhouette of a raven, obviously perched on the window sill, cast on one of the drapes. With a raucous chorus of caws, it flies off.

'Mr. Celreau. Are you okay? You look a little pale,' says Dawn from the doorway.

Visions of his first love suddenly flash through Celreau's mind. Dawn's resemblance to Angela is uncanny and never fails to stir feelings he has striven so hard to suppress. Slightly flustered by the interruption, Celreau rises and begins sorting through student essays on his desk while he tries to collect himself. He has been so wrapped up in his thoughts that he didn't hear the door open.

'Dawn! Sorry. I didn't see you there. Yes, yes, of course. I'm fine. My medical condition is causing me a bit more grief than usual. No real concern.'

'You prob'ly should sit back down, Mr. Celreau,' suggests Dawn, slowly strutting toward the desk. Dawn is wearing a tight-fitting turtleneck sweater and a short skirt that highlights her long, slender legs.

'Yes, I guess I should, just for a moment,' says Celreau, as he returns to his chair behind the desk. Making an effort not to stare openly, he can't help but be drawn by the sight of Dawn's sweet young body. She slides behind Celreau and begins to massage his broad shoulders. She presses her firm breasts against his back.

'You're so tense, Mr. Celreau. I think you're working too much. Your big muscles are so hard. You know what they say: All work and no play, makes Jack a dull boy.'

'Dawn, please stop,' the teacher asks.

'Why? Don't you like my physical therapy?'

'I do, but you know the school's hands off policy,' explains the teacher. 'There are strict rules about inappropriate touching.'

'Don't you think it's exciting to bend the rules a little, Mr. Celreau? Or, sometimes, to break them altogether?' Dawn slides her fingers gently along the teacher's neck.

'I'm not sure I follow. What exactly are you suggesting?' asks Celreau, now sexually aroused by Dawn's gentle manipulation.

'Well, for example, sometimes tigers and impalas in Africa drink together from the same drinking hole. The fierce carnivore could easily overpower the vulnerable prey. He knows he could rip and tear the poor impala to shreds and feed on its bloody carcass.'

Celreau flinches as Dawn squeezes hard on his neck muscle. 'But the tiger chooses to make an exception and shares the water this day, sparing the impala's life.'

'Interesting analogy, Dawn,' says Celreau, 'But why do you think the tiger makes this exception? Perhaps it's not hungry.'

'Not at all, Gabriel,' she replies, the use of his first name increasing the intimacy of the moment. Dawn bends to whisper in Celreau's ear. 'The tiger is famished, but it simply bides it's time. It's saving the thrill of the chase and capture of his tender young trophy for later.'

Celreau pulls away from Dawn's grip and stands quickly. Turning, he faces the teenager, visibly aroused by the sexual innuendo. 'Kill its young trophy, Miss Brady.'

'Pardon me, Mr. Celreau.'

'Kill its young trophy, Dawn. The tiger will kill its prey, not capture it!'

'Oh, yes, of course,' answers Dawn. 'That's what I meant—kill its prey. Even more exciting, don't you think?'

'I guess it all depends on whether you're the tiger or the impala,' answers Celreau over his shoulder as he walks to the door. Opening the door, he turns back to Dawn. 'Now, if you don't mind, I have some work to take care of.'

'Careful, Mr. Celreau,' says Dawn, smiling as she brushes past her teacher. 'All this hard work might turn you into a tiger.'

'Very clever, Angela. Run along now. And try to behave yourself, young lady.'

'Angela?' asks Dawn. 'Who is Angela?'

'Sorry, Dawn. Angela was, uh, is just a character in one of the novels I'm reading.'

'Too much work, Tiger, too much work,' says Dawn, laughing. She turns and exits the room. She can't know for sure, but Dawn is willing to bet he is watching the sway of her ass as she walks down the hall.

Matt & Jesse
1980

As pre-arranged, Matt and Jesse meet under the football bleachers after school. Over the years, the tree house and the bleachers have become the two main spots for the pair to talk. They discuss each other's problems and the tribulations in their lives; they share secrets, and make plans for their musical futures together. Of course, more often than not, they just have a few laughs.

'C'mon, Jess, sit down. D'you have the Raven's riddle?' asks Matt excitedly.

'Hold on to your shorts, Whitey. Gimme a second to find a clean patch of dirt to sit on.' Jesse pushes away a couple of discarded potato chip bags, a pop bottle and a half rotten banana peel. 'You'd think they could maybe throw their crap in the garbage. It's only a few yards to the trash can,' she complains.

'Okay, Mom. If you're about done the housekeeping, d'you think we can get down to business here?' teases Matt.

Jesse reaches into the pocket of her windbreaker, pulls out the riddle and hands it to Matt.

'Alright. Let's figure this out. Insatiable fangs ravage the one whom you seek,' reads Matt.

'Sounds like it could be a wolf,' says Jesse.

'Or maybe a vampire,' adds Matt.

'Maybe. Okay, go on.'

'The captor grows strong as the child grows weak.'

'Hate to say it, but that sounds like whatever it is, wolf or vampire, it's feeding on Donni.'

"Maybe, but it says captor not killer, so Donni may still be alive.'

'Yeah, maybe,' says Jesse. 'What's the next line?'

'Extending the Dark One's desperate hours.'

'Dark One's,' repeats Jesse. 'Could be a black wolf.'

'Yeah, but it still could be a vampire,' repeats Matt. 'Maybe the dark doesn't mean color. It could mean that he goes about his evil business at night. Or it could refer to the darkness in his evil soul—if he has one.'

'True. Either way, it definitely sounds like he is chowing down on poor Donni,' says Jesse.

'But why the desperate hours?' wonders Matt.

'I dunno. Maybe the wolf is sick and dying, and it is extending its life by feeding on the boy,' answers Jesse.

'Or the vampire's feeding on Donni to stay alive.'

'This vessel entombed in structures of power,' continues Matt. 'That's gotta be a coffin, Jess. This is about a freakin' vampire and not a sick wolf. Now, listen to this: Cursed by the dark and blood he desires, save for the oak tree, he cannot expire. Wow! Wow!'

'Yeah. I guess that pretty much sums it up, don't it?' surrenders Jesse. 'Vampires seek darkness and need blood to live on.'

'Bingo! We have a winner,' shouts out Matt.'

'Holy crap, Whitey. What're we involved in?'

'Well, Haida girlfriend. As your foul-breathed Raven so eloquently said, you have no idea the forces that oppose you.'

'So what part of this riddle leads us to Donni?' asks Jesse.

'It's gotta be the vessel entombed in structures of power.'

'Right, I agree, but what or where is that?'

'Hmm. What structures of power do we have in Blood Cove?'

'Off the top of my head, the police station and the church, but those're the last places a vampire would hang out,' offers Matt.

'Okay. We count those two out,' agrees Jesse. 'City Hall's another, but also not a hang-out for a vampire.'

'Although, if fat were blood, the vampire could survive a year feeding off Mayor Brady,' adds Matt laughing.

'Wait, I know,' says Jesse. 'What about the military barracks up on Look-Out Point? They could be considered structures of power, no?'

'Brilliant, Jess. The barracks have been abandoned for years, but you're right. They fit the description perfectly.'

'We gotta go up there right now and save Donni,' says Jesse, excited.

Holding up a hand, Matt says, 'Wait a minute. Exactly how do you figure we do that?'

'Waddaya mean? We know where he is, or at least we're pretty sure. Let's hike up there and find him.'

'Right. Okay. So we march up there. And then what? We knock at the barracks door and say, Good evening Mr. Vampire. Can our friend Donni come out to play?'

'Very funny! Of course we don't just walk up to him and ask. And we don't go up there defenseless. We bring a wooden stake to drive through his heart when we get the chance.'

'Oh, wonderful! A stake. And where do we get this wooden stake? I really don't think Lamontagne's Hardware Store has any in stock.'

'Buy one? Why?! You could make one easily.'

'Sure. How?'

'With an ax and any old pine 2 x 4.'

'Really! How big? How long and how sharp?'

'I don't know. Big, sharp and long enough so you can drive it through his chest and into his heart. So, what, a foot long?'

'Whoa, whoa. Come again? If you think I'm gonna stand over a blood-hungry vampire and drive a hand-made wooden stake into his body, you're nuts. Not happening!' The disgust shows all over his face.

'Well, I'm not strong enough to do it, Matt, that's for sure.'

'Not happening.'

'You have to. Donni's life depends on it,' yells Jesse in despair.

Matt and Jesse stare at each other in silence for a minute.

'Listen, Jesse. Tell you what. Let's skip school tomorrow. No one's been in the garden shed since mom died, and I'm sure I can find a stake and some sort of hammer in there. We'll hike up to the barracks at Look-Out Point and have a look around, then decide on our next plan of attack. Besides, I'm no expert on vampires, but I don't think sneaking around their caskets at night is a smart idea.'

Before Jesse can respond, her eye picks up movement near the end of the bleachers. Dawn Brady is approaching along the track.

'Shh, Matt. It's our darling Dawn,' whispers Jesse.

Dawn climbs the steps and sits halfway up the bleachers, unaware that Matt and Jesse are sitting beneath her.

Matt points silently to draw Jesse's attention to Christine approaching across the field. Christine Henderson waves at Dawn, skips up the bleachers and sits next to her friend. Jesse and Matt hardly breathe, straining to catch every word of the two girls' conversation.

'Dawn, what happened to your head?'

'It's nothing. You won't believe this, but I had a private lesson with Mr. Celreau in his classroom this afternoon.'

'Dawn, you didn't?' asks Christine.

'You just had to be there. I had Celreau so flustered,' says Dawn as she brushes her long dark hair back. 'I could see his pants bulge as I massaged his neck. He got so hard he had trouble getting up to walk me to the door,' brags Dawn, laughing.

'Your terrible, Dawn.'

'Ain't I? I'll have him licking my boots like a puppy dog by th
the week.'

'He's such a hunk. I certainly wouldn't mind him jumping my bones,'
says Christine, with a blush.

'Well, he's free game, sister.'

'Thanks, but no thanks, Dawn. That's not my style.'

'Well, your style will keep you a virgin forever, girl.'

'One day my prince will come and take me away on his golden steed,'
says Christine, gesturing grandly and laughing.

'More likely to be the Cortina Pizza delivery boy in his '79 Datsun,'
answers Dawn with a laugh of her own.

'Speaking of boys, what the heck happened to you and André the
other day?'

'The big retard got what he deserved.'

'Dawn, what did you do?'

'He wouldn't know a good thing if it slapped him in the face. I literally
had to unzip his pants myself. The big dummy. And then he had the nerve
to push me away. He almost split my head open. If he thinks he'll ever
get his hands on another babe like me, he's dreaming. Dad went freakin'
ballistic when I told him my version of what that retard did to me, with
the appropriate flood of tears, of course. He wants Kirkpatrick to charge
André with rape.'

'I knew it! That freakin' slut!' breathes Jesse, her lips almost touching
Matt's ear.

'Dawn, you know your dad. He won't just want André in jail on
charges of rape. At the very least, he'll want André convicted and sent
to the maximum security prison in Vancouver. If that happens, he'll be
locked up for years. The poor boy's so meek and vulnerable, he'll probably
be raped himself in a place like this! What are you thinking?'

'Nobody, no man at least, treats me like I'm not desirable. That idiot will have lots of time in his cell to play with himself, which he evidently prefers to me.'

'André is handicapped. He has the brain capacity of a ten-year-old. I'm sure he was terrified, and prob'ly thought you were raping him. He's a boy in a man's body. What's the matter with you? You can't blame him for the way he reacted to your coming on to him. You have to 'fess up to your dad and have him drop the charges.'

"Yeah, right! Never gonna happen.'

'Fine! Then I'll tell him.'

'Why are you being such a bitch? What do you care about that moron?'

'That moron probably saved my life. If it weren't for André showing up, I probably would have been molested and raped that night.'

'What're you talking about? You never told me this before.'

'Well, it happened ten years ago, and I was too scared and embarrassed to say anything. I knew if I reported it, nobody would have believed me anyway.'

'Who was it?'

'Pastor Dewar.'

'Get out of town! Dewar? You're kidding me, right?'

'No. It's no joke. André and I were playing hide and seek behind the church in the graveyard. André was hiding; my turn to find him. Pastor Dewar caught me wandering among the gravestones and yelled at me to come inside to his office at once.

'Soon as I stepped into his office, he got all weird and started touching me. When I tried to get away, he grabbed me, threw me on the floor and slapped me across the face. He stood over me and was undoing his pants when André walked in. He picked Dewar up and tossed him like a rag doll right over his desk and into the filing cabinets. We ran out of the church and straight home. Neither of us has ever mentioned a word about it.'

'Well, I'm sorry your date with Dewar went wrong and glad your little retarded friend saved you from the old pervert, but I'm really not sure how that affects me.'

Christine stares at Dawn, shaking her head in disbelief and disgust. 'Fuck you, girlfriend—fuck you!' Christine turns and walks down the bleacher steps.

'What? That's it? Well, fuck you, too! Go ahead. Tell my dad. He'll never freakin' believe you.'

Christine keeps walking with her middle finger raised high for Dawn to see. Dawn lights a cigarette, takes a puff and blows the smoke in Christine's direction. She waits for the other girl to be out of sight before leaving. Jesse and Matt remain silent until she is halfway across the football field.

'Why do you whiteys always have to pick on people who are different from you? And, usually, defenseless. Like André...or my people. Why do you always pick on us? Does abusing and harassing us make you feel superior? I'm sick and tired of your shit!' shouts Jesse at Matt.

'I know how you feel Jesse, it's terrible,' sympathizes Matt.

'What do you know about it? Have you been strapped or whipped for being white or speaking English?'

'Well, no, but...'

'Have you ever been told that your religion, your traditions, your culture were nonsense? Do you get watched like you're a thief every time you enter a store? Are you the butt of stupid racial jokes at parties? Well? Do those things ever happen to you?' screams Jesse, now infuriated.

'No, I haven't, Jess,' answers Matt, looking down at his hands.

'Then don't sit there and tell me you know how I freakin' feel!'

Matt looks at Jesse speechless for a moment, then says softly, 'I'm sorry, Jess.'

Crying, Jess lunges at Matt slapping him on the chest.

'I hate you! I hate you!'

Matt doesn't defend himself. As Jesse's anger loses steam and her blows to his chest subside, she collapses into Matt's arms, weeping. Matt wraps his arms tenderly around her and says in a soothing voice, 'I'm sorry Jess. I'm so sorry.'

'No. I shouldn't have gone off on you like that. I'm sorry,' says Jesse through her tears.

'It's okay, Jess. You've been through a lot, and you have a right to feel upset.'

'I got no right to hit you like that. I'm sorry. Did I hurt you?'

'Naw. I'm okay. I'm fine.'

'Matt, promise me you won't ever treat me like that.'

'Jess, you know who I am. You know I'll always treat you with respect.'

'Promise me you'll help me stand up to the bigots and bullies that pick on our people and on people like André.'

'I promise, Jess. You'll always be able to count on me.'

'Thanks, Matt. I never want to go through the prejudice and abuse my mom experienced when she was young.'

'Why? What happened?' asks Matt.

'My mom was only seven years old when she experienced her first taste of hatred and prejudice for simply being born Haida. The morning of her first day in grade two at the native day school in Skidegate, she was sitting at her desk chatting with a friend who sat next to her. The teacher had just walked into the classroom and was writing her name on the blackboard. My mom and her friend were so excited about their first day in a new grade that they began singing and clapping a traditional Haida cradle song.

Gûs lîñ kûdjû'diañ, gûs lîñ kûdjû'diañ?
What | are you for, | what | are you for?
Sgâ'na lî'ñga-i kûdjû'diañ.
Supernatural power | you are going to have | (you) are there for
Gûs lîñ kûdjû'diañ, gûs lîñ kûdjû'diañ?
What | are you for, | what | are you for?

'The teacher whirled on them, infuriated. Grasping a wooden yard stick from her desk, she lashed out at my mother. The blow struck mom across the face and knocked her sprawling on the classroom floor. Standing over her with the stick held high, the teacher yelled down, 'How dare you, you dirty little savage? Don't you ever chant that pagan nonsense in my classroom again? Did you not learn the rules of the school yet? Well, answer me, half breed. Answer me.'

'Yes, ma'am,' answered my mom. Trembling and terrified, she cowered under her desk, covering the welt on her face with her hand. The teacher dragged mom to the front of the room and made her stand with her back to the class, then pulled a whip from her desk. 'There's only one way to civilize natives and it's to beat the Indian out of them once and for all,' she said and proceeded to lash my mom like a dog.'

'My God, Jesse, that's horrible!' gasps Matt. 'Was she hurt bad, was she okay?'

'My mom told me she remembers that pain to this day. Every lash was like a sharp knife slicing into her flesh. She fell to her knees as the teacher continued to beat her. That's when, my mom says, she spotted the black bird perched on the classroom window sill. A raven. It was staring at her, and she stared back at it. She says she felt a spiritual connection, a voice telling her she was one of his creatures and she would be okay. At that moment, she said the sharp burning sting of the whip disappeared, and a peaceful calm came over her. When my mom quit reacting to the lashes, the teacher stopped the torture, thinking that my mom had passed out. She also noticed the raven on the window ledge. Running towards it waving her arm, she chased it away.

'Somehow, mom says, the raven had touched a core of resolve within her. That was the only way she could explain where she got the courage to stand up, wipe the tears from her eyes and begin to sing again…

Gûs lîñ kûdjû'diañ, gûs lîñ kûdjû'diañ?
What | are you for, | what | are you for?

'The teacher turned at the sound and stared in total disbelief. My seven-year-old mother looked directly into the teacher's eyes and continued to sing in defiance. Then my mother walked trance-like towards the teacher, never dropping her stare from the bewildered teacher's face.

Gûs lîñ kûdjûʼdiañ, gûs lîñ kûdjûʼdiañ?
What | are you for, | what | are you for?

'Looking as if she were seeing a ghost, the teacher backed away from my mother, visibly shaken. 'That's quite enough now. Get back to your seat. I said, get back to your seat,' instructed the teacher in frightened tones. My mom, not dropping a note, kept walking zombie-like towards her until the teacher had been backed against the wall.

Sgâʼna lîʼñga-i kûdjûʼdiañ.
Supernatural power | you are going to have | (you) are there for
Gûs lîñ kûdjûʼdiañ, gûs lîñ kûdjûʼdiañ?
What | are you for, | what | are you for?

'Unbelievably, at that point, the terrified teacher began to weep openly. Slumping to the floor, she begged the child to leave. My mom stopped singing and stood in silence, staring at the teacher for what seemed an eternity. The trembling teacher jumped back as my mom reached over, and grasping her hand, said in the sweet voice of a child, 'It's okay, I forgive you.'

'My mom then let go of the teacher's hand and calmly walked back to her seat. The startled teacher, still weeping and humiliated, stood up and raced from the classroom.'

'Holy crap. Did she tell her parents what happened. Did they arrest this nut-ball teacher?' asks Matt.

'Yes, she told her dad what happened. He said she had to go back to school and listen to what the teachers said.'

'What? Are you serious?'

'Mom says she didn't know it at the time, but back then if she was kept from going to the school, the family allowance payments would be stopped, and her parents could be arrested by the RCMP.'

'So what happened to your mom? Did she get whipped again by that horrible teacher?'

'Well, that's when things got interesting. At the end of that very day, the teacher was walking home through the park when she was struck by a falling pine branch. The limb struck her in the head and knocked her out cold. Her face was lacerated from her chin, across her nose to her right ear. She was lucky. An passing off-duty nurse found her and rendered first aid. otherwise, she would prob'ly have bled to death. The nurse said the teacher just kept muttering something about a cursed raven. She received thirty stitches and a hideous scar. She never returned to the school after that day.

'Mom has had a personal relationship with the Raven ever since.

'Word of the event spread through the school faster than a scandalous rumor. My mom gained a new status amongst her friends, one of respect and awe. The teachers and staff at the Indian day school never harassed her again. Certainly, there was still plenty of abuse in other classes, but none of the teachers dared confront my mom or any of her classmates. The facts, over time, were embellished and bent, enriching the details of the story, along with my mother's reputation. She's told me that her experience that day and her new relationship with the Raven empowered her, gave her the means and the courage to help other Haida who struggle against the prejudice and shame cast upon them by the white man. Eventually, her friends and family came to realize that mom had been touched by the Raven and had a very special place in the Haida community. She eventually assumed the role of Shaman and acquired a distinguished place amongst the Haida elders. My mother's experience taught me to be proud of my heritage, and to stand up for myself and for others who have difficulty doing it for themselves.'

'Christ! No wonder your mom's so bloody strong. I can't imagine dealing with that kind of crap.'

'Well, now you understand why I won't put up with any of that racial garbage at school or in town.'

'I hear ya. I am your wingman and I won't let you down.'

'You're the best, Matt.'

Jess kisses him on the cheek.

'Anyway, it's getting late,' says Matt, blushing. 'Let's head downtown. Maybe it's not too late to help with the search this afternoon.'

Celreau

1729

As the coach approaches the city limits of Budapest, Gabriel is trying to appreciate the irony. Nearly eight year ago he traveled to this very city in search of Petru only to find the bastard was no longer here. He has followed stories of the vampire's vicious debauchery across more than half of Europe and parts of eastern Asia, only to be led back to Budapest.

He has been riding with a young merchant and his wife for the last half day. The pair have been dead for an hour or so, but he is still hungry and a bit weak. Opening the coach door, he carefully steps along the window ledge and climbs up behind the coachman's seat. One sharp twist snaps the neck of the unsuspecting coachman. Gathering the reins, the vampire brings the horses to a halt at the side the road on the outskirts of the city. Gabriel feeds again. He never ceases to be amazed at how different in taste and texture each person's blood is. The coachman's has an almost spicy tang.

In a few minutes, sated and energized once more, Gabriel unharnesses the horses, and with a swat on the rump, encourages them to wander into a nearby stand of trees. He sets off to walk the rest of the way into town.

The activity on the streets at this late hour surprises him. After some thought, he realizes why the bars and taverns are so well patronized, and the noise level is so high. The weekend! The men are out on the town, gallivanting and raising hell after a week of toiling in the shops and factories. The commotion is exhilarating, and he enjoys his exploration of the main street. Drunkards stumble along the boardwalk, stopping every few yards to harass the prostitutes, then moving on to the next bar for yet another drink of ale or whiskey.

The doors of the houses and shops peppered between the taverns are locked, their windows secured with steel bars or boarded up, surely to prevent the drunks and misfits from looting or vandalizing. Gabriel cannot help but think how easy it would be to survive here with all of these defenseless fools wandering aimlessly about the city. The excitement of this virtual buffet of oblivious, vulnerable idiots just waiting to be slain spurs Gabriel's hunger. He turns and walks down a dark alleyway determined to fulfill his renewed need for blood.

Walking quickly along the dirty cobblestones, he desperately searches the darkness for a victim. A faint rumbling sound ahead, close to the alley wall, attracts his keen attention. He steps closer, thrilled to find a strapping young man asleep and snoring. Gabriel, shaking with anticipation, kneels next to the lad and slides his collar over. He stares in awe at the large pulsing veins protruding from the powerful neck. Overwhelmed, Gabriel loses his composure, exposes his sharp canines and leans in to bite.

A yelp of pain escapes Gabriel's lips as he feels teeth sinking into his own neck. He is suddenly pinned face-down on the cobblestones. Despite his strength, he cannot free himself from the powerful grip, no matter how he struggles.

Abruptly, the young man, gagging and spitting, releases his oral grip on Gabriel. 'Shit! Dead blood! Just my luck! You're a god-damned vampire, too!'

'What was your first clue, you simple-minded cretin? Get off me,' shouts Gabriel. The vampire releases Gabriel and sits back against the wall. Embarrassed, Gabriel sits up and sheepishly rubs his neck.

'Look, friend, I'm sorry,' offers the young man. 'The last thing I expected was to run into someone like me. I just reacted.'

'Forget it. No harm done,' answers Gabriel, still sulking a little.

'My name is Switzer.' The young man offers his hand.

'Gabriel,' giving the young vampire's hand a firm shake.

'No hard feelings.'

'None. You're pretty damned strong, Switzer, for a young vampire.'

'Well, I am, in fact, 60 years old. I guess that is fairly young for a vampire.'

'How could you overpower me at that age? I'm 28. I should be much stronger than you.'

'Ha! Ha! You're obviously new to this game. It doesn't work quite that way.'

'What? I don't understand. If you are 60, how can you be stronger than me?'

'The longer one of us survives, the stronger, the more powerful he gets. You have been a vampire for just a few years, I take it, so you are no match for me. Your age when you were turned, the age you will always appear to be, is insignificant and has no bearing on your physical strength. As with so many other things, becoming a more powerful vampire takes experience and time. There are no shortcuts.'

'Okay. Well, that makes me feel a little better. But only a little. I wasn't too happy about being so readily bested by a 60-year-old.'

'Just keep that in mind. Among our kind, looks can be extremely deceiving. One day you may find a teenager that will surprise you. You just never know, but you should be prepared.'

'Thanks, Switzer. You probably saved me from making a big mistake.'

'Oh, how's that?'

'I came here to exact vengeance on the bastard who turned me.

I thought it would be a simple matter of finding him and giving him a sound beating. Now, I may have to rethink that strategy.'

'Ooh, not too bitter! And it sounds more like you seek revenge rather than vengeance. You must really despise the old guy.'

'You don't know the half of it. I'd do anything to get my hands on him.'

'Again, your short time as an immortal dead makes you a little self-centered. With time you'll come to realize that your story's nowhere near unique. I know exactly why you hate this fellow. But really, you'd do anything to get near him?'

'Yes, really. He ruined my life.'

'Well, as I said, you're not alone there.'

'I need to find him. I don't care how long it takes.'

'Budapest is a large city, my friend. The chances of finding him are pretty slim.'

'I have nothing but time.'

'Ha, ha. You and me both. But seriously, my advice: get over it and move on.'

'Never! Can you help me? Will you help me? You know the area, the people around here. Maybe you even know him?'

'Listen, Gabriel, I don't usually do favors for people. In fact, I prefer to feed on the live ones and avoid the others.'

'You help me and I promise to supply you with fresh blood every night till we find the bastard.'

'Oh, sure. Aren't you the guy who doesn't even know his way around yet. But the offer is intriguing, and I find myself unable to refuse. I like you, Gabriel. Your grief and desperation are entertaining.'

'We have a deal, then?' asks Gabriel, extending his hand.

'Deal,' answers Switzer, shaking his hand firmly.

'Great! When do we start?'

'No matter how much time we have, no sense wasting any. Does this bastard of yours have a name?'

'Well, unfortunately, I know him only as Petru.'

'What! Surely you are joking?'

'No joke, I assure you. And I want my revenge. So, you know Petru?'

'I guess I do. I work for him!'

'Fantastic. You must take me to him at once.'

'Oh sure. We'll just walk over to his house for a spot of tea, then, and you two can get reacquainted.'

'Great. Let's go.'

'Are you mad?'

'I don't understand? Can you or can you not help me find Petru?'

'Listen, nobody simply drops by to see Petru. I've never even met the man face to face in all the years I have worked for the old bastard.'

'You must see him when you collect your salary, no?'

'Salary? What salary? We don't get paid.'

'But you said you work for him?'

'Just a figure of speech. It's more like barter than actual employment. I get to feed once a night in his district in exchange for all the cash, jewelry and gold fillings I retrieve from the donors.'

'But why limit yourself to only one meal? The streets here are crowded with careless, unsuspecting fools. A veritable buffet. Why not just help yourself?'

'That would be breaking the law. You don't ever want to break the law'

'What law could prevent you from feeding your fill?'

'The law of the blood covenant. Really, the only law that matters to people like us. Anybody caught breaking the rules of the covenant suffers dire consequences.'

'That just makes no sense. If what you say is true, then the more people you feed on, the wealthier he would become.'

'Petru is no fool. He has local politicians and the police chief in his pocket. In exchange for assurances that they and their families are not on the menu, they turn a blind eye on our activities. Within reason.

Petru allows us to feed on one victim every night, thereby controlling the number of transients, drunks and prostitutes on the streets of Budapest without attracting undue attention. For the privilege, we hand over any cash or valuables found on our victims. Petru, in turn, lines the pockets of the authorities with a share. It's a slick deal that has worked well for years.'

'How the hell would Petru know if you fed on several people in one night?'

'He has spies and informants everywhere. I survive just fine on one feeding. Believe me, getting caught breaking the agreement is not worth the risk.'

'Look. I have no time for this nonsense. I couldn't care less about your laws and the damned covenant. You agreed to help me find Petru. Quit wasting time. Are you helping me or not?'

'Ha. Well, you should care, friend Gabriel. And you should be worried. Petru is merciless. I've seen members who've broken the covenant and suffered greatly for it. Pain and agony like you could never imagine.'

'I have already experienced Petru's ruthlessness. What more could he do to me?'

'Petru is more than ruthless. He is outright sadistic to transgressors of his rules or those whom he feels have betrayed him. Just last week he caught his partner being unfaithful. My source told me that monster chained the lovers to posts facing each other so they could watch their lover's skin slowly melt as the sun rose above the horizon. He just stood there, watching them beg for mercy and scream in agony as their flesh roasted off their bones. The smell of the burning flesh as it dripped to the ground made witnesses physically ill. Through it all, Petru was emotionless, unmoved by the anguish and desperate pleas for mercy.'

Gabriel is visibly struggling to contain his impatience. Staring fiercely at Switzer, he demands. 'When do I get to meet him?'

'Have it your way, Gabi. You don't mind if I call you Gabi, right?' At Gabriel's nod, he continues. 'You won't be able to say I didn't warn you.

Come with me to Highland Estates. I'll introduce you to Domitor.'

'It's Petru I want to see. Why would I want to see some guy named Domitor?'

'Domitor is your gateway to Petru. He is head of Petru's security. No one sees Petru without going through him first.'

'Fine, let's get on with it, then.'

The two vampires weave their way through the tavern district, avoiding the busy streets by sticking to the alleyways as much as possible. After only a few minutes they turn onto a cobblestone lane that slopes uphill into a poor residential area. They begin the steady climb flanked by decrepit row houses, their battered shutters hanging precariously from rusty hinges and slapping in unison against weathered walls.

'Almost there. Try to keep up, junior,' shouts Switzer.

'Don't worry about me. Right behind you,' answers Gabriel. They stop a few meters from a tall iron gate where the lane begins to widen.

'Now what?' asks Gabriel.

'No problem,' answers Switzer as he effortlessly leaps over the tall gate. Gabriel smirks and somersaults over the gate, landing on his feet next to Switzer.

'Show-off,' says Switzer, laughing. 'Better save your energy. You're going to need it!'

'More where that came from,' counters Gabriel. He follows Switzer to a mansion set in the center of a large estate surrounded by yet another fence. Switzer reaches for a steel ring hanging by the gate hinge post and gives it three sharp tugs. He turns to Gabriel, 'Let me do the talking. Dom's not exactly the most sociable type.'

'Okay, sure. Let's just move it along,' says Gabriel impatiently.

A large man approaches from the other side of the gate and yells at the two intruders, 'Go away before I set the dogs on you.'

'Open up, you big ogre. It's me, Switzer. We gotta see Domitor.'

'You know you can't see Domitor without an appointment.'

'You wouldn't want to upset him now, would you? No? I thought not. Well, he will be pissed when he finds out why I was here and you didn't let me in.'

'Oh, yeah? Why?'

'I have a fresh recruit, that's why. Now, open up, you big brute.'

'A fresh one! Domitor likes fresh ones.' Reaching into his pocket for a key, the thug unlocks and opens the heavy steel gate. Switzer moves quickly to the mansion's entrance, Gabriel close behind.

'Hey, wait!' yells the guard, running sluggishly after them. 'Stop! Domitor doesn't like surprises.' Without hesitating, Switzer leads Celreau into the huge building and, turning left, down a long hallway. A door stands ajar at the end of the hallway. They enter the room to find Dom sitting comfortably on a large sofa, a drink in hand, and two scantily clad ladies clinging to him. Instinctively he reaches under the desk and draws a small pistol-gripped crossbow that he promptly aims at the two new arrivals.

'Easy, Dom!' exclaims Switzer, holding his hand up in a stopping gesture.

'Switzer, do you have a death wish?' asks Dom, as he lowers the pistol.

'Sorry, Dom, but this couldn't wait. I have a fresh one for you.'

Just then, the gate goon comes in panting. 'Sorry, boss, they slipped by me. I tried to…'

'No harm done, but if it happens again, you will be replaced. Get me?'

'Yes sir. I'm sorry, sir. I promise it won't. Thank you sir—thank you.'

Domitor dismisses him and the ladies with a shooing hand motion. Visibly shaken, the brute exits quickly with the women.

'You're looking good, Dom,' says Switzer, walking to a side table where he pours himself a drink from a crystal carafe.

'Just help yourself,' says Dom in a sarcastic tone.

'Thanks, boss. Oh, sorry. Where are my manners? Dom—Gabriel. Gabriel—Domitor.'

'Enough! Why do you bring me this filthy gypsy?'

'I'm here to meet Petru. I have no interest in speaking to his flunky. Take me to the boss,' demands Gabriel.

'How dare you? I am nobody's flunky. Obviously you don't know who I am.'

'He's just a bit ambitious, Dom,' offers Switzer. 'He didn't mean to undermine your authority. Right, Gabi?'

'Shut up!' Domitor lifts the weapon he is still holding and points the sharp wooden bolt at the newcomer's heart. 'Nobody gets to Petru without initiation to the covenant and my approval. Gypsy rat, you have thirty seconds to convince me that I should consider you as a candidate. If you fail, I'll end your fucking arrogance by putting this bolt through your heart.'

Gabriel, recognizing his misstep, backpedals a bit. 'At the risk of sounding conceited and full of myself, there's no limit to what I can do for you. You cannot name a challenge that I won't complete for you. What do you need done? Name it. Gold, jewels, blood, or perhaps somebody's life? If you need it done, I'm your man. Just give me the chance to prove it.'

Dom tightens his finger on the trigger of the crossbow.

'Don't mistake my confidence for arrogance, Domitor. Let me prove my worth. What do you have to lose? Aside from one vampire-killing bolt and a bloody mess to clean?'

'He's right, Dom. He is, after-all, worth more to you alive than dead. Give him a chance to show you.'

'Okay, Switzer, but if he fails, you go down with him.' Turning toward Gabriel, he says, 'Gypsy rat, I want Empress Theresa's crown jewels delivered to me by sunset tomorrow.'

'Good as done,' answers Gabriel without hesitation.

'Really?' asks Dom, chuckling.

'No problem,' repeats Gabriel firmly.

'Are you out of your mind, Dom?' asks Switzer. 'You know that's a death sentence. C'mon, give him something more sensible. Please.'

'Before sunset, or you and the rat both fry on the sun posts,' says Dom with finality.

'Well, it's been nice knowin' you—brief, but nice,' says Switzer sarcastically to Gabriel as they move past the mansion gate and onto the street.

'I'm not worried,' Gabriel answers without hesitation.

'Well, you should be. Damn, I know I am. Especially since my life now depends on you achieving the impossible. I was crazy to bring you to Domitor. What was I thinking? Damn! Damn! Double damn!'

'Relax. It's only a sack of jewels.'

'A sack of Crown Jewels, you mean. Located in a Royal Palace, locked in a specially made cabinet surrounded by a Royal Army of Royal fucking Guards,' answers Switzer.

#

1980

'Hush now, Donni, it's just me. I brought you some X-Men comics like I promised and I have some wonderful news!'

'I wanna go home now. Please, can I go?' pleads the boy.

'Donni, I understand that you miss your friends, and your mom and dad, but you have to be patient. Your special powers will come any day now.'

'Mister, I don't feel good. I don't want the powers anymore. Please. Can I just go?'

The man approaches the boy and kneels next to him. He places his hand on the child's shoulder to comfort him. In a soft, calming voice he says, 'Donni, I talked to your dad today, and he told me how very proud he is of you. He can't wait to see your new powers. You don't want to disappoint him now, do you?'

'No, I guess not,' answers Donni. He begins to weep.

'Of course you don't. I knew you wouldn't let everyone down, Donni. Listen. I have some wonderful news. The head of the government project is going to send you to a training camp for special kids in Vancouver. I told him how well you're doing and that we'd be getting signs of your new skills very soon.'

'I'm gonna go to Vancouver? Really?' asks Donni.

'A special agent will pick you up and drive you straight to the camp. You'll get to meet other special kids just like you. You're going to learn a lot of cool things to do with your powers. And, you know what? They have a huge pool with a water-slide…and a video room, as well.'

'Wow! That sounds like fun. When do I go?'

'It won't be long now, Donni. Maybe a week or two. We just need to continue the injections, and soon you will be ready.'

'I hate the injections. They hurt and make me sleepy,' Donni says.

'I know,' replies the man. 'That's a natural reaction to the serum. Tells me that the serum is working properly.'

'Only two more weeks—you promise?'

'Cross my heart and hope to die,' replies the man.

'Okay, but can I say bye to Ma and Pa before I leave for Vancouver?' asks Donni, wiping the tears from his cheeks.

'Absolutely,' the man assures him. 'I wouldn't have it any other way. Now, Donni, look into my eyes. Relax and take a couple of long deep breaths.'

'Please, don't hurt me, Mister…'

'I won't hurt you, Donni. Just relax and you will only feel a little sting.'

'Promise?'

'Cross my heart,' the man repeats. 'Look into my eyes, Donni. You've been up so long; you are tired, so very tired. Your eyes feel so heavy. You are safe here now. You can't keep your eyes open. You are falling asleep. It feels so good. You are asleep now. Rest—rest.'

Donni's body falls limp into the man's arms. He lays the boy gently on his mattress and looks down in excitement at the sweet innocence. The man's pulse begins to rise as he lowers his mouth to the child's neck. His lips press against the warm tender flesh, sending shivers up his spine.

He thrusts his sharp canines deep into the child's soft neck. The sharp, burning pain wakes Donni and he shrieks. He struggles in vain, trembling helplessly beneath the man's weight. Despite the struggles of the reluctant donor, the beast siphons blood from the boy's jugular. The frantically beating heart pulses blood across the vampire's tongue and down his throat, the sweet nectar firing his senses. The surge floods his every cell with adrenaline—rejuvenating, restoring the vigor and excitement of his eternal youth. Uncontrollably, he begins to shake, perspiration springing from his pores; every muscle tenses as his mind drowns in ecstasy.

He feels the boy go limp beneath him, and he knows he must stop. He has to resist the all-consuming desire for more, and more; that feeling of never being satisfied. He knows the risk. If he gives in to the feral desire, the boy will perish. He searches for the will to pull away, but he is defeated by the need. He surrenders to his lustful desire and, with desperate animal ferocity, he bites down—hard. One final drink.

Celreau
1980

The scratching at the door startles the vampire, a testament to just how absorbed in his feast he has been. Normally he would have been aware of the approach of the wolves. Enraged at being interrupted, he carelessly drops the boy on the mattress and rushes to the door. The wolves, smelling the fresh blood, are growling and clawing at the barracks entrance. Incensed at the interruption, the vampire screams in rage and frustration. He wrenches the door open and it slams against the wall. Startled by the sound and terrified by the sight of the enraged vampire, the pack scatters yelping and howling to the security of darkness just inside the tree line.

The vampire steps into the yard, roaring at the wolves the non-verbal anguish of blood lust, a language they know well. They cower together, tails tucked under their rumps in submission. The young night and the full moon beckon the wolves to the hunt. The hunger in the wolves' eyes is unmistakable and the vampire senses their excitement, their anticipation, their impatience for the night's kill. This is a need the vampire knows and understands all too well.

The largest wolf, the alpha, breaks from the pack and slowly advances toward the vampire, its thick dark fur raised along its hunched back. The alpha growls and snarls in defiance as it approaches. The vampire stands his ground, fists clenched, ready to fight should it come to that. Abruptly, the wolf rolls onto its back, spraying the air with acrid urine, surrendering its pack. The vampire screams in victory, turns and lopes into the shadowed forest ahead of the pack. The beasts, human and non, are united in a single purpose: to kill, to rend fresh meat and taste more blood.

The vampire races up the mountain path along the ridge, the slavering carnivores hard on his heels. In no time they are deep in the rain forest. Century-old cedar trees, the old forest's tall dark sentinels, fill the moist night air with their sweet aroma and cast moon-shadows across the root-webbed trail. Thick moss saturated by the evening dew fills the gaps between the roots, a silent cushion for the beasts' paws as they tear through the trees, nostrils flared with the hunt.

The vampire is suddenly overwhelmed by an unmistakable smell and stops abruptly. Prey! Sensing his heightening lust, the pack becomes frenzied. Noses to the ground, they pick up the scent. They veer off the path, down into a ravine towards the river. They are in luck; approaching from downwind, the prey is unaware of their presence, while its scent is strong in their nostrils. The river, running fast and loud, masks the sound of their descent through the thick underbrush.

The wolves move swiftly through ferns, low to the ground, ears erect, noses in the air. As the vampire tears down the incline, a sharp hemlock branch rips through his shirt, gouging deep into his flesh and drawing blood. Picking up the scent of his blood, a bitch in the pack turns on the vampire, snarling, teeth bared. The sight of blood running down his arm overwhelms the she-wolf's senses. Equally ruled by the demands of his senses, the vampire grunts in defiance. Maddened, the beast instinctively pounces at her prey, a fatal underestimation. The kick is swift and crushing, catching the animal in the throat and driving her against a nearby stump. Her shriek of pain is brief, choked off as she goes limp, dying on the forest floor. The pack, unaffected by the savagery to one of their own, await his intention, then turn to follow him downhill following the scent.

The roar of rushing water grows to deafening intensity as the pack approaches the forest edge. The vampire slows, cautiously creeping toward the clearing along the river. Eager with anticipation, the wolves close ranks behind him, nervously panting in unison as they watch their leader's every move, awaiting his orders. The vampire grins as he spots the prey, a lone woodland caribou buck, head down quenching his thirst from the icy stream.

Why the young caribou had strayed so far from the herd was impossible to know, but that error in judgment would be its last. The pack would not attack a strong, healthy buck within the protection of the herd; the risk of their antlers doing serious injury to the wolves was too great. Rather they would opt for the safe kill, a sick or old straggling member of the herd. Luck is running in two directions this night: good luck for the wolves, wretched luck for the young stray about to die.

The vampire turns to the wolf pack and motions them to their positions. Instinctively, they split into two groups, one arcing to the right, the other to the left. Bodies low to the forest floor, they snake their way to either side of the unsuspecting victim. In position, adrenaline spurring the blood pumping through their veins, saliva dripping from their glands and running down their chins, every muscle taut and ready to release, they await the alpha's signal.

The vampire breaks from the wall of foliage and sprints across the rocky clearing too fast for the caribou to react. The hungry wolves charge from the flanks, trapping the startled animal along the water's edge with no escape. Leaping onto the caribou's back, the vampire squeezes his strong arms around its neck. The wolves slash with vicious teeth, tearing at any tender area that presents itself—rump, under-belly, throat—as it kicks and thrashes in the water.

The caribou tosses its head about in desperation, its rack of antlers its only defense. A pack member, impaled by one of those deadly tines, is thrown several feet along the rocky slope. The wolf, bleeding profusely, rises and attacks, enraged. The caribou's hind leg flashes out, catching the charging wolf in full stride with its razor sharp hoof. The attacker dies instantly, its head split wide. The corpse is swept away by the torrential waters.

The wolves, relentless and undeterred by the loss, continue to rip and tear at the caribou's flesh, weakening the animal. A spray of blood and hair fills the air. The vampire, still holding fast to the young buck, stabs his teeth into the side of its throat, puncturing the carotid artery. The caribou collapses in shock onto the rocks, its dying heartbeats gushing thick hot blood down the vampire's throat. The vampire pulls away from his victim, surrendering the kill to the voracious pack. Overcome by the bliss and rapture of the hunt, he stumbles to the tree line, lies down on a bed of moss and, with a warm sense of fulfillment, watches as the pack rips, tears and devours the inert carcass.

'Get out—go away! You flea infested mongrels.'

The wolves lift their blood-stained heads from the caribou carcass and growl at this new human. The hair on their haunches grows erect and their gums pull back exposing their long, sharp fangs, guarding their feast. Without hesitation or hint of fear, the stranger rushes the wolves. Flailing his arms and splashing through the river's current, he yells, 'I said get out of here now before I beat your mangy asses to a bloody pulp.'

The unexpected verbal assault and the complete lack of fear behind the words spark fear and the survival instinct among the wolves. Surrendering their meal, they turn and run to the safety of the forest.

The vampire, startled from his sated slumber by the shouting, jumps to his feet, eyes scanning in search of the source of the offensive noise.

To his surprise, he sees no one. The only thing moving on the river bank, aside from himself, is a raven perched on the dead caribou's skull. The bird is energetically tearing off bits of the raw flesh, lifting its beak to stretch its throat and gulping them down. Abruptly, the raven stops. It turns to peer at the vampire and screeches a reverberating caw. The blue-black bird returns its wide-eyed gaze to the caribou, cocks its head and pecks the glassy eyeball from the animal's skull. In a show of leisurely indifference, the raven flaps into the air and soon disappears over the towering cedars.

A cool rain has begun to fall. The vampire scrambles up the steep river bank. Pulling himself over the lip, he stands on the ridge at the edge of the forest, gazing out over the river valley. His shirt and pants, already wet with blood and ripped from the night's kill, now cling to his body as they become soaked by the soft morning rain. Heavy black muck from the climb up the bank clings to his boots.

The vampire looks up river to the east and frowns. A faint glow is just beginning to lighten the horizon as rays from the rising sun peek between the pine trees. He instinctively turns to the narrow path leading back to town and sets off at a steady jog, ever mindful of his footing on the slippery rocks. He is startled by the sudden caw of the returned raven as it swoops from above the forest canopy. A wet slop of stinking bird dropping splatters on his shoulder. The vampire grunts in disgust, launches a curse at the mischievous bird, and hurries along his way. With another caw, as if in defiance, the raven flies ahead down the trail.

When the vampire arrives at the barracks, he rounds the corner to the side of the building, where he removes his shoes and tattered clothing. These he casts into a rusted barrel used for burning waste. Naked and wet, he walks through the rain to the front entrance and quietly slips inside. Crossing the main room to the trap door he left open during his frenzied departure, he descends to find the boy still on the mattress in the corner of the room where the vampire dropped him earlier. A rush of relief floods his senses—the boy is pale but alive, in a deep sleep.

The relief is short-lived. A curse of frustration escapes his lips. 'How could I be so careless? When will I learn to control the blood lust? Giving in to the urge when it surges so powerfully has cost me too dearly in the past. I cannot afford to destroy another human blood source. I need the fresh blood. This town is too damned small for me to risk kidnapping another donor. This boy's disappearance has already drawn too much attention. Get it together, man!'

Returning to the main floor, the vampire squints as he enters the kitchen; again he curses loudly. Rushing to the window, he draws the curtains, shutting out the offensive morning light that has been filling the room. He goes to the linen pantry, retrieves a fresh shirt, blue jeans and a dry pair of sneakers, and gets dressed. He keeps a supply of clothing stashed strategically in different parts of the building for such emergencies. Crossing to the old area rug lying in the center of the kitchen floor, he bends to pull the rug aside, revealing a trap door. He flips the ring from the door up, grasps it with his index finger and lifts the heavy door with ease. In addition to their isolation, he chose the barracks as his prison for this feature: almost every room on the main floor has an underground room accessed through a lockable trap door.

Back in the space under the main room, he kneels by the mattress and gently picks up the boy. Careful not to wake Donni, the vampire carries him up to the kitchen. Cradling the sleeping child easily in one powerful arm, he carefully negotiates the stairs to the cellar below. Reaching over head with his free hand, he lifts the globe of the old kerosene lantern hanging from the main joist and lights the wick. Lowering the globe, a dim glow illuminates the area, casting ghostly moving shadows around the room as it sways back and forth. The tiny dirt room is definitely less appealing than the other cellar; the putrid stench of rotten potatoes hangs in the damp air and moisture seeping along its walls pools to form a muddy puddle next to the steps. A thick, army-grade sleeping bag covers a rusty spring cot that stands against the dirt wall at the back of the room.

On a small wooden table next to the cot is a stack of Marvel comics, an open case of Coca-Cola, a jar of Smucker's raspberry jam and a box of dry salted crackers.

Crossing the musty room, the vampire lays the boy tenderly down on the small cot and covers him with the warm sleeping bag. Donni opens his eyes and asks in a weak voice, 'Where am I?'

'You're in the top secret lab, Donni,' answers the vampire.

'I am so tired, mister,' yawns Donni.

'That's alright; rest and you'll feel much better in a few hours. I've gotta now, but I want to tell you how incredibly brave you have been. The scientists told me they're very impressed with your progress.'

'Really?' Donni asks with a smile.

'Really! In fact, to celebrate I'll be back a little later with your favorite food—pepperoni and cheese pizza.'

'Gee, that'd be awesome,' the exhausted child says softly, his eyes closing against his will. In seconds he is sound asleep.

The vampire rushes up the rickety stairs two at a time, closes and locks the heavy hatch behind him, and carefully conceals the trap door with the carpet. He moves to the pantry, quickly donning a hooded jacket and a pair of Foster Grant wrap-around sunglasses. Stepping out of the building, he locks the door behind him and pulls the hoodie tight over his head. Running down the driveway, he leaps the two-meter security gate at the entrance and sprints up the road towards town.

The muddy road leads past Eagle's Point look-out where the dense fog blanketing the cove is rolling in off the ocean. A cool steady drizzle is falling over Blood Cove below. The vampire continues down the steep hill, turning at the bottom into the long, overgrown driveway to his home. The old stucco house is sheltered by the rocky ridge, barely visible in the shadows of tall surrounding pine trees that offer protection from the sunlight and camouflage from the road. Wild ivy climbs thickly on the building's textured walls and over the shuttered windows, clinging to the moss-filled eaves troughs at the roof edge. The weather-beaten roof is a mass of twisted shingles thickly covered by rust-colored pine needles. A raven, perched atop the rickety brick chimney, shrugs the raindrops from its feathers. It watches intently as the vampire approaches and enters the dilapidated dwelling.

Removing his muddy boots and sun glasses, the vampire steps into the living room. The textured ceiling, stained yellow from the leaky roof, swells in waves across the room, water dripping on the hardwood floor. Dark and damp, the big room is nearly empty. The only piece of furniture is a large wooden office desk against the far wall. A black leather handbag rests on the desk among an assortment of coil binders, a stack of papers, and a bunch of pens and pencils. The kitchen, to the right off the living room, is small and unused; its counters and cupboards are covered in dust, cobwebs and mouse droppings. A greasy cast iron frying pan caked with dried flies sits off kilter on the coils of a GE electric stove. Next to the stove stands a matching Harvest Gold fridge, its open door covered with magnets still clinging to notes and photos from years past.

Avoiding the abandoned kitchen, the vampire walks down the hallway to the master bedroom. The curtains are drawn and the room is dark; only the faint shape of a wooden casket on the floor is distinguishable in the gloom. The vampire hesitates, stops, turns back and enters the adjoining room. Wooden shutters cover a broken window almost completely preventing daylight from entering the room. A raven, using its sharp beak to work the shutter slats apart just enough to peer inside, observes the vampire's movements. This spare room has a closet full of sport jackets, dress shirts and pants. An assortment of different colored dress shoes lines the closet's floor.

The vampire, unaware he is being observed, reaches past the shoes to the back of the closet and pulls out a large traveling chest. Sitting on the floor, he unbuckles the security belt and opens the vintage case. With a volition all their own, his fingers find a small side compartment inside and retrieve a heart-shaped pendant on a silver chain. His fingers stroke the heart, and as if it were a magic amulet, his thoughts are transported to another place and time, a distant reality.

Angela, my sweet love, I miss you so much. I plead for your forgiveness. I know you could never forgive me, the monster that I am; but you must forgive the man that I was, the man who loved you. I am walking dead, cursed to wander this forsaken planet, a slave to my own blood lust. God has punished me for my sins and evil ways, Angela. I may be condemned to a never-ending existence, neither alive nor dead. Even if death were granted me, my love, in all likelihood my soul would be cast to suffer the fires of eternal hell. But Satan and his fiery abyss is not what I fear. It is the agony of eternity without seeing your beautiful face again that fuels pain and terror in my heart. Yes, Angela. I deserve to suffer; the beast that I am snuffed your precious life in the flower of youth. I only ask you to understand my damnation and forgive me. Is my torment not punishment enough? Please forgive me. Set me free from this god-forsaken guilt that tortures me. Angela! Angela!'

Lifting his head, the distressed vampire spots the spying raven at the window. Enraged, he drops the pendant and pounces recklessly at the bird, driving his fist through both window and shutter. Shards of glass shower around him and sunlight floods the room, sending him reeling backwards out of the room to the safety of the dark hallway. Gabriel, furious, slams the door.

Gabriel retreats to the main bedroom, sits on his mattress and inspects his injured fist. Frustrated and upset by the incident, he plucks the jagged pieces of glass from his hand. The deep cuts heal instantly as the shards slide from the vampire's pale, almost blue, skin.

Unscathed in the attack, the mischievous Raven circles the house, cawing in defiance. After a few minutes, the big bird swoops down and around the side of the house, entering through the broken window. Glancing quickly around the empty room, it cautiously flutters to the closet where the castoff pendant lies on the floor. With a swift ducking motion, the raven pinches the silver pendant in his strong beak and flutters out the window. Rising quickly, he disappears over the pines towards the river.

Matt & Jesse
1980

A cool steady drizzle falls on Matt and Jesse as they trudge past Look-Out Point to the summit of the ridge.

'We could've picked a better day to skip school,' says Matt, rain dripping from his cap.

'I don't like it any more than you, but we're runnin' out of time if we wanna find Donni alive. You got the hammer and stake, right?'

'Yeah. In my backpack. Right next to the mirror, garlic and crucifix.'

'Be serious! You've got them, right?'

'Yes, already. Don't worry.'

Mollified, Jesse looks around her. 'Shit, will you look at this fog. It's thick as pea soup. I hope we don't miss the entrance to the base.'

'I hate to tell you, Jess, but this ain't fog. We're on top of a mountain, standing in a freaking rain cloud. This crazy weather is just one more reason we should leave Blood Cove and start our new life in LA.'

'Won't it be wonderful? Blue skies, a warm ocean and music clubs on every street.'

'Already there, man, already there. Hey, look. There's the gate.'

'You sure we should be trespassing on government property?' asks Jesse.

'It's a little late to be asking that question,' answers Matt as he climbs up the gate. 'This place has been abandoned for years. No one cares if we're here. C'mon. Up and over.'

Matt and Jesse walk through the tall wet grass to a clearing where three abandoned wooden buildings loom in the mist.

'Okay, so if there's a power structure in this town, this's gotta be it,' says Matt. 'Let's split up and search around the outside of the buildings.'

'Are you out of your mind? You do realize there's a vampire on the loose, right? I'm not wandering around this fog by myself.'

'Cloud.'

'Cloud, fog, whatever. I'm not walking around here alone. Shit! What was that?' gasps Jesse, grabbing Matt's arm.

'I didn't hear nothing. It must be your imagination,' reassures Matt. Just the same, he nervously peers out into the thick mist.

'I'm sure I heard something.'

'Prob'ly just a squirrel or a magpie. C'mon let's check out the barracks for Donni.'

Matt and Jesse walk carefully around the buildings, looking through the boarded windows and broken glass for any sign of the boy.

'I guess we were wrong,' says Jesse, three-quarters of an hour later, now soaking wet and discouraged. 'Not even a trace of Donni. There's nothing here.'

'Don't give up yet,' answers Matt. 'We've really only just begun to look around here. Nowhere near a thorough search. Donni could still be here somewhere.'

As they walk around the corner of the last barracks, they come face to face with a raven perched on the rim of an old rusty burn barrel. The raven immediately begins to caw loudly.

'Ne-kilst-lass?' ventures Jesse timidly. In answer, the big bird caws one last time and flies off into the forest.

They run over, and Matt bends to look into the barrel.

'I had a feeling that bird didn't just happen to be here.' Matt bends to reach into the barrel to retrieve a piece of lined paper. 'Some sort of handwritten note.'

'So, what's it say, already?'

'Give me a sec. Don't get your undies in a knot. Hey, careful!' yelps Matt as Jesse snatches the page from his hands. 'It's wet. You coulda ripped it.'

Jesse reads the letter aloud.

Ma & Pa

I miss you a lot. It's scary out here and I don't like being alone. I can't tell you where I am because the man says it's a secret. He made it sound like a good idea, but I don't think so any more. I don't like the bites because they hurt a lot. It's cold at night and I get hungry. I'm sure you don't want me to come home, but I miss Chance. I'm sorry.

Donni

'He's alive! Can you believe it? Donni is alive,' shouts Jesse.

'Not so fast, Jess. Donni was obviously here at some point, but he could be anywhere by now. And I don't know what to make of this letter.'

'Isn't it obvious? The vampire kidnapped Donni and is keeping him prisoner. Donni wrote this letter. How it got in the barrel is another question, though.' She carefully folds the letter and slips it into the back pocket of her jeans.

'Wait a sec. There's something else in here.' Matt slides his backpack off and takes out the hammer and stake. He reaches down into the barrel with the stake and lifts out a ripped and bloodied shirt.

'Oh-my-God!' Jesse exclaims, covering her mouth with her hand. 'He must be hurt bad!'

'This bloody shirt's too big for a boy. This ain't Donni's shirt,' answers Matt.

'Thank God! Whose is it, then? The vampire's? Who else would be up here with Donni?'

'I don't know, but anybody who lost this much blood would be in bad shape or dead. Hey, look!'

'What?'

'Something just ran behind that building,' says Matt, his voice lowered.

'I told you I heard something. Do you think it's the vampire?'

'I don't know, but let's not hang around to find out.'

'Shh! Did you hear that? I definitely heard growling. I'm scared, Matt.' Jesse moves in close to Matt, her eyes wide, as big as loonies.

Matt grips the girl firmly by the arm. 'Holy Shit! Don't move!'

'Why? What is it? Matt, you're scaring me.'

'Slowly turn around, Jess. It's not a vampire. It's—wolves!'

'What the heck would they want with us? Wolves are not man-eaters. They usually avoid humans. This doesn't make any sense.'

'They must have picked up the scent of the bloody shirt.'

Jesse grabs the stake from Matt's hand.

'What the hell! What're you doing?'

Jesse swings the stick sending the bloody shirt arcing through the air towards the wolf pack.

'Giving them what they want.'

Several wolves grasp the shirt in their snarling jaws and tear it apart. No mistaking their rage.

'Let's go, quick, before they turn on us,' insists Jesse.

The kids race down the short drive to the gate, clamber over and run down the path towards town.

'I think we lost 'em,' pants Matt minutes later, struggling to catch his breath.

'Celreau's house is just up ahead,' says Jesse, pointing.

'It's just past noon. Maybe he's home for lunch,' says Matt.

'I pray he is—I'm soaked. I'd sure like to dry off and rest a bit.'

They slosh across the muddy driveway and up the old weathered porch steps to the front door. Jesse knocks, then knocks again. No response. Matt tries the doorknob.

'Shit, it's locked. He must've packed a lunch.'

'Matt! Matt!' repeats Jesse in a whisper.

'What is it?' asks Matt, turning to see Jesse pointing in shock towards the driveway. The black alpha wolf is advancing on the kids, hair hunched back, head low to the ground, mouth foaming and snarling.

'Matt!' screams Jesse. Matt reaches with his left arm and moves Jesse behind him.

'Don't panic, they can sense fear. I'll stand my ground. When I tell you to run, you run. Hard!'

'But Matt, he'll kill you.'

'Jesse, don't argue with me, damn it. When I say run, you run!'

'Okay, okay,' says Jesse, weeping.

The wolf suddenly sprints toward Matt.

'Run!' yells Matt.

Without hesitating, Jesse takes off along the house and jumps over the patio railing. She tumbles to the ground and turns just in time to see the beast latch on to Matt's hand.

'Aie-ie-yeow!' screams Matt. The wolf is shaking his arm back and forth with his powerful jaws. Matt punches and kicks at the animal in desperation.

The wolf suddenly squeals in pain and releases his grip on Matt. Celreau stands over the wolf with his fingers deep in the vicious animal's eye sockets. Celreau strikes Matt on the shoulder, sending him sliding to the end of the porch. The crazed wolf snaps his neck to the side and bites down on Celreau's arm. Celreau releases a blood-curdling roar. The teacher's eyes open wide and his gums pull back revealing sharp extended canines. His face is all feral beast. The wolf, terrified, releases his grip and squeals as Celreau effortlessly tosses the huge animal across the yard to crash against a pine tree. Matt and Jesse watch in disbelief as the wolf falls, dead before it hits the ground.

'Oh, my god, Matt. You're bleeding,' exclaims Jesse as she runs to his side.

'Damn, that burns,' answers Matt, favoring his torn arm.

Celreau approaches the children, who cower against the corner railing. 'Keep pressure on that wound,' he instructs the boy tersely.

'Stay back. Only one good arm, but I swear I'll hurt you if you come any closer,' threatens Matt bravely.

'Matt, Jesse—it's me, Mr. Celreau. It's okay. The wolf's dead. Let me look after that bite before it gets infected. I know it's sore, and there's a lot of blood, but I don't think it's as bad as it looks.' Again he steps toward Matt.

'I said get back. I'll kill you, I mean it!'

'Matt, calm down. You're in shock. I'm your teacher. Mr. Celreau. I would never harm you or Jesse.'

'You knocked Matt straight across the deck. Is that your idea of helping?' asks Jesse.

'I had to push Matt aside so the wolf wouldn't turn back on him.'

'You…you turned into some kind of beast. What the heck was that shit?' adds Matt accusingly.

'I must say that was impressive even to me. Caught me completely by surprise. But it's simply fight response.'

'What's that suppose to mean? You tossed that wolf across the yard like it was a rag doll.'

'It's a physiological reaction that occurs in response to an attack. Adrenaline flooded my body, giving me strength beyond my normal ability. I'm sure you've heard stories of a mother lifting a car to save her child who was pinned under it. Same sort of thing.'

'But your face…your eyes and teeth were like, well, you looked like a vampire,' blurts Jesse.

'That's also a characteristic of flight response. Your hormones cause all of your senses to explode in order to get you to safety. Not only are your muscles stimulated, but all of your senses, including your visual senses, are given an adrenalin boost. Your hypersensitive perceptions exaggerated my already aggressive features. C'mon now, do I look like a monster to you?'

'No. Not now anyway,' answers Matt.

'Of course I don't. Well, thank God we weren't badly hurt. Now, let me put a bandage on that wound, then I'll drive you home. Your dad will want you to get medical attention right away. Follow me. I keep a first aid kit under the seat of the Jeep for emergencies.'

'Is your arm not bleeding, Mr Celreau?'

'No, no blood. Pretty sore, though.'

'How is that even possible? The wolf bit you; at least as hard as it bit Matt. And the way you yelled,' questions Jesse.

Celreau helps Matt into the back seat of the Jeep. Jesse climbs in next to him.

'Damn lucky, I guess. The trauma to his eyes probably weakened his bite. His teeth never punctured my skin. Sure ripped up my favorite jacket, though.' He takes two six-inch square gauzes from the First-Aid kit and places them as a thick pad on Matt's bite. 'Jesse, hold this in place and keep steady pressure on it. This'll stop the bleeding and keep the bite from getting infected. By the way, what're you guys doing up here on a school day?'

'Following a lead. We had to search the barracks for Donni.'

'The military barracks? That's private property! First you skip school, then you break the law. You two are in a world of trouble,' says Celreau, infuriated. Starting the ignition, he flips the shifter into gear and backs out of the muddy driveway. The wet clouds have decided to unburden themselves, requiring that Celreau engage the Jeep's windshield wipers.

As they turn towards town, Matt explains.

'The power structures mentioned in the riddle verse have to refer to the barracks. We're sure of it, so we had to check it out.'

'Matt, didn't I tell you that riddle was nonsense?' demands Celreau, switching the windshield wipers to a faster speed.

'Jesse, read him Donni's letter,' says Matt.

Celreau listens intently to Jesse; before he can say anything, Matt demands, 'Does that sound like nonsense?'

Celreau concentrates on the road for a bit, frowning. Then, with a sigh suggesting he's made a decision, he says, 'I guess there's no point avoiding the issue any longer. You were going to get the news soon enough.'

'A vampire, right?' asks Jesse.

'No vampire. Donni ran away from home. I went for a jog along the river trail this morning before school. I spotted a shirt snagged on a dead branch jutting out over the rapids. He must have wandered too close to the river and slipped on the rocks. Mr. and Mrs. Cardinal confirmed with Sergeant Kirkpatrick that the shirt belonged to Donni. The search has been called off. I'm afraid Donni is presumed dead. The towns downstream have groups of volunteers on watch for his body.'

'No! You don't know that's what happened,' cries Jesse. 'The letter... look! It says he got bites.'

'Black flies, Jesse, most likely. They're everywhere this time of year,' answers Celreau.

'He...he said that his whereabouts were a secret. A vampire had him kidnapped,' insists Jesse, now weeping.

'No vampires, Jesse. Donni was cold, weak and confused. He lost his way.'

'But, but the structure of power, it led us to the note and...wait! The bloody shirt.'

'Yeah,' interrupts Matt. 'How do you explain a large bloody shirt we found in a barrel next to one of the buildings?'

'The verse leading you to the note was pure coincidence. The shoreline was already covered by the search party, and you two searched the area along Crooked Creek. The next logical area was Look-Out Point. As for the shirt—it's hunting season. Some hunter must have disposed of the bloody shirt after gutting and skinning his caribou or deer.'

'No. We have to keep looking. I know he's out there. Matt, tell him, please,' begs Jesse, wiping at the tears that are still leaking from her eyes.

Matt puts his arms around Jesse to console her, wincing at the pain that shoots up his torn arm.

'Let's just get home, Jess. You're cold and tired, and I've gotta get this arm taken care of.'

'I know he's alive, Matt, I just know it.'

'I know, Jess, I know.'

The Jeep enters the town and turns down Badger Avenue. The rain is coming down hard by the time he splashes up the pot-holed Fairchild driveway and parks in front of the old garage. Matt and Jesse climb out, followed by Celreau. Hopping over and around puddles in the cold rain, Matt and Jesse scurry to the porch and run into the house. Jesse's mom is sitting in the living room, knitting. Bursting into tears, she runs over to hug her mother.

'Donni's dead. We were too late. We couldn't save him. He fell into the river and drowned,' says Jesse, between sobs. 'And Matt has hurt his arm.'

'Aww, I'm so sorry, honey. The Cardinals are going to be devastated. But you did your...What? What's that about Matt?'

Still holding Jesse tightly in her arms, she looks up at Matt with concern. 'What happened?'

'Just a cut, really, and it's a long story, I'll be fine. I'm mostly just feeling sad, I guess,' answers Matt, wiping a tear from his cheek. Abruptly an expression of just remembering something crosses his face, and he turns to the door, which is still open.

'Damn! Mr Celreau. He gave us a ride home from Look-Out Point, because of the rain, and I forgot him. He's outside on the porch.'

'My Lord. It's pouring cats and dogs out there. Why is he standing out in the rain?'

'Ughh. I don't know.'

Big Mama rises from the sofa and goes to the door. Addressing Celreau through the screen door, she accuses, 'Don't you know enough to come in out of the rain?'

'Mrs. Fairchild, right? I apologize to be meeting you this way. I am Gabriel Celreau, one of the kids' teachers. And, in answer to your question, I never enter someone's residence without being invited in. Especially upon first meeting them. But now, I think it's high time I got young Matt to the clinic. I don't think the injury is serious, but we can't be too careful. We should go. If I'm not mistaken, they'll be closing soon.'

'You're right, of course,' agrees Big Mama. 'Wouldn't want the wound to get infected due to negligence. Thank you so much for your help, Mr. Celreau.'

Matt looks at Jesse as he moves to the door. 'Bye, Jesse. See you in the morning, 'kay?'

'Yeah, okay,' answers Jesse, still too emotionally upset to respond further.

Celreau
1779

'You said you'd help me, Switzer. You gonna go back on your word?'

'Do I have a choice? Really? Do I?'

'Listen, just give me directions to the palace and I'll take care of the rest. I don't need anything else from you.'

'You don't have a clue, do you?'

'What's to know? I am ten times stronger than any human. I can handle myself.'

'Do you think you're still in your village in Romania beating up whores and drunkards for a quick bite?'

'No, but…'

'There's no way you can fight your way into that castle. If you try, you'll be captured. No doubt about it. These guards have been trained by the likes of Domitor, and Petru himself, in exchange for blood favor and control of the red district. Unless you listen to me and follow my instructions, they'll take you down and have you shackled and quartered before sunrise.'

'That bastard, Domitor, set me up to fail,' accuses Gabriel.

'He set us both up.'

'So that's it? We just give up without trying?'

'There may be a way. It's a long shot, but if you follow my instructions, and we get a little lucky, I think I can get you into the palace.'

'Wait. You ever actually been in the palace yourself?'

'I may have had a fling with a young countess a while back.'

'You young-looking old dog. How'd you manage to get past the security?'

'Hopefully, for both our sakes, Gabi, the same way you will.'

Gabriel races across the courtyard and easily leaps over the five-meter security fence.

'Gabriel. Over here,' stage-whispers Switzer from behind a large oak tree. 'This way, quick!'

'Here, help me with some of these, will you?' suggests Gabriel, handing Switzer a couple of sacks.

'You did it! I honestly didn't think you'd come out of there in one piece, my friend,' says Switzer.

'Oh, ye of little faith,' kids Gabriel.

'Whoa! These are freakin' heavy! Did you steal the royal kitchen pots, as well?'

'Sorry to disappoint you, but I only stole gold, silver and precious jewels. Maybe next time. What'd you expect, anyway? Gold and silver are pretty damned heavy.'

The two vampires find their way through the darkness towards the city lights, moving as quickly as possible with their burdens.

'You must spend the night at my house, Gabi. I wanna hear all the details.'

'Sure. I need a place to lay low anyway. The palace guards'll be out searching for the lost royal treasure. They're responsible for guarding the palace and its contents, so the theft'll be embarrassing. They'll want to rectify that as quickly and quietly as possible.'

'Stop!' snaps Switzer.

'What?'

'I'm famished.' Pointing at an old man in rags passed out against the alley wall, he asks, 'Want to join me?'

'No, I'm good, but you go ahead.'

'Suit yourself. I thought you'd be hungry after all you've been through tonight.'

'Ah! Right. I fed on one of the guards before my escape.'

'Aren't you the sly one? Talk about dine and dash. Give me a minute.'

'Bon appetit,' says Gabriel, smiling.

Switzer drops his bags and kneels next to the drunk. Grasping the vagrant's arms tightly, he sinks his pointed canines deep into his victim's neck. The man's body jolts forward and his eyes open wide in pain. He gasps and grunts in desperation before quickly passing out from blood loss. Switzer feeds for a few minutes; then, satisfied, he releases the body to flop forward to the ground.

Retrieving his bags, Switzer belches loudly. 'Thanks for being patient. I was starving.'

'Nice manners,' Gabriel quips sarcastically.

'Thanks,' answers Switzer. He laughs and drops another small belch.

In short order, the pair arrive at Switzer's house. Upon entering, they sit down at the kitchen table in the dark. Striking a match, Switzer lights the candle ensconced on the wall, then empties his bags on the table. Looking down on the tangled mass of gold necklaces, rings and jewels, his grin grows to consume his face.

'You realize, don't you, that this's your ticket to meeting Petru?'

'That was the whole point, remember? And I think I earned it? Don't you?'

'Absolutely! And won't Domitor be surprised!'

'That ignoramus is of no concern to me. Petru is mine now.'

'I hope you know what you're up against, Gabi. Petru is no pushover.'

'Yes, you told me. Don't worry. I have a plan.'

'Speaking of plans—tell me about the robbery.'

'Right! Well, after you threw the meat into the courtyard to distract the guard dogs, I ran to the servants' side entrance. Right where you said I'd find it.'

'Was a soldier guarding the door?'

'Yes. I hid among the rose bushes till dark.'

'Good. Did he leave his post to go for supper?

'Yes, right on schedule, but not before another guard arrived to replace him.'

'Shit! They changed their routine. They're getting wise. Till now, the guard always walked from the servants' entrance to the guards' bunkhouse to switch. Damn! So, how'd you get past the new guard to get in?'

'I scaled the stone wall and hung tight above the door, arms and legs wedged against the walls, until the help stepped out.'

'Impressive strength for a young vampire.'

'Anyway, I took advantage of the guard being distracted by staff leaving. He was busy chatting up one of the pretty chambermaids when I dropped to the ground and stepped inside as the big door closed behind me.'

'So you followed the passageway to the kitchen, took a right down the hall past the utility room to the staircase and went up to the main lobby?'

'Right. Unfortunately another guard stood between me and the staircase leading to the second floor, where you said the jewels were kept.'

'Unfortunate for him, I'm guessing.'

'Right. Snapping his neck after creeping up behind him was no challenge. Human hearing is so limited. I dragged him into a closet and continued upstairs.'

'Oh? I thought you said you fed on him?'

'Huh? Oh, yeah, right. I did, but just a quick drink to tide me over. Then I quietly proceeded up the circular grand staircase. I flattened myself on the last few steps at the top to get a good look at the layout. I needed to be sure I knew exactly what I was up against. Your description was almost completely accurate. The second floor hallway is circular with the bedrooms arranged around the outside. The central portion is open and a crystal chandelier hangs over the foyer below. Quite exquisite, actually; I found myself wishing I had time to admire it. Anyway, just as you said, a low railing with a fancy woven skirt runs around the opening and joins the staircase banister. The treasure chest was situated in a display cabinet on the side opposite the staircase.'

'That's what I told you! What was different?'

'Oh, just one small detail.'

'What?'

'There were two soldiers guarding the treasure, not one.'

'Shit. How did you manage to kill one without the other sounding the alarm?'

'I snaked along the cold granite floor on my belly, around the curved banister towards the display case.'

'Couldn't they see you?'

'No. Well, not at first. The only light in that corridor at that time of night comes from the two torches ensconced on the walls on either side of the display, right over the heads of the guards. The rest of the corridor is heavily shadowed. I was inching forward slowly, keeping as low a profile as possible behind the railing skirt, and sticking to the deepest shadows. But when I was about halfway, one of the guards must have heard or seen something. He started to move along the hall, peering intently into the darkness. It felt like he was looking right at me.'

'Shit! What'd you do?'

'I slithered through the doorway of the room closest to me and closed the door as quietly as I could.'

'He must've spotted you? Did he go in after you?'

'Not sure if he saw me, but he kept coming in my direction. I wasn't taking any chances.'

'Where did you hide? Certainly not under the bed or in the closet? That would be the first place he would look.'

'Of course.'

'Well, where then?'

'I climbed one of the bedposts and clung to the ornate tin ceiling above the bed. He must've come straight to that room because seconds later he slowly opened the door and edged into the room. With only dim moonlight coming through the window, he'd have had to look directly up at me to see me.'

'Okay, but weren't you afraid he'd search the room thoroughly. After all, he seemed sure someone was there. Surely he would see you hanging there?'

'I'm sure he would have, eventually, but the princess distracted him.'

'Princess? Of all the damn doors to pick, you chose the princess' room? And you're telling me the guard entered without knocking?'

'It's not like I had time to be choosy. I don't know what their protocol is, but the guard's entrance woke her, and she shrieked, pulling the blanket up to her chin. The guard tried to calm her and asked if anybody else had come into her room. That's when she saw me hanging above them.'

'Holy shit? So she screamed again?'

'No. Actually, she just stared at me, evidently in shock. I don't think she believed the evidence of her own eyes. I put my finger to my lips, asking her to keep quiet.'

'That worked?'

'Yes. She probably wouldn't have remained mute for long, but I took advantage of her hesitation. Dropping on the guard, I pinned him to the floor, crushing his neck in the process. Surprisingly, the princess still hid under her blankets, making only a faint whimpering sound.'

'Lucky, or she would have alarmed the other guard.'

'She didn't have to. I was getting up from the floor after dispatching the first when the second guard rushed through the doorway, sword drawn, and attacked me.'

'Did he...?' begins Switzer, his eyes running over Gabriel's torso.

'No, but he made a valiant effort. Unfortunately for him, I had no time for games. I relieved him of the sword and beheaded the brave royal servant in one motion.'

'Touché!' shouts Switzer.

'Then I was out of the room, down the hall to the case, where I filled my sacks with the Royal treasure. Getting out of the palace presented fewer problems than getting in, and the rest you know.'

'But were the jewels not in a fortified chest secured under lock and key?'

'Yes, of course. Secure from entry by three or four strong men, but not anywhere secure enough to thwart the strength of this vampire.'

'Of course. What was I thinking? You know what, Gabi?'

'Tell me, my friend.'

'I believe the almighty Petru is about to meet his match.'

'You? You're back? What do you want?' demands the ogre at the gate.

'That's no way to talk to one of Dom's friends,' states Gabriel condescendingly. 'Now, be a nice boy and let me in.'

'I don't know. You tricked me last time and got me in a lot of trouble with the boss.'

'I have a gift for Dom. He will be truly angry with you when he finds out you turned me away.'

'Gift? What is it? What could you possibly have that would interest someone in his position. He can get anything he wants.'

'Not this he can't. I've got the Royal Jewels here for him.'

'The Royal Jewels? In that sack?'

'Yes, of course. Open the gate so I can show you.'

'Hey! You're trying to trick me again.'

'No, I'm not. See for yourself,' says Gabriel. He extends his left hand toward the guard to show off a large gold ring bearing the Royal Crest.

'Wow!' exclaims the guard.

'You like that, don't you? Want it? Sure you do. Here, take it. Go on. I've got plenty more.' Gabriel removes the ring and hands it to the guard.

'Oh, how can I ever thank you?'

'No need, my friend. You're welcome. Wanna see the rest of the treasure?'

'Yes! Ah, but wait. No tricks this time.'

'You can trust me. We're friends now, and I'd never try to trick a friend.'

The ogre opens the gate.

Gabriel moves past him and runs directly up the steps and into the mansion. Proceeding down the corridor, he enters the library and silently steps up to the large oak desk where Domitor is busily counting money. Domitor, startled by the impact of the large sack dropping on the table, stares as his stacks of gold coins spill across the desk and onto the floor. He looks up and glares at a smirking Gabriel for a moment, then his eyes turn to the cloth bag on the table. The awkward silence is broken by the gate guard running into the room huffing and puffing.

'He tricked me again, Dom. I'm sorry, I'm truly sorry!'

'Get out!' commands Dom.

The desperate guard, now on his knees, pleads, 'He pushed past me before I could stop him. I'm so sorry.'

'I said get out, you fool!' screams Dom, his modicum of patience gone.

'Thank you, thank you,' whines the guard backing away and out the door.

'You really need to train your security personnel, Dom,' teases Gabriel. 'That's something I could do for you, if you like.'

Dom, ignoring Gabriel, unties the string that secures the bag and looks inside. In disbelief, he reaches in and pulls out a handful of gold and silver necklaces and bracelets. He lays them on the table and reaches in again to retrieve a magnificent gold crown encrusted with diamonds and rubies.

Dom falls back into his chair. 'Inconceivable. I can't believe you accomplished your quest. Clearly I under-estimated you, Rat.'

'Clearly. Now lead me to Petru.'

'Not so fast, Rat. I must verify that these are, in fact, part of the Royal Crown Jewels from the Palace and not fakes you've had made. I'm not as easily tricked as my useless guard. Petru would have both our heads if he discovered these were not authentic. For your sake, Rat, they'd better be the real thing.'

'Suit yourself, but hurry. I'm anxious to meet the infamous Petru.'

'Get out! I'll summon you once the jewels have been authenticated— and even then, only when I am good and ready.'

Mayor Brady
1980

'The Mayor will see you now, Miss Henderson,' announces the receptionist.

Christine puts down her People magazine, gets up and walks past the front counter to the mayor's office. The mayor waves her in and asks her to sit down.

'Miss Henderson. Shouldn't you be in school, young lady?'

'Yes, Mr. Brady, but I need to talk to you. It's urgent.'

'I can't imagine what you need to say to me that couldn't wait till this evening. You are, after all, over at the house most nights. Almost one of the family.'

'It's about Dawn, and I wanted to talk to you in private.'

'Well, now you have sparked my curiosity and gotten my attention. What's this about?'

'Dawn lied to you. André never laid a hand on her. You need to drop the charges you have against him.'

'Nonsense! Robillard assaulted Dawn. That delinquent ripped her clothes while trying to rape her. She was able to fend the pervert off, earning a bruise on her head for her trouble. Besides, why would she lie to me about something like this?'

'I know it sounds crazy, but you don't know Dawn like I do. You're her father. She only tells you what you want to hear. Dawn was—uh, is—my best friend, Mr. Brady, but I can't let André go to jail for a crime he didn't commit.'

'What exactly are you trying to say, young lady?'

'Dawn is a…uh, well, she is a…umm…'

'Out with it, girl!'

'Dawn sleeps around.'

'Pardon me?'

'She's a slut. There, I said it.'

'How dare you come to my office and make such defamatory statements about my daughter?' The mayor's face has taken on a distinctly reddened hue.

'I'm sorry, but it's true. It hurts me as much to say it as it hurts you to hear it. Dawn's the one who led André to the seashore that day. I was with them at the park when she asked André to follow her down to the water. Yesterday, after school, she told me all about how she tried to get him to have sex with her.'

'I've heard just about enough of these unfounded allegations. I'm beginning to think you have some ulterior motive for trying to damage Dawn's reputation.'

'I'm telling you the truth, sir. André wanted nothing to do with Dawn. He has the mentality of a ten-year-old. When Dawn got aggressive, André panicked and pushed Dawn away. She tumbled down the sand embankment, ripping her clothes and banging her head in the fall.'

'That's enough! Dawn is a sweet, innocent girl. She'd never do anything like that!'

'Okay, okay. I didn't want to tell you this last bit, but now you leave me no choice,' says Christine, frustrated.

'What in the world do you mean. Tell me what?'

'Remember last week, when Dawn slept over at my house?'

'Yes, of course. She does that quite often.'

'Well, at least half the time, she doesn't actually sleep over. She tells you that so she can stay out all night and party without you knowing. And she wasn't at my house that night, either. She lied to you.'

'Where was she, then?' asks the Mayor.

'She was at Dave Adam's house. The week before, she was at Jamie Ryan's place, and the time before that, she met Mike Dawson at the 'Golden Nugget Motel.'

'Mike Dawson, the football quarterback?' asks Brady in disbelief.

'The one and only. I'm sorry you had to hear it from me, Mr. Brady, but I couldn't keep it a secret any longer. Dawn is my best friend, but what she is doing is wrong.'

His head down, the color draining from his face, the mayor slumps in his chair, his elbows resting on the desk, his hands rubbing the back of his neck. Brady shakes his head from side to side in silence.

'Mr Brady? Are you alright?' asks Christine.

'I'll call Sergeant Kirkpatrick and have the charges on André withdrawn,' mutters the mayor almost under his breath.

'Yes!' Christine shouts in excitement.

Brady looks up at her from his desk, frowning.

'I mean, I'm glad Dawn'll be okay now…with your help.'

Brady grunts as Christine stands.

'I better get back to class now. Thanks for your time, Mr. Brady.'

Christine walks out of the office, glancing back in time to see Brady slam his fist down on the table. His curse reaches her loud and clear: 'Goddammit!'

Celreau

1779

'You fool. What were you thinking?' yells Petru.

'I don't understand, Boss? Thought you'd be thrilled. These jewels are priceless.'

'Don't you realize the Royal Guard will be all over town soon, if they aren't already, searching for the Queen's treasure?'

'They got no reason to suspect us, Boss. The rat who stole them is a transient from Bucharest. No connection to us. I can arrange to have him killed, if you wish.'

'Domitor, you can be pretty stupid, but I never thought you to be a total idiot! Now shut up and listen. I'll see if I can strike a trade with the Russians—jewels for gold. They would pay a large sum to have such a treasure in their hands. Not to mention the satisfaction of thumbing their noses at the Queen. In the meantime, you'd better hope the guards don't trace the jewels back to me because you can be sure I will not go down alone. I've spent many years earning the Queen's trust, and I won't have the likes of you destroying my empire.'

'I'm grateful for your mercy, Boss. I give you my word. Not a word of this incident will be heard from my lips.'

'Alright. Now, get out of here!' orders Petru.

'As you command, Boss.'

'Wait! One more thing. Bring me this rat, the one you say stole these jewels. I have to meet the guy who can pull off something like this.'

'He probably was just lucky, Boss.'

'I don't think you'd recognize luck if you bumped into it. Luck is me not beheading you for your stupidity. Now go, before I change my mind.'

'As you say, Boss.' Domitor leaves the room grumbling under his breath.

Later that evening, Petru is sitting comfortably in his lush leather-bound chair surrounded by his unexpectedly acquired bounty of gold, silver and jewels. He examines the ornate crown closely. The deep reds of the rubies and crisp greens of the emeralds against the lustrous gold creates an almost hypnotizing motif. He cannot resist the urge to put the crown on his head. His reflection in the window brings a smile to his lips. He momentarily contemplates keeping the jewels, but realizes the risks are much too high. The exchange of the Royal Jewels for Russian gold would take several months, but time is insignificant to Petru, as his very nature gives him all eternity. His thoughts are interrupted by a rap at the door.

'Enter.'

Domitor opens the door and comes in. 'I have your rat, as you asked, out here in the vestibule, sir.'

'Does he need an engraved invitation? Bring him in, you idiot!'

'Sorry, Petru. Of course.' Domitor looks back toward the door and waves Gabriel in. 'Get in here, Rat.'

'Gabriel?' says Petru with surprise.

'What? You two know each other?' asks Domitor.

'You can go now, Domitor,' commands Petru.

'But I don't...I mean, how do you know this rat, sir?'

'I said go!'

'Fine, I'm leaving.'

'And take that waste-of-skin dummy of a guard with you.' Turning his attention to Gabriel as if Domitor has ceased to exist, he comments, 'You're looking fit, Gabriel.'

'Not as fit as a king, but I'm doing okay, I guess.'

'Ahh, the crown. Ha ha. Funny! Beautiful, isn't it?' laughs Petru, having forgotten he was still wearing the crown. He reaches up and removes it.

'How did you find me?'

'It wasn't easy, but I had some help.'

'I see. Well, you have come to exact revenge on me, then?'

Gabriel walks up to Petru and looks him straight in the eyes. 'Listen. I was young and innocent, and you caught me off-guard.'

'Sooo—you don't want me dead?'

'You terrified me, yes, so for a time I wished you dead with my whole being. But later, once I got over the shock of the attack, I found myself fantasizing about the moment; reliving every sensation.'

'I was a bit rough, but as you must now know yourself, passion and lust grow deep within the core of vampires.'

'It was a surprise. I considered you an uncle that I trusted. You were so kind and gentle with me over the years. I never knew you had feelings for me.'

'Honestly, when you were a child, I didn't find you appealing in the least. But once you had grown into a young handsome strapping man… well! One night, despite Leo's explicit warnings to keep my hands off you, I was weak. Overtaken by lust, I couldn't stop myself.'

'I understand and it's okay. I'm over it.'

'Really? Just like that, you forgive me? I must say that's very understanding of you,' answers Petru suspiciously.

'Well, you brought to the surface feelings in me I never knew I had.'

'Is that a fact? Well then, I think I have just the thing to cheer you up.

Follow me down to the cellar. I have some handsome young prostitutes for just such an occasion as this.'

Gabriel follows Petru out the room and down the hallway towards the cellar door. As he opens the door and ushers Gabriel down the stairs, Petru says with a tinge of pride, 'Gabi, I must admit that I'm flattered that you went to all this trouble to find me.'

'When I heard about the power you'd amassed and the empire that you'd built here in Budapest, I knew that this was where I wanted to be.'

'You want a part of this, Gabi?'

'Well, to be honest, I want more than just a part! You turned me into a vampire, giving me assets I could never have imagined. I have incredible strength, heightened senses, great intelligence, and an eternity in which to use them all.'

'But…?'

'I want a piece of the pie. A big piece.'

'Is that all?' asks Petru, sarcasm dripping from each short word.

'Listen, Petru. You've seen what I can accomplish. Nobody else could have taken the Jewels from the palace. Don't tell me you weren't impressed! What more proof do you need that I could be invaluable to you as an ally?'

'What do you really want, Gabriel?'

'I want to be your partner! 50–50 split.'

'Ha-ha-ha. I have to admit you are ambitious, and you have bigger stones than any of the half-wits I have around me. I'll consider your offer, I promise, but for now, let's indulge our baser lusts. Later, perhaps, if we have the energy, we'll share a meal and talk further.'

Petru opens the large oak door in front of which they have been standing for the last few minutes. The light from torches ensconced in the corners of the room reveals a wall of young men. All are muscular and naked, shackled to the stone walls. 'Nothing but the best. Take your pick of companion for the evening, my young friend.'

Gabriel tries to hide his discomfort at the sight of the gruesome sadomasochistic appliances lining the stone wall next to the restrained men.

'Ahh, I see you have noticed my collection. Feel free to choose anything you like. Perhaps you have a favorite.'

'I'm sorry. I am a bit out of my depth. I recognize the gag ball, the riding whip and the nipple clamps, but what are those strange tools next to them?'

'Let me educate you, dear boy. This first is the Choke Pear. I like to use this one on uncooperative partners. Once I insert the Pear into their behinds, the three attached segments expand by force of this screw, and they quickly become available.'

'How ingenious,' says Gabriel barely concealing his urge to gag.

'Now these are my favorites,' says Petru, taking down a pair of shears from the wall.

'They look like the head of a crocodile,' exclaims Gabriel.

'Precisely right. These are crocodile shears, originally stolen from the palace. They are typically reserved for regicides, but I like to use them on the young men who fail to satisfy me. The shears are made of iron with blades lined with sharp teeth. Now you can, of course, use these cold, but I prefer them heated red-hot.'

'And you cut off their...'

'Limp cocks,' finishes Petru nonchalantly.

'They must be blind or sexually perverted not to be aroused by you. Serves them right.'

'All this talk is making me hard. Join me and let's have some fun, Gabi.'

'Wait. May I tell you what really excites me?'

'Tell me.'

'My deepest, most shameful fantasy is that of the voyeur. There is something so erotic about being the observer, about watching others at their most intimate and vulnerable. Would you allow me to watch?'

'Oh! You like to watch? How very tantalizing. Very well. Watch and learn.'

Gabriel stands back and cringes as Petru heads for the wall.

—⟨૭⟨૨⟩—

The following evening, Domitor is in the study at Petru's mansion matching wits with his boss over the chessboard.

'Where did that idiot guard get to?' Petru demands.

Distracted, Domitor moves a rook, unaware that he is exposing his king. 'Not sure, Boss. Probably somewhere sleeping off last night's partying. Last time I saw him was yesterday at the end of his shift; said he was going out to celebrate.'

'Celebrate what?'

'Not sure. He said he was going to the pawn shop, then out to raise a little hell.'

'I've had it up to here with that lazy half wit,' says Petru, drawing a knife-edged palm across his forehead. 'Find me a replacement.'

'How about the Rat?'

'I more than half expected that from you. You're no better than the dummy!'

'What? I just thought…'

'I don't pay you to think, dammit! Gabi has more brains than you and that ogre put together. I ought to demote you to the role of gatekeeper.' Glancing down at the chessboard, Domitor's face goes sour. 'Oh, for heaven's sake. I tire of toying with you, hoping you'll give me a challenge.' He slides his bishop to the edge of the board and announces, 'Check and mate!' in a resigned tone.

'I hate this stupid game,' declares Domitor, sulking in defeat.

'That's a big part of your problem; you treat it as a game. It is survival, life and death. It's strategy; it's subterfuge, it's bluff and deception. You think it's stupid because you don't take it seriously, you moron.'

'Ugh! Enough abuse for one night. I'm done here. I'm going down to the Black Dog.'

'Fine. Don't forget to collect the protection money while you're there.'

'I won't. They're behind a week already.'

'Don't take any crap from that manager. You know the deal. If he doesn't have the money, re-kindle the fire of his memory for him.'

'My specialty, Boss. I'll break the fingers on his left hand.'

'Why his left hand?'

'That way he can still pour the drinks with his right hand. Pretty clever, eh, boss?'

'Even a broken clock is right twice a day.'

'Huh? What clock is that, Boss?'

'Never mind, you ignoramus.'

Abruptly the front door vibrates loudly to the heavy impact of what sounds like a huge fist.

'Who the hell is that? I'm not expecting anyone.'

The pounding intensifies and becomes more insistent.

'Should I get that, Boss?'

'What do you think I pay you for? Yes, you moron. See who it is, then send them away.'

Domitor opens the door and discovers the ogre in shackles held by two Royal soldiers.

'Monseigneur Petru. At once!'

'Petru is busy. Why is our doorman in shackles?'

The soldiers burst through the door, knocking Domitor on his ass in the process.

'What's the meaning of this? Do you have any idea who I am? Messing with me is a good way to end your career and, possibly, your life,' threatens Domitor outraged at the soldiers' cavalier disregard. Rising from the floor, he tries to present an imposing image in an effort to save face.

Ignoring Domitor, the guards push the ogre farther into the room. The ranking guard demands, 'Monseigneur Petru, is this one of your men?'

'Yes. My doorman, in fact,' answers Petru calmly.

'Monseigneur Petru, the Royal treasury housed in the Queen's residence was robbed last evening, and your man here was caught trying to pawn a piece of the stolen jewelry. We'll need to search the premises.'

'Over my dead body, you will,' shouts Domitor, moving to Petru's side.

'I understand, but that won't be necessary. I have what you seek. Domitor, for once just shut your trap and go get the bags.'

'Are you crazy? We can't let them have...'

Petru grips Domitor by the neck with one hand and raises him effortlessly off the marble floor.

'I said—go get the Queen's valuables now!'

Domitor's eyes bulge out from his skull as he nods in submission. When he returns with the bags, the guards escort the threesome and the stolen treasure to the carriage for the short ride back to the Royal Palace. On arrival, they lead the prisoners into the palace and escort them down the main hallway to the Throne Room. The Queen, dressed in black, rises from her throne. As she advances towards the trio, she frowns.

'Kneel before the Queen!' commands the guard, pushing them to the floor. His partner gingerly places the heavy bags on the floor.

Stopping next to the prisoners, the Queen stares down at Petru in disgust.

'How dare you, Petru?' demands the Queen.

'I just discovered the theft myself, Your Highness! I was in the process of bringing you the thief who robbed you of your priceless treasure. I knew that you'd want to deal with him yourself. Like you, I feel betrayed. The culprit was one of my most trusted servants, Domitor, whom you see before you.'

'What? No! I didn't steal the treasure. It was the sewer rat!' yells Domitor.

'Be quiet, fool!' shouts Petru driving his forehead hard into Domitor's nose. More than silenced by the blow, Domitor loses consciousness and crumples to the marble floor.

'Enough!' commands the Queen.

'You must believe me, Your Highness.'

'Of course I believe you!'

'You do?'

'Of course. Only a complete idiot would think he could break into my palace and get away with my treasure. You may be a lot of things, Petru, including a scumbag and a coward, but you're nobody's idiot'

Without thinking, Petru responds, 'Exactly. I'm happy you understand.' Then, red-faced, he hesitates and adds 'Thank you, Your Highness.'

'Now, I learned an important lesson very soon after my coronation. Responsibility for the actions of underlings rests on the head of the person in charge. You admit that this brute works for you. So, tell me why I shouldn't have you tied to a stake and burnt.'

'You have the two thieves to punish, to use an example. And the stolen treasure has been returned. I assume you're relieved to have your fortune back and sincerely hope you're feeling generous enough to show me mercy.'

'Jewels and gold! Is that what you think angers me?' She kicks the closer bag, causing coins and jewels to spill out and scatter over the floor.

'I don't understand,' declares a confused Petru, his brow wrinkling.

'You don't understand? You don't understand?'

'I'm sorry, but no, I don't.'

'Follow me. I will enlighten you.'

The Queen leads Petru from the throne room, up the winding staircase, to a bedroom not far from the empty treasury room.

Petru gasps in horror at the site of the dead princess lying as pale as snow on the bed. She is a vision, white flowers threaded into her soft hair and a rosary intertwined through her clenched fingers. A vampire bite is clearly visible upon her long swollen neck.

'No! I can't believe this. I'll tear that son of a bitch apart with my bare hands!' screams Petru, turning and exiting the room.

The guards, confused as to what to do, move forward as if to restrain Petru, but they are too slow. Petru sidesteps them and rushes Domitor.

'You bastard! How dare you murder the princess?'

'Hey! I never touched…'

Petru punches Domitor in the mouth, breaking his jaw and sending teeth clattering across the stone floor. Domitor's legs buckle as he grasps his face in pain, but his boss isn't through with him. Before he can fall, Petru grabs and throws him against the wall on the far side of the room. The semi-conscious Domitor attempts to get to his feet, already visibly recovering, but Petru is at his side. Seizing him by the neck, Petru repeatedly slams Domitor's head against the marble floor. Bone, brain matter, blood and hair smear his hands and clothing, and spray across the floor.

'You bastard! Don't die yet, you pile of loathsome scum! I want you to suffer.'

The guards succeed in catching up to Petru and once more try to restrain him. He shakes them off effortlessly. Taking his victim's arm, he viciously snaps it in two. Domitor screams, begging Petru to stop.

'I'll tear you to pieces. Nobody assaults my Queen or her kin and lives to talk about it.'

Petru is about to snap the other arm when the Queen intervenes.

'Enough, Petru! Let him go.'

'I'll tear him limb from limb, your Highness. There's no mercy for what this bastard has done.'

'I appreciate your attempt to seek justice for your man's crime, but I need him alive in order to make an example of him. And he is just barely alive.'

'What do you have in mind, then?' asks Petru, already suspecting the answer.

'The only true punishment fit for a vampire—the sun post.'

Domitor, eyes wide open, moans unintelligibly in a desperate attempt to be heard.

'Quiet!' commands Petru, snapping Domitor's other arm.

The offender has reached his limit and passes out briefly, leaking bodily fluids from all orifices. As he lies inert, his broken arms pull together and begin to repair themselves.

'Sorry, your Highness. Take him now. He's all yours. You must have him well guarded. He'll be as powerful as ever in a very short while.'

'My men will see to that. As for you—you do understand that my trust has been breached and your reputation tainted. Had this been a prince, you would be joining your man on the burning post.'

'I appreciate your leniency, your Highness.'

'Indeed. Your cut will be decreased to ten percent till further notice.'

'I fully understand, your Highness. I promise I will regain your trust.' Petru kneels to kiss the Queen's ring.

'You're crazier than a shit-house rat. What the hell were you thinking?' asks Petru when he opens his front door to Gabriel a little later that night.

'My sole concern was to pass the initiation and deliver the treasure.'

'Treasure? Fuck the treasure! You killed the bloody princess!'

'I needed to feed.'

'You had your choice of half a dozen guards. You had to choose the princess?'

'Her young blood was like sweet nectar to a bee. It was better than I could've imagined. I couldn't resist the opportunity.'

'That stunt cost me my right hand man and a big cut of my business.'

'Domitor was a fool. He's gone and good riddance.'

'Right. Easy for you to say.'

'Petru, forget Dom. Don't you see? I'm your new right hand man.'

'You? So that's what this is all about. You want to take Dom's position.'

'Not at all, Petru. I want to be your partner.'

'Partner?'

'Yes! We've already discussed this, albeit somewhat briefly. Partner and lover. I told you how I feel about you. Together we can be incredible. When we combine your business sense with my new ideas and vitality, we'll more than double your fortune.'

'I didn't think you had such strong feelings for me, Gabriel, but you know I've always had them for you.'

'I do, Petru. And I want to show you my feelings are very real, and the lustful thoughts that fill my being will not subside till I give them substance.'

'What do you have in mind?' asks Petru visibly shaking with excitement.

'I have a fantasy.'

'Tell me. Don't tease me. Please, Gabi. What is it?

'D'you have rope and a riding whip?'

'Yes. Yes, I do. In the barn.'

'Good. You've misbehaved and leave me no alternative but to punish you.'

'Punish me? How dare…ooh, I get it!'

'Quiet, slave.'

'Please, Master, spare me. I'm at your mercy,' pleads Petru dropping into the role completely.

Petru leads Gabriel outdoors and across the paddock to the old barn, his mind racing with sadomasochistic thoughts of bondage and submission. He quickly locates the rope and whip, handing them to Gabriel with eyes cast down.

'What're you planning to do to me, Gabi?' asks Petru meekly, all the while shaking with excitement.

'Shut up and take off your clothes,' commands Gabriel.

'Here? Now?'

Gabriel snaps the riding whip against Petru's thigh.

'Yeow!' Petru shrieks in pain.

'Don't you dare question my instructions again. Now, do as I command.'

'Yes, Master,' answers Petru, clearly exhilarated by the thrill of dominance and pain combined. He is no longer hesitant in the least. Gabriel can see that Petru is really into the scenario.

Petru strips, his muscular but pale body beginning to perspire in anticipation.

'Turn around and kneel.'

'What're you gonna do to me?'

'Silence, slave!' Gabriel whips Petru hard across his hairy chest, the leather tip tearing deeply into the older vampire's skin, raising a large welt. He screams, but almost magically the wound is already more than half healed.

'Damn that burns! I'm sorry, Master. I will obey.'

Upon instruction, Petru turns and kneels on the barn floor. Retrieving Petru's shirt, Gabriel rips a strip from the sleeve. He wraps the cloth around Petru's head, blindfolding him.

'Where're you taking me?...oh, shit!' says Petru, anticipating the lash.

Gabriel viciously cracks the whip across Petru's shoulders. Blood momentarily runs from the welt on Petru's back, then repairs itself in an instant.

'I'll teach you to obey, even if I have to slice you open like a melon.'

Gabriel picks up the long rope and ties one end snuggly around Petru's neck. Tugging the other end like a leash, he pulls Petru out of the barn towards the forest.'

'We're going for a walk in the forest where we'll have privacy, and I can do with you as I desire.'

'Mmmm!' mutters Petru in pleasure.

The full moon dimly lights the forest path to the edge of a meadow. When they arrive, Gabriel positions Petru against a large oak tree facing east into the open meadow. He wraps the sturdy rope several times tightly around Petru and the tree trunk. Immobilized and totally vulnerable, Petru chuckles, nervously anticipating the next act in this sexual fantasy.

Yanking the makeshift blindfold from Petru's head, the younger vampire steps back. 'So, you demented old faggot. How does it feel, eh? To know you're about to be abused, subjected to painful and humiliating torture, and there's shit you can do about it?'

'You're in control, Gabriel. I've behaved badly. Punish me as you will,' answers Petru, trying to hide a smile of anticipation.

'Oh, you can count on it. How does this feel, you twisted bastard?'

Gabriel slashes the whip across Petru's face with all his might, drawing an ear-piercing yelp from his victim. Even as Petru's head shakes side to side in pain, the open wound is closing.

'You're a vicious master. Thank you. May I have another?'

'What? Another, you sick fuck?! You think this is a game?' Gabriel cracks the whip repeatedly across Petru's chest and abdomen. Skin and blood spray in all directions, beginning to paint the tall grass at the base of the tree deep crimson.

'Had enough?' asks Gabriel facetiously.

'Are you kidding? You're amazing. I've never felt so fully exhilarated by a partner.'

Gabriel, enraged that his ministrations are not having the effect he has anticipated, tears a piece of his victim's shirt and stuffs it into Petru's mouth. Then he abandons himself to his fury, whipping Petru from head to toe, each lash harder and deeper than the last. Despite the gag, Petru screams in pain, wincing at each strike of the leather. Gabriel lashes Petru over a hundred times. Exhausted from the exertion, Gabriel drops his arm and looks closely at the bloody and disfigured body tied to the tree.

'How does it feel to be vulnerable and abused, helpless to defend yourself, you sadistic son of a bitch?' demands Gabriel.

Petru, his head lolling forward chin on chest, grunts under the gag. Gabriel approaches and pulls the rag from Petru's mouth. Almost unrecognizable, Petru raises his head and, grinning evilly, answers, 'More, Master. Please, please. Don't spare the rod. Punish me as I deserve.'

Shock and disbelief etch Gabriel's face; the perverseness and paraphilia of Petru is more than he has imagined. He has been aware that Petru is a powerful vampire, but the strength and resilience required to endure and recuperate so quickly from this onslaught is beyond what he was expecting. And even more unexpected and disheartening is the tortured vampire's attitude. Petru not only seems to truly enjoy the flogging, he appears to have been expecting it.

'You're a demented freak.'

'Now, is that a nice thing to call your lover? Gabi, d'you think I don't know what you are up to?'

'Fuck you! I have you at my mercy, helplessly tied to this tree. Don't try to act as if this was your idea.'

'Helpless? I'm never helpless, you young pup. It's you who don't understand. Gabi, Gabi, Gabi. I was born at night, yes, but it wasn't last night. Your attempt at feigning homosexuality was feeble at best. To be fair, I wasn't exactly sure at first, but your sad dissembling in the dungeon, suggesting that you had a fetish as a voyeur, pretty much gave it away. No gay vampire can be truly satisfied by such a simple diversion. We may play and tease, but ultimately we cannot resist the flesh.'

'Say what you will. I've got you right where I want you, and now you'll pay for what you did to me.'

'I know you harbor deep-rooted animosity towards me for raping and feeding on you. And not everybody accepts the change as the gift it is. I understand that.'

'You call this eternal affliction a gift? D'you expect me to thank you for the loss of my innocence, my mother and the only woman I'll ever love? Well, I'm sorry, but this is a curse, not a gift. And you can keep your twisted understanding and sympathy. I don't want them.'

'No, Gabi, I know you don't. You want delicious revenge.'

'Yes! I do.'

'So, tell me, then. How does it feel? Is it all you hoped it would be? Go ahead. Do your damnedest, and I'll revel in every minute of it. And when I tire of this game, I'll show you what real power is. I'll show you again, as I did in the past, what it is to be a vampire.'

'The power is mine, now, and this game is far from over,' replies Gabriel.

'Ha, ha. You make me laugh. I have ten times your strength, young man; you could never overpower me.'

'That hardly seems fair.'

'Time you faced it, Gabriel. Life isn't fair.'

'Perhaps, but sometimes the balance shifts a tad in our favor.' Gabriel smiles as he draws closer to Petru, his wide grin exposing his sharp canines.

'Don't you dare feed on me. I am your keeper. You've no right to bleed me.'

'Might is right. As you say, life isn't fair.' Pouncing to land next to Petru, Gabriel sinks his canines deep into Petru's thick neck.

'Damn you! Release me,' screams Petru. Straining against his bonds, he struggles vainly to escape Gabriel's vicious bite and the rope that binds him to the tree. His thrashing against the bonds makes the entire tree shake, but it is well anchored. It's thick, gnarly roots deeply penetrate the densely packed clay on which it stands. Gabriel feeds ferociously for several minutes. Invigorated by the feast, he releases his hold on Petru and steps back.

'So tell me, then. How does it feel?' taunts Gabriel.

'Go ahead. Enjoy your moment, Gabriel. When I regain my strength, and I assure you that will be much sooner than you think, I am going to teach you a lesson you'll not forget, no matter how long you live.'

'Interesting. You still haven't grasped the reality of your predicament, Petru. Unfortunately for you, your days of teaching anything to anyone are over. Tonight I'm the teacher and you, my arrogant degenerate, are about to be schooled.'

'Like I said, junior, go ahead and take your best shot. But remember, this rope won't hold me for long. I can already feel the power building. Once I am free, your agony and suffering will surpass tenfold anything you can inflict on me.'

'I must say your misguided optimism is truly beginning to entertain me. I'd really like to spend what's left of the night listening to you run off at the mouth, but the glow in the eastern sky just there above the tree line is getting brighter by the minute.'

'What? Shit! Sunrise! Damn you! Untie me, at once!'

'Nothing would please me more than to stay and watch the sunrise with you, but sadly I can't. You know how the sunlight affects my young delicate skin.'

'This isn't funny.' Stress is raising the pitch of Petru's voice, making it reedy. Obviously, the thought of being exposed at sunrise had not entered his mind.

'I was just playing around. You know no one cares for you as I do. Don't do anything crazy now. The game is over. Untie me!'

Gabriel pulls the hood of his cape over his head to protect himself from the light now touching the tips of the tall pines above them.

'Ask me nicely!' demands Gabriel.

'Please untie me,' begs Petru, squinting in terror at the growing morning glow.

'That's it! Beg me!' commands Gabriel.

'I beg you, Gabi, please release me. I don't want to burn here alone in the forest. I don't want to die.'

'What a performance, Petru, truly deserving of a wider audience. I hope you don't mind, but I've invited a few friends that I know will appreciate this moment. Not to put too fine a point on it, they're literally salivating in anticipation.'

Gabriel cups his hands to his mouth, leans his head back and releases an ominous howl.

'What're you doing? Let me go, damn you!'

'Shhh, listen. D'you hear them? My, but they sound hungry, don't they?'

'You son of a bitch! I could've made you filthy rich.'

'It was never about the money, fool. It was all about this sweet moment of revenge. I may be a son of a bitch, but I'll never be your bitch again.'

Gabriel spits in Petru's face and runs toward the safety of the shadowed trail leading back through the forest to the mansion. Petru, bound, naked and weak, stares in dread at several pairs of piercing eyes peering at him from the edge of the meadow.

'Bring it on, you mangy, flea-bitten mutts,' shouts Petru. 'I think I still have enough strength to survive an attack from mongrels like you. But I need to be quick about it. That sunlight is much more dangerous than you, and it won't wait.'

In desperation, still unable to break free of his bonds, Petru begins shouting for help. His hope that someone will hear him is unrealistic, he knows, but he cannot help himself. In short order he gives it up as a lost cause. He is miles from the nearest houses. The morning rays are quickly crawling down the pine trees and now shine just a few feet above Petru's head.

Petru has never been one to entertain regrets. He has lived his life full speed ahead and don't look back. Until now. In these moments, he finds himself suddenly full of regrets. He is sorry he didn't run with the wolves, despite having had plenty of opportunity. His lusts always drew him instead to the boys in his dungeon. He regrets never having left anything for the lupine forest dwellers when he fed. Wolves are not scavengers, they are predators; they kill their food, then feed. But when Petru finishes with his victims, all that remains is an empty carcass.

But chief among his regrets right now is that he ever laid eyes on the young Gabriel. If he hadn't, he would not have been tempted, and he wouldn't be in this predicament.

Before he can expand on that thought, his attention is drawn back to the wolves. As a unit, they rise from their crouch, move several paces closer, then sit. Nervously they sniff the morning air searching for that all-too-familiar scent of fear. Puzzled by their prey's intrepidity, they stare at him, suspicion in their feral eyes. Abruptly, their nostrils flare and they seem to relax on their haunches.

Then Petru smells it. Hair burning. The wolves, with their keener olfactory sense, have caught the scent first. Craning his neck back, he sees that the rays of the rising sun have moved down the tree trunk and made first contact with the hair on his head. In an effort to avoid the killing rays, he contracts his neck, pulling his head as low between his shoulder blades as possible. That only helps for a moment, then the descending rays once again make contact, and his hair begins to smolder. Seconds later, Petru feels the first tingling of his scalp—a tingle that almost immediately becomes searing heat and excruciating pain. His scalp ignites and begins to separate from his skull in flaming flakes: he screams, a sound that has nothing human in it.

The smell of cooking flesh spiced with the scream of the wounded prey sends the wolf pack into an eating frenzy. Driven by instinct, they attack Petru; sharp teeth ripping and tearing at his charring naked body. Unlike humans who pick and choose the most tender and choice morsels of meat, the wolves indiscriminately tear at Petru's body. His penis is instantly amputated, the scrotum simultaneously ripped from his crotch. The wolves tug on the calve muscles, ripping ligaments and tendons from bone. Petru's head is fully ablaze. He thrashes against his bindings in a last desperate attempt to free himself. By the time the sun and flames have reached his upper torso, he is in shock. What little is left of his consciousness surrenders his soulless body to the fire and earth.

Gabriel, back in the mansion and safely away from exposure to the morning's deadly rays, listens in utter satisfaction. He wishes he could witness the merciless slaughter of Petru by the ravenous wolves. A bright flash on the blinds covering the windows, followed by the sounds of wolves yelping, startles Gabriel. He covers his eyes. Both light and sound quickly subside.

Gabriel smiles at the thought of Petru's body igniting like a torch from the intense heat and the uneaten parts sifting to the ground in a heap of ashes. He laughs out loud now, imagining the wolves retreating into the forest, bellies swollen with digesting chunks of Petru.

'I'm speechless. Not in a million years did I figure you'd get to Petru, never mind succeed in killing him!' exclaims Switzer.

'Well, you certainly made things easier for me. And don't think that I'm not grateful for your help.'

'You're welcome. But really, did you have to kill the princess?'

'I was thirsty.'

'You're insane. You know that, don't you?'

'No. I'm not insane. I just don't care because I have nothing left to lose. That's all.'

'Nothing to lose? Think again, my friend. Just look at all the things around you that're now yours. You own everything in this mansion—including the gold and silver coins in the vault. And then there's the take from the red section of town.'

'Take it, it's yours.'

'Waddaya mean, it's mine?'

'All of it. It's all yours.'

'Seriously? All mine? You'd give all this up just like that? After all you've been through? Why?'

'Consider it a gift. To me, they are just things, unimportant in themselves. Wealth holds no attraction for me. I've seen too often the evil effects of having too much money and power. When I came here, I sought only revenge on one such man—Petru. He destroyed my life and those of the people I once loved. And he enjoyed doing it!'

'There must be someone left that he hasn't reached or touched? Someone you care about, whose life you could improve with a little money.'

'Sadly, no. My dear mother's lost to me, and Angela is gone forever.'

'What about friends, Gabriel? Everybody makes friends during their lifetime.'

'I've never had friends. In my youth, I was kept hidden and alone in a vampire-infested inn.'

'You had no childhood friends to play with? That is truly sad.'

'Well, there was one girl.'

'Ah! There you go. I knew there had to be someone.'

'Yes, I guess you're right. Her name was Tati. She had long beautiful brown hair and hazel eyes. We spent a few weeks each summer together, playing in my courtyard. Tatiana didn't seem to have a care in the world. She feared nothing.'

'Sounds amazing. Whatever happened to her?'

'Her parents were both vampires living in Hungary. They had to move away because of growing suspicion from the locals. You can't stay in one place too long if you don't age. People begin to notice.'

'That's too bad. Where'd they move to?'

'Paris.'

'Nice gray, cloudy city. The perfect destination for a vampire to visit at this time of year.'

'I guess.'

'Mais, oui. Aren't you even a little curious about her?

'I suppose I am, yes.'

'Very well, then. Les jeux sons faits, mon ami.'

After Switzer retires to the suite of rooms in the mansion he has commandeered for himself, Celreau sits in the dark on a window seat in the parlor. The cool night air wafting through the open window sets a mood, and he finds himself thinking of those summers with Tati, the last in particular.

He and Tati had been inseparable. They would spend the days together, laughing and playing in the yard. Tati's mother forbade her to leave the yard, but Tati could always persuade Gabi to sneak off and run through the forest with her. She loved to explore the forest, climb trees and sing at the top of her lungs. She was the only visitor to the inn that ever made Gabi laugh. He only felt truly happy when she was around.

Then they turned sixteen. They would never spend another summer together. Tatiana's parents had decided to move to Paris because their local community was becoming suspicious. As a consequence, the yearly pilgrimage to Romania was no longer an option. Gabriel was heartbroken when Tati gave him the news. That was the day they carved their initials in the old oak tree, and the day Gabriel got his first kiss.

'Gabi, can you keep a secret?'

'I guess so?'

'You promise?'

'Sure.'

'Anna and I are crossing over.'

'Crossing over?'

'You know, becoming vampires.'

'Are you crazy?'

'No. We talked about it and agreed it would be fun.'

'Fun? What's fun about being a freak?'

'Just think what it would be like to live forever. Think of all the fun we'd have being stronger and smarter than everybody. You could stay up all night playing and never get tired.'

'I'd rather live and play during the day. Besides I don't want to kill and feed on people. That's just gross.'

'You get over that, I'm sure. We're not planning on converting for a couple of years, anyway. We've thought about this quite a bit. We decided we want to be adults when we are turned. Right now, as kids, we don't get any respect. We have no rights and don't even control our own lives. Like all kids, we change so fast as we grow that a pair of girls who suddenly stop getting older will attract too much attention. As adults, we'll be able to take jobs in the city, hiding in plain sight. And we'll be free to move about, making it easier to hide the fact that we don't age.'

'You're both out of your minds.'

'No, we aren't! We want you to join us, Gabi? Let's all do it together.'

'Give me one good reason why I should?'

'Because I like you and, well, if you don't, I'll remain young and you'll grow old and feeble.'

'Tati! There you are,' interrupts Anna, running towards the pair. 'Mother is worried; you were supposed to be back at the Inn for supper thirty minutes ago.'

'Anna. Tell Gabi to convert with us. He won't listen to me.'

'What's wrong, Gabi? Are you scared?' teases Anna.

'No. I just don't want to. It's a stupid idea. That's all'

'Don't you want to be with Tati and me forever? Just think of all the fun we could have together.'

'Yeah, I guess so.'

'Voilà! Meet us in Paris in two years and we will be 'Les trois Aventuriers.'

Tati and Anna join hands and dance around Gabi singing together…

Pale though her eyes,
her lips are scarlet
from drinking of blood,
this child, this harlot

born of the night
and her heart, of darkness,
evil incarnate
to dance so reckless,

dreaming of blood,
her fangs—white—baring,
revealing her lust,
and her eyes, pale, staring…

'Vive les Aventuriers!' yells Anna

The following evening, Gabriel is preparing to board the luxurious chartered carriage that will transport him to Paris. The coachman skillfully holds six strong horses in check while his passenger gets settled. The horses neigh and champ at their bits, impatient to set out on the long road ahead.

'Hmm. I see I'll be riding in style,' comments Gabriel.

'Only the very best for you, my friend. It's a long journey to France, and you must cross most of that country to get to Paris. Consider the extra expense of traveling in style as a posthumous gift from Petru.'

Gabriel laughs and offers his hand to Switzer.

'I'm afraid that just won't do,' remarks Switzer. Stepping forward, he hugs his departing friend.

'Farewell, friend,' says Gabriel, climbing into the coach. He sits on the soft leather seat and smiles at the two strapping young men, tied and gagged, sitting across from him.

Switzer pokes his head through the door. Nodding toward the pair of captives, he says, 'Thought you'd appreciate some refreshments for the trip.'

'Nice touch,' answers Gabriel, chuckling.

'The very best. I dipped into Petru's personal reserve straight from the cellar.'

'Much appreciated, Switzer.'

'Bon voyage et bonne chance, mon gars.' Switzer closes the door and steps away from the coach.

Dawn
1980

After a one-sided discussion about her promiscuity and the damage to her father's reputation as mayor of the city, Dawn walks out the back door with a 'Whatever, Dad.' She sits down beside a planter on the porch step. Reaching behind the planter, she takes a cigarette from her stashed pack of smokes and lights up. Inhaling deeply, she smiles, her thoughts returning to that morning and the classroom when she had teased Celreau so deliciously. He is such a hunk, so freakin' hot, she thinks to herself. He must be a wonderful kisser. André Robillard? Really? What was I thinking? I'm way too hot for that Métis retard and the rest of those immature boys. I've had enough of stupid, zit-faced teenagers. It's time I hooked up with a real man. Celreau will be totally into a gorgeous woman like me.

She stands and flips her cigarette butt across the back yard. As she is about to turn and walk back into the house, she is startled by a raven gliding over the fence, just missing her head. The raven lands in the grass next to the porch.

'Holy shit! What the…' gasps Dawn. The big bird is carrying something gold-colored and shiny in its big black beak. Dawn approaches the bird carefully, trying to get a closer look. To her surprise, the object turns out to be a gold pendant necklace.

Dawn taunts the bird, 'Drop it, you mangy bird!'

The raven cautiously waddles away from her, then takes flight as Dawn steps toward it. The bird lands on the clothes line pole and peers down at her.

'I said drop it—goddammit!' The raven calmly repositions his grip on the post and ignores Dawn. Frustrated, Dawn reaches down and picks up a small stone from the rock garden. She pitches it at the bird, but the rock, missing its target, rings off the aluminum post. Even so, the raven launches itself into the night with a loud caw, dropping the pendant as it flies off.

'Yes!' exclaims Dawn as she eagerly picks up and examines the golden prize. She is awed by the gold heart pendant and delicate chain. They are stunning. She knows at once that it is very valuable and very old. Her hands tremble in excitement as she fastens the necklace around her neck. 'This was no coincidence; this has got to be a sign,' she says to herself aloud. She exits the yard through the side gate onto Main Street and turns east, in the direction of Look-Out Point.

Main Street leads out of town in both directions. She knows if she follows Main east, it will lead eventually to Look-Out Point—right past Celreau's house on the hill. Gliding soundlessly above, unnoticed, the curious Raven follows her, landing on the General Store sign next door to Mademoiselle Chic clothing store, the only boutique in Blood Cove with any taste. M.C. carries only the latest styles and fashions from Vancouver, and Dawn buys all her clothes here. To Dawn it seems that the rest of the population would be happy to purchase their clothing from the hardware store, if they could. She stops to look at the mannequins in the storefront window, then crosses the street to the coffee shop. The Raven watches from its vantage point.

Dawn is pleasantly surprised to catch sight of Mr. Celreau sitting at the corner window table of Ruth's Café. Almost at the same moment, he raises his eyes from his book and looks directly at her. She smiles and waves. He waves back as she walks into the coffee shop.

'Mr Celreau, how are you?'

'Okay, Dawn, and you?'

Dawn pulls a chair close to Celreau and sits down. 'Just okay, Mr. Celreau? You sound sad. Anything I can do to cheer you up?'

'Thanks, Dawn. I've had a rough day, but I'll be fine. I don't know if you heard, but little Donni Cardinal is presumed dead.'

'Oh my, what happened?'

'He ran away from home and apparently slipped into the river along the valley trail. I found his shirt on a branch in the rapids.'

Dawn puts one hand on Celreau's hand and the other on his thigh.

'Oh my, that's horrible. No wonder you're upset.'

Celreau pulls his hand away and turns to Dawn. 'I don't mean to be rude, but I'd really appreciate some time alone.'

Pouting a little, Dawn coyly reaches up and begins to wrap her new gold chain around her finger. 'I just thought you might want some company.'

'I appreciate your kindness, but…'

Dawn lets the chain drop from her finger and the heart pendant slips from under her shirt to rest on her chest.

Celreau sits riveted, staring in shock at the gold pendant.

'Mr. Celreau, is something wrong?' asks Dawn.

'I was just admiring your pendant. It's very beautiful. I don't think I've ever seen you wearing it before.'

'Thank you. You're very sweet. It's very precious to me, so I don't like to wear it to school.'

'Would you mind if I asked where you got it?'

'I, uh, well, uh, my daddy bought it for me on my sixteenth birthday. But I'm seventeen already.'

Celreau reaches between Dawn's breasts and takes the heart pendant between thumb and forefinger. He examines it in disbelief, thoughts of Angela flooding his mind.

'Mr Celreau?'

'Uh, yes. Well, with your figure, you could easily pass for eighteen, Angela.'

'Angela? Again?'

'Dawn. I meant Dawn. Sorry. Your dad must love you very much. This is a magnificent piece of jewelry. Where'd you say your father purchased it?'

'I didn't say, actually, but I think, huh, he bought it in, like, Vancouver.'

'Vancouver? That's interesting.'

'Why interesting?'

'This piece is made of twenty percent pure yellow gold. Canadian jewelry is made from a ten percent mixture of gold and silver. This necklace is possibly Asian, but most likely European.'

'Well, lucky me, huh? You really think I look eighteen?'

'I think you look amazing. Most men only dream of being with a young lady as beautiful as you.'

Dawn slides her hand higher on Celreau's thigh. Leaning forward, she whispers in his ear, 'Gabriel, I'd love to make your dreams come true.'

Lowering his voice to match hers, Celreau points out to Dawn, 'I can't be seen leaving here with a student. I have to protect my reputation, you understand?'

'Yes, of course.'

'Good. Meet me in the alley behind the café. I'll drive my Jeep around.'

Dawn smiles as she squeezes Celreau's thigh. 'I'll be waiting. You won't be disappointed.'

Celreau watches with mixed emotions as Dawn leaves the coffee shop.

Moments later, an excited Dawn climbs into the Jeep and closes the door. Celreau speeds down the alley and turns up Main towards Look-Out Point.

Dawn breaks the silence, smiling. 'Sweet ride.'

'It's the only way to travel in this part of the country.'

'Where we going? Want a smoke?'

'No, thanks.'

'Mind if I do?'

'No, go ahead. Crack the window, though.'

Celreau steers the Jeep into the turnabout at Look-Out Point and parks overlooking the bay. During the summer, the place was wall-to-wall cars with steamed windows and teenagers in various stages of undress. This time of year, the Jeep had the lot to itself.

Pulling a pack of cigarettes from the small purse she always carries, Dawn lights a cigarette and takes a long, deep drag. She rolls down her window and shakes her blond hair loose in the evening breeze. Returning the cigarette package to her purse, she pulls out a mickey of Sour Puss raspberry liquor. After taking a swig, she offers the bottle to Celreau.

'No, thanks. Too sweet for my tooth. I am partial to ten-year-old single malt Scotch.'

The sky is a myriad of pinks and purples as the sun sets behind solemn gray clouds. Beams of sunlight jet at sharp angles across the sky and reflect off the ocean below. The pair watch the sun make its final descent into horizon.

'What a fantastic view! Isn't the sunset romantic?' asks Dawn scrunching up to the teacher as closely as the bucket seats will allow.

'Yes, it is. My favorite part of the daylight hours. To be honest, I prefer the night.'

'You are so mysterious. Are you a werewolf?' asks Dawn, as she flicks her cigarette butt out the window. 'Are you going to rip my clothes off, ravage me, then eat me?' she teases.

'Maybe I will. No one can hear you scream up here. No one knows where you are, and you have nowhere to run. Aren't you frightened, my lamb?'

Dawn feels goosebumps all over her body. Excitedly, she leans over and whispers into Celreau's ear, 'What makes you think I want to escape? I may be the wolf, dressed in lambs' clothing. Maybe you're my prey.'

Celreau turns to look at Dawn. His eyes are drawn to Angela's pendant around her neck, and in a rush, his mind fills with lustful thoughts for his lost love. His excitement suddenly becomes evident. Passion saturates his empty soul and his body quivers as he leans toward the temptress beside him.

'I'll take my chances, but are you willing to take the same risk?'

'There's only one way to find out,' whispers Dawn. She slides her hand into his lap and unzips him. Squeezing the shaft gently, she eases his erection out of his pants.

'My lamb, the beast is hungry and ready to feast.'

'Mmmm, I like the sound of that,' says Dawn. 'Take me, you animal!' She uses her free hand to wriggle out of her pants, then her panties, and straddles Celreau. She moans in ecstasy as she feels Celreau, long and hard, bury himself within her.

Moving rhythmically up and down on his shaft, she slides her sweater over her head, exposing her firm breasts. She kisses Celreau on the mouth and enjoys his tongue as it tangles with hers, exploring. She leans back against the steering wheel. Celreau teases her breasts with his tongue as he moves his hands over her body.

'Oh, God,' whispers Dawn panting. 'You're so hard. God, you make me feel so free.'

Celreau kisses her neck gently and whispers, 'I love you, Angela. I love you so much.'

Stopping in mid-stroke, Dawn demands angrily, 'Wait! Angela? Not again. I'm Dawn. Who the hell is Angela?'

Celreau grips Dawn tightly around her arms. Overwhelmed by mixed feelings of passion for Angela and primal hunger for blood love, his senses leave him.

'Answer me! Who the fuck is Angela? Ow! You're hurting me,' shouts Dawn now visibly frightened. Her fear turns to terror as she watches Celreau's face transform. His lips and gums withdraw exposing his long sharp canines. Bloodshot, his eyes widen as he focuses on Dawn's long pale neck.

'What the hell are you? Lemme go, you freak,' shouts Dawn, struggling to pull away. Pinned between the vampire and the steering wheel, she struggles in vain. He sinks his canines deep into her tender skin, piercing the artery.

'Noooo!' Her scream fades as her thoughts blur. She loses her hold on consciousness and her head falls heavily to her shoulder. The vampire drinks deeply of the rich red blood flowing freely from her carotid artery. Sliding into an erotic trance, he continues to thrusts his penis hard into Dawn.

A flurry of black wing feathers flapping inside the Jeep snaps the beast back to reality. Cawing raucously, the Raven thrashes around the cab and lands on the vampire's thick black hair. The bird sinks its sharp talons deep down into the beast's scalp and jabs its beak repeatedly into his eyes. The enraged vampire swings his hand back blindly, just missing the Raven as it flutters toward the window. The bird makes its exit into the cover of the forest, but not before it splatters the interior of the Jeep with a stream of white, stinking bird shit.

The vampire covers his burning eyes with his hands and grimaces in disgust at the putrid odor. 'Damn you, Ne-Kilst-lass. You've interfered and frustrated me for the last time. I'll kill you, you filthy fowl. You hear me? I'll kill you!'

A defiant caw-caw drifts above the tree-line and echoes in the valley.

The vampire forces himself to regain control, to calm his rage. His facial wounds and the eye damage heal visibly as he watches in the rearview mirror. The excruciating pain subsides. He zips his pants, then opens the Jeep door and steps out, dragging Dawn's unconscious body out onto the ground. He hears a strong heartbeat when he presses his ear to her bare chess. Carefully he removes Angela's necklace from Dawn's neck, squeezing the heart pendant in his hand.

'Angela, why do you torment me so? I took your life and killed your family. Damn you! Don't you understand? Don't you see? I'm a beast, a monster, a demon. Leave me alone! I never loved you! D'you hear me? I never loved you. I wanted only to drink your blood, just like every other wench I have killed. Leave me alone; can't you just leave me alone?'

He dresses Dawn, then pours what remains of her bottle of Sour Puss over her clothing. He slides the empty bottle back into her purse. Opening the Jeep's hatch, he gathers her limp body into his arms and lays her down in the rear of the truck. After the short drive to town, he turns into the back alley behind Dawn's house and douses the headlights. The young girl moans as he collects her from the back of the Jeep and carries her to the back deck, where he lays her on the porch swing. Quickly returning to the Jeep, he speeds away.

Celreau

1779

The journey by horse carriage from Hungary to Paris is long; agonizingly long and bone-wearyingly rough. In very short order, Gabriel finds himself wondering how much worse the ride would have been had Switzer not paid the additional cost to hire a better quality carriage. The trip weighs heavily on Gabriel's hunger and his patience.

Immediately upon departure he realizes that the two poor souls gifted by Switzer will not sustain him through the trip to Paris. He rations his usage of the pair, alternating daily, drinking only enough to maintain his strength without fatally draining his hosts. Inevitably, weak and dehydrated after only a few weeks on the road, both prisoners perish. Unsure of the route to Paris, he decides against consuming the coachman and driving the carriage himself. He manages to sustain himself by partaking of foot travelers and farmers working their fields. Occasionally, he is desperate enough that he turns to livestock for sustenance.

One evening Gabriel swings out of the carriage door while the carriage is in motion, climbs forward along the side and plops down next to the coachman.

'What's your name, coachman?' asks Gabriel.

'Shit, you scare me! You're not going to 'urt me, are you, Monsieur Gabriel? S'il vous plait, I beg you. I'll do anyt'ing you wish.'

'Calm down. You're in no danger—for now, anyway. I'm losing my mind alone in the coach. So again, young man, what's your name?'

'Merci, t'ank you, monsieur. Sorry. My name is Jean-Paul Thibodeaux, monsieur.'

'You're a Frenchman. How'd you end up in Petru's care?'

'I was born in Paree and for many years worked as a stable boy for le Duc d'Orléans.'

'He is a nobleman?'

'He is the king's cousin, monsieur.'

'Impressive. Carry on, then.'

'Anyway, I work 'ard and learn evryt'ing about the 'orses. Nobody work 'arder. Soon I am become personal coachman for le Duc.'

'Even more impressive. So why would you leave Paris?'

'Sadly, une affaire du cœur. I fell in love with his beautiful daughter, Lisette.'

'Well done!'

'Oui…I mean non. Only a suitor of noble blood is allowed near a Duc's daughter.'

'So?'

'He caught me making love to Lisette and threatened to be'ead me if he ever set eyes on me again.'

'You left Paris without her?'

'I 'ad no choice, Monsieur Gabriel. Le Duc d'Orléans is a man of his word. I stole his best 'orse and fled to 'ungary.'

'Ha ha. So, Thibodeaux, essentially you chose a horse over a woman.'

'Mon Dieu! Monsieur Gabriel, I never t'ought of it dat way. Tabarnac, you're right! What was I t'inking?'

'You know what, J.P.? You're alright.'

'You seem hokay, yourself,' the coachman replies with a smile. 'So, why you go to Paree, Monsieur Gabriel?'

'To find a woman.'

'You could not find one in Budapest?'

'Not just any woman. The one I seek was an old childhood friend. She and I were kindred spirits. Her light-heartedness amused me.'

'Une affaire du cœur, aussi?' asks JP curiously.

'I suppose, but it was all quite innocent at the time…and so long ago.'

'Women, dey draw us like shit draws flies. It's a sickness, non?'

'Hmm. I don't know about that.'

'You traveled almost a mont' by 'orse an' carriage to meet a woman! You don't t'ink dat is a disease?'

'I suppose, when you put it that way, perhaps it's a sickness. One thing's for sure: we have a difficult time recovering from them once they've infected us.'

'Your chérie, 'er name?'

'Tatianna.'

'Pretty name. What district of Paree does she live in?'

'No idea, really.'

'Vous êtes drôle.'

'Careful, J.P. Your impertinence is stimulating my appetite!'

'My apologies, Monsieur Gabriel, but Paree, she 'as half a million citizens. 'ow d'you t'ink it's possible to find your demoiselle?'

'Believe it or not, I've done it in the past. Now, exactly how I'll do it, I don't know. Perhaps you'd be willing to assist me.'

'Mais, oui, I will 'elp in any way you t'ink I can.'

'Well, if we team up, my ingenuity with your knowledge of the city, and a bit of good fortune thrown in, I think we have a better than even chance of locating her.'

'May I be so bold, monsieur, as to ask what's in it for me?'

'You have guts, J.P., I give you that. Fair enough. If we succeed in finding Tatianna, I promise to reunite you with Lisette and provide safe passage back to Hungary, sparing you from the guillotine. You may live in Hungary with my friend, Switzer. He will keep you safe.'

'Mon Dieu! Lisette et moi, togeder again! A dream come true. I cannot t'ank you enough, M. Gabriel.'

'Don't thank me yet. We have to find Tatianna first, and by your own admission, that won't be easy.'

'What we are waiting for, den? Allons-y!'

'Ha, ha. I say again, you're alright, J.P.'

J.P. guides the horses and carriage through the dimly lit backstreets of Paris. The rhythmic clop-clop of the horses' hooves echo from the stonework houses that hug the empty street. On the seat next to him, Gabriel begins to grumble. Restless, he squirms uneasily.

'Evryt'ing, it is hokay, Monsieur?' asks J.P.

'No! Shut up and keep moving,' snaps Gabriel angrily.

'Brute!' mumbles J.P. under his breath.

'There!' Gabriel points ahead to a lone man walking at the edge of the street.

'What?' questions J.P., confused.

'Stop the cart, you fool!'

Bringing the carriage to a stop behind the pedestrian. J.P. asks again, 'What I did? What's wrong?'

'Wait here. Don't move,' commands Gabriel. He leaps from the carriage to land almost on top of the innocent pedestrian who is just beginning to look up with a questioning expression. Gabriel grabs him and drags him into a nearby alleyway. His struggles and calls for help are brief, ending with a series of mushy impacts as Gabriel repeatedly bashes the man's head against the stone wall.

J.P., frozen in his carriage seat, watches in horror at the terrifying scene before him—his new friend, now a ravenous beast, biting into his victim's neck. Time seems to stand still as the beast feeds. At last, Gabriel surrenders the lifeless body, wipes the fresh blood that drips down his chin and turns toward J.P. Two strides and a pounce puts him back in the carriage seat next to his driver.

'Off we go, then,' says Gabriel with a wide, bloody smile.

Still frazzled from the terrifying scene, J.P. sits wide-eyed and unresponsive, staring in disbelief at Gabriel.

'J.P. Alons-y, mon gars, alons-y,' urges Gabriel.

Shaking his head, J.P. turns his eyes to the horses.

'Sacrebleu,' exclaims J.P. softly, slapping the lead horse's rump with a snap of his whip.

The carriage travels east, turns onto rue Honoré and is forced to an abrupt halt by a debris barricade that stretches the width of the thoroughfare. Several obviously lower-class citizens stand on the wall of debris waving pitchforks and sticks in the air, some shouting. Others are singing.

'What's all this commotion about?' asks Gabriel.

'De poor people, dey are sick and tired of de monarchy taxing dem while de King and Queen, dey live in luxury in de palace. Dey even begin to talk about révolution. Dey jus' want to eat. If you 'ave a few centimes for dem, we will not be troubled.'

'Fair enough.' He takes a small leather pouch of coins from an inside vest pocket and hands it to J.P. who tosses it to the young man who looks to be the leader.

'Laisser passer,' the young man shouts. A group of his men pull the edge of the barricade aside to let the carriage pass.

'Well done, J.P. A resourceful fellow, you're already turning out to be an asset.'

'T'ank you, monsieur.'

'Please call me Gabi.'

'Mais certainement, monsieur, I mean, t'ank you, Gabee.' After a few seconds he adds, 'Gabee, I can ask you a question?'

'Yes, of course.'

'In de alley back dere. You were mad at me, No?'

'Oh, that. No, I was just hungry.'

'So, I will be your dinner one day, too?'

'Good question, J.P. I wish you no harm. I could tell you that I'll never hurt you but…'

'But?'

'But, I can't, in all honesty.'

'Why not? You jus' say dat you would not 'urt me?'

'Not intentionally, but imagine a young wolf abandoned by its mother. A farmer finds the lost pup on his property and takes it home. He raises it; he gives it shelter, food and love.'

'Hokay. 'e is a lucky puppy.'

'Yes, J.P. The pup grows up and develops into a big, strong, healthy wolf. It becomes very attached to its owner and faithfully follows him everywhere. Then one day, while on a long hunting excursion with his owner, the wolf gets very hungry. Suddenly, without warning, the wolf attacks his master and drags him into the woods. Despite the farmer's struggles and yells, the mad creature holds fast to the man's neck until he chokes to death. The wolf then rips into its victim's body, tearing and feeding on his master's flesh. Once his appetite is satisfied, he methodically digs a hole in the forest floor and buries the bloody remains.'

'Mon Dieu, dat is 'orrible. Does 'e not recognize 'is master? Why would 'e do such a awful t'ing to someone who raised and cared for 'im?'

'Later that evening, the wolf comes back to lie by the shallow grave and whine over the loss of his dear friend.'

'I am confused. I don' understand. Why would 'e kill 'is best friend?'

'That's the point, J.P. The wolf cannot escape its true nature. As long as he's well fed, he can resist the urge, but when faced with real hunger, or any other stress, it quickly reverts to its feral ways. It becomes the wild animal it was always meant to be.'

'Excuse me if I don' find your story comforting, but 'ow can I be certain I won't end up like de poor farmer?'

'To be brutally blunt—just keep me fed. You'll be safe as long as my dietary needs for that special liquid are met.'

'Say no more, den. I'm already planning your dinner menu.'

'From what I have observed, Paris is a virtual smörgåsbord for vampires, so your task should prove relatively easy.'

'I 'preciate your 'onesty, Gabee. So. Where do we go from 'ere?'

'Well, let me ask you this. Where would a free spirited lass like my Tati spend her evenings?'

'What be de lady's pleasures?'

'It's been quite a while, but if my memory serves, theatre, dance and music were her principal interests. Music above all.'

'I know jus' de place: La Danse Macabre.'

J.P. steers the carriage right at the next corner and guides the horses up rue Montmartre. Within a few blocks, businesses begin to give way to entertainment establishments. Soon he reins the horses in and halts the carriage in front of a nightclub, La Danse Macabre in fancy script above the entrance. Loud voices and music billow from within the nightclub.

Gabriel raises his eyebrows at J.P.

'What makes you think that, of all the places in this city that offer musical entertainment, I'll find her here?'

'For someone who loves music, théâtre and danse, monsieur, dis is de place to be in Paree.'

'I hope your instincts are correct. Only one way to find out.'

The pair enter the dimly lit club. Crossing directly to the bar, they order red wine and survey the scene while they sip.

'D'you see 'er?' asks J.P.

'What?'

'D'you see Tati?' shouts J.P. over the loud music.

'No. I'm going to walk around the room. Don't go anywhere.'

The club is packed with people milling about, drinking and chatting, while at the same time watching dancers and musicians perform on a small stage. Most are intoxicated, but the mood is jovial. Gabriel wanders among the tables working his way towards the front of the large hall, his eyes constantly scanning for Tati. Satisfied that she is not here, he turns towards the entrance. Applause erupts as the performers leave the stage to be replaced by a new act. Tapping J.P. on the shoulder, Gabriel nods towards the exit.

'Let's go. Your instincts were wrong. She isn't here.'

Halfway to the door, Gabriel is stopped in his tracks. The new voices from the stage are ones he could never forget. He is not surprised to turn and find Tati and her sister dancing and singing on stage.

'It's her! It's Tati!' exclaims Gabriel.

'Sacrebleu!'

'Well done, mon gars. You did good, J.P.'

'T'anks, but you were not completely 'onest, monsieur. You said dey were good looking, but dey are not. Les mademoiselles are beautiful.'

'Indeed.' For the next several minutes, Gabriel stands transfixed, watching the pair perform and remembering events he'd thought long forgotten.

The young ladies, coming to the end of their performance, take bows to enthusiastic clapping, then step down from the stage for intermission. They make their way to a nearby table occupied by a young man who greets Tati with a kiss. He has drinks waiting for them and they sit down. Gabriel and J.P. wander through the maze of patrons to discreetly take a position near the table. Finger to lips, Gabriel makes a shhh sign to J.P. and begins to sing...

Pale though her eyes,
her lips are scarlet
from drinking of blood,
this child, this harlot

Tati and Anna turn and gasp as they recognize Gabriel. Anna smiles and continues the song…

born of the night
and her heart, of darkness,
evil incarnate
to dance so reckless,

Laughing, Tati supplies the next bit…

dreaming of blood,
her fangs—white—baring,
revealing her lust,
and her eyes, pale, staring...

'Vive les Aventuriers!' yells the threesome.

'Gabi, what are you doing here, and how on earth did you find us?' asks Tati excitedly.

'I have a great scout. Meet my traveling friend, J.P. Jean-Paul, meet Tati and her sister, Anna. These lovely mademoiselles kept me sane during my crazy childhood.'

'Enchanter,' says J.P. He bows briefly from the waist to Tati, then reaches for Anna's hand and bends to kiss it.

'Okay. You can let go of her hand now, J.P.' says Gabi.

'Pardon? Oh, yes, of course,' answers J.P., embarrassed.

'This is my boyfriend, Pierre,' interjects Tati, breaking the awkwardness of the moment.

'Capitaine Trottier,' says Pierre as he stands and leans across the table to grasp and squeeze Gabi's hand with force. 'Are you here to enlist? I am just returned from New France to recruit soldiers to defend our Louisiana holdings against the British and their red savage allies, the Chickasaw.'

'To be honest, I arrived in your beautiful city just today. I traveled here from Hungary to visit Tati.'

'You'd like me to believe you traveled all the way to Paris to see an old girlfriend and were lucky enough to find her in a city of millions? Considering the odds of that, and the new regulations, I think it's more likely you've been seeing Tati behind my back. You hope to wed her knowing that married men are exempt from conscription into the army.'

'Believe what you wish. What I told you is fact.'

'I believe you are a liar and a traitor, and I do not trust you around my girl.'

'Pierre! Gabi is an old friend. Don't be jealous.'

'I have no qualms with you or your government. And how can I be a traitor when I am not even a French citizen? And to be quite honest, I have no interest in a war against anyone, white or red.'

'If not a traitor, then you're a coward,' responds Pierre.

'Pierre! That's enough. You're being ridiculous,' says Tati, not happy about being ignored.

'Believe me, friend. I'm not in the least interested or intimidated by you or your monarchy.'

'You dare challenge me, a Capitaine in the French Royal Army?' shouts Pierre, drawing his pistol and pointing it at Gabi. 'The King endeavours to amass the greatest empire the world has ever known. At this point in France's history, no one is allowed a lack of commitment. You must choose—imperialist or traitor. Which is it?'

Tati steps in front of Gabi. 'Stop Pierre! You're making a scene and a fool of yourself.'

'Ahh! I see how it is. You protect your old flame.'

'I've had enough of your foolish pride and childish jealousy.'

'So now I'm childish, am I? That's easily remedied. Make your choice—him or me? Which is it?'

Tati stands speechless, but defiant. After a moment, she straightens. 'Fine! You are dead to me. Get out of my sight!'

Pierre raises the pistol to Gabi's head once again. 'It's not over coward. You can't hide behind a woman's skirts forever. When you least expect it—expect it.'

Visibly upset, Pierre leaves the bar without another glance in Tati's direction. For her part, she turns to Gabriel and kisses him long and hard.

'What the...?' exclaims Gabriel.

'The night is young. This is Paris. Let's go explore,' says Tati.

'But your boyfriend—aren't you upset?'

'Lots of fish in the sea.'

'Allons-y,' shouts J.P., grinning and taking Anna's hand. 'Me, I am all for de exploring.'

"Well, I'm no stick in the mud, either.' Bowing low with a flourish to Tati, Gabi invites, 'Lead the way, you crazy lass.'

The four link hands and run from the club into the street.

'Vive les Aventuriers!' yells J.P.

The foursome spends the late hours, and the very early hours, partying at several pubs and cabarets in the arts district. Tati and Gabi spend much of the time, when they are not dancing, laughing and acting silly, reminiscing and catching up, while J.P. and Anna flirt and kiss. The pace and the booze is dizzying until J.P. complains of developing a headache from the noise and tobacco smoke. He suggests a walk in fresh air so he can clear his lungs and his head. Tati leads them across the street to a park. They stroll along the pathway and into a grove of oak trees, where the two couples choose separate benches; things are soon heating up quite nicely.

'Gabriel,' calls J.P. in a stage whisper that verges on comical.

'What do you want? Do you need help over there?' jokes Gabriel laughing.

'T'anks for de offer, my friend, but I t'ink I'm doing hokay. Me and Anna, we are going down to de river for a walk. We will catch up wit' you two later, yes?'

'Sure. Have fun. We'll be back at the carriage if you come looking for us.'

'Hokay, but it might be a while,' answers J.P.

'Right. Can I talk to you in private for a second?'

'Sure,' says J.P., meeting Gabi just out of earshot from the girls.

'You know Anna is a vampire, right?'

'But of course. Don't worry. I'll be fine.'

'I'm not worried, J.P., but you should be.'

'I know, I know—once a wolf, always a wolf.'

'Exactly.'

'I be careful. Hokay?'

'Alright. Go. Go!'

J.P. and Anna begin to walk away. They notice somebody strolling up the path behind them. They ignore the stranger and continue toward the river. They only get a few yards down the lane when they hear a terrifying scream.

'What de 'ell is dat?' asks J.P.

'Looks like the lovebirds are having a night time snack,' answers Anna, laughing.

J.P. strains his eyes to see through the inky night. Hesitantly taking a few steps back toward where they left the other couple, he grimaces in horror at the sight of Tati and Gabi on the ground ravaging the poor soul like a pair of hungry Hyenas.

'Want to join them?' asks Anna chuckling.

'Merde, non. Let's go.'

'Okay. I guess I can feed on you a bit later,' answers Anna under her breath.

'W'at? W'at did you say?'

'I said we can catch a bite a bit later.'

'Hokay, later. I don' got much of a appetite right now.'

Just after sunset the following evening, Gabi is ready to go and meet Tati. As is his habit, he has taken a suite in a hostel that had a vacancy on the north side of the building, away from the daytime sun. Stepping into the street, he realizes that they hadn't set a time and place to meet. La Danse Macabre seems like the obvious place to start looking. He has only walked a couple of blocks, enjoying the fresh evening air, when he meets J.P. visibly unsteady on his feet, J.P. struggles to remain upright as he stops to greet Gabriel.

'Bonsoir, Gabee.'

'Hi. You wear the masque of the dead, my friend.'

'I guess you could say dat,' answers J.P. turning his head to show his fresh bite wound.

'Jesus! What were you thinking?'

'I don't know. We make mad, passionate love and before I know it…'

'Did I not warn you about Anna?'

'Hokay! You can say you told me so, if you must. I just don' wan' to argue. I am sick like da dog, me.'

'Of course you are. One of the first symptoms. It'll get worse before it gets better. Go home and rest. By the way, d'you know where Anna is?'

'Not sure. I lef 'er back at the park and 'eaded over to Lisette's place.'

'Lisette? You didn't hurt her, did you?'

'I didn't get der. Suddenly I was so sick to the estomac dat I could not 'ardly stand, so I 'eaded back. Why would you t'ink I might 'urt 'er?'

'Never mind right now. Get back to the room and try to get some rest. I'm going to the Macabre to see if I can find Tati. We'll talk when I get back, okay?'

'Hokay, Gabee, I am sorree. I jus' need some res' and I'll be hokay, non?'

'I hope so. You should be, but we'll soon find out.'

'Huh?' returns J.P.

'Nothing. Go, go…and no matter what, stay in your room,' demands Gabi.

❧

Both Anna and Tati are in the club. What they are doing when he finds them catches him off-guard, causing him to do an almost comical double-take. Tati and Anna kissing! Really kissing.

'Evening, ladies,' says Gabi, surprising the sisters mid-kiss.

'Gabi, what a nice surprise. We weren't expecting you,' says Tati.

'Apparently not. I didn't know you two were a couple.'

'Gabi, are you jealous?' asks Anna.

'No. Of course not. I mean, after last night I'd never have suspected and didn't think sisters would ever…well, you know…'

'Gabi, quit being such a prude and buy us a drink,' says Tati.

'Besides, Tati doesn't mind sharing. Do you, Tat?' adds Anna.

'Speaking of sharing, I just saw J.P. I don't have to tell you he was in pretty bad shape. He was headed home to rest.'

'Oh? He told me he was going to, uh, visit somebody tonight,' answers Anna defensively.

'Oh, right. Lisette. He didn't make it; too physically drained.'

'Lisette, eh?' questions Anna.

'An old lover that he still yearns for.'

'Pfft!' scoffs Anna. 'Love is for fools.'

'I'll drink to that!' shouts Tati raising her glass.

'Let's go out for a bite and meet back at my apartment for a little ménage-à-trois,' suggests Anna.

'Sounds exciting,' Tati responds with a deep, passionate kiss. Pulling back from Anna, Tati turns to Gabi and gives him the same treatment.

'See? Sharing is fun,' says Anna, with an mischievous grin.

Early in the morning, J.P. staggers through the door, surprising the threesome mid-orgy. Gabriel is lying naked on the floor with Anna straddling his face. Tati, facing her sister, is riding Gabriel's cock.

'Hi, J.P. Come join us,' says Tati smiling.

'T'anks. I'd love to, but I'm not feel good. A bit weak and dizzy.'

'Must be the late nights with strange women,' says Anna sarcastically.

'Oui, maybe dat's it,' J.P. rubs his neck, looking more than a little uncomfortable.

'Tarry with us a while, J.P. We'll be going out for a bit of breakfast as soon as we have been satisfied by Gabi!' says Tati riding her partner even harder.

'Naw. But you enjoy. I'm 'eaded to the 'ouse of a friend and thought I'd stop in on Gabi on my way by.'

'What friend is that?' asks Anna between moans.

'Jus' an old friend. Nobody you know,' answers J.P.

'Oh, really? Fine. Suit yourself,' says Anna, slightly perturbed by J.P.

'Bye, lover,' moans Tati.'

'Au revoir,' answers J.P. As he goes out, he closes the door behind him.

'Say hi to Lisette for us,' say Anna and Tati in chorus, laughing hysterically.

J.P.

1779

J.P. stumbles through the dark streets, his destination one of the most exclusive residential areas of the city. This is the Paris of opulence and privilege, reserved for the special few, the wealthy beyond belief. Dukes, earls, counts and marquis live here. Only by extreme good fortune had he, as a young man, found himself working here, first as a stable boy and, eventually, as a coachman. The Duke of Orleans, traveling by carriage and late for an important royal function, made the fortuitous decision to cut through the poor section of Paris to save time. A broken bridle forced his coachman to stop the team and seek repairs.

The liveryman was away tending to the plow harnesses of a local farmer, infuriating the already upset Duke even further. When J.P., still a young boy at the time, approached and offered to repair the bridle, the Duke had no confidence that boy could accomplish the repair. But he was desperate not to miss his Royal meeting and impatient to get back on the road. Having no alternative, he ignored the scoffing of the coachman and allowed J.P. to approach the horse. Using a knife from his pocket and the leather belt from his waist, J.P. quickly mended the bridle. The Duke, grateful and impressed, handed the boy a couple of Francs and offered him employment.

That very week, J.P. started as stable boy in this posh district. A number of years later, after excelling at his liveryman duties, he was promoted to coachman. He was working in that capacity only a few days when he met the Duke's daughter, Lisette, who had just returned from several years at an elite private girls' school. Soon they were more than friends. Their secret romance was eventually discovered and reported to the Duke. J.P. was immediately dismissed and warned that he would be executed on sight if he ever tried to contact or come near Lisette again.

Tonight, however, J.P. longs for his beloved Lisette. The touch of her soft milky skin, the curves of her young firm body haunt his mind. He wants her now more than ever, and he will be deterred by nothing.

Some of last evening's nausea has been lingering, and he is suddenly engulfed by a wave much worse than the others. He pauses to lean against an ornate steel fence, doubles over and vomits through the rails into a flower garden. Kneeling for a few minutes, weak and dizzy, he stares foolishly at the phlegm and stomach contents dripping from somebody's prized roses. He regains his composure slowly, wipes the residue from his lips and regains his feet. An eerie feeling knocks him back to his knees. Grasping the sides of his head, he is overwhelmed by what appear to be random thoughts, ideas bombarding his consciousness. He strains to open his eyes only to be blinded by an assault of bright light and color. The sound of his own racing heart pounds like a steel drum in his ears. J.P. collapses on his side and curls into a fœtal position. He knows that he is about to die of a heart attack or some sort of brain seizure. He surrenders himself to his fate and passes out.

'Hey, mon gars. Réveillez-vous! Wake up!' insists the policier, nudging the tightly curled J.P.

'Huh? What?' J.P. manages to open his eyes and sit up.

'You drunk, mister?'

'No. No, Officer. I am so sorry. Suddenly I was feel weak and sick to my estomac, then I seem to 'ave passed out.'

'So you say, but you look fine to me now. You can't loiter around here. This is a very exclusive neighborhood, you know. What're you doing here, anyway?'

'C'est incroyable! I am feel pretty good!' says J.P., largely to himself.

'What's that? Speak up,' commands the policeman.

'Sorry. I say I was on my way to visit ma belle amie, Lisette, when I took ill.'

'Lisette Loiseau?'

'Mais, oui! You know 'er?'

'I know her and her father, le Duc d'Orleans, quite well.'

'Wonderful! I am free to go, den, am I not?'

'No! You claim to be visiting your girlfriend at four o'clock in the morning? You, someone who obviously has seen better days, want me to believe that Mlle Loiseau is not only your girlfriend, but expecting you at this ungodly hour?'

'Yes. Well, non.'

'Which is it?'

'You see, Officer, she is expecting me, but I am not exactly her boyfriend. Her fadder does not approve. I was 'eaded to the Duke's residence earlier in the evening to encourage a change of 'eart, but I am become sick and black out against dis garden fence. I was jus' get my senses back when you arrive. And now, I should 'urry over before she become distraught. She get so worry.'

'A likely story. I'll escort you to the Duke's to confirm your story. I hope, for your sake, you're telling the truth. If the young lady doesn't know you, that lie will earn you twenty lashes, and free room and board with a family of rats.'

'But of course, Officer. I appreciate your concern. No need to worry—you will see. My Lisette will be so 'appy.'

Under police escort, J.P. proceeds to the duke's mansion only a few blocks from where he passed out. The policeman has to knock at the door several times before getting any response.

'You better not be handing me a line, buddy. If I wake these people in the middle of the night, and they don't confirm your story, you will not see the light of day for a very long time.'

The housekeeper opens the large oak door a crack and frowns at the two men.

'What's the meaning of this? D'you know what time it is?' demands the housekeeper in a stage whisper.

'I'm sorry to disturb you at this ungodly hour, but I found this person loitering in the neighborhood and he claims to know Lisette, to be coming to see her, in fact.'

'Lisette is asleep. She certainly is not entertaining any men at this time of the night. Especially not the likes of him.'

'So, you don't know this man?' asks the policeman.

'No! Now, please leave before you wake up the household.'

'Sorry to have disturbed you. My sincere apologies.'

The housekeeper's goodnight is cut off by the closing door.

'Okay, you jackass. It's off to the rat hole for your lying ass.'

'No! You can't. I swear I know Lisette. We're very close. Dat housekeeper hate me, dat's why she say she don' know me.'

'Shut it and get moving,' says the policeman. Grabbing J.P. firmly by the collar, the officer spins him around, and the pair start down the walkway. Their attention is drawn to the sound of shutters opening in a window above.

'J.P.? J.P., is that you?'

'Lisette! Yes, my darling, c'est moi.'

'I'll be damned!' exclaims the policeman. 'You know this character, mademoiselle?'

'Yes, of course. He's a friend of mine. I'll be right down.'

'You are extremely lucky, young man. Barely saved by the skin of your ass.'

'I tol' you I know 'er.'

'You did. And apparently you do. Next time you visit 'La Provence,' I would suggest you come with an escort and at a reasonable time of day. Goodnight.'

'Bonsoir.'

Lisette bursts though the front door and throws her arms around J.P., almost knocking him off his feet. The two hug and kiss passionately, as if each cannot get close enough to the other. After a few moments, Lisette pulls back with effort from her lover.

'Come. But be very quiet. Papa makes no pretense about liking you, and he'll lynch you in the garden if he catches you here with me in the middle of the night.'

They start up the sweeping staircase towards the second floor and Lisette's bedroom. A sound from below freezes them in their tracks. Seconds later, the housekeeper walks from the kitchen into the foyer below. Stopping, she stares at the front entrance with a puzzled look.

'I could've sworn I just locked that door. The demands of this family are wearing me out, but I'm not so tired that my mind is going, is it?' grumbles the housekeeper to herself. She walks to the entrance and locks the large security bolt once more. 'I'm getting too old for this. Visitors in the middle of the night! I need a holiday.'

She walks back past the staircase to the side entrance to the servants' quarters.

Already halfway up the stairs, the couple continue to the top, then proceed on tiptoes down the hall to Lisette's bedroom.

'Phew! That was close. Are you crazy coming back here?' asks Lisette.

'I 'ad to see you again. I need you, Lisette. I mus' be near you.'

'You know that's not possible, my love. You'll be killed.'

'I don' care. It's wort' the risk. I can't continue living like this. Every day without you is not worth living.'

You're a fool—romantic, yes, but a fool nonetheless. Papa will never allow you back here. You must find a way to forget me, mon amour.'

'You don' understand. I can never get you out from my mind. It's make me sick; I can' eat or sleep no more. I barely made it here tonight. Your love is the only cure.'

'Ah, mon amour. You are mad. You risk your life for me. How could I refuse your love? Come. Come and make love to me. I am yours, if only briefly. Tonight is ours and nobody can take that from us.'

J.P. picks Lisette up in his arms, kisses her deeply and turns towards the bed.

'Well! Isn't this just too romantic. I think I may have to throw up,' says a female voice from the far side of the room. The two lovers turn to see Anna climbing in through the open bedroom window.

'Anna! What you are doing here? And how did you fin' me? Did you follow me?' asks J.P. in one run-on question.

'Hello, lover-boy.'

'Anna, what you are doing here?' repeats J.P. lowering Lisette to her feet.

'I thought you might want to share tonight.'

'Who is this woman?' demands Lisette obviously upset.

'She's, uh, just a friend,' comes the nervous answer.

'Just a friend? Really?' Anna's voice drips sarcasm. 'Even after the other night?'

'Jean-Paul, what is going on? How did she get up here? What does she mean by share. Share what?'

'I'm not sure…exactly. I only met her the other day. I don'…' mumbles J.P.

'Let me clear this up for you, my little French muffin,' says Anna, walking towards the couple. 'J.P. and I are going to share a late night snack together.' Anna smiles exposing her long sharp canines.

'Mon Dieu! She's a vampire!' screams Lisette.

'Silence!' commands Anna. The vampire backhands Lisette across the face. The blow lifts Lisette off her feet and deposits her unconscious on the bed.

'Anna, no! Not my Lisette.'

'Doesn't she look lovely lying there half-naked? She looks so appetizing, don't you think?'

J.P. stares down at his unconscious girlfriend.

'She's beautiful. So sweet, her skin so milky white, so fair.'

'That's right. Now lay down next to her with me. Feel her young firm body.'

'Yes. Yes! It feel so nice.'

Anna takes J.P.'s hand and places it on the side of Lisette's long tender neck.

'Doesn't she feel nice and warm?'

"Yes, so warm and soft.'

'Feel the pulse of her blood pumping through her veins.'

'Yes. I feel da pulse strong under my fingers. Dat beat make me feel very strange, Anna. What it is? I—I feel so hungry. I've never been so hungry. I have this urge to—to…'

Anna gently cups the back of J.P.'s head and draws his face down to Lisette's neck.

'Feed, feed. Sate your hunger. You're one of us now.'

J.P., disoriented and confused, overwhelmed by a primal urge at once so foreign and completely natural, sinks his canines into the alabaster neck of his dear Lisette.

J.P. finds himself sitting on the floor next to Anna, back against the bedroom wall. He has no concept of how much time has passed.

'What 'ave I done?' he laments, looking across the room at a pale Lisette lying inert on the large brass bed.

'I'm no doctor, but I'd say you just bled your sweetheart dry,' answers Anna flippantly.

'No! No!' J.P. stands, tears beginning to spill from his eyes. 'What 'ave I become?'

'Oh, drop the melodrama. Don't be so damned feeble. There're thousands more like her in Paris.'

J.P. rushes to the bed and stretches beside the cold Lisette, caressing her limp body.

'Lisette. Lisette. Please wake up, ma chérie. Lisette?'

'Ha! You're so pathetic. Face it, you weakling. You killed her. She's as dead as this bedpost.'

'You! You! You do dis to me. None of dis would 'ave 'appened if not for you.'

'You can thank me later. Besides, if I remember correctly, lover boy, you asked for it! Take a look on the bright side—maybe Lisette has a sister?'

'You 'eartless bitch. I ought to…'

'Listen, you ungrateful little Frenchman. Don't you be threatening me. You wanted to be like us. You wanted the power, the everlasting life. And now? Now that you have it, you can't handle the truth of what you have become.'

'The trut'? The trut' is dat I did not become dis beast. You turn me into dis animal, slave to its lusts. You're da reason dat my Lisette is dead.'

'No. The truth, lover boy, is that you are a vampire. You lusted for blood, and realizing you had the power, you took it. And Lisette's life in the bargain!'

'I'll kill you!' screams J.P. Pouncing off the bed, his fists clenched tightly, he leaps at Anna.

'Not so fast, lover boy!' She thrusts her legs forward, catching J.P.

squarely in the chest, lifting him off his feet and catapulting through the open window.

The sound of a dull impact is followed by muted gasps of surprise and several short screams. Anna rises and calmly crosses the room. The night is silent before she reaches the window. On the roadway below the window, a lady stands hand at her throat staring in shock at J.P.'s quivering body staked to the garden fence. Several wooden pickets protrude from his bloody chest, one directly through his heart.

Celreau
1779

'That was nice,' says Tati, a smile of contentment slipping over her features. Gabriel, exhausted and sweaty, rolls off her naked body to lie beside her on the rumpled sheets.

'Nice?' questions Gabriel, his breathing slowly returning to normal.

'Yes. You're a decent lover. I feel pretty satisfied.'

'Well, thank you. I guess.'

'I wonder if Anna caught up to J.P.? She's always so curious. She's not even really interested in that Frenchman.'

'Why did she chase after him, then?'

'Curiosity. She wants to meet Lisette. She probably wants to see how pretty Lisette is.'

'That's stupid. And pretty damned vain, don't you think?'

'Don't call my sister stupid. Who do you think you are? You've no right to judge her.'

'I…I just meant I don't understand why she's jealous of a woman she doesn't know; a woman who's in love with a man for whom Anna has no amorous feelings.'

'I told you. She's just curious. Why're you being so odd about this?'

'Forget it, Tati. Let's change the subject.'

'Fine with me.'

'I'm so lucky I found you, Tati. I haven't been this happy in a long, long time.'

'I'm having fun, too.'

'Before I found you again, I hated my life. I cursed the return of darkness every night, knowing that I would take yet another innocent life to feed my blood lust.'

'It's what we do. We couldn't change the way we are now even if we wanted to, so we may as well enjoy ourselves doing it!'

'You see? That is precisely what I love about you. Your enthusiasm for life and your positive outlook are contagious. I feel you've given me a new purpose, a reason to carry on. We're going to be so happy together. Imagine! An eternity of partying and making love.'

'Hold on there, loverboy. Where'd you get the idea that I want to spend an eternity with you?'

'I thought you and I were soul mates and…'

'Well, you thought wrong. I mean yes, we've had fun together. The last few days were entertaining, but let's not get carried away here.'

'But we made love together. I know I felt a connection. I really…'

'Listen, Gabi. I like you, I do, but all we've had here is a couple of crazy fun days together and some sex. And to be honest, the sex was okay, at best.'

The hurt is evident on his face. 'I don't understand. Let me try again,' grovels Gabi. 'Give me another chance. I know I can satisfy you. I know I can change your mind. We're meant to be together, Tati. I just know it. Please. Just one more chance, please,' begs Gabi desperately.

'Isn't that a pathetic sight? Let's have a little self-respect, Gabi, a little dignity,' says Anna from the front door.

'Sorry you had to see this sad performance, sweet sister. Unfortunately for loverboy here, your lovemaking has spoiled me so. After you, no one will ever measure up. I am tainted.'

Anna crosses the room, stepping around Gabi, and kisses Tati passionately on the mouth.

'I s'pose you'll just have to keep trying, my little vampire.'

'You know I will, Anna,' answers Tati with a laugh.

'How can you be so heartless? I love you, Tati. I always have.'

'I think I'm gonna vomit. Please make him go away,' pleads Anna.

'Shut up, you sick fuck. I'm not talking to you.'

Tati slaps Gabriel sharply across the face sending him to the floor on his back.

'I warned you about bad-mouthing my sister.'

'I'm sorry, Tati. I…I love you.'

'Love! Haven't you learned yet? Vampires don't love, they lust.'

'Waddaya mean?'

'Think, loverboy. Since you became a vampire, what has become of the three people who once loved you? Your mother doesn't want you, and in fact chose an old vampire over you. Petru, whose love was tainted, you incinerated. And your dear Angela, the love of your life, you bled to death. Need I say more?'

'How can you be so heartless? Have you no sympathy for what I've endured?'

'C'mon, Tati, end this. Please! I'm tired of his whining,' Anna begs her sister. 'What you ever saw in him, I don't know. He's as dull and pathetic as his friend was.'

'Waddaya mean was? Have you done something to J.P.?'

'I put the poor Frenchman out of his misery. He, like you, was so demented that he couldn't appreciate the finer things our life affords. Like a good meal. His sweetheart was so young and tender—her blood so fresh and thick. I helped him take his first drink and how does he show his appreciation? He attacks me! Unfortunately for Frenchy, that was his first and last taste.'

'J.P. was my friend. He was a good companion. Why couldn't you leave him alone?'

'Oh, boo-hoo. I've had enough of your clingy sentimentality. Honestly, Gabriel, you've become a terrible bore,' says Tati. 'It's time for you to leave.'

'Gladly. And you can be certain that if you ever think you see me up the street or in a café in the future, you will be mistaken. The distance from you will never be great enough.' Gabriel slams the door behind him as he leaves the house.

'Good riddance,' exclaim the two sisters in unison, bursting into laughter.

Unsure and worried about J.P.'s probable fate, Gabriel rushes to Lisette's house, where his suspicions are confirmed. He arrives to find J.P. bent backwards almost in half, suspended in the air, two wooden pickets protruding from his chest. Gabriel can't help but think about bad luck. If the fence had been wrought iron, like so many in the neighborhood, J.P. could have pulled himself off the impalers and walked away.

A police carriage stands in front of Lisette's residence, and a number of gendarmes are positioned along the white picket fence to protect the murder scene. He is surprised to see Tati's former lover, Capitaine Pierre Trottier talking to the police inspector. Staying in the shadows, Gabriel creeps up behind the carriage to listen to the conversation.

'You put me in quite a precarious situation, mon Capitaine Trottier. With the revolution gaining momentum every day, your reputation as a leader of the resistance makes your presence in this district highly suspect. It undermines my authority.'

'I assure you, Inspector, I bear no malice towards any of the nobleman in this district. They have their roles, as I have mine, and we're all merely pawns moving at the whim of the monarchy. I simply happened to be riding through this district on my way to the centre-ville. And, as you can see, I am unarmed.'

'Under the circumstances, I will give you the benefit of the doubt. I think you can understand, however, that I will leave your name out of the police report.'

'Of course. For my part, I'll do my best to assist you. In the future, I promise to avoid this district in order not to upset the noblemen.'

'That would make my life much simpler, I admit. Merci encore, Monsieur le Capitaine, for staying around at this hour to give me your expert witness account. How extremely fortuitous that you were able to identify the murderer as this Celreau fellow. Careless of him to let himself be seen standing in the very window out of which he has just thrown someone. My officers will capture the killer before he can escape the streets of Paris. The've already sealed off the surrounding area to prevent his escape.'

'Happy to be of assistance, Inspector. It was mere coincidence that I was passing at the moment the poor soul met his fate. I recognized Gabriel Celreau because I had occasion to confront him but a few days ago for molesting a mademoiselle in public, if you can imagine.'

'Brute!' exclaims the inspector.

'I tried to enter through the front door to capture him, but it was locked, of course. By the time the maid let me in, he had escaped out the back exit. When I mounted the stairs to the bedroom to investigate, the sight of the young girl lying dead at the foot of her bed was nothing less than horrific. God knows what ungodly acts that pig performed on the poor child.'

'I assure you the guillotine is his destiny,' proclaims the officer.

'I should've done us all a favor and slain the swine at our first meeting, but against my better judgment, and in consideration of the onlookers, I demanded his apology to the young lady and let him go with a firm warning.'

'Your nobility is beyond question and reproach, Capitaine. Please feel no shame nor remorse. One cannot expect to know a stranger's character at a glance.'

'I appreciate your support, Inspector. My men and I will help in the search for Celreau. I will contact you if we see any trace of the fiend.'

'Sacrebleu! He is heavy like a bull,' exclaims one of the policemen straining to lift J.P.'s body from the fence.

'No. I think his innards are stuck to the pickets impaling him. We need to lift him high enough to get him off the points of the pickets,' offers his helper.

'On the count of three, put your back into it. Un, deux, trois! Lift!' shouts the officer.

J.P.'s body jerks free from the pickets, which instead of white are now smeared red with gore. With the sudden release, the officers lose their grips, and J.P. tumbles to the ground with an audible thud.

Startled, the horses rear, bumping the carriage backward. Caught off-guard when struck by the rear of the jostled carriage, Gabriel sprawls on the street.

'Scoundrel,' yells Trottier at the sight of his prey prone on the cobblestones only feet away. But Gabriel is exposed and vulnerable for less than a wink. Springing to his feet, he is down the street and disappearing into an alley before Trottier reacts.

'After him,' commands the officer.

Trottier is already in hot pursuit of Gabriel, leaving the Inspector to marvel, 'Mon Dieu but the man can run.' Precious seconds later, his gendarmes follow on horseback.

Gabriel effortlessly one-hands a backyard fence, then in another single leap, he lands sure-footed on the roof of the house. Looking over his shoulder, he is relieved but not surprised to see the officers on their horses coming towards him, but still quite a distance down the same alley.

'Humans are quite sluggish, are they not?' shouts Trottier from the fence below.

'Trottier! What is your concern?'

'Don't play stupid with me, gypsy pig-dog. You know damned well that you stole my woman.'

Trottier pounces suddenly, landing feet-first on Gabriel's chest, dropping him flat on his back on the near-flat roof. Lips pulled back and canines fully descended from his gums, forearm across Celreau's neck, he pins his enemy to the roof. Gabriel, now face to face with Trottier, calmly points out, 'You know as well as I do that Tati is nobody's woman. She would have tossed you on the trash heap sooner or later.'

Gabriel knees Trottier in the stomach, catapulting him over his head to slam hard against the chimney at the corner of the roof.

Shaking the dust off, Trottier looks up at Gabriel in defiance.

'She was faithful to me till you showed up in Paris with your pathetic poems and ugly face.'

'Face it. She'd already grown tired of her plaything. She simply opted to trade you for a new, more exciting model.'

'Awwrrr,' yells Trottier, too angry for words. He charges towards Celreau.

Easily side-stepping, Celreau trips his attacker with his leg and cross-arms him, sending him tumbling.

'Don't feel bad. She recently tired of me as well.'

Trottier, further enraged but unharmed by the fall, hops to his feet. 'You're a liar. She loved me. You cast a gypsy spell upon her that set her against me. She became vulnerable and confused, and you deceived her into hating me.'

'Au contraire. She deceived and manipulated you, as she has deceived probably a few dozen others before you. I am afraid, dear Pierre, that our sweet Tati loved neither you nor me. She is nothing but a heartless vampire tramp.'

'No! No! You're wrong. She loved me. We were destined to be together. She was my reason to carry on, my candle of light in this endless

God-forsaken hell. You—you bastard, you destroyed the only joy of my dreadful and cursed existence.'

'Well, welcome to my nightmare,' answers Gabriel.

'I am your nightmare,' shouts Trottier, running straight at Gabriel.

Again Gabriel avoids an intended tackle. Grabbing Trottier's arm firmly en passant, he uses his attacker's momentum to swing him at shoulder height. Mid-spin he releases le Capitaine, sending him over several rooftops to disappear into an alley. Gabriel turns and leaps to the next rooftop, then down into the street, heading towards the river Seine.

Trottier, catapulted over the city skyline, windmills his arms and legs in the cool night air, desperately attempting to regain control and right himself. Before he can succeed, he slams to a dead stop—against the brickwork factory wall. The loud snapping of his bones as they fragment like dry kindling from a fire echoes in his skull; pelvis, collar bone and several ribs splinter. The excruciating pain courses through the vampire's body. The four-storey fall from the craggy stone wall to the cold cobblestone alleyway is accompanied by yet another brittle snap. Pain-riddled, he opens his eyes and examines his broken right leg resting at an odd angle in front of him. He winces in anticipation of the inevitable torture that his mangled body is about to inflict upon itself.

A familiar burning sensation rushes from the soles of his feet up his spine. Trottier curls into a fetal position, squeezes his eyes tightly closed and clenches his jaw. The fiery sting races from the base of his neck, up the brain-stem and explodes like fireworks. He feels like his brain has been shattered and ejected as tiny fragments from his skull. Involuntarily he stiffens, his arms snapping to his sides. The broken right leg slingshots back into place, wrenching a scream of agony from the vampire.

The creature, for that is all he is right now, lies spread-eagled on its back like St. Andrew upon the cross. He loses control and fills the night air with the putrid smell of soiled trousers. His tendons and ligaments begin to spasm. They tighten and, with pops, snaps and a nauseating grinding sound, force the broken bones back into alignment. Barely conscious, he growls and moans. His realigned bones and cartilage mesh rapidly. Just when the beast thinks it can take no more of the punishment, healing ends.

Trottier returns to himself and sits up. His body shows no signs of having been injured, and he feels energized. In fact, he admits to himself, he never felt better. He wipes a dribble of saliva from his mouth and, grinning evilly, he curses Gabriel. 'Mark my words, Gypsy,' he yells. 'My time is eternal and my revenge will be sweet.'

At the docks along the river's edge, Gabriel encounters a weathered sign that names the area Quai des Celestins. The sweet smell of tobacco draws his attention from the sign to the source of that pleasant aroma. Across the street an old man is smoking a pipe outside a sailor's tavern, L'auberge des marins. Famished, Celreau crosses to the poor bystander, and without hesitation drags him into the nearby alley. His appetite satisfied, Gabriel tosses the body onto a pile of refuse, returns to the street and enters the tavern.

The bar is dimly lit and surprisingly busy, loud at this late hour. He sits at the bar and stares, discouraged, at his reflection in the large ornate mirror behind the bartender. Feeling depressed over the failure to connect with Tati, the last person that could make him feel human and alive again, he sinks into despair.

'Drink?' asks the bartender, snapping Gabriel from his reverie.

'Huh? What?'

'Beer? Whiskey? Wine? Name your poison, garçon.'

'Beer. Yeah, beer. Why not? I only wish it were poison!'

'Chin up! Tomorrow's another day, mon ami.'

'Gee, thanks for those words of wisdom,' quips Gabriel sarcastically.

'De rien,' replies the bartender.

Four men have been standing at the entrance surveying the room since they came in just after Celreau. Something about the way they carry themselves and watch the patrons makes Gabriel suspect they are up to no good. They spend a few minutes talking in hushed tones and indicating with nods various male drinkers before separating. On the surface they appear to move randomly and sit wherever there is room. Gabriel can tell, however, that everything they are doing is part of a plan, something they have done many times in the past. He is not surprised when one takes a stool next to Gabriel and introduces himself.

'Napoléon Dufay,' says the gruff character, holding out a large callused hand.

'Gabriel Celreau,' answers Gabriel, shaking the hand with little enthusiasm.

'My friends call me Léo. May I buy you a drink, Gabriel?'

'Pleased to meet you, Léo. Please, call me Gabi and, sure, I'll take a refill, thanks.'

'Bartender, two double whiskeys,' barks out Léo.'

'I'm drinking beer,' points out Gabriel, holding up his cup.

'Beer? Have a whiskey. It'll put hair on your face.' Stroking his thick black beard for emphasis, Léo laughs loudly at his own joke. He takes the glasses of whiskey from the bartender and hands one to Gabriel.

'To your health,' exclaims Léo, tapping Gabriel's glass and tossing back the drink.

'À votre santé,' responds Gabriel following suit.

'Bartender! Two more whiskeys—doubles—and keep them coming,' shouts Léo.

A dozen rounds later, Gabriel looks around the bar. All of Léo's men have been ordering double whiskeys for their guests, who are very much intoxicated now, barely capable of staying upright in their chairs.

'You sure can handle your liquor, I'll give you that, young man,' mutters Léo. His own words are now distinctly slurred.

'Alcohol doesn't do much for me. What're we celebrating, by the way?'

'Celebrating? We're not celebrating anything. I'm just being cordial, that's all.'

Losing his balance, Léo upends his stool, sending it spinning into a nearby table of six. On his back on the floor, he peers up at Gabriel who kneels to help him back to his feet.

'You alright?'

'Merde! Yes, yes, fine. I'm okay,' answers Léo, embarrassed.

'Look, Dufay. As someone I once knew used to say, I may have been born at night, but it wasn't last night. What're you and the rest of your buddies up to?'

'Okay, listen. I could get in serious trouble, but since you literally drank me under the table, you've earned my respect. I'll tell you. We're a press gang, hired by a boarding master to shanghai this drunken lot. We're to get them to a barge anchored on the canal outside. They'll be tied and taken upriver to Rouen at the mouth of the Seine. For this we're paid handsomely. Some call it blood money, but one must make a living, non? At Rouen, they'll be loaded onto the St Jean Baptiste, set to sail for New-France in a week. The ship's in dire need of sailors and seamen, but few will sign up for such an extended voyage across the Atlantic. And the crimp is indeed a healthy sum.'

'Let's not disappoint them, then,' suggests Gabriel.

'Are you implying that you want to volunteer for this God-forsaken voyage?'

'No! Of course not. If I go willingly, you'll not receive payment for my capture. Bind me in your usual manner and take me aboard with the others.'

'Why would you do this? You don't owe me anything? What's in it for you?'

'It's complicated, but believe me, you'll be doing us both a favor.'

'Aww, complicated. A woman, non?'

'You are intuitive, my friend, but in fact more than one woman is involved.'

'Mon Dieu. You need say no more. You must get ready, then. The time is at hand.'

'What do I do?'

'Just play along.'

Dufay puckers his lips and lets out a loud whistle. The members of his press-gang react immediately to the signal. Tackling their inebriated guests to the floor, they tie the unfortunates' hands behind their backs and gag them with a handkerchief. Then lifting the drunks to their feet, they funnel them out the tavern door without much struggle.

Gabriel plays along as planned and, bound and gagged, he is escorted along with the drunks down to the river's edge. They follow the banks of the Seine to Le Pont-Marie, where a moored skiff awaits them. The captives are manhandled aboard the large row-boat. Most of them sit for but a moment before toppling over to the bottom of the boat.

Dufay unties Gabriel and removes his gag.

'Man the oars, Celreau, and don't try anything stupid or you will become fish bait. You hear me?' shouts Dufay with a wink.

'Yes sir,' answers Gabriel with a wink of his own. The three climb into the rowboat and push off. Gabriel begins to row. When the boat is a few hundred meters from the bridge, he looks up to find Trottier standing on the shore, his fist high in the air. Despite distance and wind, he can hear the man's angry words, 'Celreau, you can run, but you cannot hide!'

Gabriel scoffs at the threat and continues to row without hesitation. A steady rain has begun to fall, and the day quickly becomes unpleasant.

At first Gabriel rows the boat with ease. The rain continues, and the night quickly becomes unpleasant. The men shiver and complain, but the growing downpour only invigorates Gabriel. Cool and comfortable, he continues to row at a steady pace. In short order, a storm has developed with heavy winds and large white-capped waves. Gabriel struggles to keep the boat steady. His drunken companions become nauseous, more than one losing the contents of his stomach to the river as the boat is tossed about. Gabriel overhears the press-gang leader shout to Dufay that at this pace they will miss their rendezvous with the Jean-Baptiste.

After several miserable hours, the storm abates. Gabriel looks up and frowns at the sight of colors painting the morning sky on the horizon. Concern turns to worry and stress about the inevitable, but he smiles in relief when thick layers of stratus clouds overtake the dreaded light.

Finally they pull alongside the St Jean-Baptiste—several hours late! The men climb the ropes to the deck where they are met by armed mariners. The captain of the ship informs the leader of the press-gang that, unfortunately because of their late arrival, he has purchased the required men from another press-gang. He has need of only one more man to complete his crew.

'That's preposterous! We have traveled all night through a storm in order to meet your quota of men. You know we deserve no blame for the delay.'

'I'm sorry, Dufay, but you were late. We're on a tight schedule, and not knowing where you were or if you would arrive at all, I was forced to take the men available. And still I am a man short. I require an ordinary seaman capable of managing inventory below deck. Any of your lot have any schooling at all?'

Dufay's captives all look down at their feet, avoiding eye contact. All except one.

'I volunteer,' barks Gabriel before Dufay can react to the Captain's request.

'Step out here and name yourself,' commands the captain.

'Gabriel Celreau, sir.'

'Can you read and write, Celreau?' demands the Captain.

'Yes, sir. In two languages; educated in both English and French, sir.'

'Impressive for a simple laborer. Well, Celreau, you just volunteered your literate derrière for three months in the dark, damp belly of my ship. I hope you enjoy your stay.'

'Thank you, sir. I'll make do.'

Gabriel turns to Dufay, who accents his nod with a wink.

'Well, get aboard, man. We have to get out to the ship. We sail with the tide.'

'Yes sir,' answers Gabriel, once again returning the wink.

$\mathfrak{M}\mathrm{a}\mathrm{ft}$

1980

Pastor Dewar walks up to the pulpit, opens the bible and reads a passage: Exodus 20:2-17

...And God spoke all these words, saying, "I am the Lord your God. You shall have no other gods before me. You shall not make for yourself a carved image, nor any likeness of anything that is in heaven above, nor that is in the earth beneath, nor that is in the water under the earth. You shall not bow down to them nor serve them, for I, the Lord your God, am a jealous God...

The minister pauses for a moment and shakes his head side-to-side before looking up at the congregation assembled in the church. He heaves a big sigh of dismay and repeats—

"You shall have no other gods before me. You shall not make for yourself a carved image, nor any likeness of anything that is in heaven above, nor that is in the earth beneath, nor that is in the water under the earth.

'My dear friends, how in heaven can I make things any clearer than that? This, the Second Commandment from God, Our Father in Heaven, is well known. Yet what do I see as I stroll through the streets of Blood Cove? Ravens carved on totem poles, eagle and whale tattoos on arms and shoulders, pagan rattles and masks adorning your houses. Wake up, sinners! This warning is not a simple suggestion from our Lord and Savior. This is a commandment.

'Just look at the horrible events that have plagued our community in the last week. Young Donni Cardinal lost in the wilderness; the young darling of our little town, Dawn Brady, savagely attacked by a delinquent. I ask you, are these simply random and unlucky coincidences? No! Noooo, I say! I assure you, they are not. The retributions of living a sinful and savage lifestyle are self-evident. The dire and tragic consequences associated with breaking the law of god are painful indeed, but they are necessary. God is teaching all of us a lesson. Sinners, it is not too late, indeed it is never too late, to change your satanic ways. Repent of these primitive and unchristian beliefs, turn your back on the devil and be baptized in the name of Jesus Christ. In this way, you will purify your heart. You too can have a heart as white, as pure as snow.'

Once the sermon and communion are completed, Matt is more than ready to leave. The hypocrisy of this man who dares call himself a minister sickens him. Matt wants nothing more than to expose Pastor Dewar's attack on Christine, but he knows he would be wasting his time. He has no proof, and Christine is not about to subject herself to a lengthy and embarrassing trial in front of the community. And André is certainly not a credible witness. Matt is committed to making sure Dewar gets what he deserves, but all in good time. He struggles with impatience.

After the procession, Dewar customarily stands outside the front entrance, shaking hands with members of the congregation as they exit. Mayor Brady and Sergeant Kirkpatrick stand with him today. Matt's dad, Frank, stops to chat with them for a minute. Matt slides past Dewar and walks over to Jesse sitting on the church steps waiting for him.

'Hey, Matt. How was mass? Are you all forgiven and all clean of sins and shit?'

'Yeah, I felt shame and it's all good now. Ha ha.'

Overhearing Matt and Jesse, an infuriated Pastor Dewar runs to them screaming, 'How dare you? How dare you ridicule the word of God and laugh at the teachings of the Church? I expect this kind of disrespect and impertinence from your savage friend here, but not from you, Mr. Taylor.'

'Really?' responded Matt. 'And what would you know about respect?'

'How dare you question my integrity, young man? Frank, are you going to stand there and let your son talk to me in this manner?'

'Well, uh, no. Matt, apologize to…'

'Maybe I should ask Christine Henderson about your fine lessons on the subject of respect,' taunts Matt.

'What are you talking about? This is nonsense.'

'Son, I don't think you should talk t…' Frank begins.

'You know damned well what I am talking about. If you like, I am willing to describe all the juicy details of your private lesson with Christine.'

'I haven't a second more to waste on this rubbish. I have work to tend to.'

'Excuse me, Father. I believe you owe Jesse an apology.'

'Pardon me?'

'Well, she is one of God's children, is she not?'

'Matt. That's enough!' snaps Frank.

Ignoring his father, Matt begins, 'The way I remember it, Christine and André were playing hide and seek in the graveyard when…'

'Stop! Enough. I apologize. I am, after-all, a minister and must do as I preach.'

'Ha, that's a joke. C'mon, Jesse. Let's go to the general store for a cone.'

'What was that all about, Pastor?' asks Kirkpatrick, watching the two youngsters walk away.

'Proverbs 22:15: Folly is bound up in the heart of a child, but the rod of discipline drives it far from him,' quotes Dewar as he edges by Frank.

'Frank, I think you should have a talk with that boy about manners. If she were here, I know Doris would not put up with such insolence.'

Celreau

1787

The voyage across the rough Atlantic, destined for Quebec City in New France, is long and arduous. This is especially true for Gabriel, who can only come up on deck after dark or on particularly overcast days. The position of Inventory Officer is exceptionally well suited to his circumstances. He lives below deck for the duration of the voyage, surviving on blood from two goats stowed on board for the sole purpose of satisfying the Captain's demand for fresh goat's milk for breakfast. When the goats get weak from his overindulging, Gabriel allows them time to regain their strength by supplementing his diet with the blood of rats, of which there is no shortage.

Keeping records of the inventory is a simple task for Gabriel. His favor with the Captain increases dramatically when he reports that, under orders from the First Mate, crew members were stealing rum. Everyone but the Captain seems to be aware of their drunken soirées.

The Captain immediately makes an example of the First Mate, sending him to the plank. Upon arrival in Quebec, he grants Gabriel release from the ship, but not from his employ. He puts Gabriel to work managing his property along the St-Lawrence River. With a show of gratitude, Gabriel accepts the offer. This arrangement removes the need to escape from the ship. He certainly hasn't endured the tribulations of this passage just to spend another three months on the ship to return to Europe and his past life.

Upon arrival in Quebec City, Gabriel is escorted to the section of land he is to manage. The property, once owned by a fisherman named Abraham, known locally as The Scotsman, is located on a plateau just outside of the walls of the city. Over the past few years, most of this land overlooking the magnificent Cap Diamant has been acquired by the Ursuline Catholic Order of nuns and divided into sections. The sisters granted one of these sections to the Captain as reward for his efforts and contributions toward the settling and expansion of New France, and his financial contribution to the sisters' efforts to educate young women in Quebec City.

Gabriel settles in, content to work the Captain's land for several years. First things first—shelter from the deadly rays of the sun. He constructs a small, windowless stone house. His predominant crop is potatoes: low maintenance and easily tilled during the night. He becomes quite wealthy in surprisingly short order. The money acquired from his labor, and his fair share of the sale of the autumn harvest, he stashes in a strongbox buried in the garden. His operating expenses are lower than most other landowners' since he requires no fuel to heat his cabin, and his grocery budget is nonexistent. The hunger Gabriel experiences is satisfied by the blood of unfortunate Huron tribesmen who live along the river just outside the city. He feeds primarily on the young, and on loners who stray from their small settlements. He disposes of the cadavers by dumping them into the broad St-Lawrence, which conveniently carries them quickly down river. Complaints and reports of missing natives fall on deaf ears among the white authorities. Natives, after all, are known to be untrustworthy, tellers of tall stories.

On a spring morning in year eight, the Captain, newly returned from his latest voyage from France, approaches Gabriel with a business proposition.

'Gabriel, you've proven yourself a hard and faithful worker, and for this I am truly grateful.'

'I appreciate your thoughtful words, Captain, and thank you for the chance to serve you.'

'Listen, Gabriel. This last trip, I came upon a wonderful opportunity, one that could turn us into very rich men. To get the best out of the arrangement, we'd have to become partners. No more employer/employee relationship. Equals. And, if we handle it properly, we would accumulate great wealth in the bargain.'

'Why would you consider taking me as your partner? I have nothing to offer you.'

'Au contraire. Look at me. I am almost fifty now, old and weak. You are strong as a bull and still, incredibly, as young looking as when you walked off my ship. I have money and the connections, but lack your strong back. This undertaking will not succeed without you.'

'There is some truth in what you say. So, what am I to do, that you need my strong back?'

'In Europe, hats made from the beaver pelts of New France have become all the rage. Manufacturers require increasing numbers of pelts and suppliers cannot meet the demand. I have a contact in France willing to pay a handsome sum upon delivery for thick pelts. As many as we can deliver.'

'You want me to become a trapper?'

'No! I want you to become a trader! You will travel the upper St-Lawrence by canoe to the Great Lakes where the Algonquin Indians are eager to trade fur pelts for metal goods, like knives, hatchets, kettles. They trade their best pelts for firearms, ammunition and liquor. I will supply the canoe and all the trade goods. You will meet and bargain with the natives and return with a canoe-load of pelts.'

'And my share?'

'We split 60/40, payable upon my return from France with payment I receive for the fur pelts. The sixty percent is for me, of course; I have much greater expenses. I assure you this is a very generous offer and...'

'I'll take it.'

'...and not many would get this chance at such a lucrative opportunity. Huh? What did you say?'

'I said, I'll take it. When do I depart?'

'Well. Okay. Good. But understand, Gabriel, the trip to Upper Canada is not without perils and natural hazards; wild animals, forest fires, river rapids and the constant harassment of black flies and mosquitoes.'

'Those are of little concern, Captain. Is that all?'

'Well, huh, no, to be quite honest. Perhaps worst of all are the Iroquois. These savages live throughout the boreal forest and are renowned for their vicious attacks on white settlers. They have a reputation for torturing their victims, not to mention raping the females.'

'Torture? What type of torture?' Gabriel is curious.

'There have been stories of Iroquois stripping their victims naked, burning them with a firebrand, then beating them until their bodies are blood-stained and lacerated. They often cut off fingers, toes, and even penises, and watch their victims scream in agony. They have been known to take some of the men they view as worthy opponents and hang them suspended from hooks that pierce the flesh of their chests.'

'Really? Go on,' encourages Gabriel.

'Well, in the evenings, the poor souls are made to lie down on the forest floor, their arms and legs stretched in the shape of Saint Andrew's Cross and bound to four stakes. Pegged down and immobile, they are prime pickings for rodents, varmints and bugs of all sorts that creep out of the dark to gnaw on their flesh. In the morning, weak from the previous day's torture and driven mad by the night of terror, they are promptly tied to a scaffold and burned alive.'

'Very interesting. Alright. I will need a large birchbark canoe with a couple of extra paddles.'

'We have a deal, then, partner?'

'That we do, Captain. That we do.'

1795

Gabriel adjusts easily to his new role as coureur des bois. Soon he is spending most of his time in his canoe far from civilization. He makes countless excursions on the Ottawa River, paddling as far north as Temiskaming, navigating treacherous rapids and portaging his birchbark canoe around sections that are unnavigable. Upon his return, his canoe is always so laden with bundles of thick valuable beaver pelts that he paddles perched precariously atop his load. He soon makes enemies among the Voyageurs, the other major fur traders in New France. The Voyageurs travel in large canoes with ten to twelve men, barter with the indians for pelts, then trade the pelts to the North West Company, which then transports them back to Europe. This system has been working well for some time, and the North West Company is well on the way to establishing itself as the prime trading partner in the area. Until Gabriel begins operations.

Voyageurs and the North West Company are infuriated by the competition created by Gabriel, and by the fact that he cuts out the middle man. He trades with the Algonquins for pelts and delivers them directly to the Captain for transport to France. This arrangement generates a hefty sum of money every trip, money the competitors felt should be theirs.

In time he gains near-legendary status among the Algonquin peoples because of his remarkable strength and courage. Stories of the mighty Frenchman repelling an Iroquois attack from an Algonquin village spread all the way back to Ottawa and Montreal. Jesuit Missionaries who have been sent to live amongst the tribe to facilitate the trade with the North West Company try to undermine the natives' growing respect for Gabriel's heroism by spreading stories that the Frenchman was possessed by Satan. They quoted as evidence the fact that he was known to hide from daylight, to travel the river at night, and once had been discovered drinking blood from a freshly killed deer. These seemingly farfetched rumours only intensified the natives' respect and awe for the mighty French trader.

Upon his return to Quebec City from one of his successful excursions up the Grand River, Gabriel is welcomed with the unexpected news of the Captain's passing. He is told that his partner had fallen quite ill and quickly died of consumption. Gabriel is quite upset, not so much by the Captain's sudden death, as by the prospect of having to find a new agent for dealing with the French buyers. A new intermediary almost certainly would not agree to the same percentage share of the profits as the captain had. Within a few days of his return, Gabriel is surprised by a letter from a Montreal law firm delivered to his house summoning him to appear in Montreal at their offices. The letter informs him that he has been named as beneficiary in the Captain's last will and testament, the details of which would be accorded him at the meeting.

After two days to see the latest load of pelts stored for later shipment, Gabriel travels to Montreal by horse and carriage. He uses the 5-day travel time to consider his situation, and he comes to realize that he has no further interest in the fur trade. The endeavor had represented a means to acquiring a substantial amount of money, which was now satisfied by the inheritance. Upon arrival in Montreal, he quickly completes the paperwork to finalize his ownership. He severs his ties with the Algonquin fur traders and advertises his property for sale. As it turns out, the French military has begun expropriating land, including a portion of Celreau's inheritance, for the construction of a citadel on the plateau overlooking the river. The plan is to build, along with the citadel, two redoubts that would act as the first line of defense against an invading army.

Gabriel's prime farmland sells quickly. And none too soon. The conflict between the British and the French over ownership of the young colony quickly deteriorates into open war. Ultimately, in 1759 the French are defeated on the very plains they had taken from Celreau.

1859

The autumn day of his arrival is overcast and drizzly, as it has been most of the five-day trip. Over the last few decades, Celreau has used the wealth he amassed in the fur trade to finance an expansion into construction and transportation. Grown weary and bored with plating the eccentric businessman, he is in Montreal to see his lawyers to finalize the sale of his assets. He is ready for a change.

Despite rain and muddy roads, he manages to arrive at the lawyers' office on time. The gray stone two-storrey building is situated next to the Montreal seminary. A young Métis boy is sitting in the drizzle on the front steps of the school. The boy's deep set brown eyes are emphasized by the sallowness of his complexion. He seems to be praying, his gaze focused on some unknown in the distance. Curiously intrigued by the boy, Gabriel shakes off the temptation to address him and, instead, proceeds into the barristers' offices.

An hour later, when Gabriel steps out of the building, he is surprised to see the Métis boy sitting in the same spot on the steps, seemingly still in prayer. Gabriel succumbs to his curiosity and addresses the boy.

'Hello. Are you okay, young man?'

'Yes, of course, I'm fine. Why do you ask?'

'I'm sorry. I thought you were troubled by something.'

'Troubles? I have no troubles...I give all my troubles and sins to God for him to bear.'

'Interesting. Mind if I join you?'

'Suit yourself, stranger.'

Gabriel sits down on the wet granite next to the boy.

'This arrangement with your God—how very convenient. How I wish it were that simple for me.'

'Tell me, stranger, have you accepted Jesus Christ as your savior?'

'I'm afraid I am beyond help, and even if your Jesus could help me, I could never repay him.'

'If you accept him as your savior and repent your sins, he'll forgive you. He asks for no payment. The scriptures tell us, For the wages of sin is death, but the gift of God is eternal life in Christ Jesus our Lord.'

'Well, if that were true, I'd be dead a long time ago, and I can assure you eternal life is no gift.'

'Do you mock my God and savior, sir?'

'Of course not. I'm only trying to understand him.'

'Ah. I can respect that. Unfortunately, understanding God is beyond the capacity of mere mortals. Acceptance of his divine superiority is all we can hope to achieve, and that comes only through faith.'

'Listen, ah, sorry I didn't get your name. I'm Gabriel, by the way.'

'Louis. A pleasure to meet you, friend,' answers Louis.

As they shake hands, Louis gasps in horror. His hand burns like it's being stung by a hundred angry hornets. The excruciating pain radiates up his arm into his body. Incomprehensible visions flash through his mind: mutilated corpses hung on meat hooks, naked bodies tangled in perverse sexual acts, a man biting down on a shrieking rat. He jerks his hand from Gabriel's grip and slides away on the step. He doubles over and vomits.

Turning back to Gabriel, he shouts defiantly, 'You! You are evil. Away with you, Satan. You have no power over me, as God is my shepherd.'

'Calm down. I assure you I am not Satan. I won't harm you.'

'Perhaps not, but you've done some terrible things. I've seen the evil within your being.'

'I have committed some horrible crimes. I've murdered many innocent people, some of whom I loved very much. I'm not proud of these acts, but they are beyond my control.'

'If you're sincere, I can help you, but first you must repent, Gabriel. Redemption can only be realized through repentance. Confess your sins so God can forgive them and set you free from Satan's grasp.'

'Confess to whom? You?'

'No. You confess to God through me. I'm only a seminarian, but the Lord is all loving and will understand. Tell him what evil lies within you.'

'To be honest, Louis, I am skeptical. On the other hand, I've nothing to loose.'

'Good. Now bow your head and close your eyes.'

The vampire does as instructed.

'Gabriel, I urge you to have confidence in the one true God. May the Lord be in your heart and help you to confess your sins with true remorse.'

Gabriel draws a deep breath. 'I have committed too many terrible acts to recount. I prey on innocent people. I kill them and drink their blood. My intention is not to inflict pain, but I have this hunger, this urge for the only food that provides me sustenance. I don't expect you to understand. It's a damned curse that I must bear for eternity.'

'Gabriel, God hears your plea and feels your sorrow. He understands your need for blood.'

'Listen to me. You're not understanding. I am a vampire. I drink blood!'

'So do I, Gabriel.'

'What? You're not a vampire!'

'No, but I am a Christian, and every Sunday Christians meet in church and feed on blood—the blood of Christ. We drink of his blood and eat of his body.'

'I've heard of this rite, this communion, but I never thought of it that way.'

'You see, we have more in common than you think.'

'Now what?'

'That's it. Now I give you absolution. May God give you pardon and peace, and I absolve you from your sins in the name of the Father, and of the Son, and of the Holy Spirit. Now you say amen.'

'Amen.'

'May the Passion of our Lord Jesus Christ, the intercession of the Blessed Virgin Mary and of all the saints heal your sins, help you to grow in holiness, whatever good you do and suffering you endure. Go in peace.'

'That's it?'

'That's it'

'Well, I appreciate the effort, Louis. Now I should be going.'

'You're quite welcome. Don't give up hope. Where you off to?'

'Not sure. To be honest, I just received a large sum of money from the sale of a number of business assets, and I'm not quite sure yet what I plan to do'

'You should get an education. The seminary is quite a good school.'

'Well, I may just consider that.'

A man, obviously a priest by his garb, opens the building's front door and looks down the steps at the boy. 'Riel, are you waiting for a written invitation? The class starts in five minutes. I swear you always have your head in the clouds, daydreaming. You will never amount to anything with that attitude, young man. You must take life more seriously. Now, inside with you.'

'Sorry, Gabriel. I must get back to my studies. It was nice meeting you.'

'Hey, you never know. Maybe I'll see you around soon.' Gabriel winks at the boy.

—☙☙—

And he does see the young scholar several times over the next few days. Gabriel is fascinated by the boy's informed view of the world, his broad range of knowledge, and most particularly, his complete dedication to gaining as broad and advanced an education as he can. Through their discussions, Gabriel is forced to admit to himself that he has sorely neglected his own education, allowing himself to go through life largely ignorant and narrowly focused. He becomes determined to correct this lack. Taking Riel's advice, he registers at the Montreal seminary before returning to Quebec to deal with outstanding business loans and his personal holdings.

Henry

1910

Free of debt and encumbrances, Gabriel wastes no time returning to Montreal to begin his education. He rents a small basement apartment near the university and is fortunate to locate and hire a bright young student willing to tutor him during the evenings. Having never attended a formal school, he is a little apprehensive about what to expect. His modicum of education was learned from his mother at their kitchen table. And that was a long time ago.

He schedules his study time late in the evening, after returning from feeding, when he is most alert. His urges must be completely satisfied and under control so he can concentrate, not to mention ensuring that his young teacher is in no danger.

Gabriel becomes obsessed with the accumulation of knowledge. His rate of advancement is unprecedented, his mind like a sponge. In short order, he completes Ph.D.s in several subjects, including literature and history. He attends the minimum allowed regular classes, claiming his mind is much sharper in the evening. The priests at the seminary turn out to be more flexible than he expects. Especially with good students.

Usually seen in the classrooms and laboratories during later hours, he agrees one time, to arrive early to sit for a class photograph.

Eventually he joins the staff at McGill College and is a successful and popular lecturer for several years. Abruptly, he decides to pursue graduate studies toward a Ph.D. in sciences at the University of Toronto. The fact that one of his original tutors has drawn attention to the vampire's unchanging youthful appearance has no small influence on his decision.

His new lecture hall in Toronto is fitted with window blinds and soft lighting at his request. The Dean is most accommodating when told of Gabriel's skin disorder and the fact that exposure to direct sunlight could kill him.

Once again, Gabriel attacks his studies as if he were driven, juggling teaching duties with his academic studies, impressing students and faculty alike. As before, he makes short work of the degree, and upon receiving his doctorate, he accepts the administration's offer to assume the role of Dean of Science.

In celebration, he heads straight to his go-to spot, a dingy tenement called The House of Industry, for a celebratory feeding. Situated in a densely populated slum district called The Ward by its inhabitants, Industry House is used to house the indigent, mostly unemployed immigrants, homeless and orphans.

Standing in the dark lot at the rear of the rundown building, Gabriel waits patiently next to the maintenance shed, his usual spot for his next victim. Within minutes his newest victim, a young man, approaches from the back laneway and turns up the beaten path towards the tenement. Gabriel pounces!

Although unsuspecting, his prey reacts instantly. To Gabriel's surprise, the man fights back, delivering quick, well-placed punches to the vampire's head and solid kicks to the body. Gabriel, more off-balance than hurt by the blows, falls backward over a hedge, coming to rest against the property fence. Terrified, the man takes advantage of the opportunity to escape down the laneway, running as quickly as he can and still stay on his feet. After a few minutes and several blocks, he turns into another lane and stops to catch his breath. Sweating, still shaking, he looks back, squinting through the darkness for signs of the monster. Satisfied that his assailant is not pursuing him, he breathes a sigh of relief and turns to come face-to-face with Gabriel.

The young man freezes, a gasp escaping his lips, as Gabriel's hand wraps around his throat. He is lifted off the ground, his throat squeezed shut and his esophagus crushed. The man's eyeballs bulge from their sockets and blood trickles from his ears. The last thing he hears is the loud pop of his bursting Adam's Apple.

Gabriel drags the limp body into a growth of thick willows growing along the laneway. His own body trembles from mixed emotions: anger, excitement, hunger. Overcome, he digs into the man's chest with his bare hands. He breaks through the ribs with his powerful fingers and rips out the still pumping heart. He holds the warm bloody organ over his head like a trophy. His eyes roll back in ecstasy as the blood pours freely down the torn artery to drip into his mouth. All his senses thrill to the metallic iron flavor of the warm blood. As the flow ebbs, he wraps his lips around the aorta and sucks the rest of the bloody nectar into his mouth. Tossing the dry appetizer aside, he picks up the body and hangs it upside down in a tree. He bites deep into the cadaver's neck and drains the remaining blood.

Satisfied and fully energized, Gabriel leaves the alley, stopping at the entrance to rinse his bloody face and hands in the rain barrel standing at the corner of the building. He makes his way down Elm Street to Bay, then up Yonge to the city center. Another hunger must be satisfied—the need for social contact. He enters a pub on Yonge Street and sits beside one of three men at the bar, each of whom is obviously alone.

After several drinks, he is becoming friendly with the eccentric businessman sitting beside him. The gentleman, more than a little inebriated and obviously in the mood to bend someone's ear, is telling Gabriel a love story that resonates with the vampire. A long time has passed since Celreau had something touch him so deeply.

'Mary must be a very special woman,' says Gabriel, patting his new drinking partner on the shoulder.

'She's the love of my life,' answers the misty-eyed business man.

'You're a very lucky man, Henry. A woman like that comes along only once in a lifetime.'

'You, too, have known such a woman, Gabriel?'

'I have, but the moment was fleeting, I'm afraid.'

'You lost your true love? How terrible!'

'There isn't a minute in the day when she isn't on my mind. I only wish I could have loved her more.'

'I'm sorry, my friend. I hope the passage of time has softened your memories of her and healed your broken heart.'

'I'd give all of my worldly belongings to be with her again.'

'Gabriel, can I confide in you?'

'Yes, of course. What is it?'

'My darling wife is very ill—a weak heart.'

'Oh, no! How serious? Will she be alright?'

'She's confined to a wheelchair and may only have a few years to live.'

'I am so sorry to hear that, Henry. There must be something that can be done. I know some talented physicians in Montreal who could take a closer look, if you like.'

'All that can be done has been done, but thank you for the offer.'

'Henry, listen. I've been very fortunate and have accumulated considerable wealth. I have the resources to pay for the best surgeons for your Mary. I'd be honored if you'd allow me to put these resources at your disposal.'

'I appreciate your offer, truly, but the doctors have determined that my poor sweet Mary was born with a bad heart. She's been fortunate to live even this long. I'm afraid no amount of money will help her failing heart now.'

'Is there anything I can do to help, Henry?'

'Well, I…no, I couldn't ask. You would not understand.'

'Go ahead, ask. What is it?'

'It's a crazy idea!'

'Please tell me. If I can help in anyway…'

'You'll think I am insane. I want to build my Mary a castle.'

'A castle?'

'Yes! But not just any old castle—a castle built for a queen. I'd build it on Davenport Hill overlooking the city. A castle like no other in the world. It would have two towers, one topped by a British rampart, the other with a French conical roof. And that's not all: a grand hall with Italian marble flooring, mahogany walls and vaulted ceilings; a magnificent library two storeys tall and stocked with all of Mary's favorite books; a conservatory lined with marble chosen to depict a cross-section of our great country and filled with a multitude of exotic plants surrounding a water fountain; a wine cellar, a secret garden and stables for the horses. Mary loves horses. The stables would be connected to the castle by a tunnel so my frail darling would not have to expose herself to the elements. I would name the castle Casa Loma.

'House on the hill. That sounds amazing, Henry.'

'You think I am crazy, don't you?'

'Not at all.'

'Seriously?'

'Listen. I'd give my entire fortune to bring my Angela back from death. Your Mary is here, alive, with you. I see nothing crazy in wanting to build her a castle and treat her like the queen she is.'

'Exactly. You really do understand!'

'Yes. More than you will ever know. So, this castle. Tell me about it.'

'Like you, I was a very ambitious man in my youth. Much of that ambition was rooted in my meeting Mary, quite by chance. I was walking through High Park on a sunny spring day, a shortcut on my way to an appointment. And there she was, so striking that I broke stride. She stood at the edge of a flower bed admiring the daffodils. And I, well, I stood admiring her for several moments. Love blossomed almost at once, and within a few months I made her my bride.

'She's my love. I know we were made for each other is an overused term, but in our case, it's true. We talked about traveling the globe together one day, visiting the Seven Wonders of the World. Making dreams like those come true is not cheap. I devoted the next years of my life, working day and night, to amassing as much wealth as possible.

'To my good fortune, with the advent of affordable electricity, city council made a commitment to light the streets of Toronto. I took a gamble and invested all of my savings in a dam to generate electricity.'

'Risky, but it turns out you made a wise choice,' interjects Gabriel. 'Lampposts line the streets of the city, making it a much safer place at night. And you are now, I presume, a successful businessman.'

'If the definition of success is the accumulation of wealth, I guess I achieved my goal. But somewhere along the way, unfortunately, making money distracted me. I lost sight of what was truly important to me. My Mary. I almost lost her; those long lonely nights that I spent working late began to tear us apart. If not for our deep love for each other and Mary's eternal patience, I don't think our marriage would have survived.'

'Your wife sounds like an amazing woman, Henry. Surely the voyage around the world was fair compensation for all those empty hours and hard times in the past.'

'We never left Toronto. Mary fell ill just about the time I decided I could afford to take her on her trip. Our dreams of travel ended.'

'Oh, that's terrible, but she regained her health, obviously, and you are still together. So you can, once again, begin to look to the future.'

'Not entirely. Her health has improved to some extent, but she 'll always be frail and suffer a weak constitution. Worse, though, her spirit's been beaten down. She's eternally depressed. This beautiful woman, once so alive, has lost all vitality. No will to live.'

'So this is why you want to build Casa Loma. How wonderful!'

'Yes! Her biggest wish was to visit the beautiful castles of Edinburgh in Scotland. Well, I want to make her wish come true. I'll build her a castle, a castle like no other in the world.'

'So. When do we start building?'

'You'll help me fund the project?'

'Absolutely. I have, however, one small condition.'

'Name it. Anything.'

'You grant me secret quarters in the stables and a promise that you'll never reveal its existence to anyone. Not even Mary.'

'The stables! Why would you want to live in the stables, man? Are you in some sort of trouble, a fugitive from the law? Is there something I should be worried about?'

'Sorry, Henry. Nothing that exciting. I suffer from Cutaneous Porphyria, a rare and incurable skin disorder. I was diagnosed as a child. When exposed to the sun, I develop burning blisters, my skin swells, and I am stricken with severe cramping. Too much exposure over time can lead to paralysis, and sometimes, psychosis. The stables would offer me the a perfect environment insulated from the sun.

'I'm so sorry. I can't imagine having to live like that. But why all the secrecy?'

'Please indulge me, Henry. Please don't ask me to explain more than to say that the condition is truly rare. Everywhere I go, once the medical establishment learns of my condition, I'm hounded incessantly by researchers. This's one of the reasons I seldom stay very long in one place.'

'So be it. The secret room is yours as long as you need it, my friend. Let's toast—to the loves of our lives,' shouts Henry, raising his glass.

'To Casa Loma,' replies Gabriel.

Long before construction of Henry's castle is complete nearly three years later, Gabriel is ensconced in his new hideaway. His room under the castle, off a secret underground corridor leading to the stables, is one of the first sections completed. Curious workers are told the room is to be a large root cellar where fresh vegetables, as well as fruits, relishes and vegetables canned by the kitchen staff, will be stored over the long Canadian winter. That Mary is an avid gardener is well known. She has five acres of gardens, much of it devoted to her love of flowers, but she also grows a variety of vegetables. So, a root cellar is the perfect disguise.

The space ultimately serving as root cellar, however, is somewhat smaller than the original design. After the workmen have moved on, Gabriel and Henry themselves work on the sly to erect a wall, dividing the room in two. Gabriel's requested sanctuary is small and dark, exactly as requested. They go to great pains to ensure the door into his room is unobtrusive. Indeed, only someone who knows its exact location could find the entrance, and even then, only with some difficulty. Upon completion of the castle, the two friends are the only people who know of the room's existence.

Lady Pellatt

1923

In addition to tending her garden, Mary enjoys sharing its lovely surroundings. She is quite involved with the Girl Guides of Canada and regularly invites groups of Girl Guides to visit, tour her new home and the gardens, then take tea and sweets.

'Tea is served,' calls Lady Pellatt to the group of Guides assembled in the courtyard. The girls, giggling and chatting, make their way into the Palm Room and take their seats.

'I hope you enjoyed the garden tour this morning. After tea, we will visit the stables, the conservatories and, finally, you will all have a chance to climb the circular staircase to the top turret. Does anybody have any questions so far?'

'Will we see any ghosts?' calls out a voice from the back of the group.

A group gasp fills the room.

'Who asked that question, please?'

'I did,' answers a young redhead, raising her hand.

'What is your name, dear?'

'Margaret. Margaret O'Leary, Ma'am.'

'What an odd question, Margaret.'

'Everyone says that a ghost wanders around Casa Loma. Our neighbor, Mrs. Brown, told my mom that her cousin, Jake, was a carpenter here for over a year. He told her that he saw the ghost with his own eyes. He spotted the ghost one evening walking into the library. Jake went into the room after it, but the ghost was gone— disappeared into thin air.'

'That is complete nonsense, Margaret. You shouldn't listen to such silly stories.'

'Jake's right!' says a strong booming voice from the back of the tea room.'

The children shriek, startled by Mr. Pellatt standing behind them.

'I knew it!' says Margaret.

'Henry, you're not implying that we have ghosts in the library, are you?'

'No, of course not, dear. It was me that Jake saw entering the library.'

'But Jake looked in the library and nobody was there?' explains Margaret.

'I have a hidden compartment in one of the bookcases. I occasionally like to have a little fun, especially with people as superstitious as Jake.'

'There you have it, Miss O'Leary. No ghosts! Just my dear husband, Henry the trickster,' says Lady Pellatt.

'Oh, but we do have ghosts,' exclaims her husband.

'We do?' asks Lady Pellatt.

'Yes, of course. I keep them locked up under the castle by the stables!' says Henry with an evil grin.

'Henry!' Lady Pellatt's voice is quite stern.

'Have a nice afternoon, ladies. Enjoy the rest of the tour.' Henry exits the Palm Room laughing loudly.

The girls finish their tea and leave the Palm Room for the stables. Dark, ominous clouds are rolling in from the southwest accompanied by the rumble of thunder overhead.

'Helen, please take the girls out to the stables before it begins to rain,' directs Lady Pellatt to her staff member. Assisted by Mr. Pym, the stable hand, Helen rushes the group of excited girls to the side entry of the castle and down a ramp leading to the horses.

'Whoa! What a smell! That you, Margaret?' jokes one of the girls.

'Yeah, I'm wearing your mom's perfume,' answers Margaret.

'Ha. Well, maybe it'll protect you from the big bad ghosts, scaredy cat.'

'We don't need protection with you around. You're so ugly that you will scare all the ghosts away.'

'Margaret O'Leary! That is quite enough. Stop this ghost nonsense at once. You're scaring the younger girls. This is no way for a Girl Guide to behave,' scolds Lady Pellatt.

'She started it.'

'Perhaps she did, young lady, but I am ending it. Do you understand?'

'Yes, Ma'am.'

The girls enter the stables, and as a group, begin to walk along a row of stalls to look at the horses. When they reach the third stall, a big black mare extends her neck as far as she can and lowers her head, obviously inviting the girls to pet her.

'Oh, isn't this big black one friendly! What's his name?' asked Lisa, one of the older girls.

'That he is actually a she, my dear. That is my Duchess. And yes, she is easily our friendliest horse. She just craves attention. Go ahead and pet her. She especially loves being rubbed behind her ears.'

A flash of lightning briefly brightens the passageway; a few seconds later, a colossally loud clap of thunder shatters the air. Frightened, the horse in the stall next to Duchess rears up and slams its body hard against the wall of its stall. The girls shriek; a few immediately burst into tears.

'Oh, brother!' scoffs Margaret, only partially under her breath.

'Calm down, ladies. It's only a small storm. There is nothing to be afraid of. We are safe here. Casa Loma is equipped with the latest protection against lightning strike. And we all know thunder cannot hurt us,' assures Lady Pellatt.

The lights flicker, casting shadows along the stable walls.

'Oh my God! I want to go home! The ghost's here,' gasps one of the younger girls. 'I want to go home!'

The solid wood stable door, caught by the swirling squall outside, swings shut with a thunderous bang. Again the girls scream, most of them cowering together. Margaret is the exception. She rolls her eyes in disbelief and disgust at her companions. Inquisitive rather than frightened, she decides to do a little exploring while Lady Pellatt is distracted. She remembers that the stable was supposed to be connected to the main house by an underground tunnel. She quietly slips down the row of stalls to another section of the stables to see if she can find it.

'Alright, young ladies. I have had quite enough of this foolishness. I am so disappointed by your conduct today. You have been acting quite unlike the ladies you are supposed to be becoming. I regret that I must end the tour now.

'My goodness! You are Girl Guides, and you will behave like Girl Guides. Get hold of yourselves and follow Mr. Pym to the bus waiting at the front door of the main house.'

The girls, led by Pym, make their way back up the ramp and out the door, Helen pushing Lady Pellatt in her wheelchair.

'Ma'am! Margaret is missing,' exclaims Mr. Pym, as Lady Pellatt emerges through the stable doorway.

'Are you certain?'

'Yes. I did a head count twice. She must have wandered off.'

'That little brat. I am going to have a stern chat with that young lady.'

'Shall I go find her?' asks the stable hand.

'No. She can't have gone far and undoubtedly will be back momentarily. I'll wait for her. You help get these kids out of the rain into the bus before we lose another one.'

'Yes, Ma'am.'

The children, led by Mr. Pym, head back to the bus in the driving rain, with Helen bringing up the rear. Mary turns her wheelchair away from the door and wheels herself back into the stables. She is more than a little vexed with Margaret. Sure, these girls are young, but not so young they cannot follow a few simple rules. Learning that sense of responsibility is, after all, a big part of what they are learning at Girl Guides. They have all been told explicitly to stay with the group, to go nowhere without permission.

Now this contrary girl has gone exploring alone without the knowledge of an adult. Lady Pellatt is contemplating a suitable punishment when she hears a scream. Spinning her wheelchair towards the sound, she realizes it's coming from the tunnel leading to the house. She hurries to investigate.

Dawn
1980

Dawn opens her eyes and stares up through the darkness at the tiles of her bedroom ceiling. She frowns. Despite the total absence of light, her eyes focus clearly on the tiny star-shaped design on the tiles—a pattern she usually can barely see during daylight hours. She feels strange.

Uneasy and confused, she closes her eyes and searches her thoughts for memories of last night. Abruptly her mind is overrun by lustful images blended with flashes of violence, arousing odd feelings of excitement and passion. She shakes her head in an attempt to clear her senses of these erotic thoughts.

She moves on the bed and a sharp pain, like the slash of a hot razor, slices across her right forearm. Reflexively she jerks her arm tight across her abdomen, and digging her heels deep into the mattress, she recoils against the headboard. Cradling her wounded arm in her left hand, she glances around her in search of the source of the pain. A thin slice of sunlight is peeking through a slit in the blinds, cutting at an angle across her bed. She jumps out of bed, crosses to the window and closes the blind tightly, snuffing the beam.

Backing to the wall, she slides down to the floor and sits quietly, her arms wrapped around her legs, head resting against her knees. She is suddenly aware of a cascade of sounds: traffic, a boy bouncing a ball on the sidewalk up the street, a blender whirring in the neighbor's kitchen, her parents talking in the living room. These sounds and voices are unnaturally clear and loud, as if they were all in the bedroom with her.

Dawn covers her ears, but the aural intrusion continues unabated. Unexpectedly, her attention shifts to the musty smell of mildew and rot entering through her window. The putrid stench turns her stomach, causing her abdominal muscles to clench. Rising, she walks over to her dresser and leans forward, examining herself in the mirror. The scar on her neck is more than obvious. She rubs it as she tries to recall the evening's events. But before she can really get started…

'Dawn.'

Startled by the voice, she blurts, 'Who's there?'

'It's me, Gabriel,' says the Raven, imitating Celreau's voice perfectly.

'Where are you? I can't see you.'

'I'm at home, Dawn, communicating with you telepathically.'

'What? How? I don't understand.'

'I'm talking to you mind-to-mind.'

'I don't get it. How's this possible?'

'You're like me now. You'll soon discover the many great powers you now possess.'

'Powers? What powers?'

'Powers of the supernatural and the undead. Your new unending life as a vampire.'

'I'm a vampire? Yeah, right! Vampires aren't real. They're just in horror movies. What're you trying to pull? You think because I'm a teenager, I'm gullible?'

'I assure you, Dawn, I know you're a very bright young woman. I am a vampire and I am very real. Our encounter last night turned you into one as well. Have you noticed how your senses have become hyper-sensitive? Enhanced? Everything you see, feel, smell, taste is much more vivid, more detailed?'

'Yeah, I did! That explains the weirdness. I thought I was going nuts— or someone slipped me some hallucinogenic drug. Everything seems weird. I hear noises, see illogical, impossible details and smell disgusting things. I have a wicked headache and I feel like I'm going to hurl.'

'That's all temporary. You'll learn to control your senses and use them to your advantage. Combined with your physical strength and beauty, you'll be amazing.'

'No! I don't want to be a vampire. It's impossible. I can't be a vampire. Go away. You're not real. What's wrong with me? I'm hallucinating.'

'Sweetheart, you're fine. There's nothing wrong with you. You must try to understand. You and I will be together for eternity.'

'Together? You and me?'

'Yes. Don't you see? I love you.'

'No, I don't see. Last night you attacked me! Now you say you love me.'

'What you perceive as an attack was me consummating our relationship and initiating you into my world.'

'Your world? I don't know. This is happening too fast.'

'I understand. It's a lot to take in, but believe me. We'll have fun and be happy together.'

'Why should I trust you? Last night you tricked me so you could get into my pants and now you say you love me?'

'Don't try to play the young innocent now. You're no virgin. And you're the one who asked me at the coffee shop to let you make my dreams come true.'

'Yeah, but that doesn't give you the right to...'

'Listen, Dawn. Ever since the day you came on to me in the classroom, I can't stop thinking about you.'

'I knew it!'

'I wanted to take you into my arms and kiss you, but I couldn't take the risk of someone walking in on us. Your beauty, intelligence and strength are all I want in a woman, and none of the girls in Blood Cove can compare to you.'

'Well, I have to agree with you on that one.'

'Just think. All the girls you know will grow old, fat and wrinkled. You, on the other hand, are going to remain young and beautiful forever, sweetheart.'

'I will never get wrinkles?'

'Never. Your beauty is now eternal.'

'Wow! Now that is awesome!'

'Join me, Dawn, and together we will be lovers for eternity.'

'I love you, but I'm not sure. It's scary.'

'Don't worry; I'll teach you everything you need to know. We're a young, beautiful, powerful couple, and we'll have anything and everything we want in our eternal life together. I'll always be by your side.'

'Yes, I want that. I love you, Gabriel.'

'Wonderful! I can't wait to feel you in my arms and feel your sweet lips on mine.'

'Me, too, but I don't feel good right now.'

'You don't feel well, sweetheart, because you're weak from hunger.'

'That can't be true. I've been in bed all day and I don't feel hungry at all. Strange.'

'Your appetite will no longer be the same. You'll never again feel hunger as you did in the past. At dusk, meet me at the barracks across from Look-Out Point and we'll feast together.'

'Tonight? Why not right now?'

'You can no longer venture out in broad daylight. The sun's rays will weaken you, or worse.'

'That explains the burn on my arm. But it's already healed!'

'Wonderful isn't it?'

'Pretty freakin' awesome!'

'Darkness is now your friend, Dawn. You're my princess of the night.'

'You really love me?'

'I always have. I was just too scared to admit it. I can't wait to feel you in my arms again. Promise you'll meet me this evening.'

'I promise, but I want you now.'

Dawn carefully peeks out between the blinds.

'Can you see outside? It's overcast now. Can't I come right now?'

'Not wise, Dawn. You are weak. You might not make it.'

'Please? I'll wear my hoodie and sunglasses. I'll be okay. Really, I feel okay…please?'

'Alright. Come on up, but keep covered and stick to the shade of the pine trees along the road.'

'I'll be right there.'

'Wonderful. See you in a bit, then. Love you, Dawn.'

'Love you, too.'

Balancing on the clothes line in Dawn's backyard, the Raven caws, puffs his feathers in satisfaction and, in one motion, swoops across the Brady's yard and over the fence towards Look-Out Point.

Celreau

1923

Gabriel thinks to himself: They've left, finally! I can get out of here. I really must find a way to stop Lady Pellatt bringing visitors down here. I'll need to have a chat with Henry about these damned tours.

Opening the hidden door to the root cellar, he freezes face-to-face with Margaret. What is she doing here?

Startled by the stranger coming out of a door that hadn't existed a moment ago, Margaret reacts as most young girls would—she screams. The sound is deafening.

'Quiet! Shut up, damn you,' orders Gabriel.

Margaret bolts from the root cellar, down the corridor toward the stables, screaming near-continuously. Gabriel tries to give chase, but stumbles over an apple crate and tumbles to the cellar floor. Regaining his footing quickly, he overtakes the frightened girl just as she reaches the entrance to the stables. He covers her mouth to stifle her screams, hoping they had not attracted attention.

'Be quiet! I don't want to hurt you.'

Desperate to escape, Margaret punches and kicks her captor,

struggling to free herself. A shoe, lost during one of her badly aimed kicks, lands in a mound of hay by the nearest horse stall.

Gabriel swears under his breath as he catches sight of Lady Pellatt making her way through the dimly lit stables toward them. Damn! She didn't leave with the girls! He needed to hide before the Lady saw him holding the struggling Guide.

Instinctively, he drags the girl to the darkest corner of the empty horse stall. Margaret, still flailing, manages to get a solid bite on Gabriel's hand. The vampire grunts from the sharp pain and swears at Margaret. She manages a last yelp as he wrenches her head in anger, snapping the youngster's neck. Margaret goes limp in his arms.

'Margaret, quit your nonsense and come out here at once,' demands Lady Pellatt.

Gabriel looks down at the dead child. Waves of grief and guilt overwhelm him.

'Why didn't you listen? Look what you made me do,' he whispers to the corpse. To himself he adds, She didn't make me do anything. I've sunken to killing a poor, innocent, defenseless child. Nothing but a wild animal—a beast—is what I am. I can't take this anymore. He begins to weep softly.

'Miss O'Leary,' calls Lady Pellatt. 'Are you in distress? If not, please stop acting up immediately. The rest of the girls are on the bus, waiting. Please come out this instant.'

Moving her wheelchair along the row of stalls, she looks into each as she passes in search of the delinquent child.

'I know you're in one of these stalls, Margaret. You are really trying my patience, young lady. You leave me no alternative but to have a word with your mother about your behavior.'

Hiding in the dark holding the warm limp body, a different urge is becoming kindled in the breast of Gabriel. Again he whispers to the corpse in his arms. 'You're so beautiful and sweet. Thick flowing red hair. Your young alabaster skin with its dusting of freckles, so soft, so tender in my hands. Your long supple neck, so inviting. You are so frail, so delicious, so enticing. I want, I need...'

Lady Pellatt gasps at the sight of Margaret's shoe on the mound of hay next to the last stall. She maneuvers her chair into the opening of the stall and leans forward, peering into the darkness.

'Margaret, I can see you hiding there. Come along, dear. The game is over. Let's join the others before the storm gets worst.'

As if to punctuate her words, a flash of lightning illuminates the stables. Briefly, the vampire is exposed, hunched over Margaret's limp body. He turns his bloody face to Lady Pellatt and snarls, his long canines dripping blood. Mouth and eyes wide open, the good Lady is horror-stricken by the sight of the terrifying creature ravaging the young girl.

'Lady Pellatt, did you find the girl?' shouts Pym, approaching from the side entrance with Helen. 'We're all aboard the bus and ready to roll.'

At the sound of the approaching voice, the vampire drops Margaret in a heap and sprints from the horse stall, knocking the Lady's wheelchair over in the process. He runs down the corridor towards his hideout. Pym, behind him, sees only his fleeing back.

Pym's first impulse is to chase the receding form, but he is distracted by the sight of Lady Mary lying in the entrance to the last stall.

'Oh my God! You okay, mum?' asks Pym as he kneels on the stable floor next to his mistress. She stares up at him with a look of horror on her face. She mumbles incomprehensibly, pointing to Margaret's body at the rear of the stall. The left side of her face sags, then she passes out.

'She's having a stroke!' exclaims Helen.

'What's she pointing at?' asks Pym, getting up and walking into the stall. 'Jesus Christ!'

'What is it? Is it Margaret?'

'Stay with Lady Pellatt.'

'Is Margaret okay?'

'No! She's dead.'

'Dead! Oh my God,' cries Helen, sobbing.

'Stay with Lady Pellatt. She's in shock. Keep her warm, do you hear me?'

'Yes, I understand. Go. go!'

Mr. Pym runs down the corridor in pursuit of the murderer.

Having reached the root cellar, Gabriel curses at the sight of the overturned crate. Concerned about leaving a clue to the existence of his lair, he hurriedly stoops to begin picking up all the apples, which are scattered across the floor and the cellar entrance. But he abandons the idea when he hears the sound of running footsteps approaching.

'Shit!' He steps back into the underground corridor and sprints to the wine cellar, carefully turning his face away from his pursuer.

'Stop and identify yourself, man,' shouts Mr. Pym, passing the root cellar in hot pursuit.

Entering the wine cellar, Gabriel hurries to the back of the room, where he opens a sliding mahogany panel behind the last wine rack, revealing a narrow staircase known only to him and Henry. He closes the hidden door carefully and climbs the steep stairs to Henry's Study on the main floor.

Pym arrives at the wine cellar's open door. He enters and quickly checks between the several rows of racks. The room is empty. Exiting the room, he sprints up the main staircase next to the wine cellar to the main floor. Cautiously, he begins his search for the intruder in the Oak Room. Finding it empty as well, he moves along the teakwood hallway searching the Great Hall, the Library, the Dining Room and the Conservatory in turn.

Gabriel peeks through the crack in the slightly open door to the Study Room and watches Pym enter the Conservatory. While Pym is busy searching among the countless beds of flowers and plants in Lady Pellatt's Conservatory, Gabriel sneaks into the hallway and up the main stairs.

Relentless in his search for the fiend who attacked his beloved mistress, Pym leaves the Conservatory, headed toward the Service Room and Sir Pellatt's private study. A terrified scream from above brings him running out of the study and up the stairs. A crash and a loud moan from below bring him to a halt momentarily just short of the second floor landing. On the landing, a young servant girl stands at the railing, her hand over her mouth, crying hysterically. She is starring and pointing down at the Great Hall below.

'Ellie, what is it? What happened?' questions Pym.

Before Ellie can answer, Pym looks over the railing and down to find Sir Pellatt's butler, John, skewered on the spear of a decorative suit of armor that stands along the wall below the staircase. The butler's still-writhing upper torso and legs hang on opposite sides of the bloody iron spear that protrudes from his midsection.

Mounting the remaining three steps to the landing, Pym takes Ellie by the shoulders and turns her towards him.

'Ellie, where did the man go?'

Again, she begins to sob uncontrollably.

'Ellie! Snap out of it, damn it!' shouts Pym. 'Where did the stranger go?'

Ellie, still mortified, manages to point up the stairs.

'Okay, good. You did good, Ellie. Stay here. I'll be back.'

The moment he releases his grasp on her, Ellie collapses to the floor in a faint.

Pym has no time to attend to the servant. He looks along the hallway for a weapon and chooses a solid bronze staff from the entrance wall to the Windsor Room. Adrenaline pumping through his veins, he runs up the last flight of stairs to the top floor of the castle. He stands shaking on the upper landing, breathing heavily, his pulse racing. He knows he has the intruder cornered; there is no way out but past him back down the stairwell. Trying to compose himself, he wipes at the sweat running down his brow.

A strange thumping sound is coming from down the hallway that leads from the stairwell. Pym takes a deep breath and slowly inches his head around the corner to inspect the situation. The hall is clear except for what looks to be a torso lying halfway out of the elevator. He cautiously approaches the body, his arm raised high, holding the staff above his head, ready to strike.

Pym feels his gorge rise at the gruesome sight before him. His assistant, Charles, is lying on his back, half in the elevator, pinned across his belly between the elevator ceiling and the hall floor. The elevator, trying to continue on its way, jolts down on Charles, then kicks back up a few inches before crushing down again. The man's bulging eyes look up at Pym in desperation, blood spurting out from his mouth with every blow.

'Help me!' mutters Charles through his spittle and blood.

'Jesus Christ!' exclaims Pym, dropping the metal staff and desperately pushing on the elevator 'up' button.

A servant runs out from one of the adjacent rooms and begins to scream at the ghastly scene.

'Shut up! Get hold of yourself. Go get help. Hurry!' Turning back to the elevator, Pym urges, 'Go up! Up, up damn you!' while slapping repeatedly at the button.

The elevator lurches upward, releasing its hold on Charles. It stops in the fully open position with a loud ring. Kneeling next to Charles' bloody body, Pym tries to assess his condition.

'Charlie, listen to me. You're going to be okay.'

Charles, staring into Pym's eyes, shakes his head in submission.

'Charlie, don't you give up on me. Damn you, Charlie hang on. Help is on the way. Do you hear me? Charlie?'

Charles forces a grin, closes his eyes and releases his last breath.

'God damn it!'

Pym feels a cool draft from the tower room at the end of the hall. Enraged and hell-bent for revenge, he picks up his staff and storms carelessly down the corridor into the tower. He looks around the room, ready to clobber the assassin. He swears in disbelief at the empty room. Rushing to the open window, he is just in time to see the murderer in the distance, escaping through the garden.

Matt & Jesse
1980

'Extra butter, Jess?'

'Absolutely. You need to ask?' As she stuffs a handful of popcorn in her mouth, Jesse mumbles, 'Let's hurry and get some mini donuts before our show starts.'

'Sounds like a plan,' mumbles Matt, imitating Jesse and laughing. 'The Lumberjack Fair gets better every year. We gotta try the Twister after. It's an awesome new ride.'

'Yeah, I hear it whips you around pretty good. But just wait. Disneyland, man! We'll be able to go as often as we want,' says Jesse excitedly. 'Space Mountain, Pirates of the Caribbean…'

'Haunted Mansion!' they shout in unison.

'Do you think we'll ever actually get to L.A.?' asks Jesse, changing the mood.

'What're you talking about? Course we will. We've been planning it forever. We got a gig here today, don't we?'

'Yeah, but this is Blood Cove. I mean, do you really think we're talented enough to get paying gigs in California? I know you got talent, but my vocals are just, well, so-so.'

'Don't be ridiculous. You have a wonderful voice and your original compositions are awesome. Together we can really rock it. L.A. producers will be knocking down our door to offer us recording contracts. You'll see.'

'Thanks, Matt. Sometimes I just need to be reminded, you know?'

A loud Ladies and Gentlemen reverberates from the overhead speakers.

'Just a reminder for those of you who are interested in Mrs. Graham's famous butter tarts: better get over to her booth 'cause they are going like the truly sinful treat they are. And now, I am delighted to introduce to the Lumberjack stage this afternoon, two of Blood Cove's wonderful young talents. Please help me give a warm welcome to the our own Arrowhead.'

'Shit! They're introducing us early. We'll have to take a rain check on the mini donuts. We're on!'

Matt and Jesse run through the crowd and up the steps to the back of the main stage. Jesse nervously adjusts her blouse and combs her fingers through her long black hair. Lifting his Martin guitar out of its vinyl case, Matt slides the strap over his head. He flashes Jesse a smile. Hand in hand they walk up to the mic at the front of the stage, greeted by a few cheers and half-hearted applause.

'My name is Matt and this is Jesse. We are Arrowhead. We'd like to perform for you an original composition by Jesse entitled Bound by Blood. We hope you enjoy it.'

An hour later, more than satisfied with the response of the audience, the pair talk to the handful of people waiting to congratulate them, then go in search of mini donuts.

'Look at this crowd. The mayor must be happy with the turn-out,' says Jesse.

'Yeah. And I have to say he sure did a good job of keeping Donni's disappearance hushed up and out of the paper.'

'He never would have gotten away with it if Donni were white,' points out Jesse.

'I think you're right. If it weren't for Kirkpatrick, I don't think they would've bothered with a search party at all for a Métis.'

'I hate both that slime ball mayor and his slutty daughter. They almost had André locked up for rape.'

'Thank God Christine told Brady what really happened with André. I don't think Dawn's innocent little girl act will work as well anymore,' says Jesse.

'Anyway, she's quite the prize, huh?' asks Matt.

'Yeah. A real piece of work.'

'André could never have defended himself? He can barely speak,' Matt adds, sadness and pity in his tone.

'He doesn't say much, but he's as strong as an ox. What I wouldn't give to see André kick Brady's fat, arrogant ass,' Jesse says with passion.

'Unfortunately, André wouldn't hurt a fly, would he?'

'Probably not, but André could have a breaking point, like anyone else. And when push comes to shove, he'll defend himself or anyone else he feels needs help.'

'Hey, wait. Looks like the ax-throwing demonstration's starting soon. André and the others are warming up. Let's go say hi,' suggests Matt.

André and a few other woodsmen are getting set for the lumberjack ax-throwing demonstration on the main stage. Matt and Jesse slip into the crowd that has gathered to watch. By the time they get close, André is already in the competition ring getting ready for his first throw. He stands tall and confident, his full attention focused on a large slice of cedar log standing on end thirty feet away. The muscular Métis takes careful aim at the colorful rings painted on the flat surface of the log. He swings the big double-bladed ax back over his head, and in one fluid motion, thrusts his powerful right arm forward, catapulting the ax through the air to pierce the target deeply in the bull's-eye. The crowd gasps, then cheers at the perfect strike. André smiles and walks proudly over to the target to retrieve his ax.

'Woohoo! Great throw,' yells Jessie, jumping and flailing her arms. André spots the two youngsters in the crowd and waves with a sheepish grin.

'Hey, Jess, look. Celreau's here.'

'Where?'

'Over there, on the sidelines near the target.'

'Mr. Celreau. Hello, over here. Hello,' yells Jesse.

'No use, Jess. He can't hear you over all the noise.'

While they have been trying to get the teacher's attention, André has returned to the competitor's ring and is set for another throw. The crowd goes silent as he slowly raises the ax over his head. André is a statue, unmoving and completely focused on his target. Faster than the eye can follow, his ax arm arcs forward. Mid-swing, a huge raven appears seemingly out of nowhere, its wings beating furiously inches from André's face. André flinches away from the bird as he looses the ax. The misguided weapon ricochets off the edge of the cedar log and into the crowd.

The horrified crowd has no time to react as the ax hurtles recklessly toward them. The wooden handle and its sharp double blades whoosh and whistle, the ax spinning end over end—directly at Celreau. Bystanders gape, stunned to see Celreau standing poised and calm, the ax handle grasped tightly in his hand, its sharp blade only inches from his nose.

The crowd watches in shock as Celreau coolly walks over to André and hands him the ax.

'Best to be a bit more careful, big fellow. Next time, someone could lose an eye—or worse.'

'Y-y-yes, s-sir,' stutters André, clearly baffled. He's never made such an error. Celreau winks at André, turns and disappears into the crowd.

'Holy crap!' Matt exclaims. 'You saw that, right? There's no way he...'

'You bet I did! No human could have the reflexes and speed to catch that ax in mid-air,' answers Jesse. 'But a vampire could. This explains him being able to deal with that wolf yesterday on his porch. All that baloney about hormones Celreau tried to hand us.'

'I knew his arm wound was worse than he let on. That wolf bit straight through his jacket into his arm. Not a scratch!' adds Matt. 'And the Raven just now—it had to be Ne-Kilst-lass. He was trying to kill the vampire.'

'Exactly! We've got to find out everything we can about Celreau. He isn't human, so where did he come from? Do you remember where it was he claims he taught before coming to Blood Cove?'

'I heard the school principal brag that he was an honors student then part of the teaching staff at some snooty university in Toronto,' says Matt.

'Must be on the run. Why else would anybody with those credentials move out to the boonies to teach?' wonders Jesse.

'We should check his school records,' suggests Matt.

'School's closed till Monday. And anyway, there ain't a chance in hell the principal will share Celreau's private info with us,' replies Jesse.

'Shit! You're prob'ly right. Wait a minute. I know.'

'What? What?'

'We could check out old yearbooks from the last school he taught at. Maybe we can get some clues about Celreau and where he was before teaching there.'

'Sounds like a plan, but where can we get old school yearbooks?' asks Jesse.

'The library!' They both say at the same time.

'Jinx—you owe me a coke,' says Jesse, laughing.

Henry & Celreau

1923

'Come in. Come in,' says Henry from the comfort of the leather chair in his favorite room in the house—his study. A house servant ushers the uniformed officer into the room, then closes the door as he leaves.

'How may I help you, officer?' asks Henry, getting up from his chair.

'Inspector Tremblay. Yvon Tremblay, from the RCMP Crime Investigation Division.' The officer reaches across the desk to shake Henry's offered hand. 'Nice to meet you. Have a seat, Inspector.' Henry motions to the chair.

'Thank you.'

'Cigar?' offers Henry.

'No, thank you. I don't smoke.'

'Whiskey?'

'Sorry—on duty.'

'Well, if I can't offer you anything, how may I help you, Inspector Tremblay?'

'Well, to be accurate, you did offer and I declined.'

'True. So again, how can I help you?

'Just a few questions for my investigation into the young girl's death, sir.'

'Call me Henry, please. I already gave the city police my statement several hours ago. Why is the RCMP becoming involved, and somewhat after the fact?'

'We are following up on similar homicides that have occurred in the greater metro area in the last couple of years.'

'Similar? You mean other children have been murdered?' Henry is incredulous.

'No, it's not the age of the victim that interests us. Rather, the condition of her body when found has striking similarities to others who have met a violent end recently.'

'The victims were all strangled?'

'Margaret did not die of asphyxiation. Her neck was broken.'

'So, you're telling me that all the victims died of a broken neck?'

'No. Not all of them.'

'Exactly what are you telling me, Inspector? I'm not a very patient man, particularly at this moment. What's the connection between Margaret's death and the other murders?'

'The coroner's report stated that Margaret's body had no blood in her system.'

'Well, obviously she must have been stabbed, then?'

'There were no knife wounds on her body. Only two small, almost circular, punctures on her neck.'

'You're not implying that she was killed by some sort of vampire? Are you?'

'That, sir, is precisely what I am implying.'

'Preposterous. Vampires are but characters of fiction and legends, invented to titillate and to keep children in line. You can't be serious, Inspector.'

'Sadly, I most certainly can, and am. Deadly serious. Over four hundred murders in the last two years—children, students, homeless, prostitutes—all found dead with fang marks on their necks and void of blood.'

'My God! No wonder Mary's in such a state. God only knows what she saw that afternoon.'

'Mr. Pellatt, have you been in contact with anybody in the last year or last few months that may have had a strange disposition or odd habits?'

'I'm a business man, Inspector. I meet interesting characters most every other day. Can you be a bit more specific?'

'This vampire is highly intelligent, probably well educated, possibly wealthy and unusually strong. The suspect could appear very pale and sluggish one day, yet alert and energetic the next. He would conduct most of his affairs in the evening and rarely be seen during the day.'

'Interesting characteristics, but no, I can't say that anybody comes to mind.'

'Vampires are very real Mr. Pellatt. They're dangerous, cunning creatures. I advise you to be careful who you associate with. Aside from those few characteristics I just mentioned, there's little that distinguishes these undead from normal human beings.'

'I appreciate the advice, Inspector. I assure you, I will be vigilant. I must say that, despite my respect for your rank, I have difficulty believing the veracity of vampires.'

'Well, here's my card. Call that number anytime should anything come to mind. Anything at all. Give me a call.'

'I will.'

'Goodnight,' says the inspector leaving the office and closing the door behind him.

Pellatt reaches for the crystal decanter on his desk and pours himself a shot of whiskey.

'Do come in, Gabriel.'

Gabriel slides the secret mahogany wall panel further open and enters the room.

'Good evening, Henry.'

'You make a habit of listening in on my private conversations?'

'I just now came up to speak to you. Was somebody here?'

'Indeed. An RCMP inspector was interviewing me in regards to the murder last night. What do you want Gabriel?'

'Yes, well, I heard about that terrible tragedy and wanted to know how Lady Pellatt was recovering.'

'The mental/emotional trauma is immeasurable. As a result, she had a stroke that paralyzed the right side of her body. She's resting comfortably at Toronto General Hospital, under the best medical care available.'

'She's fortunate to have you to care for her, Henry. You're a wonderful husband. Did she give the police a description of the intruder?'

''fraid not. Unfortunately, because of her paralysis, she can neither write nor speak.'

'My God! That's terrible. I just wish I could have been here to help.'

'Indeed. Where were you last night, Gabriel?'

'I was studying late at the university and didn't get back till after the storm ended. I saw the ambulance leave. I used the secret entry to the stable, as usual, and stayed out of sight while the police were questioning the staff. I overheard all the details.'

'You have someone who can confirm your alibi?'

'Henry, are you questioning my honesty? Why would I need an alibi? D'you suspect that I had something to do with this? Really? Is this what our relationship has deteriorated to? After all I've done for you and Mary? How could you even entertain the idea that I could be involved?'

'You keep very strange hours, my friend.'

'What? Strange hours? What do you mean?'

'I mean, you're always out and about at night, every night, but I've never seen you during the day.'

'I told you, I take night courses at the university, Henry, and with my skin disorder, you know I can't risk exposure to the sun.'

'And another thing. In twenty-three years, I don't recall ever seeing you actually eat anything. It's the strangest thing.'

'Eat? Of course I eat, Henry. I eat every day in town. What's this nonsense all about? If you have an accusation, make it!'

'You showed up out of nowhere and offered me, a stranger, a small fortune in exchange for a hidden room in my fruit cellar. Now, don't you think that's a bit odd? Tell me—who are you hiding from?'

'Yes, Henry, that was our agreement and no questions asked, remember? And I have no reason to hide from anyone.'

'Damn you, Gabriel! I am aware of our agreement. A young girl has been murdered on my property, and my wife almost died. The police are asking me crazy questions about vampires, and, in the meantime, I am harboring you in my castle. I really don't know what to think anymore!'

'Vampires? What? Are they crazy?'

'That's what I thought, but what do I know?'

'Listen, Henry. I am your friend, and I have never given you any reason to believe otherwise.'

'I suppose, but you must understand. I have some very difficult decisions to make.'

'Decisions? What are you trying to say?'

'I'm sorry, but in view of the circumstances, I have no choice but to increase security around the castle. Gabriel, I'm afraid you will have to find a new residence elsewhere.'

'But we have an agreement! I funded the construction of the castle in exchange for my secret room! A deal is a deal, Henry!'

'Inevitably the guards will spot your presence and sound the alarm. The police'll be notified, and when a search ensues and your secret room is located—or worst, you get captured—I could be arrested for harboring a fugitive. My involvement with you could even implicate me in the Girl Guide's murder. The nature of our arrangement would be disclosed, and my integrity as a reputable businessman in Toronto destroyed.'

'Henry, you know I'm innocent. As your friend and partner, I beg you to reconsider your decision. This is complete nonsense. I would never think of hurting your beautiful wife.'

'Understood, but what about the girl?'

'Margaret? She is, ah, was nothing but a child. I may be a lot of things, Henry, but I'm no molester.'

'Margaret? Was that her name, Gabriel?

'What? I, ah, I heard…

'How do you know the murdered child's name?'

Gabriel pauses for a second to collect himself. 'Like I said earlier, Henry, I overheard the police questioning the staff. They used her name during their questioning.'

'Hmmm. Yes, I guess you could have.'

'Listen, Henry. I completely understand your concern, but think about it. To be fair, I've been living here for almost twenty-three years now, and not once has anybody gotten even a peek at me.'

'True, you have been inconspicuous.'

'And what better security than to have me living along the underground corridor that leads directly to the heart of your residence.'

'I suppose that is advantageous and does decrease the odds of a break-in from below.'

'Absolutely, Henry. I can promise you nobody will break in on my watch.'

'Very well, but I give you fair warning: if any suspicion of your presence in the castle arises, you must leave Casa Loma for good. Understood?'

'Understood. You will not regret your decision. I'll be as invisible as a ghost.'

Celreau

1924

The car advances up the front driveway of Casa Loma and parks. Pym gets out and retrieves the wheelchair from the rear compartment of the sedan. Helen exits the rear driver's-side door, opens the rear passenger door and positions the wheelchair as close to the opening as possible. Reaching in, Pym lifts Lady Pellatt from her seat, carefully lowering her into the wheelchair. Helen tucks a shawl around the legs of her mistress.

'We're home, Lady Pellatt. After three weeks of sleeping in that awful hospital bed, won't it be delightful to sleep in your own bed again?' asks Helen, guiding the wheelchair to the front door of the castle.

Lady Pellatt forces a lop-sided grimace. Her entire face, along with the right side of her body, is afflicted with paralysis, the sad remnants of the stroke triggered by the physical and psychological trauma of the stable incident.

Henry steps out from the front passenger seat and joins his wife. He bends to kiss her on the cheek.

'Honey, this evening we will share a delicious meal as far removed from that atrocious hospital fare as possible. After supper, I thought we could relax in the conservatory and listen to the gramophone—like you love to do.'

Pym, ahead of Helen pushing the wheelchair, opens the front door to the castle. Lady Pellatt immediately begins to struggle, her left leg kicking against the restraints holding her in the chair.

'Mary, what's wrong? What is it dear?' asks Henry.

'I think she's having a seizure,' offers Helen.

Mary turns to Henry with a look of terror and begins to scream and cry.

'No, it's not a seizure. She's frightened! Pym, close the door, for God's sake!' shouts Henry. 'Honey, it's okay. I'm so sorry. I understand, of course. After your ordeal, the castle still troubles you. What was I thinking? Sweetheart, would you be more comfortable in the Carriage House?'

Mary's crying changes to a sob. She struggles to nod.

'Helen, please escort Lady Pellatt to the Carriage House and keep her comfortable. Pym, please instruct the house staff that we'll be moving to the Carriage House for the time being.'

The cool October rain trickles under Henry's collar and sends shivers through his body. He closes the car door, pulls his overcoat tightly around his neck and jogs across the wet cobblestone driveway to the front door. He flinches, startled by Gabriel stepping from the shadows at the side of the building.

'Dear God, you will be the death of me!'

'Sorry, Henry. I need to talk to you.'

'Talk to me tomorrow, man. It's late and raining cats and dogs, for Pete's sake.'

'I just need to know that Lady Pellatt is okay.'

'Her condition is improving slowly. She's able to speak a few words, but it's going to take time.'

'She can speak? Did she say anything?'

'No, no. Only the odd word, but let's go inside. I'm getting soaked by this wretched rain.'

'I don't think that's a good idea.'

'Don't worry. It's late, so Mary will be in bed, and the servants will have retired to their quarters for the night.'

'Are you sure nobody is...'

'Come in. Come in. I'm not standing out here all night.'

Gabriel follows Henry through the entrance into the foyer. Henry removes his overcoat and tosses it on a chair in the corner.

'Gabriel, you're not wearing a coat. It's freezing outside. Why didn't you use the tunnel?'

'It's too risky. I might be discovered. After the break-in, you hired all that extra security, so my movements are constrained.'

'I'm sorry, but you understand I had no choice. I'm away on business most of the time, and Mary's safety is my priority.'

'Of course. I know the guards' schedules and routines, so I am able to come and go undetected, as promised.'

'I appreciate that. Let's go to the kitchen. D'you want a tea?'

'Uh, sure, thank you,' answers Gabriel, looking around the room nervously. He sits at the kitchen table, while Henry sets the kettle on the stove to boil.

'Henry, I feel helpless. I wish I could do something for Mary.'

'I appreciate your good intentions, but you know that's out of the question. The nurse and staff are doing everything possible to keep Mary comfortable while she recovers. Adding something new to her routine could disrupt the equilibrium they have established. We must not jeopardize their progress.'

'You said she started talking. That's a good sign, right?'

'Yes. It's a sign that she's healing, regaining control of some of her affected muscles. She only says a few words, however, most of them unintelligible.'

'I'm sorry, Henry, I really am.'

'Don't be sorry. You had nothing to do with it, right?'

'I'm just upset.'

'Well, of course you're upset. We all are. We all love Mary very much.'

'Yes, I do love her dearly; she's kind and loving, not only to you and your household, but to everybody she meets. But you see, Henry, Mary is like everyone that I have come to love in my life. Everyone close to me ends up hurt or killed. I am a curse to everybody I ever loved. All of their lives destroyed, snuffed out because of me. I can't help but feel guilty for what's happened to Mary.'

'Enough! The notion that you've had some sort of hex put on you by some evil power, some witchcraft, that induces misfortune in peoples' lives is pure nonsense. I told you, I don't hold you responsible for the incident, and I don't want to discuss it any further. Now, I think our thoughts are better directed towards Mary's recovery, rather than focused on our own selfish issues.'

The high-pitched whistle of the boiling kettle interrupts the conversation. Henry prepares the tea and hands a cup to Gabriel.

'Thanks. Sorry. Of course, you're right, I'm being selfish. Mary needs our support right now,' says Gabriel.

'Wonderful. The kettle is already on,' says Helen, entering the kitchen.

'You're up late, Helen,' comments a surprised Henry.

'Mary has an upset stomach and can't sleep. She's wide awake. I'm making her a cup of Chamomile tea to settle her tummy.'

'Thank you for taking such care of my sweetheart.'

'It's my pleasure, Mister Pellatt. Who's your friend?'

'Oh, sorry, Helen. Where are my manners? This is my business partner, Gabriel. Gabriel, this is Mary's assistant, Helen.'

'Nice to meet you, Helen. I am glad Lady Pellatt is in such good hands.'

'Gabriel, come to the bedroom and meet Mary. She is wide awake and would certainly love some company.'

'Maybe some other time. It's late and I don't want to disturb her at this hour.'

'Hogwash. You heard Helen. Mary is wide awake. A visit will cheer her up. She hasn't had company for days. Perhaps this's exactly what she needs.'

'I don't know…'

'I insist.'

Gabriel follows Helen and Henry down the hallway to Lady Pellatt's bedroom. A small lamp on the bedside table dimly lights the room. Mary is sitting up in bed, leaning back comfortably against a few puffy pillows.

'Ma'am, I have your tea, and Henry's here with a friend,' announces Helen.

Henry walks up to the bed, bending to kiss Mary on the cheek.

'How are you this evening, my dear? Are you comfortable?'

Mary smiles and nods, murmuring, 'Hmm hmm.'

'You're looking better every day, sweetheart. You'll be all better very soon. Before you know it, you'll be back in Casa Loma sitting amongst the beautiful flowers in your conservatory.'

Mary frowns at Henry and shakes her head from side to side in disagreement.

'No? It's too early for the move back to the castle? Of course, you're right, sweetheart. We can stay here as long as you want. Don't you worry. I'll have Mr. Pym transfer some flowers here for you to enjoy.'

Mary relaxes, smiles at Henry and mutters what is meant to be a thank you.

'Mary, look. You have a visitor.'

Mary squints her eyes and tries to focus through the dimness at the stranger standing inside the doorway.

'This is Gabriel Celreau, dear. He's one of my business partners and a good friend. Without Gabriel's help, the construction of Casa Loma wouldn't have been possible.'

Mary leans forward for a better look.

'Gabriel, move in a little closer, so Mary can see you.'

'Please forgive me, but I really shouldn't get close. I'm fighting a cold and would hate to spread my germs to Mary,' answers Gabriel.

'Helen, turn on the ceiling light, please,' instructs Henry.

Helen flicks the main light switch on as Gabriel shouts, 'No!'

Almost simultaneously, Mary shrieks and begins trembling uncontrollably. She locks her petrified gaze on Gabriel.

'Honey? What's wrong? This is Gabriel. He is a friend,' says Henry, sitting next to Mary on the edge of the bed, his arm around her.

Mary raises her left arm and points a shaky index finger directly at Gabriel.

'Ma—Mar—Ma—Mar,' stammers Mary, struggling to keep her outstretched arm steady.

'What are you saying, Mary? I don't understand!'

'Ma—Mar—Ma—Mar,' repeats Mary, struggling to speak.

'Helen, run and get Mr. Pym. We need to get Mary to the hospital now!' orders Henry.

Helen brushes past Gabriel, runs out of the room and down the hallway.

'Henry, I'd better go. I'm obviously upsetting her.'

'Wait. Not so fast. Don't you move, Celreau.'

Henry turns to Mary and brings his face close to hers.

'Honey, look at me.'

Mary stares into Henry's eyes, obviously terrified.

'Nobody's going to hurt you. Calm down. Breathe.'

Mary shakes her head side to side and again tries to speak.

'Ma—Mar—Ma—Marg—et.'

'Margaret? Margaret who? O'Leary?' asks Henry.

Mary nods repeatedly and points again at Gabriel. Henry stands, turning to confront Gabriel.

'Why, you son of a bitch! How dare you? How dare you hurt my loved ones after all I've done for you. I suspected you were involved somehow.'

Helen, entering with Mr. Pym, runs to Mary's side to calm and comfort her.

'Henry, what's going on here?' asks Pym, a look of puzzlement creasing his face.

Gabriel delivers Pym a quick elbow to the face. The stable hand's nose snaps, a spray of blood cascading down his chest onto the surrounding carpet. Unconscious, he drops with a thud to the floor.

Gabriel has not taken his eyes off Henry.

'You just couldn't leave it alone, Pellatt. You had to screw up a good thing, didn't you?'

Helen shrieks and embraces Mary. Gabriel raises his hand slowly to his neck and wipes Pym's blood. He slides his bloody fingers into his mouth and sucks them with a revolting slurping sound.

'You're a sick fuck! You strangled an innocent little girl with no remorse and then bulldozed over Mary—the very woman you said you loved. I wouldn't call that love!'

Sliding his fingers from his mouth, Gabriel smiles.

'If you had controlled your guests as we agreed, that wouldn't have happened. Would it?'

'You're a god-damned psychopath.'

Gabriel's smile disappears and his eyes turn dark. His canines extend slowly from his gums.

'No, Henry, I'm no psychopath. I'm a vampire.'

Mary, overwhelmed by the sight of the monster before her, grasps at her chest and collapses in Helen's arms. Henry rushes to the bed, gently lifting Mary into his arms.

'Mary? Mary?' Getting no response, he touches her neck softly. 'No, don't leave me, darling. I need you. I love you,' says Henry weeping.

He rests Mary's lifeless body back on the mattress. Weeping, he crawls across the bed, past Helen. He pulls a small pistol from a holster under his vest and points it directly at Gabriel.

'You'll die for this!' shouts Henry, enraged. Gabriel walks towards the bed, calm, in no hurry.

'Always the brave one, Henry. Let's see…a commanding officer of the Queen's Own Rifles, a Knight Bachelor and a Major General. Impressive list.'

'Stop, damn you!' shouts Henry.

'Sorry, Henry, but I don't take orders, even from you.'

Henry squeezes the trigger, firing into the vampire's chest. Gabriel falls backward onto his ass with his back resting against the wall.

'Nice shot, Henry, and not at all surprising. I would expect nothing less than a bullseye from an ex-rifleman.'

Henry drops the pistol, shocked by the sight of the vampire's chest wound healing before his eyes. The vampire regains his feet and walks to the foot rail of the bed.

'How is this possible? You should be dead.'

'How I wish you were right, Henry. How I wish you were right.'

Grabbing Henry's foot, he pulls the bewildered former friend towards the end of the bed. Helen grabs Henry's hand and desperately tries to pull him away from the vampire.

'I got you, Henry, hold on,' yells Helen.

'Let go, Helen, he's too strong. Save yourself. Run, run!'

'No. I won't let you die this way.'

The vampire is dragging them both across the bed towards him, when a chair crashes down on his head from behind. He falls to the floor, momentarily disoriented. He rubs the back of his skull, cursing. Looking up, he finds Pym helping Henry and Helen off the bed.

Gabriel moves to a crouching position and pounces. His large canines dive deeply into Pym's neck. Screaming, struggling to escape, is futile. The vampire delivers several vicious punches to the servant's already bloodied face, rendering him once again unconscious. Still feeding, Gabriel drags his prey back to the door, preventing Henry and Helen from escaping. He quickly drinks the body dry, then throws what's left of Pym like a rag-doll into the hallway.

'That was a fine appetizer. I feel invigorated. Who's next?' He turns his dark soulless gaze on Helen. Sliding his long tongue out through his bloody lips, he licks the blood from his chin and advances towards her.

'No! You pig, leave me alone. Henry! Please do something,' pleads Helen.

'Let Helen go. Take me. I'm the one you want.'

'I told you, Commander. I don't take orders from you. Remember?'

The vampire grabs Helen by the collar and Henry by the throat. He raises Henry off the floor and, holding him at arm's length, begins to squeeze.

'Watch carefully, sweetheart. I want to set the mood before I pleasure myself with you. Consider it foreplay, if you will.'

'You'll never have me alive.'

'Suit yourself, sweet thing. Dead or alive, matters little to me.'

Gabriel's powerful grip tightens around his prisoner's neck. Henry's mouth, working in a vain attempt to pull in air, gapes wide with a croaking sound. His tongue lolls loosely, his eyes bulge from their sockets, and his ears begin to ooze a mixture of thick white fluid and blood.

'Let him go. Your choking him, you sick bastard!' screams Helen.

Gabriel simply grins at Helen. He brings Henry's thick neck to his mouth and sinks his teeth deep into the exposed tissue. Ripping out a large chunk of skin and muscle, he turns and spits the mess into Helen's face. Returning to the open wound, he bites deeply into the carotid artery, the flesh clamped between his lips. He stares into Helen's terrified eyes while siphoning dry her master's body.

This course of his meal completed, he releases his grip on Henry. The body hits the bedroom floor with a dull thud.

'What a delightful evening, my dear. First an appetizer, then the entrée, and now for dessert.'

'You're not having me without a fight, you loathsome brute,' says Helen.

As Gabriel reaches for her, Helen surprises him with an unexpected attack, jamming her thumbs into his eyes. He screams, releasing his hold and grasping for his eyes. Helen breaks free and runs for the door. She slips on the blood-smeared marble floor and crashes head first into the door jam. On her tummy, she lies semi-conscious in the doorway.

Gabriel manages to open his stinging eyes and walks over to the prone Helen.

'Is that any way to treat your lover, sweetheart?'

'Fuck You!' mumbles Helen.

'As you wish.'

The vampire takes down his pants and straddles Helen from behind. He pins her down with one hand on her back and rips off her skirt and underwear with the other hand. She shrieks as Gabriel forces his erect penis into her. He thrusts his cock hard and fast, tearing into her dry vagina like a wild animal mating for survival.

Realizing that, once satisfied, the vampire is going to kill her, she decides to yell for her life.

'Help me! Help me!' she screams as loud as she can.

'Shut up, you stupid wench,' commands Gabriel.

'Help me. Somebody help me!' continues Helen.

Gabriel reaches down, grabs a handful of Helen's hair and slams her face into the marble floor.

Callaway
1980

The peaceful lull of his day is suddenly broken by a blast of chatter and laughter. Callaway looks up from his Rolodex and frowns over the half-lenses that rest halfway down his nose. Two young teens have just come in. He is more than a little irritated at their lack of respect for the quiet that he nurtures in his library.

And that's how he thinks of it: his library. Melville Callaway, long retired from teaching at Blood Cove Public School, has worked at the town Public Library now for the past ten years. Known to the town folk as 'Melville the Maven,' Callaway's wealth of knowledge and wisdom have earned the old bachelor a reputation as a scholar and a source of nearly unlimited information.

Callaway's irritation quickly changes to curiosity as the children begin to search randomly through the bookshelves.

'May I help you? Looking for something in particular?' asks the librarian.

'We're looking for a book about vampires,' answers Matt.

'Hmm. That's very interesting. Well, you're not likely to find them in this area, unless your vampire is planting tomatoes or cucumbers. You see, you are searching in the applied science section, 600-699 of the Dewey Decimal cataloging system, specifically the 634 series, which is dedicated to gardening.'

'Uh, okay, interesting,' says Jesse.

'Not!' whispers Matt.

Jesse elbows Matt in the ribs.

'Where should we search, then?' inquires Jesse politely.

'This way to the social sciences, 300-399. Let's see now. If my memory serves me right, third row, bottom shelf, 398 and voilà! Myths, legends, customs and folklore of your vampire, at your disposal.'

Matt and Jesse kneel down and begin excitingly thumbing through the pages of several books. The librarian stands over the children curiously peering over their shoulders.

'Thank you so much,' says Jesse, when she notices Callaway is still present.

'No problem at all. My pleasure,' answers the librarian, showing no signs of moving away.

'Yeah, thanks a bunch, mister,' says Matt.

'You are welcome. Vampires, then?'

'Pardon me?' asks Jesse.

'Vampires? A peculiar study for a couple of kids on a school holiday.'

'Well, some people like teapots, and others're into ceramics. We just happen to like vampires,' says Matt facetiously.

'Matt,' snaps Jesse. 'Don't be a jerk!'

'What?' questions Matt, wide-eyed.

'Jerk, indeed,' says Callaway. ''Well, you are in luck. I just happen to be an aficionado on the subject of vampires, and the supernatural in general.'

'A what?'' asks Matt, his brow furrowing in puzzle.

'Aficionado. It means very knowledgeable. Somewhat of an expert, if I may be so indelicate. When I was a youngster, I saw the talented Bela

Lugosi perform in the most famous vampire movie of all time, Dracula. I was hooked on vampires from that day forth.'

'You're an actual expert on vampires?' asks Jesse.

'Indeed. I have read most everything on the subject: wooden stakes, coffins, garlic and mirrors...Go ahead. Ask me anything you like. What do you want to know?'

'Okay. How do we kill a vampire?' asks Matt.

'Quite. Straight to the chase, then. As you probably are aware, a vampire is cursed to forever hide from the sun. He will only venture out at night or during overcast days. If you can expose him to the direct sunlight for a short period, he will be severely burnt and eventually die. Trapping him in this situation is not an easy task, as he will be fast and cunning.'

'Of course! That explains the drapes and sunglasses,' exclaims Jesse.

'And picking this overcast town as his home,' adds Matt. 'No wonder we don't see him outside very often.'

'What's this then?' inquires Callaway.

'Nothing. Sorry. Please continue,' pleads Jesse.

'The classic or traditional method of killing a vampire is, of course, to drive a wooden stake through its heart. Vampires heal quickly from all other injuries, but they will not recuperate from this attack. If you are prepared and act quickly, without hesitation, you will catch him off guard and be successful. Make an error and you will certainly be the one who dies.'

'The wolf bite. His hand healed so fast. It all makes so much sense now,' says Matt excitedly. 'It's all coming together.'

'As the lethality of exposure to the sun might suggest, fire is also a wonderful weapon against a vampire,' continues the librarian seemingly unaware of the children's interruption. 'The fire has to be big and extremely hot in order to overwhelm the innate healing processes of the vampire.

'Now, you must be mindful—a vampire has incredible power and speed. Its reflexes even surpass those of a wild animal, so the chances of catching it and tying it down are slim to none. I would suggest, therefore, that you use fire in conjunction with the application of the wooden stake. The combination should render your vampire worries a thing of the past.'

'Remember the way he tossed that wolf across his front yard? That was more than just adrenaline,' says Matt.

'No doubt. And no human could catch an ax flipping through the air, either.'

'I say, to whom are you referring? If you don't mind me asking, of course?'

'Uh, oh, just a horror movie we watched, Mr. Callaway,' lies Jesse.

'Indeed. Well, they can be quite frightening, to be certain. Vampires are a nasty breed. They have been known to take their victims captive in order to fuel their appetite. The prisoners are kept locked up and maintained in a semi-healthy state, in order to provide the vampire with a dependable and accessible source of fresh blood.'

'Don't the prisoners become vampires after being bitten so many times,' asks Jesse.

'Vampires know that over-feeding will result in the infection of the victim, who then becomes a vampire, or in the death of the host, in extreme cases. I dare say, both situations mean the loss of the source of blood. Smart vampires exert some self-control and stop short of over-using the host.'

'I sure wouldn't want one breaking into my house in the middle of the night looking for a drink,' Matt says, only half joking.

'Not to worry, son. As a point of interest you should know, vampires cannot enter your premises without being invited in.'

'Holy cow! Now that puts the cherry on the cake.'

'It does?' The librarian is clearly confused.

'Just one of Matt's stupid expressions, Mr Callaway.'

'Stupid. Hmm. Indeed.'

'That explains Celreau standing out in the rain at your mom's house,' whispers Matt.

'I got it Sherlock, I got it. Now hush!' answers Jesse.

'Gabriel Celreau, I presume,' interrupts Callaway.

Jesse looks at Matt with a stern look.

'Shit, you heard that?' says Matt

'Dear boy, my life in the library revolves around whispers. Yes, I heard that.'

'You know Celreau, then?' asks Matt.

'I do. A most intriguing fellow.'

'That's putting it mildly. If you only knew,' answers Matt.

'Son, you underestimate my knowledge. I am privy to much more information than you might think.'

'Matt didn't mean any disrespect, Mr. Callaway, did you, Matt?' says Jesse. Her withering glare makes Matt wince.

'No, of course not. I meant that Mr. Celreau is a bit weird. We can't help but be curious. Actually, we're trying to find out where he was before he came to Blood Cove. Can you help us?'

'I must admit that, despite your manners, the pair of you display an inquisitiveness that I find quite entertaining. I was much the same so many years ago. As a young boy in Edinburgh, my thirst for knowledge led me to some interesting adventures, and a bit of trouble I'm afraid. Nevertheless, what doesn't kill you makes you stronger, I always say. However, I digress. Where was I, then?'

'Celreau,' points out Jesse.

'Aw, yes, Gabriel Celreau. Or should that be Count Celreau, your alleged vampire? He was a mystery to me, too, so I delved into his recent past. He arrived in Blood Cove without notice and was hired at the elementary school under curious and most inauspicious circumstances.'

'Which circumstances?' asks Matt.

'Stephen Williams, the history teacher at the time, was an intelligent young man, but very much an introvert.'

'Introvert?' asks Jesse.

'He did not socialize, kept pretty much to himself.'

'Any idea why?' asks Matt.

'Stephen was gay, and although he did not flaunt this, his effeminate mannerisms and sensibilities set him apart from the other teachers. When the community began to suspect he was homosexual, he was ostracized, treated like he had the plague. It wasn't long before the rumors began, and the gossip mill started circulating claims that Stephen had aids; many went so far as to suggest he was a pedophile.'

'That's not fair! What a bunch of bigots,' exclaims Jesse.

'People can be cruel when forced out of their comfort zone. Interestingly, Stephen had met Celreau and the two quickly became friends. They were often seen spending hours chatting at the café in town. Celreau didn't seem intimidated by Stephen. In fact, Celreau was the only person associating with him at the time.'

'That was nice of Celreau, then,' says Jesse.

'Quite. But soon a group of parents, fearing for the welfare of their children, forced the school council and the board to investigate. All of the claims were unjustified, but Stephen was understandably devastated by the inquiry.'

'What happened to him?' asks Matt.

'Vanished. Just didn't show up at school one day, leaving all of his belongings in his apartment. No one was sure where he went. Some suggested he committed suicide, but a search for his body produced no results.' Visibly changing topics, Callaway goes on, 'All that aside, the School Board was very fortunate Mr. Celreau had recently joined the teaching staff. Turns out he is qualified in many areas, and as he was already teaching French and science, he conveniently took over for Stephen as the new history teacher.'

'That was lucky!' says Matt.

'Lucky, indeed' answers Callaway, the tone of suspicion evident in his voice.

'So, do you know where he came from?' asks Matt.

'If memory serves, he graduated from the University of Toronto.'

'How can we be sure, Mr. Callaway? Do you have any of his records here at the library?' asks Jesse.

'I'm afraid not, children. His personal files would be available only at Blood Cove Elementary School.'

'But the school is closed till Monday. And even then, they would never give out that information to Jesse and I. It will be too late by then, anyway. Sheesh!'

'Jesse and me,' corrects the librarian.

'Huh?' questions Matt.

'You said Jesse and I. The proper grammar is Jesse and me,' explains Callaway.

'Right. Whatever!' grumbles Matt.

'Matt! Stop being rude. Mr. Callaway's trying his best to help us. He can't have all the answers.'

'I do enjoy a jolly good challenge, and besides, there are more ways of killing a cat than by choking it with cream. Let me think for a moment.'

'C'mon, Jesse, lets go. The old man is off his rocker,' whispers Matt.

'Give him a chance. When was the last time we had an adult take us the least bit seriously?' whispers Jesse.

'Dewey Decimal, grammar, choking cats, what next?' mumbles Matt under his breath.

'Eureka!' shouts Callaway, startling the children. 'Dan Hathaway, my old mate from Glasgow. He is now a professor of Literature at the University of Toronto. He can check Celreau's records for us.'

'Mr. Callaway, you're a genius,' enthuses Jesse.

'Genius? Thank you, young lady, but I wouldn't go to that extent,' says Callaway, blushing.

'Indeed,' whispers Matt.

'Let me ring him at once and see if he can help us solve our mystery,' suggests Callaway. He turns and strides to his office situated behind the main service counter. Matt leans toward his friend.

'We need to get Donni's letter over to the cop station now!'

'Just a few more minutes. We have to wait until Callaway gets off the phone. We need to know how he makes out.'

'We don't have time for Callaway's mate to send us the records, and I'm sure the letter will convince Kirkpatrick that Celreau is a suspect. I just know Donni is up in the barracks. We need to get a look inside the place.'

'Be patient, Matt. One more minute won't make a difference. Hush. Here he comes.'

'I have some interesting news. I reached Professor Hathaway, and he informs me that Mr. Celreau was not a student at the University of Toronto.'

'That's not possible. You said yourself that he graduated from U of T,' insists Matt.

'Indeed, I did, but I stand corrected. Gabriel Celreau did not graduate from the University of Toronto. He was, in fact, a professor of history there for a period of five years.'

'How is that possible? That would mean he started teaching as a professor when he was twenty years old,' says Jesse.

'And wouldn't he have spent at least three years getting his education degree?' adds Matt, confused.

'Make that more like five or six. Hathaway said that Celreau had a PhD, as do all the professors. It is required for teaching positions at the university level,' says the librarian.

'He started his post-secondary education at the age of fifteen?' asks Matt.

'Inconceivable, I know. Probably a mix up of sorts. That is precisely why I asked my old friend to send me copies of Celreau's academic records, so we can solve this conundrum.'

'Couldn't your friend get in trouble?' asks Jesse.

'Hathaway owes me a big favor from early in the history of our relationship, and this is an easy way for him to wipe the slate clean. He was more than happy to oblige. He will courier the package to me ASAP, and I will trans-ship it to your house immediately upon receipt.'

'You need my address, then?' asks Jesse.

'You have a library card. I have your address on file,' explains Callaway.

'Thank you for your time and help, Mr. Callaway. You have been very helpful,' offers Matt politely.

'Bye, and thanks,' says Jesse.

'Happy vampire hunting,' answers Callaway with a wink.'

Celreau

1924

Gabriel is fully intending to pay for a seat on the night passenger train bound for Winnipeg, but the sight of three city policemen pacing attentively around the Canadian Pacific station force him to alter his plans. So much for a relaxing overnight ride in the luxury coach. The news of the Casa Loma massacre, as the papers have labeled it, evidently put the police on high alert throughout the city; bus stations, airport and rail stations are all under surveillance for the Pellatts' murderer. Gabriel leaves the area, walks five hundred meters up the street, crosses a field to the railroad tracks, then doubles back to the train. Passengers are waiting patiently inside, while suitcases, pets and boxes are loaded into the cargo car. Gabriel, obscured by the shadows behind one of the unloaded carts, waits for just the right moment. As the baggage handler turns his back to collect another heavy shipping box, Gabriel leaps into the cargo car and slips back into the dark interior.

Gabriel makes himself as comfortable as he can, settling in for the long ride. He is reasonably content for several hours after the departure from Toronto, but eventually, with nothing much else to occupy his mind, his appetite gets the better of him. He scrounges through the boxes and cases for the dog enclosures he knows are there. Although the dogs have been well behaved and quiet, his sensitive hearing and nose have made him aware of their presence from the moment he set foot in the car. He discovers half a dozen kennels in a row along the far end of the car. As he approaches, all the dogs rise and back to the far ends of their cages, away from him. Hair bristles at their necks and they bare their teeth.

Gabriel opens the first enclosure and reaches to retrieve his supper. The Cocker Spaniel within snarls and bites down hard across his fingers, eliciting a yelp more of outrage than pain.

'Merde!' swears Gabriel. 'You mangy little mutt. What a pathetic effort for your last act.' Ignoring his bleeding hand, he reaches in once more. Ready for the dog's speed this time, he snatches the animal by the neck and pulls him out of the kennel. He gives the mutt a quick shake, breaking its neck with a sharp snap. He brings the animal to his mouth and digs his fangs into its furry neck. Within seconds, Gabriel has drained the dog dry of blood. With a grunt, he tosses the carcass across the rail car and steps to the next kennel. He looks through the opening to find a cat lying asleep on its blanket. 'Fluffy' reads the tag hanging from the feline's collar. Gabriel scrunches his face in disgust.

'Damn! Is this what I have sunken to—feeding on pets? What am I doing? There's gotta be a hundred travelers on this passenger train.'

Invigorated by his snacks, and anxious to fill his lustful needs, Gabriel slides the door of the cargo car open. Reaching for the top of the doorframe, he swings his legs outwards to catapult his body up and over, onto the car's roof. The night air rushing past is refreshing, and he takes a deep breath. Getting to his feet, he runs down the center of the moving cargo car and leaps through the darkness onto the roof of the following car—a passenger car.

'Mother, did you hear that bang on the ceiling?' asks a young boy sitting in a window seat.

'Yes, Mathieu. Probably just a branch or something, blown onto the roof by the wind, dear. Nothing to worry yourself about. Try to get some rest. We have a long ride to go yet.'

'Okay, Mom. If you say so.'

Gabriel crawls to the edge of the car and lowers himself head first over the side. He grabs the edge of the metal window frame and, inching his powerful body down to the glass window, looks in.

The middle aged man, asleep and resting peacefully in his berth only a moment ago, explodes through his sleeper car's glass window, and wakens to find himself suspended in mid-air by his ankles and starring down at the sparks flying from the tracks below. He looks up in horror at the creature dragging him to the roof. Minutes later, his drained corpse is cast from the train. 'Mom, Mom! A man just fell past my window!' yells the young boy.

'Mathieu, don't be silly. You saw no such thing,' replies his mother.

'But Mom, I saw a man fall and he bounced into the ditch.'

'That's quite enough, young man. You've let your wild imagination run away with you again. Here, switch places with me. I'll sit by the window for the remainder of the night.'

'Aw, Mom. I saw it. I did. I know what I saw.'

'Enough said. Understand?'

'Yes, Ma'am.'

The mother slides over and sits in her son's seat. She looks out the window a little apprehensively at the shadows slipping by in the night.

Gabriel, fed and content, wipes his blood-stained face with the handkerchief he has lifted from his victim, then throws it into the night. He climbs down the side of the moving train and carefully crawls into the private sleeping compartment through the broken side window. Gabriel rifles through his victim's belongings. In the closet, he is surprised to find a shelf of fine clothing, neatly pressed and folded. A quick try-on verifies that they fit reasonably well. Fully dressed, he slips on a pair of highly polished leather shoes found under the foot of the bunk. He takes a moment to admire himself in the closet mirror, then steps out into the narrow passageway. A glance left and right, then he turns left toward the doors connecting to the dining car.

When he enters the dining car, he surveys the decadent luxury before him and smiles. A crystal chandelier hangs above a dozen oak tables covered in fine linens and silver place-settings. Passengers are seated in plush leather chairs, consuming their fill of gourmet meals—roast chicken, rack of lamb, baron of beef, complete with bottles of fine French red wine. Each table is dimly lit by an electric table lamp with silk shades that match the vase of fresh flowers. Gabriel walks between the tables looking for a place to sit. As he passes a table occupied by a woman and a young boy, a glass of milk, accidentally elbowed off the table by the boy, drops on his foot and spills milk over the cuffs of his pants.

'Mathieu, look what you've done! I'm so sorry, sir,' says the woman. Taking a cloth napkin from the table, she kneels to clean Gabriel's pants.

'It's okay. No harm done. It was an accident,' assures Gabriel.

'I don't know what's got into him tonight. First he goes on with some nonsense about bodies falling from the train, and now this,' shares the woman, desperately dabbing milk from Gabriel's shoes.

'Well, boys will be boys. Please, Madame, don't bother. I have another pair of shoes,' says Gabriel, offering his hand to help her up from her knees.

Regaining her feet, she turns to her son. 'Mathieu, apologize to Mr…?'

'Sorry, How rude of me. My name is Gabriel, but please call me Gabi.'

'Nice to meet you, Gabi. I'm Isabelle. Please let me buy you a drink to make up for the inconvenience we have caused you.'

'Enchanter, Isabelle. As they say, no point crying over spilled milk, and I assure you the pleasure is all mine. Isabelle. What a beautiful French name.' Gabriel bends to kiss the back of her delicate hand. Looking up, he locks eyes with her. She freezes, suddenly light headed, unable to move or speak—a prisoner within her own body.

Mathieu, sensing something strange is happening to his mother, tugs at her dress.

'Maman? Maman?' he insists. He looks up to see Gabriel's eyes turn black. Terrified, he demands in a much louder voice, 'Maman!' Getting no response, Mathieu panics and kicks Gabriel hard in the shin.

'Oye!' exclaims Gabriel, flashing his large canines at the boy. Terrified, the boy retreats to the back of the bench, unable to take unbelieving eyes off the vampire.

'Mathieu?' whimpers Isabelle. She shakes her head, as she regains her senses.

Gabriel's canines retract instantly, and his eyes revert to their usual shade of brown.

'Are you okay, Isabelle?' he inquires, turning to her calmly.

'Yes, I think so, but I feel a bit woozy.'

'It's probably caused by the movement of the rail car. The rocking motion sometimes causes vertigo. Please sit down. I'm certain you'll feel better in a moment.'

'Mathieu, are you alright?' asks his mother, as she sits. 'You look like you just saw a ghost.'

'I want to go back to our seat, Maman.'

'That would be rude, Mathieu. You spilt your drink on Mr. Gabriel. The least you can do is sit quietly and keep us company, while I buy him a drink.'

'But Maman. I saw...'

'No, Mathieu. No buts. Sit still and be quiet. Comprends-tu?'

Mathieu frowns, curls his legs up underneath him and stares out the window, glancing obliquely at Gabriel every few seconds.

'Excuse me,' says Isabelle with a hand gesture to gain the attention of the passing waiter.

'May I please order a glass of champagne, an orange juice for my son, and whatever the gentleman would like?'

'I'll have whiskey, please,' states Gabriel.

'Sorry, sir. Hard liquor is not available.'

'What kind of bar doesn't keep whiskey in stock.'

'My apologies, sir, but it's on account of the prohibition.'

'But the prohibition has ended, has it not?' questions Gabriel.

'Yes, sir, but it's still very much in effect in the USA.'

'What, precisely, does that have to do with the price of rice in China?'

'The black market, sir. The trade of high-priced Canadian liquor to the Americans has made it next to impossible to get any hard liquor here in Canada. We haven't received an order in months. May I offer you a glass of Niagara Falls Merlot?'

'You may offer, but I will usually decline. I would really prefer a glass of Canadian rye whiskey on the rocks.'

The waiter bends to Gabriel's ear. In subdued tones, he breathes, 'For a small gratuity, I can put you in contact with a gentleman who's in a position to furnish the desired beverage, if he so chooses.'

'Name it?'

'A small portrait of our beloved Prince of Wales would do nicely, sir.'

Gabriel reaches in his pocket and slides the waiter the flesh-colored five dollar bill.

'Very well, then. Who is this well-supplied individual?'

The waiter tilts his head in the direction of a man sitting alone at the far end of the car, smoking a large cigar.

The waiter returns to his station at the bar, and Gabriel turns to the lady and her son.

'Isabelle, I will take a pass on your offer of a drink, but it has been a pleasure meeting you. I hope you enjoy the remainder of your travel,' says Gabriel standing up.

'Oh! You're not staying for a drink?'

'I have some business to which I must attend. Perhaps another time.'

'I'll hold you to that.'

'I expect you will. Au revoir, Mathieu.'

Mathieu grunts.

'Mathieu!' scolds his mother.

'Boys will be boys,' repeats Gabriel, chuckling as he leaves the table. Heading to the rear of the car, he approaches the man with the cigar.

'This seat taken?' asks Gabriel.

'Help yourself, pal. I ain't using it.'

'Thanks. How are you today?'

'Listen, bud. If you're one of those traveling salesmen, you're wasting your time.'

'No. Of course not. A little birdie told me that you can line me up with some liquor.'

'The bar is at the end of the rail car—help yourself, bud.'

'Squeezings of the grape are not my choice of drink. Kinda tastes like piss and gives me the runs.'

'I hear that!'

'So, can you help me out?'

'Maybe—maybe not. Who are you and why you asking me?'

'The waiter gave me the heads up. Not the first time this has happened, unless I miss my guess. Don't worry. I'm not a cop.'

'I expect not. The waiter's pretty sharp, and he'd have smelled you out if you were the law. So, what's your business, then?'

'If pressed to put a label on it, I'd say I'm in the evening entertainment business.'

'Awww! Got ya,' says the man with a wink.

'I'm Gabriel,' extending his hand.

'Jake.' He reaches over the table to shake the extended hand.

'Where you figurin' on opening shop?' asks Jake, wincing and rubbing his hand.

'I'm on my way to Winnipeg. The city's booming and full of hot-blooded men in need of my services.'

Jake pulls a silver flask from the inside pocket of his vest. Taking a swig, he extends the flask and gestures to Gabriel to help himself.

'Don't mind if I do.'

'You rounding up some local girls for your operation?' asks Jake, his interest growing.

'Some, but I have many in Toronto eager to join me in the new establishment.' Gabriel takes a drink from the flask, coughs and smiles.

'Yeow! A fine example of premium whiskey, my friend.'

'And there's a lot more where that came from,' answers Jake with a hush and a wink.

'You must be one resourceful son of a bitch, Jake.'

'Let's just say that I'm well connected. And not just 'cause I know people. I'm always thinking ahead, prepared to take advantage of any opportunity that arises. And I'm way ahead of you. I'm willing to wager that a steady supply of said whiskey to your new business would prove to be mutually beneficial. Am I right?'

'Indeed. Tell me, Jake, is there a place where we can discuss the details in private?'

'Meet me in my cabin in an hour. A14.'

'Perfect. That'll give me time to grab a bite before the meeting. See you then.'

Gabriel rises and walks to the bar. He looks down the aisle to where Isabelle is seated, her son now sound asleep, still curled up across the opposite bench. She sips the last of her champagne and looks around the room nervously. Noticing Gabriel, she smiles, gets up and walks over.

'Gabriel, would you be kind enough to watch Mathieu while I go to the washroom.'

'Of course, I would be happy to. The little angel is asleep. I don't think he'll be a problem.'

'Thanks. He's so exhausted from the excitement of the trip, he won't even know I left. I won't be long.'

Brief moments later, Isabelle returns to find Mathieu and Gabriel gone. Anxiously, she looks to the bar in the hopes of discovering Mathieu there next to Gabriel. Neither is in sight. Her heartbeat accelerates, and her palms begin to perspire.

'He must've taken Mathieu to the washroom,' thinks Isabelle, trying to remain calm. She hurries to the washroom and asks the attendant to check inside for her son.

'Sorry, Ma'am,' says the attendant upon his return. 'There is no child in the washroom.'

'Did you check all the stalls?' asks Isabelle impatiently.

'Yes, Ma'am—twice. There are only two stalls and they're both occupied by grown men. Where did you last see your son, Ma'am?'

'He was asleep over there, at that table. I should never have left him alone. Dear God, what was I thinking, asking a stranger to watch him?'

'Perhaps he woke and went back to the passenger car to find you,' suggests the attendant.

'Yes, of course. Yes, he did mention he wanted to go back.'

'He is probably there waiting for his mom right now. Try not to worry. There are only a half dozen cars on this train. He'll show up. Really nowhere for him to go.'

'Yes. You're right. He must be back in our berth. Thanks.' Isabelle rushes from the dining car and crosses to the sleeper car. She is startled by the sight of Gabriel stepping from a room ahead.

'Where's Mathieu? What have you done with him?'

'Isabelle, I was just coming to find you. Calm down.'

'Don't tell me to calm down. Where's Mathieu? Where's my son?' she demands.

'Shhh, shhh. Be quiet. You'll wake up the passengers? He's in my room.'

'In your room? I only asked you to watch him.' She pushes past Gabriel and tries to open the room door.

'It's locked. Let me in at once!'

'Of course, Isabelle.' Gabriel pulls a key from his pocket and opens the door.

Isabelle elbows past Gabriel into the apparently empty room. As she turns to confront Gabriel, a loud click announces the locking of the door.

'Why did you lock the door? And why is the window broken? What is going on here? What have you done with my son?' shrieks Isabelle, leaving no gap for Gabriel to reply.

Isabelle turns back to the bed and pulls off the blankets. Empty.

'Where is he? What've you done with my son, you pervert?' accuses Isabelle, kneeling to look beneath the bed.

'I didn't do anything. I swear. Let me explain.' He steps toward her, raising a palm in a calming gesture.

Ignoring him, she notices light coming from under the small bathroom door in the corner of the room. Rising, she hurries to the door. It, too, is locked.

'Mathieu needed to...'

She desperately tugs on the handle, trying to force the lock.

'Isabelle, stop! You're going to break the door,' says Gabriel putting his hand on Isabelle's shoulder. She bites Gabriel's hand—hard.

'Ow!' screams Gabriel, releasing his hold on Isabelle.

'Damn it, Isabelle! Mathieu had to...'

Isabelle gives the door a hard pull with all of her strength and it snaps open with a splintering sound.

'Mathieu,' gasps Isabelle.

'Mom, I'm on the toilet!' says an embarrassed Mathieu.

'I tried to tell you. Mathieu needed to go 'number two' really badly and the public washroom was occupied,' explains Gabriel.

Responding to the soft knock, Jake opens the door and invites Gabriel into his sleeper.

'Perfect timing. I was just about to have a drink. Can I pour you one?' offers Jake.

'Yes, please. I see you have the deluxe sleeper. Very nice.' Gabriel crosses to the leather chair at the end of the bed.

Twisting the cap from a new bottle of whiskey, Jake pours two full glasses. Handing one to Gabriel, he holds his glass high and makes a toast: 'Here's to women's kisses, and to whiskey, amber clear; not as sweet as a woman's kiss, but a damn sight more sincere.'

'Cheers. I take it you're a preferred customer of the rail line.'

'This room's reserved exclusively for me—meals and room service included.'

'Marvelous. How often do you travel, then?' Gabriel tosses back his drink in one swallow.

'Three times a month—Moose Jaw to Toronto return.'

Jake, not wanting to be outdone, follows suit and gulps down his whiskey with a grimace.

'Moose Jaw? Why supply that one-horse town when you can supply Winnipeg, where the population is a hundred times greater and demand for hard liquor is high?'

Jake gestures to Gabriel's empty glass and asks, 'Another?'

'Absolutely.'

'You ask a lot of questions, my friend?' says Jake, a bit perturbed. He fills the glasses to the brim and hands Gabriel his glass.

This time, Gabriel raises his glass and recites his own toast: 'I'll drink to the girls who do! I'll drink to the girls who don't! But…I won't drink to girls who say they will and turn out to be girls who won't!'

Gabriel clinks his glass to Jake's and tosses the drink back, again in one swallow.

'Ha ha,' laughs Jake nervously. 'That's funny.' He downs his drink and moves toward the bottle, staggering a bit. 'We have no interest in the chicken shit Canadian market.'

'But Moose Jaw is in Saskatchewan. Not following you, Jake.'

Gabriel takes the bottle from Jake's somewhat unsteady hands and refills the glasses. He raises his glass with yet another toast: 'May Dame Fortune ever smile on you, but never her daughter, Miss Fortune.'

Gabriel gulps his rye back.

'Indeed,' agrees Jake. 'Cheers.' Down goes his rye.

'Moose Jaw's our link to the U.S. and the big bucks,' says Jake now slurring his words.

'Okay, but why not Estevan? It's on the border.'

'This's precisely why you deal in whores, and I deal in quality whiskey.'

Gabriel fills the glasses once again. 'To whores and whiskey!'

Jake and Gabriel down their liquor together. Feeling unsteady, Jake sits down on the bed. 'The main junction of the U.S. and Canadian railroads is in Moose Jaw. You get me?' Jake exaggerates a wink.

'So, you supply Minot and Grande Forks?' baits Gabriel.

'Fuck, no! Chicago, man. That's where the money is! Have you not heard of Al Capone?

'You're in cahoots with Scarface. Wow! You do play with the big boys!'

'They don't call me Big Jake for nothing,' answers Jake proudly, expanding his chest, then reeling a little.

'Well, I guess that explains how you can afford the luxurious accommodations. A dozen cases per shipment at three hundred percent profit, three times a month is a lofty sum.'

'A dozen? Pffft! Try a hundred cases,' scoffs Jake. 'The shipment is stockpiled in secret underground tunnels in Moose Jaw. When we get an order from the Chicago head office, we transfer the cases to a southbound U.S. Soo Rail car that's been specially modified to include a hidden under-floor compartment.'

'What a sweet business,' says a smiling Gabriel.

'You betcha. The whiskey keeps flowing south and the cash keeps coming north.'

'So what have you got in mind for me?' asks Gabriel.

'I always order a dozen extra cases for a little side action, if you know what I mean.'

'A guy's gotta make a living,' suggests Gabriel with a sly head nod.

'If you purchase the lot for your new Winnipeg establishment, you would have a steady supply of whiskey for your clientele, and I, in turn, would only have to contend with one customer. A sweet deal for the both of us. Am I right?'

'Jake, may I make a suggestion?' asks Gabriel.

'You have a better idea?'

'I think so. I suggest I unload the one hundred and twelve cases at our next stop in Brandon, and you carry on to Moose Jaw with a message for your boss.'

'What the fuck you talking about?'

'Tell him that, from now on, he will deliver thirty percent of the take from the whiskey sales to me or no supplies will get through!'

'Is this some kind of a joke, or are you drunk? Or, maybe, just plain stupid?'

'I am sober, Jake, and quite serious. D'you understand our deal? Yes or no?'

Jake slides off the bed and walks over to Gabriel.

'No!' barks Jake. In a blur of motion, a knife appears in his hand, slipped from his belt, and drives deep into Gabriel's stomach. As fast as he is, he is no match for the vampire. Before he can withdraw the knife, Gabriel has him by the wrist. The sound of splintering wrist bones is accompanied by excruciating pain, and his hand goes limp. Gabriel pushes him back against the bed, then looks down at the knife protruding from his bloody shirt. Ripping his shirt open to expose the wound, the vampire looks up at Jake and smiles. He grips the knife by the hilt and draws it out slowly. Jake stares in disbelief as he watches the puncture wound healing miraculously.

'What the fuck? Who the hell are you?'

'I'm your new partner, remember?' answers Gabriel. 'See that my message gets to Capone. Understand?'

'Listen, I don't want any trouble. I'll do whatever you say. Yeah, I'll give him the message.'

'You see, we're already becoming an excellent team.'

'Yeah, sure, a team, you an' me. I'll deliver the message, no problem, okay?'

Gabriel runs the knife blade across his left wrist, slicing it open with a quick cut. Blood spurts from his wrist and spills to the floor.

'Jesus, you just opened up your wrist. Are you nuts?'

Gabriel drops the knife. Rising, he grabs Jake by the jaw. With one hand, he lifts him effortlessly off the floor and deposits him on his back on the bed.

Jake kicks and punches in desperate futility. He is no match for Gabriel's strength. Holding his wrist over Jake's face, Gabriel forces his victim's jaws apart and drips blood into the gaping mouth.

'When you wake up, you'll be in Moose Jaw. Don't forget your assignment!'

Jake can do nothing but stare up into Gabriel's dark eyes and gag on the blood flowing down his throat. He becomes light-headed and surrenders his fight to the darkness that fills his soul.

Celreau

1925

The familiar air horn blast sounding the arrival of an incoming eastbound train fills Brandon station, stirring Gabriel from his makeshift straw bed. Rising, he moves to the window of the old abandoned shed next to the town's main grain elevator, across from the rail station. Gabriel has picked this shed because it is only a few meters from the tracks. About a month ago, when he unloaded Jake's confiscated whiskey crates from the train bound for Moose Jaw, the shed proved convenient.

The arrival of tonight's train has Gabriel excited. He watches intently as passengers step down from the rail cars and walk across the boardwalk into the station for a much-needed break and a decent meal. Most are families moving back east. They have given up after enduring years of the unrewarding, back-breaking work of farming the prairies, and they are looking forward to the prospect of a new life in the bustling city of Toronto. A few are businessmen from Winnipeg traveling to Toronto with offers of new wealth and real estate opportunities within the growing city. All are inconsequential to Gabriel. All of his attention is reserved for the last passenger stepping off the evening train.

Jake walks to the edge of the station platform, leans against a post and lights a smoke.

'Howdy partner,' says Gabriel walking out of the shadows.

'Gabriel. Wait, don't hurt me,' pleads Jake.

'Hurt you? Now, that's a fine how-do-you-do,' jests Gabriel.

'Well, I don't feel so good since our last meeting. I got a few aches I never had before,' complains Jake.

'Sorry to hear that, Jake. Maybe it was something you ate?'

'You son of a bitch!'

'Enough of the pleasantries. Are you here to make a trade, or are you looking for a return trip on ice?'

'Yeah, uh, I mean no. Shit, here you go.'

Jake draws a thick manila envelope from his coat and hands it to Gabriel. Opening it, Gabriel smiles at the countless large bills filling the envelope. The accompanying letter begins…

'Celreau–

The message my man Jake delivered last month with your business demands disturbed me, to put it mildly. So I sent my four boys to deliver my answer by hand. I was more than a little disappointed by your response— having the four shipped back to me in crates, dismembered and packed in ice like so many mackerels, was an embarrassment. I didn't think that was very smart.

I'm sure you understand that, at that point, I was no longer just disturbed. You had succeeded in pissing me off. Who the fuck did you think you were, doing that to my boys? Under the circumstances, my reputation was at stake. If I didn't deal with you, what was to stop other upstarts from pulling the same stunt? I had no choice. A message had to be sent. You had to be eliminated.

I admit, getting my nine best guns returned to me in that many more ice-packed crates the other day got my attention and forced me to reconsider.

Broken up like that, those big guys sure fit into very small spaces!

Clearly, you have skills. Not only are you capable of coming up with and presenting a business plan, but you have the guts and the hired muscle to enforce it against anyone who doesn't like it. I can respect that.

I agree to your terms. From now on, we are partners. We are going to have a long and prosperous relationship. Expect the first shipment in Moose Jaw on the next train from Brandon.

Capone'

Gabriel tucks the letter back into the envelope and smiles at Jake.

'Well, I guess this makes it official. I'm your boss.'

'Hell will freeze over before I work for you!'

'That's no way to start your first day on the job.'

Gabriel reaches forward and wraps his powerful hand around Jake's throat. Lifting the terrified gangster kicking and choking off the wooden platform, he pulls Jake close so they are face to face.

'We'll start with something easy. Your first assignment is to help me load the crates of whiskey on the train to Moose Jaw tomorrow evening. Am I clear?'

Jake's eyes bulge from his reddened face. Unable to speak, he desperately tries to nod his head in agreement.

Gabriel releases his grip, dropping the big guy to the platform. Jake cowers and soothes his sore neck with his hands.

'Ten p.m. sharp. And don't be late.'

Tremblay

1925

'Inspector Tremblay, a pleasure to meet you. I hope your rather long trip to Brandon was a pleasant one,' offers the Chief of Police.

'It was tolerable, at best, but the modes of transportation to Brandon are limited. Though not much more comfortable, the trip by train was, at least, faster than it would have been by horse and buggy,' sneers Tremblay.

'Well, I assure you that your accommodation here during your stay will more than compensate for your discomfort.'

'Thank you, Chief. I appreciate you meeting me here after hours. I know your time is valuable, but I hope you understand that I'm pursuing an active case that may be related to the murders. I don't have the luxury of waiting till morning for your briefing. This criminal always seems to be just one step ahead of me.'

'Please, call me Stuart. How may I assist you with your investigation?'

'Well, Stuart, I received a telegram summarizing the report of your police investigation into the deaths and mutilation of a woman and child found aboard the eastbound train several weeks ago. The details were incredibly gruesome.'

'It was a horrific scene—the worst homicide crime scene in my thirty-year career. The woman and child were dismembered, their bodies devoid of blood, and their extremities strewn about their berth. I know how this is going to sound, but it's almost as if this animal drank their blood, like some kind of vampire.'

'Vampire? Are you serious, Chief? This is no time for levity.'

'No, no! I mean no disrespect. It just seems inconceivable to me that a human being could be so cruel and deranged. Imagine ripping the arms and legs from a young child. We found the boy's torso in the washroom and his head in the closet, for Christ's sake. I've never seen anything like it and pray to God I never do again.'

'And no suspect?'

'We have a suspect, but no identity. He was seen chatting with the deceased earlier in the evening, not long before she and her son were murdered. We have a description, but none of the other passengers on board knew his name nor anything else about him. Oddly enough, nobody even recollects him boarding. The murder was only discovered after the arrival of the train here at the station. Unfortunately, the suspect apparently de-trained before we had time to secure all the exits.'

'I presume you have searched for him in town—hotels, boarding houses, barns, out-buildings in the area.'

'Of course, Inspector. Sadly, we've found neither hide nor hair of the monster thus far.'

'I see. You don't mind if I take a look around, just to double check, do you?'

'No, of course not. I assure you my men are well trained and quite efficient.'

'I don't doubt it, Chief, but it's probably safe to guess that, as a homicide officer in Toronto, I have just a smidgen more experience in this field than the municipal police force of Brandon.'

'I get your point. I suppose Toronto, with all its freaks and derelicts, must give your force more opportunity to investigate murders than they'd like. I see no harm in you confirming our findings,' concedes the Chief.

'I thought you would see it my way, Stuart. I won't be here but a couple of days at most.'

'Fine. Keep me posted on anything you find.'

'Of course. But as you said, your fine officers probably left no stone unturned.'

Tremblay spends the following morning questioning several townspeople, to no avail. Moving his investigation to the east end of Main Street, he examines the railroad station and its surroundings. A weather-beaten old caboose standing on a short section of track parallel to the main line attracts his attention as a potential hiding place for a felon. He climbs the rusty steel steps, turns the door latch and pulls the stiff creaky metal door open. An old desk and chair sit just inside the door beside a dented Buck stove. Ignoring them, he is drawn to a pile of rumpled blankets on the floor between the firewood box and what appears to be a closet or washroom. As he approaches, the bundle moves sharply. The old vagabond, startle, sits up, holding one hand up in self-defense.

'I don' want no trouble. I's jus' restin' my old bones fer a minute. I'm on my way. I don' want no trouble, please,' begs the homeless man.

'Relax, old timer. I just want to ask you a couple of questions and you can go back to your siesta.'

'I don' live here, mister. I swear. I jus' come in for a quick nap before moving on. I don' cause no problems.'

'It's okay. Calm down. What's your name?'

'Elmer. Elmer Johansson.'

'Okay, Elmer, tell me something. You seen anything strange or suspicious around here in the last few weeks.'

'Listen, mister, like I tol' you, I don" want to cause no trouble. I jus' came in here a few hours ago.'

Tremblay reaches into his pocket and pulls out a roll of bills. He slips five dollars from the roll and hands it to Elmer.

'Would this help you remember anything, Elmer? There's enough here for a nice warm dinner at Ruth's Diner and some left over for a bottle of your favorite Chardonnay. So, what do you say?'

With a trembling hand, Elmer takes the cash from Tremblay and stuffs it in the pocket of his dirty pants.

'There's a new guy around lately. Never seen him before. He stays in the shed down the tracks across from the station. He's not very big, but he's a lot stronger than he looks. Keeps pretty much to himself, too. Never seen him during the day; only at night.'

'Why d'you say he's strong?'

'Listen, mister. I don' want trouble.'

'Yeah, yeah. You don't want trouble.' Tremblay slides another bill from his roll and hands it to the beggar.

'Thanks, mister. Well, he carries hundreds of crates back and forth to the cargo train every couple of weeks.'

'By himself?'

'He had another man help him once, but...'

'But? But what? Speak up, old man.'

'He...well...he got mad. I don' know. They was arguin', and the next thing I know, this guy rips his helper to pieces. Horrible, mister—horrible. Pulled the head clean off his shoulders and tossed it into the bush. Thought I was just having a nightmare, pinched myself to be sure. The guy kneels down over the poor man's body and licks the blood from his neck, like one of those African hyenas.'

'Okay, that's enough. Sounds to me like you were into some bad hooch. Get back to your bed and don't repeat any of this nonsense to anybody, hear me?'

'Yes, sir. Nobody. I won't. It was just a nightmare. Just a nightmare.'

Tremblay steps down from the caboose ladder and walks along the tracks towards the shed Elmer just described. A beaten path runs from the tracks to the old building. Coming up to the side window to have a look inside, he curses. The window is boarded up solid. Moving to the front entrance, he tugs hard on the door handle, but it does not budge, apparently locked from the inside.

'This is the RCMP! Open the door!' commands Tremblay.

He kicks at the door several times, but it resists his efforts. Looking more closely, he sees that the door has recently been reinforced with new heavy hinges and solid fur boards. Frustrated, Tremblay re-crosses the tracks to the rail station in search of an ax.

Gabriel, just inside the door of the shed, ear to the door, waits a few minutes for the intruder to go away.

'Damn! It was too good to last. Must've gotten sloppy. Somebody must've spotted me moving one of the shipments. Time to hit the road, damn it all!'

When Tremblay returns to the shed with a large fireman's ax in hand, he curses at the sight of the door standing ajar. He drops the ax and moves in warily. The room is stacked from dirt floor to ceiling with wooden crates. A peculiar odor wafting from the corner of the room strikes his nose. He grimaces. A make-shift bed of straw fills a narrow space between the rows of crates. Lifting one of the wooden crates from the pile, he pulls the top off to find a dozen bottles of Canadian rye whiskey neatly packed in sawdust. As he reaches for one of the bottles, he is distracted by a sound coming from a couple of 45-gallon steel drums in the corner of the shed. Tremblay's curiosity is aroused; the foul odor is coming from the same vicinity.

Blood and slime discolors the floor in that corner and is oozing down the side of the barrels. He touches the side of one of the drums. His sensitive fingertips feel a faint tremor. Puzzled, he pops the cover from one of the drums and winces in disgust at the stench. The drum is brimming with a stew of decomposing human body parts. The sight of thousands of maggots slithering through and around the rotting flesh make him gag. Disgusted by the grizzly find, and frustrated for letting Gabriel get away, he kicks the container over. Disfigured heads, toes, arms, fingers, and many unrecognizable bodily parts in various stages of decomposition slosh across the floor and out the door. Tremblay curses. He walks over and around the mess he just created, trying to avoid the remaining bits on the way out of the shed. Exiting, he steps directly onto a partly decomposed femur. The decaying flesh peels off the leg bone sending the detective's feet out from under him, dropping him on his ass in the cesspool.

Kirkpatrick
1980

'D'you have an appointment?'

'Well, no, but it's urgent that we see Sergeant Kirkpatrick right away,' pleads Jesse.

'Urgent,' repeats the receptionist.

'Yes, urgent!' blurts out Matt.

'Name, please'

'Matt Taylor and Jesse Fairchild. Please hurry. It's important,' presses Matt.

'A matter of life and death,' adds Jesse.

'Yes, I'm sure it is. Take a seat.'

'But it's urgent,' says Matt, close to shouting.

'Young man, take a seat. I'll call you when the Sergeant is free.'

'C'mon, Matt. Let's sit down. Don't want to get kicked out.'

'Yeah, whatever,' answers Matt, scowling.

The pair sit on hard wooden chairs in the waiting area and flip through magazines without really focusing on content. A few minutes later, Mayor Brady steps out of the Sergeant's office, followed closely by Kirkpatrick.

Jesse and Matt spring to their feet and rush past the receptionist towards the Sergeant.

'Hey, you two. Stop! You can't go in there,' shouts the receptionist as she rises to go after them.

'Well, look at this, Tom. If the two little heathens haven't come calling. Now that they've set Pastor Dewar straight, maybe they want to teach you a thing or two about how to run your station.'

'I'd like to see them try, Mr. Mayor,' says an unamused Kirkpatrick. To the receptionist coming up behind the children, he says, 'Beatrice, please accompany these children back to the waiting room. They have no business leaving it unescorted.'

'Sorry, Tom. They rushed by me before I could stop them.'

'Sergeant, we need to talk to you. It's urgent!' yells Matt.

'Whatever it is, it can wait till I am done my meeting with Mayor Brady,' explains Kirkpatrick in a stern voice.

'It's about Donni. He's alive!' shouts Jesse, desperation in her voice.

'Nonsense. Donni drowned and his body washed down river. Now go sit down.'

'You know what, Tom? It's okay. Our meeting is done anyway. I'll show myself out.'

'You sure, Cliff?'

'Absolutely. Good luck with Mr. Taylor and his little injun.'

'Fuck you,' says Matt.

'Watch your language, young man,' says Kirkpatrick.

'I will if he will,' returns Matt.

'Have a pleasant meeting, Tom. You may have your hands full,' says the Mayor. He chuckles all the way to the door.

Kirkpatrick half smiles. Then, turning on the children, demands, 'Alright, you two. What're you up to now? You know darn well the Cardinal case is closed.'

'Give him the letter, Jess,' says Matt.

'We found this letter in a fire barrel next to the barracks,' explains Matt, as Jesse hands it to the Sergeant.

Kirkpatrick unfolds the letter and frowns as he reads.

'It proves that Celreau has kidnapped Donni and has him locked up in the barracks,' continues Matt.

'We have to drive up to the barracks now, before it's too late,' urges Jesse.

'Not so fast. How do I know you two didn't write this letter and aren't leading me on a wild goose chase?'

'What? No! We wouldn't do that. You have to believe us. You can check, if you want; we don't have handwriting like that,' pleads Jesse.

'This is serious business. If I discover that this is some sort of trick, you'll both be charged with giving false evidence and find yourselves in juvenile detention until you reach legal age. Am I clear?'

'We just want to find Donni, sir. We know he is up there. Please help us search the barracks,' begs Jesse.

'Go home for now. Once I confirm with Donni's parents that this is in fact his handwriting, I'll consider searching the military barracks.'

'We want to come too!' exclaim the kids together.

'Go home. I have your number. I'll contact you.'

'But you will come get us to help in the search…?'

'Enough! Now run along. I have an investigation to re-open, and for your sakes, I pray to God I'm not wasting my time.'

'The sergeant doesn't really intend to pick us up, if he decides to go up to the barracks, does he?' asks Jesse.

'Nope. Not a chance.'

'Figured as much. Maybe we can get your dad to drive us up to the barracks.'

'My dad? Yeah, right. Even if he's sober at this time of day, there isn't a chance in hell that he will get his butt off the couch to drive us anywhere.'

'Well, there's no harm in asking. What's the worst that can happen? If he says no, we can always hike up there.'

'I hate asking my old man any favors.'

'I know, I know. I'm sorry. Betcha a bag of Twizzlers I can get him to drive us.'

'Good luck with that. Ever since mom passed away, he hasn't been the same man. It's like he gave up on life—on me.'

'He loves you, Matt.'

'He sure has a strange way of showing it. Nothing I do makes him happy. Nothing! He is totally disappointed in me. He thinks I'm a wimp.'

'How could he be disappointed in you? You are an honor student and an awesome talented musician.'

'He wants me to work at Kodiak Lumber like he did. I would rather stick pins in my eyeballs than set foot in that stinking old mill.'

'There isn't much else to do in this town but work at the mill. Maybe he is worried you might end up on the street living on unemployment.'

'What good did it do him? He's a miserable old drunk. He's managed to spoil every Christmas holiday I can remember. He even embarrassed me when he showed up slobbering drunk at my honors class presentation. I'm sick of him and his issues. The sooner we get out of Blood Cove, the better.'

'A little patience, Matt. Won't be long before we're free of this town, playing our music in a land where it's always summer. Then you'll never have to bother with your dad again, if you don't want to.'

Arrived at Matt's house, the pair climb to the porch and enter through the back door. To their surprise, they find his dad sitting at the kitchen table—sober. Frank is reading the Klondike Star newspaper, a cup of coffee on the table beside him.

'Hi, Mr. Taylor,' says Jesse, leaning to kiss him on the cheek.

'Humph,' grumbles Frank. 'Damned taxes're going up again. They don't even plow the roads. Where does my damned money go, is what I'd like to know?'

'I think Mayor Brady spends it on coffee and donuts,' says Jesse smiling.

Frank gets up, walks to the counter and rinses his empty coffee cup in the sink.

'That wouldn't surprise me one bit. That overpaid blow-hard spends half his day at the coffee shop wasting taxpayer's money.'

'Nice day today huh, Mister Taylor?' asks Jesse.

'I guess, seems okay. Why?'

Jesse walks up to the stove and takes the dishtowel hanging from the oven door. Crossing to the sink, she reaches past Frank, picks up the cup from the sink and dries it.

'Oh, nothing really. I just thought, maybe, well, perhaps…'

'Well, out with it already. What is it?' asks Frank.

'Just thought it would be nice to go for a ride,' answers Jesse.

'Ride? Ride where?'

'Up to Look-Out Point would be fun,' says Jesse, handing Frank his cup.

'Why in the world would I want to waste gas driving up there?'

'Forget it, Jesse. I told you he was a lost cause. C'mon, let's hike up there before it gets too late.'

'Watch your mouth, boy,' threatens Frank.

'Matt and I were exploring around the military base just across from the look-out the other day and scared up some grouse. Matt told me how you love partridge hunting. I just thought we could drive up there, and you could shoot us a couple for supper.'

'Grouse, you say? How many?'

'At least a half dozen. They were pecking the ground on the trail to the barracks.'

'Eating pebbles for digestion. Gastroliths they're called,' adds Frank.

'Matt says you can shoot a dime off a fencepost at twenty yards with your .22 rifle.'

'Thirty yards with my Cooey, no problem.'

'Well, let's bag a few of them birds, then. My Ma will be happy to cook them up for us for supper. She wraps the partridge breasts in back bacon and bakes them in the oven with sweet potatoes. It's delicious.'

'I'll get my rifle. This is the perfect time of day to find them out on the trails,' says Frank, already headed for the hallway.

'Thank you, Mr. Taylor,' shouts Jesse as she turns to Matt and winks. 'Make them strawberry-flavored Twizzlers, and make sure they're fresh, Whitey.'

'You amaze me all the time, Haida girl. Strawberry it is, then,' says Matt with a smile.

Bélanger
1942

The cool November wind sweeps down the recently famous Yukon River. The hull of the S.S. Klondike, forced against the pier by the north-rushing current, responds with a high pitched squeal. Massive ropes stretch and growl in unison, strained but more than adequate to resist the pull of the river. The moored vessel heaves, yet remains secure against the weathered wharf. Passengers, weary from the long river voyage from Whitehorse, begin to debark the stern-wheeler, descending the narrow ramp to the docking platform. They shuffle down the icy plank carrying large suitcases, crates and bags that represent, for many, all their worldly possessions.

The Frenchman, unhindered by luggage, threads his way through the knot of struggling passengers. Free of the crowd, he leaves the dock to follow the muddy path up the river bank to town. A battered sign, in desperate need of repair and a coat of paint, is planted at the top of the ridge and welcomes the stranger to Dawson City—Paris of the North. The gold rush has been over more than thirty years, but hopeful prospectors, wannabe millionaires, still migrate to Dawson City in hopes of finding the next mother lode.

He trudges up the street into town, ankle deep in muck, making wet, sucking sounds with every step. A couple of children playing in a mud puddle in front of their home are quickly ushered from the street by their concerned mother. With a worried frown, she stares at this stranger, then follows the children inside and sharply slams the door. The metallic clang of the latch locking the door resonates loudly, like a warning. The door is adorned with an oversized wooden cross that rattles with the impact. It begins to swing like the pendulum of a grandfather clock. The stranger frowns.

Continuing towards the center of town, he sees that most houses display similar crosses and crucifixes on their doors. Some have braids of garlic hanging from the front gates and mirrors nailed to walls next to windows. The message on the bulletin board of the church across the street summons followers to a prayer vigil and exorcism the following evening. Still frowning, the stranger shakes his head.

Crossing the street, he walks along the side of the church to the graveyard at the back. A dozen freshly dug graves pepper the fenced lot.

He skips over the metal railing to take a closer look. The graves are circled by lines of sprinkled oats and rice. His gaze locks on the grainy circles for a moment. Shaking his head again, perturbed, he frowns in disbelief and leaves the graveyard.

The Frenchman has been in town for nearly twenty-four hours when he returns to the church. He enters through the side door, descends the stairwell to the basement meeting hall, and finds a chair among local parishioners.

'Yer not from around these parts, are ya?' questions the old man sitting next to the stranger.

'Pardon?' asks the Frenchman, leaning towards the old fellow.

'You mus' be new in town, eh?' asks the old timer.

'Fresh off the boat,' answers the Frenchman.

'Hmm,' mumbles the old man, switching his attention to the minister who has just entered and is moving to the front of the room.

'Good evening,' says the minister, holding his arms stretch outward from his chest.

'Good evening, Pastor,' the gathered townspeople answer in unison.

'And the Great Dragon was thrown down, that ancient serpent, who is called the 'Devil' and 'Satan,' the deceiver of the whole world—he was thrown down to the earth, and his angels were thrown down with him.'

'Kill the serpent!' yells an old lady rising from her seat.

'Many of you here tonight have felt the sadness, the desperation and the pain of losing a loved one—your child, sister, brother, father, mother, or perhaps a close friend. Their innocent lives snatched away by some possessed creature.

'Peter tells us, Be sober, be vigilant; because your adversary the Devil, as a roaring lion, walketh about, seeking whom he may devour. But I am here standing before you tonight to assure you that we will not be victims of this assault.'

'Amen,' shouts a member of the congregation.

'We will fight the scourge that threatens our community. We are not alone in this battle against evil. We have God on our side.'

'Amen,' says the crowd. 'God is good.'

'Amen. And the Good Book tells us, Put on the whole armor of God, that you may be able to stand against the schemes of the Devil.'

'Lord, alleluia,' shouts a man from the group.

'Are you ready to put on your armor and stand against Satan?'

'Yes. Yes,' shouts the crowd, excitement building.

An old lady in the front row suddenly runs towards the minister. Her eyes roll back into her head and foam spills from her mouth. She begins to babble incoherently.

'Praise the Lord,' shouts the minister. 'Do not fear her; she speaks in tongues. She has been touched by God. The lord is among us. Praise the Lord. Gentlemen, please assist our blessed sister to safety and bring out the demon woman.'

Two men escort the old lady from the room. When they return, they are dragging a scantily dressed young woman in shackles whom they deposit in front of the group. She drops to her knees snarling and screaming at the angry crowd. Glancing around, she sees the Frenchmen in the crowd. Her shouting stops momentarily as their eyes meet. An evil grin forms across her lips. The old man next to the stranger raises an eyebrow at the woman, then looks suspiciously to the Frenchman.

'Now lay the heathen woman upon the table, so we may cast the demons from her body,' commands the minister.

The men grab her, and with no attempt to be gentle, lay her on her back on the table. They hold her down by the legs and arms.

The minister, back straight and head high, approaches a nearby stand and lifts an aspergillum from a silver bowl. Walking around the woman, he sprinkles holy water over her while saying a prayer:

Most glorious Prince of the Heavenly Armies,
Saint Michael the Archangel,
defend us in "our battle against principalities and powers,
against the rulers of this world of darkness,
against the spirits of wickedness in the high places."

The demon lady pulls her arm free of the man's hold and swats the aspergillum from the minister's hand.

'Imbecile! Your silly prayers have no power over me,' yells the woman.

Undeterred, the minister slides a crucifix from the chain around his neck and holds it to her face. He continues…

We drive you from us, whoever you may be,
unclean spirits, all satanic powers,
all infernal invaders, all wicked legions,
assemblies and sects.

'Take that cross out of my face fore I stick it up your ass,' hisses the woman.

'God the Father commands you. God the Son commands you. God the Holy Ghost commands you.'

'Fuck you!' A chilling screech escapes her grimacing lips, her body writhing against the restraining grips of her captors. As the seizure becomes more violent, her torso arches, her head thrust below the end of the table. The two men desperately struggle to hold her spasming body on the table as it begins to change. The crowd, in shock, stares as the woman completes the transformation, showing her true vampiric nature; her brows extend, her eyes turn straw yellow, the veins in her neck bulge and vicious fangs descend from her upper jaw. The thin muscles of her sinewy arms become steely, and black claws extend from her finger tips.

Visibly shaken, the minister steps back. When he continues, a distinct tremor can be heard in his voice.'

'Depart you cursed, into the eternal fire prepared for the Devil and his minions.'

One shake of her arms catapults the two men across the room. She sits up, and with a sharp kick, snaps the shackles binding her legs.

Sliding off the table, she steps up to the minister, who cowers, extending his crucifix toward her in his trembling hand.

'Yea, though I walk through the valley of the shadow of death, I will fear no evil: for thou art with me; thy rod and thy…'

Sharp claws swipe his neck, decapitating the minister in mid-verse. Blood sprays the front row of the congregation, who sit frozen in shock and fear. The head tumbles across the concrete floor as the body slowly topples across the lap of one of the townswomen.

Terror grips the crowd. Suddenly, everyone is running into everyone else, scrambling for the safety of the rear exit. The old man sitting next to the Frenchman is bumped out of his chair by a fleeing parishioner and falls at the stranger's feet. The Frenchman is the only person still seated. The vampire walks toward these two remaining souls, knocking chairs aside as she advances. Frightened, the old man looks up at the Frenchman in desperation.

'Save yerself, man. Run! I'm old. I lived my life.'

Ignoring the Frenchman, the vampire reaches for the old-timer, but is brought up short by a steely grip around her extended wrist. Her eyes, wide with surprise, follow the arm back to the Frenchman who is still sitting on his chair.

'Not this one!'

The vampire snarls and hisses at him.

'Stand down, wench. You are no match for me. You don't want this old man. Go! You have a whole town of young, healthy people. Go now or you'll never go anywhere again!'

Pulling her arm from his grasp, she runs out the rear door into the night.

'Who're you that a vampire takes orders from ya?' asks the old man, cringing from the Frenchman.

'My name is Marcel Belanger. I report for the Winnipeg Free Press, and I have a few questions of my own. If I am satisfied with your answer, I may be willing to answer yours.'

'Ask away, my friend. I owe you my life.'

'Good. What can you tell me about Gabriel Celreau?'

'Gabriel Celreau. Ya sure know how to pick 'em! Where do I start? Well, 'bout a year and a half ago, this stranger shows up in town with nothin' but the clothes on his back and a duffel bag. He checks in at Mrs. Elsie's boardin' house. The next few evenings he's seen, by me and a bunch o' others, snooping 'round town. Gettin' the lay o' the land, I guess you could say. Next thing I know, he sets up shop in the old Yukon Hotel; been vacant for years.'

'He re-opened the hotel?'

'Well, not exactly. Come with me and I'll show you.'

The old man leads Belanger out of the church, east down Main Street.

'He opened a gambling house—Journey's End Casino and Nightclub—complete with good time girls. Rumor is, he paid cash for the buildin'. Guy who sold it to him swears his duffel bag was stuffed with hundred dollar bills.'

'Business must have been pretty slow, what with the gold rush being over and all?'

'You'd think so, but with the war in Europe startin', many young men come north to hide from recruiters and duck conscription into the army. Celreau had a dozen call girls shipped up from Edmonton to waitress and entertain the men. Tweren't long before word got out. Dawson had a new, first class gamblin' house and bordello. Shit! Miners, prospectors, trappers, even businessmen traveled from Whitehorse, and even as far as Yellowknife, to get in on the action. The place was redone all fancy-like on the inside. He put in a solid oak bar, a Burlesque stage, a restaurant and a large casino. The upstairs had a large room that was shared by the call-girls and six bedrooms for their appointments.'

The old man can't resist a wink.

'Sounds like a success story. What happened next?'

'The nightclub bustled with business most every night for about a year. That's when things started gettin' strange 'round here.'

'Be a little more specific. What do you define as strange?'

'Johns who went missing after leavin' the whorehouse, bodies cut in pieces found in the woods, shallow graves, vampires,' lists the old man.

'Most of such seemingly odd occurrences can usually be logically explained. I am sure the same applies in this case.'

'Really? Gimme a fer instance.'

'Okay. Isn't it possible that some of the young men, when surprised by the arrival of the army recruiters in Dawson, fled into the surrounding forest or downriver to hide? Most were inexperienced with wilderness survival, so they probably got lost, ran around in circles until they died of exposure or starvation. The timber wolves would make short work of such easy pickings, scattering the remaining body parts. The few lucky ones who managed to survive and evade the wolves would have been tracked down quickly by bears. Grizzly bears are essentially killing machines, but prefer eating their prey alive. Those men, once the grizzlies got scent of them, were basically walking dead. They may or may not have heard the charging animal. The bears instinctively sink their teeth into their victim's head crushing their skulls in the process. They feed and then bury what is left of the carcass for later. The discovery of these burial sites could easily be mistaken for a shallow grave by an inexperienced city inspector.'

'I s'pose all that's possible, but what about them vampires?'

'What about them?'

'Six men in two weeks were killed by these ungodly creatures. All of them in the club the night before, gettin' their jollies with them good time girls.'

'You're sure these killers were vampires?'

'C'mon. You saw that thing a few minutes ago. And all them bodies with two bite marks in their necks and drained of blood. Vampires, alright!'

'Did the RCMP investigate the murders?'

'Yeah, but they said they couldn't find nothin' that could be used to charge the girls. Except for prostitution, o' course.'

'Those murders were never solved?'

'The RCMP boys was a week in town investigatin' the cases and questionin' everybody, but they left with no arrests made. They figured the murders were prob'ly done by a mad trapper or some bum passing through. They reckoned, whoever twas likely skipped town and 'scaped down river.'

'What did the town do about the nightclub?'

'Have a look for yourself,' says the old timer pointing at a pile of burnt rubble across the street.

'You burned the club down?'

'No choice. Once the RCMP left, we had a town meetin' and took matters in our own hands. We were desperate. Just a matter of time before innocent folk and their children would be attacked by these creatures. That very night, we surrounded the buildin' and torched it, along with all of them vampire vixens. The screams coming from that bonfire were not from anythin' of this earth, nothing natural. It was pure evil—the Devil incarnate.'

'What about Celreau?'

'His body was never found. Reckon he perished in the fire along with his brood.'

'You assume?'

'Yes. Unfortunately, if the vampire we saw at the church tonight managed to escape the blaze, maybe Celreau did too.'

'Good deduction! A little late, though, don't you think?'

'I'm no damned cop, ya know. Just tryin' to stay alive. Okay, I've answered all yer questions. Your turn. Who are ya that a vampire does what you tell her?'

'I appreciate your help, old timer. At your age you must've learned that life isn't always fair. Have yourself a nice evening.'

Belanger turns and walks away.

'Hey, come back here. We had a deal. Why did she listen to ya? Answer me, damn it.' After a hesitation, he adds, 'Ya French bastard!'

Pamela
1946

Cool coastal rain falls in relentless diagonal sheets from the graphite sky ominously hanging over Vancouver. Crossing the intersection at Prior and Main, she splashes along the sidewalk and up the steps to Café Brulé, absolutely her favorite spot in the city. She fumbles her umbrella closed, gives it a shake and squeezes through the Café door into the warm, comforting aroma of sweet croissants and creamy lattes. She walks directly to the back and takes her usual seat at the table next to the window looking out on The Bank of Montreal across the street. The handsome young waiter, clad in black and white, places her customary cup of Orange Pekoe tea on the small round table before her. She nods a smile, whispering an almost inaudible 'Merci.' She stirs a teaspoon of amber honey lazily into the tea. Her chin propped on her hand, she stares unseeing past the droplets clinging momentarily to the pane of glass. The beads of water shimmy, struggling in vain to maintain position on the glass. Slowly they stretch, coalesce with others and grow. In seconds they surrender to gravity and, like race cars, they streak downward to the bottom of the foggy window.

Pamela Walden, forty, single, and very much alone in this cold damp city, can't help but feel her life and enthusiasm slipping away like the droplets on the glass. Youth is slowly giving way to wrinkles, gray hairs and a little flab around the middle. To avoid depression, she takes refuge in focusing on her work, comforted by the thought of financial security provided by a pension earned through years of dedication to her career. Still, Pamela daydreams of romance, and travel to far exotic places; of walking hand-in-hand with a lover along the Champs-Elysées in Paris, or sailing away on the clear blue Mediterranean Sea and making love on the sun-baked beach of a deserted Greek Island.

A soft touch on her shoulder startles her, jolting her back to reality.

'Excuse me, miss.'

Pamela looks up into the eyes of a tall handsome man. 'Uh, yes?'

'I don't mean to disturb you, but I wonder if you can help me?'

'Well, I am expecting a friend any moment now,' answers Pamela cautiously.

'This will take less than a moment. I just need a woman's opinion on an important matter,' implores the man, his questioning eyes softening.

'If it's important and quick, I guess I can provide an opinion,' says Pamela, curious despite herself.

'Wonderful. My parent's fortieth wedding anniversary is approaching, and I've been saving for a few years to send them on a vacation.'

'How very sweet of you.'

'Actually, it's the least I can do for them. They put up with a lot from me over the years.'

'I'm sure you couldn't have been that bad.'

'Horrible. A brat!'

'I see. So this trip would be a bit of atonement, a way of mending any hard feelings between you.'

'In part. I've told them several times that I truly appreciate all they've done for me. But I want them to know it in their hearts, and actions speak louder than words, right? Anyway, I am torn between sending them to London, Paris or Rome. What destination would you suggest?'

'My, your parents are very fortunate to have such a thoughtful son.'

'As I say, I owe them. I really want my mom and dad to enjoy this holiday, but I don't know which city they would enjoy the most? I am hoping your opinion will solve my dilemma.'

'Well, I don't know about your father, but every woman dreams of visiting Paris at least once in her lifetime. The allure of dining at a sidewalk café, while being serenaded by romantic accordion and violin music, is irresistible,' says Pamela, blushing.

'Of course! Why did I not think of that? Paris it is. Thank you so much.'

'You are quite welcome. I'm glad I could help.'

'My parents will be thrilled. Thank you again. Oh! I'm sorry. I didn't get your name. I'm David.' He extends his right hand.

'Pamela,' she answers, grasping his hand lightly.

The young man bends to softly kiss the back of her hand. She blushes and hesitantly pulls her hand away.

'Okay. Ahem. Well, enjoy your tea. I must go. I have airline tickets to purchase. Goodbye, Pamela. Nice meeting you.'

'Goodbye, David.'

'Pam, you done something different with your hair?'

'No, not really. Just brushed it a bit different. Why?' Pam nervously pats her hair.

'I'm not sure. You look, I don't know, radiant.'

'Really! Oh, don't be silly, I'm just in a good mood, that's all.'

'No, that's not all, girl. C'mon, you keeping secrets from me?'

'Well, to be honest, I may have met someone,' answers Pamela excitedly.

'Oooh! Why, you little vixen. You must give me all the juicy details. Who is he? Is it Fred in recruiting?'

'No, of course not. He picks his nose!'

'Jack in internal affairs? I know you've got a crush on him.'

'Ethel McMillan, I do not and don't you be spreading any such rumors!'

'Well, if you don't want me spreading rumors, tell me who your new man is.'

'Oh, all right. But you have to promise not to tell.'

'I promise. Now give.'

'His name is David. I met him at the café across from the Bank of Montreal.'

'Is he a stud?'

'He is tall and quite handsome. And he has an accent that I couldn't place, but sounded vaguely French.'

'Ooh. He sounds mysterious. Did he kiss you?'

'Ethel! We just met—but yes!'

'I knew it. What was it like?'

'Just on the hand, but his lips were so soft and tender.'

'Ooh-la-la! On the hand? How European! Well, that's a start, I guess. When are you meeting him again?'

'I…I don't know, really. He had to go and…'

'You let him get away? Oh, Pam. What am I to do with you?'

'He will come back. If it's meant to be, he will.'

'Good grief, Pam. I can't believe you let him get away.'

'He'll come back. Everything happens for a reason. He'll be back. You'll see!'

─෨෬─

Saturday morning. Pamela slips from her bed and, as usual, cleans her apartment while still in her pjs. Then she dresses, puts on her face, and spends the afternoon listening to Brahms on the record player, while knitting a scarf she is determined to complete in time to give to Ethel for Christmas. For supper, she broils a chicken breast sprinkled with rosemary, with a garden salad on the side. Preoccupied with thoughts of her encounter with David earlier in the week, she only manages a few bites of her meal. Making a decision, she quickly washes and dries her dishes, feeds the cat and sets out for Café Brulé.

Shivering, Pamela tugs her wool sweater tighter around her neck to repel the cool, humid air that wafts in through the coffee shop door every time a customer enters or leaves. A cup of hot tea in her right hand, she is reading from a book held open on the table with her left. A poem by her favorite poet, William Blake:

NEVER seek to tell thy love
Love that never told can be;
For the gentle wind doth move
Silently invisibly.

'Mr. Blake, only you really understand me,' thinks Pamela.

I told my love I told my love
I told her all my heart
Trembling cold in ghastly fears
Ah! she did depart.

'Why? Why, would he tempt me and then simply…leave?'
A gentle hand touches Pamela's shoulder, startling her. She turns to

stare in disbelief. David is standing next to her. His soft, sensuous voice continues where she left off:

Soon as she was gone from me
A traveler came by
Silently, invisibly—
O, was no deny

'David! What are you doing here?'

'I didn't know this was an exclusive coffee shop?'

'Of course it's not. I was just wondering…um, how'd you know what I was reading?'

'I'm sorry. I just had to sneak a peek over your shoulder to see what had you so captivated. William Blake is indeed one of the greats. I knew him as a young man.'

'What? How could you? That would make you about a hundred and fifty years old!'

'No…uh…of course not. I didn't know the man, Blake. What I meant was that I came to know his poetry when I was a young man.'

'Oh. Well, of course. How silly of me. So you enjoy poetry?' asks Pamela.

'Very much. Ever since I was first seduced by Gabriel Hugo and Jean de la Fontaine in elementary school in Paris, I have been hooked.'

'Paris, France?'

'Ha ha. The one and only. The city of lights, or my preference—the city of love.'

'My, yes. They do call it that, don't they,' answers Pamela, blushing and looking away.

'May I join you, Pamela?'

'Please do. My apologies. Rude of me not to offer.'

'I'm so glad I bumped into you again.'

'Why? I mean, you are?'

'Yes. I am new in town and a familiar face, especially one so pretty, is a nice treat.'

Pam's blush deepens. 'Uh, where are you from, David?'

'Montreal. I'm here on business.'

'What sort of business?'

'Well, to be honest, it's classified. I really can't say.'

'Oh, well, if it's classified, I guess…'

'I'm sorry. I didn't mean to sound standoffish or pompous.'

'You were, a little, but it's okay. Like you said, it's none of my business. I understand. I do. Well, I really should be getting home. It's getting late.'

'I'll escort you back, then.'

'No, it's too much trouble. I'll be fine, but thanks for the offer.'

'It's no trouble. Truly, I insist. It's dark and you never know what kind of characters are about at this time of night.'

'Really, it's okay. I walk home alone at this hour all the time.'

'Please indulge me. If not for you, for me. I would feel better knowing you made it home safely.'

'Suit yourself. I'm only a couple of blocks away anyway.'

'Perfect. I need to stretch my legs.'

The pair leave the Café and head north on Main Street.

'May I ask you a question?' asks Pamela after a few moments, breaking an awkward silence.

'Of course, anything.'

'Did you come to the coffee shop tonight with the sole intention of meeting me?'

'I'll answer your question if you promise to answer one for me. Deal?'

'Deal.'

'No, I came to the Café because I had a craving for a Cappuccino, but yes I was hoping I would find you there.'

'Oh my! I don't know if I should be flattered or frightened?'

'I assure you that you have nothing to fear. To be honest, I felt alone and wanted some company. When you're new in town, a big city can seem so cold and standoffish.'

'I can understand that feeling. This city is so beautiful in the summer under a bright warm sun and blue skies, but in the fall, the endless cold drizzle and gloomy skies can lead the most positive spirit to the depths of despair.'

'You know, you have more than a little poetry in you, Pam. Now, my question?'

'As I agreed, I'm afraid. Go on.'

'Did you come to the coffee shop tonight with the sole intention of meeting me?'

'That's not fair David. That was my question to you.'

'A deal is a deal!'

'Very well. No. My craving was for a Chai Latte, but yes, I was hoping to find you there,' answers Pamela, blushing.

'Well, aren't we clever?' David laughs out loud.

'Aren't we? Of course, great minds think alike,' adds Pamela laughing along. A moment later, she sobers and adds, 'Well, this is me,' pointing up the steps leading to a small brick house.

'I really appreciate you spending time with me tonight, Pamela. I'm glad we ran into each other. May I call you sometime? Perhaps you'll let me take you to dinner and a movie one evening?'

'Dinner with me? I mean, I don't know, I'm busy and I have a cat and...'

'Pamela, it's dinner and a movie. Your cat will be fine, I'm sure.'

'Yes, of course he will. I guess I could, sure.'

'Wonderful. I will come by Tuesday around six.'

'A weekday?'

'Why not? You have to eat, right? And we'll catch an early movie. Besides, it will help break up the week. Waddaya say?'

'Okay, Tuesday at six. Well, goodnight.' Pamela turns towards the steps.

'Pam?'

'Yes?'

'You forgot something.'

'No, I don't think so,' she says, turning back to face David. 'I have my purse, jacket…'

David puts his arm around her shoulder and kisses Pamela tenderly on the lips. Stunned, she stiffens. It's over before she can react.

'Goodnight, Pam,' David says, smiling.

'Th-thank you. I-I mean, yes, goodnight David,' stammers Pamela, abruptly exhilarated and light-headed.

Pamela examines herself in the mirror. She can't help sneering at the crows' feet around her eyes. She has heard them called laugh lines, but in her opinion, nothing could be that funny. Raising her hand to her neck, she wiggles her double chin with her fingers. The droop of her saggy breasts is depressing. With a sigh, she thinks to herself at least they don't hang down to my navel.

Pamela is only too aware of the toll that time has taken on her body. She often dreams of marriage and having children, but beauty is fleeting. Time is running out.

Maybe I'm crazy, but David may be my last chance. I must play my cards right; confident, but not desperate. No man wants to become involved with a desperate woman. Come on, Pamela, get yourself together. Don't mess this up.

She moves to the bed and sits on the edge of the mattress. She gently pulls up her stockings, careful not to put a run in them. She picks out her prettiest garter belt, sliding it up and over her hips to secure her stockings in place. She can't help but fantasize about David sliding the garter off with his teeth before making crazy love to her.

The doorbell rings, startling Pamela back to reality. Sliding off the bed, she straightens her dress and crosses to the door. Touching up her hair with her fingers, she takes a deep breath and opens the door.

A smiling David greets her with a bouquet of roses.

'I hope you like them. It was roses or daisies, but I figured your taste would be for roses. Am I right?'

'I love roses. Thank you. This is really sweet of you, David.'

'My pleasure, Pam. I'm glad you like them.'

'Come in. We have lots of time before the show begins. Would you like a glass of wine?' offers Pamela.

'Sure, that would be great, thanks.

David walks into the living room and sits on the Chesterfield.

'Nice place you have here. Have you lived here long?'

'Over ten years,' Pamela answers as she walks to the kitchen. Uncorking a bottle of Merlot, she fills two small water glasses with the red wine, wishing she had fancier stemware. 'It's close to work and a safe, quiet neighborhood.'

Returning to the living room, she finds David searching through her record collection.

'Nice selection of music you have—Jimmy Dorsey, Glenn Miller, Tony Martin, Billie Holiday. Mind if I put one on?'

'Great idea. Go ahead,'

David deftly slides the fragile shellac record from its paper sleeve. Gently, he centers it over the spindle and lowers it onto the turntable. Twisting the dial to On, he lifts the tonearm from its cradle and lowers it to the disk. Immediately the room is filled with a rhythmic hiss overlain by a romantic melody.

Our lady known as Paris
Romantic and charming
Has left her old companions
And faded from view

Pamela looks up at David from the Chesterfield and smiles. 'I just adore Tony Martin. The Last Time I Saw Paris—interesting choice. I've been meaning to ask you something, David. You said your parents were…'

David puts his finger to his lips, interrupting her with a 'Shhhh.' He steps across the room to offer his hand. 'May I have this dance, Mademoiselle?'

'Mais, bien oui, Monsieur.'

David takes her right hand in his left. Circling her waist with his right, he gently pulls her to him and leads her around the room gracefully moving to the music.

'You dance divinely, David. I feel like I'm floating!'

'It's not every day that I have the pleasure of dancing with such a beautiful woman.'

'I bet you tell all your dance partners that?'

'You're a beautiful woman, Pam,' whispers David into her ear.

'Oh, go on,' giggles Pam nervously.

'Your eyes are green as emeralds; your hair is like fine silk. And your soft tender skin? Irresistible!'

Pam feels his hot breath on her neck followed by the tender brush of his lips. Dave pulls Pam tightly into him. His left hand moves up her arm and into her hair. He gently caresses the back of her neck with his powerful hand. His lips slide from her neck to her mouth, and he kisses her hard, passionately. Pam submits to his erotic grasp and feels her body melt into his arms. The ease with which he picks her up almost makes Pam swoon. He carries her to the bedroom, where he gently lays her on the bed and lies next to her. Looking directly into her eyes, he says 'I've never wanted to make love to a woman as much as I do right now. I haven't been able to stop thinking about you since the first time I set eyes on you in the coffee shop.'

'Oh, David! I feel the same way. It's almost like we were meant for each other. Since I met you, my nights have been sleepless, filled with crazy thoughts, sinful thoughts. As if my insides were on fire. I can't stand it anymore—and I don't want to.'

'You don't have to wait any longer.'

'Make love to me, David! I never want to be without you again.'

'I think I've died and gone to heaven.' Pam is lying on her back trying to catch her breath.

'You're a beautiful, sensual woman, Pam. Every man's dream.'

Pam rolls onto her side and rests her head on David's broad shoulders. She slides her fingers through his chest hairs.

'May I ask you a question?'

'Yes, of course. What is it?'

'Something has been bothering me. It's nothing I'm sure, but…'

'What is it, Pam?'

'Well, remember when we met at the restaurant and you asked me if I knew a nice destination for you to send your parents on holiday as a surprise?'

'Yes, of course I do, and thank you for your suggestion. They can't wait to travel to Paris.'

'But you said you were born there.'

'Well, yes, but we moved to Canada when I was seventeen. My parents have always wanted to return for a visit, but could never afford the expense.'

'But Paris is the obvious choice, so why ask about Rome or London, especially from a total stranger? Please tell me it's not just a line you use on all the women you meet.'

David turns onto his side, facing Pam. He reaches over and slides his fingers down her arm and over her breast.

'Ha ha. No, I assure you the tickets are real. I have a sizable bank withdrawal to prove it. Although Paris was the logical choice, my parents have never been anywhere. I wasn't sure, now that I can afford it, that I shouldn't take the opportunity to show them a little more of the world. They are not getting any younger, after all. I guess the decision was weighing on my mind, and I just wanted a second opinion. And, yes, maybe I wanted a reason to meet you. I didn't mean to upset you, Pam. And you really did make the decision easier.'

'Hmm. You must see how, from my perspective, it can all seem a little contrived.'

'Perhaps, but aren't you glad it all worked out?'

David runs his index finger gently around her nipple.

'Yes, I am. Very!' answers Pam, giggling.

'Forgive me?'

'Nothing a movie and hot popcorn won't remedy.'

'Buttered?'

'Is there any other kind?'

'You got a date, beautiful. Let's get dressed.'

Dawn

1980

Dawn jogs along Riverview Avenue and turns up Main Street past the hospital. Her newly acquired hypersensitivity bombards her brain with smells, sights, sounds. Looking up Main, she is amazed that she can read the sign at Lamontagne's hardware, on the other side of town, as clearly as if it were only a few paces away.

'Wow! Gabriel wasn't kidding. This is really cool.'

She feels like a stranger in her own skin, uncomfortable yet invigorated and strong. A loud thundering blasts her eardrums. She covers her ears, but despite the cushioning affect of her palms, she can still hear the tumultuous roar of Spirit River. Still a quarter mile away, the sound of the river rushing down from the mountains is ear-splitting, the current splashing and slapping along its banks and spilling past the old mill into the ocean. She remembers what Gabriel said about the effects of her new powers. She tries to calm herself, to relax until the sound subsides.

'Jesus, that hurts. I hope I gain control of these senses pretty quick. I'm sure Gabi'll help me with it when I see him. Once I get this shit under control, we'll be unstoppable together.'

She grins and breathes in the cool autumn air. She smells the sweet perfume of pine trees and salty sea air on the afternoon breeze. She draws a long deep breath; a strong, revolting smell assaults her olfactory system and drops her to her knees—urine. Dawn, overwhelmed by the acrid stench, doubles over on the sidewalk and vomits. Wiping her chin, she looks across the street in the direction of the offensive scent. In the cemetery behind St Jude's church, she can see a wolf pack weaving among the gravestones. The black alpha male raises its leg repeatedly, spraying the tombstones, while the other grey wolves squat and pee randomly, marking the burial ground.

'Damn! Just when I thought I could handle this. God that burns. What a stench! I wonder what those wolves are doing in town? Oh shit. There's Dewar.'

Dawn gets up quickly and ducks behind a car parked on the street. Shielded by the vehicle, she watches Dewar ushering a half dozen choir boys out of the church. They stop and listen to him intently for a moment, then descend the steps and run off down Main Street toward their homes. Dewar smiles and hurries back into the church.

The young alpha catches scent of Dawn and watches her closely. Leaving the pack, it jumps the graveyard fence to the sidewalk and advances cautiously towards Dawn. The rest of the pack watches and paces nervously in the cemetery. Getting to her feet, Dawn moves away from the vehicle, walking directly towards the gray wolf. Snarling, it stands stiff legged and tall, its fur bristling, ears erect and forward. Its tail is held vertical, curled over its back.

'Calm down. I can help you get what you want. After all, we want the same thing,' says Dawn, moving in closer. With a snarl, the alpha male curls its lips to display its incisors.

'Do we really have to do this the hard way?'

The wolf crouches to attack.

Her patience gone and her temper rising, Dawn's transformation begins. Her brow extends and the blood vessels around her eyes swell and protrude from her face. Her eyes turn yellow, and fangs lengthen, descending from her gums. Her fingernails extrude into long, sharp claws. Flash-fast, she grabs the challenger by the snout and throws him in a high, wide arc into the street. A loud yip escapes its throat when it bounces on the asphalt. In pain, the wounded lupine crawls slowly back to the sidewalk, where it lies whimpering and licking its wounds, its tail tucked between its legs.

The soft sound of the church door opening sets both in motion—Dawn back behind the parked vehicle, the wolf over the fence into the cemetery. Dewar again exits the church, this time holding a young choirboy by the hand. The boy is crying and Dewar kneels down to talk to him. He pulls a lollipop from his pants pocket and hands it to the young lad. Still visibly upset, he heads up the street clutching the lollipop.

From the shadows among the headstones, the wolves lock their gaze on the Pastor. The alpha leads them along the juniper bushes at the side of the old church towards the front entrance and Dewar.

Dawn watches the hunt scene unravel with mixed emotions. She thinks, at first, that she should warn the old Pastor, but changes her mind when she remembers the pedophile's sickening attack on her best friend, Christine. She struggles momentarily with her decision; her new feral instincts decide for her. She is overtaken by a strange primal wave, an overwhelming urge to join the pack in the pursuit and ravaging of their prey. Her pulse quickens, her muscles tighten and her senses come alive. The Pastor, oblivious to the stalking of the wild pack, turns to the front door to find he has allowed it to close. It is locked. He fumbles in his pocket for his keys, slides one into the slot and unlocks the door. Streaking around the corner, the pack makes a mad dash for the old man. Opening the door, Pastor Dewar slips into the main vestibule, closing the solid wood door without knowing how close he'd come to losing his life.

Dawn, disappointed by the failed attack, crosses the street towards the pack. Fearless and confident with her newly acquired strength, Dawn stops short of the group, and speaks directly to the alpha wolf.

'You've seen what I can do. Don't make me hurt any more of you. We should be allies.'

Her fangs extend and she growls ferociously, turning full circle to confront the surrounding wolves. Terrified by the superior adversary, they back away. The alpha flattens its ears, lowers its body and arches its back in submission.

'Good. Now get yourself together so you can concentrate on your prey.' Climbing the church steps, she opens the big oak door and lets the gray wolf and its followers in.

Father Dewar walks up the center aisle to the front of the church, turns left at the altar railing and steps into his chamber. He kneels, facing the wall, in the corner of the small room and breaks down. He shakes with body-wrenching sobs. The tears flow freely.

'I'm a monster, an abomination! Satan's pawn. Why? Why am I so weak? I deserve to be punished for the evil I am inflicting upon these poor, innocent children. They're so innocent. But only my Lord has the right to punish me. Mere mortals don't have that right. They are themselves sinners; how can they presume to judge me? But they will, if they find me out. Matt and his redskin friend are already on to me, after that incident on Sunday. How could I let them bait me that way? Sweet Jesus, give me the willpower to resist the Dark One.'

Resolutely, Dewar makes the sign of the cross, struggling to compose himself. After a minute, he wipes the tears from his cheeks with his sleeve and takes a deep breath. Pulling off his jacket, he unbuttons and removes his shirt, dropping both in a pile on the floor. Trembling, he slips the rosary from around his thick neck and slides his fingers gently along the beads to the ornate crucifix. His shaking hand rises to his lips, and he kisses the tragic image of Jesus. Reaching left to the drawer of a side table, he digs under several articles and retrieves a whip hidden at the back of the drawer. He extends the crucifix out in front of his face with his left hand and begins to pray.

'My Lord and Father, creator of all, please forgive my sexual transgressions.'

With his right hand, the preacher whips the cat-tail lash over his shoulder, flinching as the knotted strand cuts into his already callused and scarred back.

'Please divert the attack of the Wicked One who brings lust and temptation into my life.'

Again he lashes himself over the shoulder, lacerating his skin.

'Let the Devil have no bond nor authority over me. Cover me with the blood of your Son, Jesus, and release the angels of Heaven to minister unto me.'

The third lash digs deep into his flesh, sending a spray of blood over his pants and the floor.

'Dear Lord, allow this humble penance to cleanse me of unrighteousness, relieve me of sexual temptation for these innocent boys, and reconcile me with your holy mission once more. In Jesus' name, Amen.'

Without warning, the door of the chamber opens. Dewar, startled by the intruder, drops the whip and reaches for his shirt.

'Sarah, damn you! How many times have I told you not to come in here without knocking? You have no business in here.' exclaims Dewar, embarrassed and angry.

'I'm so sorry, Pastor. I thought the place was empty. You should already be at the seminary. Oh dear, you're bleeding. Let me get you a towel.'

'I'm fine. Please just leave me alone.'

'Pastor, let me help you. Talk to me. I can help you get over this obsession.'

'Damn you, Sarah. You better not mention this to anyone. Do you hear me? No one!'

'I would never say anything that might hurt you, Pastor, but you have to stop the self-mortification. You know our Lord forgives you, if you repent. Penance is not required for reconciliation.'

'Who do you think you're preaching to, Sarah? Let me be. Get out of here! This is nothing I can't handle.'

'I only mean to help you, Pastor. This self-mutilation has to stop. Your back is a mess, and it's bound to get infected.'

'God damn it, Sarah! Are you happy now? You've made me take the Lord's name in vain. I don't know how to make it any clearer. Get out of my chambers. Go lock up and go home. Please!'

'As you wish, Pastor. I will pray to our heavenly Father that He hasten your recovery and bring you peace of mind.'

Dewar steps into the adjoining washroom, fills the sink half full with cool water from the tap and rinses his face. Leaning forward, his elbows on the sink, he looks into the mirror. Deep and guttural, almost a growl, he curses the reflection of the pitiful old pervert looking back at him. He spits at his reflection in disgust.

'This will not happen again, damn it! No more. Hear me, Satan? I will not succumb to your vile temptations any longer. I am stronger than you!'

Dewar puts his shirt back on. As he's buttoning it, he hears a muffled sound that he is sure is a cry for help. He hurries from the bathroom, through his chamber and out into the nave, trying to locate the source of the sound. He runs along the altar railing, past the pulpit to the center aisle, glancing frantically around himself. He is becoming concerned for the safety of his assistant, the only other person in the church. In the dim lighting, he can barely make out a gray shadow on the granite floor midway up the center aisle. As he approaches, it becomes a pool of fresh blood. He is still trying to assimilate the possible implications of the scene, when he hears a faint call.

'Pastor.'

The patch of blood leads to his right between the pews, where he finds Sarah lying on the floor in her own blood, struggling to breathe. Her dress is torn to shreds. Pieces of flesh hang from her mutilated face.

'Oh my God, Sarah. What the hell happened?' asks the pastor, moving towards the disfigured victim.

'No. Run, run,' whimpers Sarah, her weak voice wet and bubbly.

Dewar, confused and seeing no immediate threat, continues towards Sarah. He must get her to the hospital. Then he stops, frozen in place.

A gray timber wolf jumps onto the pew from the shadows of the side aisle and looks menacingly up at Dewar. Its snout is covered in fresh blood. Its hackles raised and its lips contracted, it moves towards the frightened pastor. Dewar back steps quickly along the pew, stumbling over the kneeler, into the center aisle. Turning back towards the altar, he is halted by another gray blocking his way. This wolf bares its fangs and snarls, advancing deliberately towards this new prey.

Terrified, Dewar turns and runs up the aisle toward the main doors. He slips on Sarah's blood and lands hard on the church floor, his head making a sickening sound as it slams first into the side of a pew, then into the granite. Dazed and disoriented, he struggles desperately to get back up, slipping and sliding in the slimy pool of Sarah's blood. He manages to regain his feet. Dizzy and in pain, he limps towards the main vestibule. He can't believe his eyes when a large black alpha wolf appears blocking his route. Looking left, he finds yet another member of the pack growling at him from between a pair of pews.

No other choice available, the wounded preacher limps to the right. His only chance of escape is up the rear staircase to the choir loft. The gate to the stairwell stands open, as usual. Rushing in and pulling the gate closed behind him, he is feeling the beginnings of relief when he is pulled to the floor from behind. The black wolf, snout between the bars of the gate, has a firm grip on his pant leg. Using all the strength he can muster,

Dewar kicks the black wolf in the snout with his free foot. Squealing in pain, the alpha steps back, shaking its snout to release the piece of pant leg from its teeth. Locking the gate, the pastor frantically scrambles backwards up the stairs.

Covered in sweat, adrenaline still racing through his veins, he sits on the top step for a moment to compose himself. His heart pounds under his rib-cage. His hands are trembling. Clenching them tightly, he pulls them to his body for comfort. Head between his knees, he closes his eyes and takes several slow, deliberate deep breaths. Calm is just beginning to vanquish anxiety when the revolting sound of the wolves gnawing and chewing on Sarah rises from below.

Suddenly fear and panic turn to anger. Sarah was not only his personal assistant, she had become, over the years, a dear friend and confidante. Now she is dead, horrifyingly mutilated, and being ripped to pieces by this pack of mangy wolves. Dewar jumps to his feet. Grabbing a folding chair from the stack by the gate, he moves to the railing and stares in disgust at the feeding frenzy below. A pair of wolves tug on a severed arm; another wolf pulls strands of tendon from a hip; others rip flesh from the torso. Like all canines, they are not chewing; everything is swallowed whole. Lifting the chair over his head, he roars as he heaves it at the ravenous pack.

'Awwwwrrggh!'

The chair caroms off the back of a pew and lands in the aisle with a crash. The wolves briefly halt their ravenous gorging, look up at the Pastor, then return to their feast unperturbed. Discouraged and helpless, Dewar sits in the first pew by the railing and begins to weep.

'Awwww. Somebody needs a hug.'

Dewar jerks with surprise at the unexpected female voice. He turns to peer into the dark recesses at the back of the choir loft. He is just able to make out a shadowy figure.

'Should I get you a sweet, innocent choir boy to comfort you?'

'Who's there?'

'No? Maybe you'd prefer Christine Henderson to satisfy your sick urges.'

'What's the meaning of this? Come out of the darkness, so I can see you!'

'No? Perhaps you're right. She has been a bit moody lately.' The figure steps forward so he can see her face. 'How about the mayor's sweet daughter?'

'Dawn Brady? What are you doing up here?'

'You don't sound very happy to see me.'

'You have to get out of here. You're not safe. A pack of murderous wolves has invaded the church. They've already slaughtered my assistant.'

'How touching. You're concerned with my safety. But I'm not the one in danger. In fact, the wolves are here because I let them in. I've been waiting up here for you.'

'That's not possible. They would have attacked you.'

'But you see, it's not me they want.'

'What are you talking about? I don't understand.'

'Let me explain, Pastor. As you may know, wolves are opportunistic, they look for situations that present food with the least effort and risk. This means they select vulnerable prey—the weak, the old and the sick. You, you twisted pervert, fit all of those categories.'

'Dawn, why would you say such terrible things? I am none of those things. What's gotten into you?'

'Shut up and let me finish! Often weakness is not obvious to human observers; your congregation, for instance; but wolves pick up cues that are too subtle for humans to notice.'

'That's enough of this nonsense. I don't care what you know, or think you know, about me, or even what Christine may have told you. You can't prove anything. Nobody will listen to you, especially after those false accusations you made about André.'

'You're probably right, but the wolves know your weakness, Pastor. They sense your sickness.'

'Damn the wolves. I escaped from those mangy dogs.'

'Do you really believe you could outrun or out-maneuver a pack of timber wolves? Especially after you fell and were injured? Actually, they herded you right to me, as instructed.'

'To you? That's preposterous. Why would they lead me to you?'

'Because today, I am the leader of the pack, the top dog, the alpha.'

'You're out of you mind. D'you think you scare me. I ought to take you to my chamber and...'

'The choir boy was your last victim, Dewar, and damned straight you should be scared.'

Dawn's fangs descend from her gums, her eyes turn yellow, her fingernails extend into claws, and her arms ripple with muscle.

Dewar stares at the young girl's transformation. Dawn grabs the terrified pastor by the collar and pulls him to her.

Face to face, she screams, 'This is for Christine, you sick fuck!'

Sinking her sharp canines deep into his neck, she siphons his fresh, warm blood. Dewar struggles in vain to escape the young vampire's powerful grip. Blood loss to his brain renders the pastor unconscious in moments; his body goes limp as the life is drained away.

Exhilarated by her newly acquired powers and by the satisfaction of her first blood conquest, Dawn lifts Dewar's body over her head. She calls down to the pack.

'Enjoy your meal, my brothers. You've earned it.'

She tosses Dewar's cadaver over the railing to the pack below. The body hits the bloody granite floor with a wet thud, and the wolves instinctively pounce on it and rip. The air is filled with the sounds of tearing flesh.

#

1980

Celreau, weak and light headed from hunger, carefully steps down into the cellar. He spots the donor cowering on his mattress in the corner of the room. Donni is clinging to a blanket, looking at the vampire in fear.

'Hi, Donni,' says Celreau, trying for a calming tone in his voice. The boy, too terrified to reply, tightens his grip on the blanket.

'I delivered your letter to your parents. They're so thrilled that you're making such great progress.'

Without answering, Donni begins to whimper.

'They asked me to tell you that Chance misses you, but he's doing great.'

'You're a liar!'

'Donni, be nice now. I wouldn't lie to you.'

'You're a liar and you hit me. You're a bad man.'

'Oh, c'mon. That little slap? I asked you to be quiet and you didn't listen. If those strangers would have discovered our hide-out, our whole project could have been ruined. The government people demand that we keep this location a secret. Look, I'm really sorry about hitting you, Donni, but you must understand that I had no choice.'

'I don't like you. Just leave me alone.'

Celreau grabs Donni tightly by the arm. 'Listen, son. You have to be sensible. Now be brave, lay back, relax and take your injection.'

'No, I won't,' screams Donni, and he kicks Celreau.

'That's enough, boy. Be quiet and sit still,' orders Celreau, noticeably flustered. The vampire leans towards the boy and bites down on his neck. Reacting to the sting of the bite, Donni flails in a desperate attempt to escape. Celreau tightens his hold on the donor, sinking his fangs more deeply into the boy's tender flesh. Struggling in vain, Donni loses consciousness and goes limp on the mattress. Delighted by the familiar iron taste of the warm blood seeping along his tongue and down his throat, Celreau feels the blood pool at the bottom of his stomach and gently ooze into his duodenum. Energy is suddenly flooding his body.

His thirst for blood now quenched, Celreau releases his hold of Donni's neck. He resists the primal urge to gorge himself at the risk of infecting or killing his host. He lays Donni in the recovery position on the bed and covers him with a blanket.

A squeak in the floorboards overhead startles Celreau. He turns to see Dawn looking down from the open trap door.

'Dawn! You startled me,' says Celreau.

'I came as fast as I could.' The words were spaced around the panting in her voice. 'The road was wet and muddy.'

'Wait there. I'm coming up.' When he reaches the top of the stairs, Celreau is surprised by Dawn wrapping her arms tightly around him.

'We're going to be so happy, Gabriel.'

'We are? I'm not sure I understand. What's this all about?'

'You're kidding, right?'

'Kidding? Kidding about what?'

'You said that you'd always be by my side, you'd teach me everything I need to know.'

'Really? I said that?'

'Yes, really! Just a couple of hours ago, when you were talking to me in my head. You said that we're a powerful couple and that we'll have anything and everything we want in our eternal life together.'

Celreau shrugs his shoulders and stares at Dawn in confusion. 'I haven't seen you at all today.'

'Quit it, Gabriel. You're not funny. You invited me up here for a feast, remember?'

A loud caw interrupts the couple. Celreau spots the Raven hopping along the walkway outside the barracks door.

'Damn you, Xhuuya, I should've known,' swears Celreau under his breath. He runs out the front door and chases the Raven away. Turning back towards the barracks, movement in the direction of the front gate catches his eye. He sees a small group of people preparing to enter the property. Before he can be seen by them, he hurries back inside.

'Gabriel, what's going on?' asks Dawn.

'Nothing. Listen, Dawn. I was just teasing you earlier. We'll be great together. I'm so glad you agreed to come join me.'

Dawn runs to Celreau and hugs him. 'I knew you were just messing with me.'

'Indeed. Now follow me. I have a surprise for you.' Celreau leads Dawn back to the cellar and points down at Donni. 'I know you're weak and famished. Your first meal sweetheart. Enjoy!'

Dawn looks back at Celreau with her blood-stained canines now exposed.

'Ah. I see you've started without me, sweetheart.'

'Just an appetizer, and I had to share with friends. I'm still famished.'

'Well, enjoy. Bon appétit.'

She pounces to the cellar floor and onto the defenseless boy Sinking her canines into Donni, she ravenously drains his lifeblood.

In turn, Celreau wastes no time. Out the front door, he runs down the path to the gate.

Pamela
1946

David and Pam are standing just inside the door of the Roxy Theatre looking out at the light rain falling on the street. Evidently it was raining harder while they were in the theatre because water is running in streams down the gutter.

'I'll flag a cab,' suggests David.

'Don't be silly. It's just a little drizzle. C'mon, live a little, or are you made of sugar?'

Pam takes David's hand and pulls him into the rain.

'You're crazy, you know that?' asks David with a laugh.

'I love the rain. It's so refreshing—so rejuvenating. Don't you just love the rain?'

'I never really thought about it, although if you live in Vancouver, it's probably best to learn to appreciate it.'

'Don't be such a fuddy-duddy. C'mon, run—catch me if you can!'

Pam runs splashing along the sidewalk. David quickly overtakes her. Wrapping his arms around her, he scoops her up and kisses her deeply.

'Oh, David. I feel so alive, so amazed not to have seen the freshness, the potential of the world around me. I feel like a butterfly that just escaped from it's cocoon.'

'Alright, Miss Butterfly, we better head back to your place before your wings turn to fins.'

'Why sir! Aren't you at least going to invite me over to your apartment for a night cap?'

'I'd love to, darling, but I live in a boarding house, and the landlady won't allow female guests after hours. She is a mean old hag!'

'Which boarding house?'

'It's an old hotel, the Sylvia, on Gilford. It's been converted into a boarding house.'

'I know the one. My mom worked in the kitchen there for over fifteen years when it was a hotel.'

'No foolin'! Small world, eh? Anyway, the old battle-ax is pretty strict, and it's getting late. Let's get you home.'

'I suppose we should head back. I've probably had enough excitement for one day. Actually, come to think of it, I had more excitement today than I've had all year.'

They walk together hand-in-hand for a few blocks without talking. Then, in a soft voice, Pam asks, 'David, how long are you in town for? I know you can't tell me why you're here, and I respect that, but can I expect to see you again?'

'I'm sorry. I realize how terribly insensitive I must seem, but you understand that the confidentiality of my client is imperative. Anything I disclose to you could potentially endanger my case, my reputation, and even your own safety.'

'I understand. And I respect your privacy. I do. Don't worry about it.'

'Pam, please don't take it personally. It's just complicated, you know?'

'Actually, no, I don't know. That's the point. But hey, don't lose any sleep over it. I'd just like to know if you plan on skipping town soon, or if this—whatever this is—matters.'

'Of course it matters. More than you can know. Okay, you know what? I'm sorry. You're right. What am I thinking? I know that I can trust you.'

'You do? I mean, that's great. You know that anything you tell me stays between us.'

'I'm a private detective. I was hired by a wealthy prominent family from Victoria to find their son. The army informed them that he was killed by mortar fire at the battle of Vichy in France, but they are convinced he is still alive.'

'Why don't the parents believe the army's report?'

'For one thing, I know that someone recently has been using his I.D. That means one of two things: either the parents are right and their son is alive, or someone is impersonating the dead son. A few weeks after the devastating news, a young man with an amputated leg arrived on their doorstep looking for their son. They were stunned to hear that he and their son had spent the long voyage home beside each other on the hospital ship. The pair had landed in Halifax together about a month earlier. The young veteran said that their son suffered a gun shot wound to the shoulder during the conflict, but was very much alive. The medics commented that his rate of healing was nothing short of miraculous.'

'That's strange. The military is very careful with the handling of these cases. Identification of deceased soldiers is checked and double checked. This seems very odd to me.'

'How do you know this, Pam?'

'This also seems a little strange, but I happen to work in the army administrative offices in town. I handle these sorts of files all the time.'

'No! Is that the offices on Water Street, the same ones that house the recruitment center? You're pulling my leg?'

'No. I've worked there for years.'

'No kidding. I was there just last week. My attempts to acquire some information from your office were unsuccessful. They turned me down flat. Apparently information of that sort is classified.'

'I'm sorry, David, but that's policy. The information's only available directly to the next of kin. Who served you at the counter?'

'Some tall redhead wearing a ton of make-up and the attitude to go with it.'

'Oh, that's Ethel. She can come off like a bitch sometimes. Her bark is worse than her bite, though. She fills in for me when I'm on break, or something.'

'Well, unfortunately, that leaves me with only one option. I'll have to steal the files in question.'

'Are you crazy? That's a federal building, David. They have soldiers guarding it year round. You do know soldiers carry guns, right? And if you are caught, you'll go to a federal penitentiary for a long time.'

'Yes, I know. That's how important this is and why it's imperative that I get into the building undetected. Without those files, my mission will fail.'

'Wait, maybe I can help you get access to the filing room.'

'Out of the question!'

'But David, I have a key and full access to the filing room.'

'They'll be just as hard on you for helping me to steal classified military documents as they'll be on me. If we get caught, we'll both go to prison.'

'We won't get caught. I promise.'

'I can't possibly expect you to put your career, and maybe your life, at risk, Pam.'

'David, listen to me, please. Let me help you. I've worked in that office for what seems a lifetime now, and the greatest excitement I get every day is listening to Ethel tell me about her new make-up, or the scarf she just bought at Simpson Sears. This would be so exciting and great fun. What do you say?'

'I say I think your nuts to consider helping me, but if you really think we could pull this off together…'

'Oh, David. Thank you, thank you, thank you,' shouts Pam wrapping her arms around his neck. 'This's going to be so much fun!'

As she leans forward to kiss him, David takes her by the shoulders and holds her away, looking very stern. 'No, this is not going to be fun. What we are considering is very serious, and if we don't go about it exactly right, we're both going to jail. I don't want to go to jail, and I certainly don't want to see you behind bars. A delicate flower like you would never survive.

'We have to prepare. We'll only get one shot at this, so we have to get it right the first time. Now, tell me in detail the daily routine of everyone that works in that department.'

Fontaine
1980

Matt and Jesse are leaning against the station wagon, arms crossed, both staring in silence at the military site ahead. The evening has turned cool, and they exhale small billowy breaths that rise and dissipate in the evening air.

'Perfect timing. They should be out on the trail right about now,' says Frank, excitingly sliding his Cooey from its weathered case.

'I sure hope so,' says Jesse.

'Of course, if it were sunny, it would be better,' adds Frank, fumbling bullets from his jacket pocket. 'But when does that ever happen in this suck-ass part of the country?'

'I remember a couple of years back, I think on July 1st, the sun came out for about an hour,' says Matt sarcastically.

'Canada Day, right?' adds Jesse laughing.

'I doubt that, boy. I'm surprised you even remember how to tie your shoes,' blurts Frank as he slides the loaded clip into the base of his rifle.

'Whatever. At least I wasn't passed out, slobbering drunk, on the kitchen floor,' mumbles Matt.

'What was that, boy?' questions his dad.

'Nothing,' answers Matt.

'That's what I thought. Now let's get on the trail before it's too late.'

They are about to climb the barbed wire fence next to the security gate when Sergeant Kirkpatrick's suburban pulls up behind their car, followed closely by the corporal's Jeep. The policemen step out of their vehicles carrying shotguns and approach the group. Ignoring Matt and Jesse, Kirkpatrick addresses Frank.

'Evening, Frank.'

'Tom.'

'Who's your sidekick?' asks Frank.

'This is Corporal Fontaine, on loan to me for the duration of this investigation.'

'Nice to meet you.' The Corporal extends his hand.

Pointedly ignoring the offered handshake, Frank says, 'I thought we were cutting back. No wonder my taxes keep going up! By the way, you couldn't find a white guy?'

'My ancestors were here a thousand years before yours arrived, mister. I don't appreciate…'

'Fontaine, let it go. Frank, don't be disrespecting the Corporal. He is more than qualified, and we're lucky to have him.'

'Whatever you say,' grunts Frank.

'Where you heading?' asks Kirkpatrick.

'Grouse hunting. Why? Is that a crime now, too?'

'No, but trespassing on private government property is a federal offense,' states Corporal Fontaine.

'You're not serious! This base has been abandoned since '45. You'd know that if you were from around here, Tonto.'

'Frank! Enough. I won't warn you again.'

'Hell, everybody passes through this area all the time—hunters, hikers, picnickers—to get to the river valley.'

'That doesn't make it right or legal, Frank.'

'Don't you have anything better to do than harass innocent tax-paying citizens out chicken hunting? Why're you two up here, anyway?'

'Did these kids talk you into coming up here, Frank?' asks Kirkpatrick.

'Why, yes, as a matter of fact they did. How did you know?'

Kirkpatrick frowns and looks over at Matt and Jesse.

'You told us you would come and get us before coming up here,' blurts Matt before the Sergeant can say a word.

'What in God's name is going on here?' asks a confused Frank.

'Frank, I'm afraid these kids didn't bring you up here to hunt grouse. I'd say it's more like a wild goose chase.'

'Matt, I should have known you and your savage were up to no good. Why was it so all-fired important for me to bring you up here? Out with it, then.'

Matt stares at his father, speechless, holding back tears.

'I said out with it, boy!' yells the father.

'Mr. Taylor, this is no time for you to puff out your chest and prove you're a big man by putting down your son,' interrupts Jesse. 'We're wasting time. Donni is prob'ly lying in that barracks half dead. If we don't hurry, it'll be too late to save him.'

Frank grabs and shakes Jesse by the sleeve. 'Shut up, you lyin' injun,' he shouts at her. 'I'm not talking to you, am I?'

'Let me go! You're hurting me,' shouts Jesse defiantly.

'Let her go,' commands the Corporal, stepping forward.

Frank raises his hand signaling Fontaine to stop.

'Frank,' commands Kirkpatrick. 'She may be right. Let her go.'

'What? You're going to defend this little misfit after she lied to both of us?'

'I'm not defending her, Frank, but I'm afraid she may be right. We have new evidence that suggests Donni may still be alive, held captive in the barracks.'

'I knew it,' says Jesse as she pulls her arm free from Frank's grip.

'Tom, look. Seems we have more company,' says Fontaine, pointing towards the military base.

The small group turns and watches as Gabriel Celreau waves and walks up to the gate.

'Well, this's quite the welcoming committee' says Celreau, smiling as he climbs over the security gate.

'Gabriel, what're you doing out by the barracks?' asks Kirkpatrick.

'I'm just out getting some exercise, Sergeant. I try to get a good hike in at least once a day. The river trail is quite nice this time of year.'

'See, Tom,' Frank says to the Sergeant, a self-satisfied look on his face. 'I told you everybody uses this darn trail. You spot any grouse along the way?'

'As a matter of fact I did, Mr. Taylor. I startled a few hens just over at the trail head.'

'Excuse me for interrupting your conversation, Celreau, but I have to ask you to accompany the Corporal down to the station to answer a few questions?'

'Questions about what? Trespassing? Isn't that a bit extreme?' asks Celreau, chuckling.

'It's just standard procedure. We just want to ask you a few questions in regards to Donni's disappearance, and if everything checks out, you'll be free to go.'

'Donni? I thought that case was closed.'

'It was, but so far the body hasn't been recovered from the river, so we need to tie up some loose ends in order to close the file. You understand.'

'I suppose the fact that I was the one who discovered Donni's t-shirt along the river would make me a suspect, right?'

'Like I said, Gabriel, it's just standard police procedure. A few questions and you'll be free to go.'

'No problem. I certainly understand rules and policies, but I'm usually the one enforcing them.'

'Wonderful. I appreciate your cooperation. Please go with Corporal Fontaine, and I'll see you at the station house shortly.'

The corporal leads Celreau to the Jeep.

'Place your hands on the roof of the vehicle,' demands Fontaine.

'You got to be kidding me,' says Celreau looking over his shoulder at Kirkpatrick.

'Indulge us, please. It's standard practice, Mr. Celreau,' says Kirkpatrick.

Celreau reluctantly places his hands on the Jeep's roof.

'Spread your legs.'

'Whatever turns you on,' says Celreau, sarcastically.

The corporal quickly frisks Celreau, then removes handcuffs from his belt.

'Hands behind your back,' orders Fontaine.

Celreau looks back at Kirkpatrick in disgust. Kirkpatrick nods to Celreau. The corporal secures the handcuffs around Celreau's wrists.

Looking Fontaine straight in the face, Celreau says, 'Wow. You made your mother real proud today.'

The Corporal opens the Jeep door. 'Get in, smart–ass!'

Pamela

1946

Two days later, David arrives at the military administration office on Water Street at 10:00 a.m. sharp, as planned. He is wearing a pair of coveralls and carrying an oblong red tool-box. Mounting the granite steps, he passes the guard, enters through the large oak doors and approaches the front reception counter.

'Good morning, sir. How may I help you?' asks Pam nervously.

'Good morning. I'm with 'Secure Lock and Key.' I understand you have a lock that's giving you problems,' answers David with a wink.

'Yes, of course. We've been expecting you. Please follow me.'

'Miss Walden.'

'Yes, sir?'

'Who is this gentleman?'

'A locksmith. He's here to repair the lock on the file room door, sir. The lock's been acting up for over a week.'

'I don't recall receiving a requisition for this repair?'

'Well, I believe Ethel put it through. It should've crossed your desk last week, sir.'

'Last week, eh? Didn't get it. Where's Ethel?'

'She didn't show up for work this morning. She's probably home sick.'

'Sick indeed.'

'Well, with all of the rain we've been getting and all the colds and flus, I'm surprised more of the staff are not ill.'

'Poppycock. I haven't been sick enough to miss work in more than twenty years. Besides, I expect employees to call in when taking sick days. I'll have a talk with her when she gets back.'

'Yes sir. Of course.'

'Well, you're not getting paid to stand around. Get that lock fixed and get back to work. And get this civilian out of here.'

As the pair approach the file room, Pam pulls a key from her pocket. She is shaking so badly that two attempts to unlock the door are unsuccessful. David takes the key. 'You'd think there really was something wrong with the lock.'

A moment later, they are inside, closing the door behind them.

'Wow!' Pam gasps. 'That was so close. I'm so excited, I can't stop shaking.'

'You did very well, Pam. Now, take a couple of deep breaths,' suggests David looking past Pam at the roomful of filing cabinets.

'Okay, okay. My heart is pounding. Okay, I know—breathe.' In a few moments, her breathing has returned almost to normal.

'Better?'

'Yes, much. What do you need me to do?' asks Pam, her excitement starting to mount again.

'Steer me to the filing cabinets containing files of soldiers deceased in the last twelve months.'

'Oh, that's easy. Right here along this wall,' points Pam.

'The whole row?'

'Yes. I'm afraid so. War comes at a terrible price. Most of these soldiers were barely out of high school.'

'Alphabetical order?'

"Yes, starting at this end. Family names first—of course."

David begins to walk down the aisle, hunching over to look at the labels on the drawers.

'What name are you looking for, David?' questions Pam following closely behind.

'Sorry, Pam, but I'd rather not say. You have already done quite enough, and I don't want to risk getting you into deeper trouble. If we're caught, you have deniability this way. Aah! Here we go.'

Opening the top file drawer partway down the row, he begins to finger quickly through the folders. He pulls one halfway out to check the name. 'Voilà!'

The filing room doorknob turns. Pam stifles a shriek, freezing in place.

'David!'

He lets the folder drop back into the drawer. Turning quickly, he pulls Pam into an embrace as he falls back against the cabinet, slamming the drawer shut. He kisses Pam with passion.

The filing room door swings open to reveal Pam's boss standing in the doorway with his hands firmly on his bulky waist.

'Well, well, well. Isn't this a fine how do you do!'

'Sir, I can explain. It's not what it looks like,' says Pam desperately.

'Save it, Miss Walden. I would expect this kind of behavior from Ethel. But I never in my life would have expected this from you.'

'Please don't fire me, sir. I need this job. I'm so sorry. Please, please don't fire me,' pleads Pam beginning to cry.

'Calm down, Miss Walden. This is not the first time shenanigans have occurred in this room. Believe me, if these walls could talk—well, never mind.'

'You mean I'm not fired?'

'No, you're not fired, but consider yourself on probation, young lady.

And I admit it is nice to know you are not the cold fish everyone seems to think you are.'

'Thank you, sir. You won't regret it, I promise.'

'Indeed. Now get back to reception, and escort Romeo off the premises. I will hire a professional locksmith myself to fix the door.'

'I appreciate your understanding, sir,' says David on the way through the office towards the door.

'Hmm, indeed. Don't even think of sending me an invoice. Is that clear, young man?'

'Absolutely transparent,' answers David, stepping out the office door.

Trottier

1980

Matt, Jesse and Frank follow Kirkpatrick down the path toward the barracks. 'Everybody stay together and keep your eyes open. We're looking for any sign of Donni,' instructs Kirkpatrick.

They walk the perimeter of a couple of abandoned buildings before Matt points and exclaims, 'Look!' Breaking from the group, he races towards the open door of one of the barracks several buildings away.

'Stop,' shouts Kirkpatrick.

'What?' answers Matt, stopping in his tracks.

'Matt, what did I just say about staying together?'

'Yeah, 'kay, whatever. What're we waiting for?'

'Get back here and keep quiet.'

Matt shuffles back to the group and stands next to Jesse.

'Matt, you stay here with Jesse and don't budge till I get back. Understand? Frank, you're my back-up. Come with me.'

'Uh! Tom, I should stay here and keep an eye on these two.'

'They'll be fine out here, Frank. I need you to come with me in case I run into trouble inside.'

'I...I really think I should stay here and protect the kids, Tom.'

'Really, Frank? Protect them from what?'

'Well, uh, it's getting dark and, uh, there're wolf packs known to wander these woods,' says Frank sheepishly, looking down at the ground.

'Wolf packs! Yeah, okay, sure. That's mighty courageous of you, Frank. Fine. Stay here. You probably wouldn't be much help in a pinch anyway.' Turning to the others, the Sergeant repeats, 'Stay here. Nobody sets foot in the building until I return and give the all clear. Understand?'

'Yes sir,' answers Matt.

Kirkpatrick grips his shotgun tightly, muzzle pointing ahead, and cautiously steps through the doorway. The building is dark. He slips the large flashlight from its leather harness attached to his belt, and flashes the bright beam around the main room. Immediately evident are the fresh footprints on the dusty hardwood floor. Some lead to a kitchen on the right, and others towards a hallway across the room. He follows the set of prints down the hallway. He finds the first room empty except for an old chest against the wall, so he continues to the only other door on the hall. The door is closed. He slowly turns the knob and inches the door open. He is startled to find an open casket lying in the middle of the room. He is assaulted by a smell that makes him gag.

'What the hell?' whispers Kirkpatrick. He feels goose bumps all over his body, and his heart rate begins to rise. He anxiously flashes the light around the room, then back down the hallway. Walking towards the closet, he cocks the hammer on his shotgun. He places the flashlight on the floor with the beam directed at the closet door. Leveling the shotgun at the opening with his right hand, he takes a deep breath, then whips the closet door open with his left.

Involuntarily, he jumps back. A body obviously badly decomposed, is lying on the floor of the closet. The stench is much worse, and he feels his gorge rising. Leaning the shotgun against the coffin, he tries to collect his senses. Covering his mouth with his forearm, he approaches the cadaver. A quick inspection and a search through ragged pockets reveal no clue to the identity of the deceased. His attention is attracted by what appears to be a leather briefcase in the corner of the closet next to the corpse's feet. He opens it to discover a couple of history books and several manila folders containing pages of hand-written notes.

It's not possible, thinks Kirkpatrick as he opens the cover of one of the books. 'My God!' exclaims the Sergeant aloud. The name of the author and the signature on the title page were the same—Stephen Williams.

The Sergeant straightens up and heads back down the hallway.

Damn! I've always suspected Celreau had something to do with Williams' disappearance. He was way too smug when I questioned him about his friend. There was something very odd about that son of a bitch from the get-go. And now he's involved with this mess somehow. I have to get back to the station and make sure we can hold Celreau until I get answers to some crucial questions.

Kirkpatrick retrieves his flashlight and is crossing the living room headed for the door when he is halted by a strange noise coming from the kitchen area. What the hell is that? It's like no sound he has ever heard.

Cautiously, Kirkpatrick enters the kitchen, scanning the room with his flashlight. The light beam illuminates an open trap door to the right of the floor's center. He listens intently to what sound like very loud sloshing and sucking noises coming from below. Stepping down into the cellar for a closer look, he is horrified at what he sees—Dawn staring back at him, long canines protruding from her bloody mouth. Donni Cardinal lies pale and lifeless on her lap.

'Dawn, whats wrong with you? My God, what've you done?'

She stands and walks towards the stairs, dragging the limp boy behind her with one hand.

'I'm having supper, Officer Kirkpatrick. Donni is such a good little boy, but strangely enough, I'm still famished.'

'Dawn, stop now and drop the boy,' commands Kirkpatrick.

Dawn begins to climb the cellar steps, still dragging the dead boy effortlessly behind her.

'I said stop, Dawn. Stop or I'll shoot.'

Kirkpatrick points the shotgun directly at Dawn's chest as he retreats to the kitchen. Undeterred, the young vampire reaches the main floor and continues her steady advance on the frightened officer.

'Drop the boy,' orders Kirkpatrick, his voice trembling. 'Drop him now or I'll shoot. Do you understand?'

'Fine, be that way,' answers Dawn. She drops the boy's body with a thud to the kitchen floor.

'Good. Now stop where you are and lie flat on the floor,' commands Kirkpatrick.

'I don't think so.' Pouncing, she grabs the shotgun from the officer before he has time to react. Kirkpatrick falls backwards onto his ass and watches dumbfounded as Dawn bends the barrel of the gun like it was made of rubber.

'You see, Tom, the mayor's sweet, innocent daughter is all grown up.' She grips the officer's throat and lifts him gagging and choking to his knees.

'Nobody tells me what to do anymore. Certainly not you! Understand?' Grinning, Dawn raises the officer effortlessly into the air above her head. Kirkpatrick's limbs flail in desperation, his lips turn blue and his bulging eyes roll back into his head. He loses unconscious and hangs limp in Dawn's tight grip. 'Your Métis boy was barely an appetizer. You're just what I need to top off my appetite.'

The novice vampire lowers Tom to her face and bites into his thick neck. 'Pathetic humans,' says Dawn, as she finishes. Turning, she throws the officer across the room and out the open door, Kirkpatrick's head cracking against the door frame.

Pamela
1946

Pam tucks the folder under her arm and locks the office door behind her. Saying goodnight to the guard, she exits the federal building through the front door and she skips down the granite steps to the sidewalk.

She smiles smugly, then laughs out loud. She has never felt so alive! Nor so wicked! Exhilarated, she purposely splashes through the shallow puddles on the wet sidewalk.

We taught that old fart a lesson, didn't we? Who says Pam Walden would never make love in the filing room. Cold fish, eh? Ha! And the stupid bugger fell for it. Putting a dainty hand to her chest, she mimics a high-pitched, shy voice, 'I'm so sorry, sir. I will work late tonight with no overtime to make up for my misbehavior.' Switching to a deeper, more dumb-sounding voice, she answers, 'Good, young lady, and I hope you have learned your lesson.'

David will be so proud of me when I give him the files he was after. Lucky the folder was crooked in the cabinet drawer or I never would have found it. I can't wait to see his face when I hand it to him.

Pam turns down Gilford and up the street to the boarding house. I can't believe I'm doing this. I just stole a confidential file from the admin offices of the Canadian Army! Up until a few days ago, I wouldn't have replaced a typewriter ribbon without authorization. I feel like a different woman since the day I met David. I've never felt so alive, so excited, so happy. This is going to make him happy, too.

And that's all I want—to make him happy. Don't ask me how I know, but I am going to marry that man. I never thought it possible, but I know this is it. Ethel has always told me one day the right guy would walk into my life. I've waited for years! Just when I was ready to give up, Pow! Who knew?

Pam skips up the steps to the front door, which she finds locked. Sighing, she steps back a bit to look up at the second floor. Yep, as often was the case when she was a child, the window on the second floor landing is partly open. The branch from the old elm tree next to the building is thicker and even closer to the window than it was all those years ago. Many was the time that she gained access to the locked hotel by way of the elm tree and that window, to visit her mom who was cleaning the rooms.

The debate is short—go home to change into slacks and a shirt more suitable for climbing, or be entirely unladylike and shinny up the tree in her dress. She is too excited to wait. Turning her back to the street, she lifts the hem of her dress, reaches under and unclips her nylons from her garter belt. She kicks her shoes off, then gently roles the stockings down her legs, and places them in her purse. Nylons are too darned expensive to ruin needlessly. She leaves her shoes off.

Slipping the file into her blouse, she steps toward the old elm tree.

'Hello, old friend. Remember me?'

Without really having to think about it, Pam climbs the tree trunk, making her way up the old limbs to the branch that extends toward the window. Sitting sideways, feet dangling, she slowly slides over until she is right in front of the window. She leans forward, balancing herself with one hand, and eases the window wide. In a moment she is inside brushing leaves and bits of bark from her clothing.

This floor has three bedrooms and a common washroom. Pam disregards the first room; the strident sounds of a screaming baby testify that it is not David's room.

Through the open door across the hall, she sees an old man laying on a bed in his underwear smoking a cigarette. He lowers his newspaper and looks directly at her

'Hey, sweetheart. Don't be shy. C'mon in,' invites the old man.

'Sorry, wrong room,' returns Pam.

'Awww. That's okay. Join me for a beer, kitten.'

'Thanks, but no thanks.'

'Suit yourself,' scoffs the stranger raising the newspaper.

'Actually, I'm looking for my friend, David. He rents a room here.'

'Not sure how that's my problem,' answers the old man, without looking up from his reading.

'I thought perhaps you've seen him and could direct me to his room. He is tall, dark hair, lives alone.'

'Across the hall's the only other bachelor in the joint, but I don't think he's lonely, sweetie, if ya know what I mean.

'Listen, kitten. You can believe whatever you want, but your Prince Charming entertains more ladies in that room than Valentino. Either way, I really don't give a rat's ass.'

'Okay. Well, thank you.'

'Hum,' mutters the old man.

Pam crosses the hall to the last room on the floor and puts her ear to the door. Nothing.

'David? Are you home? David, it's me, Pam. Open up, please.'

She tries the doorknob, which turns freely. The door swings open. A strong putrid odor of rotting garbage makes her step back momentarily. She feels around the door frame for the light switch and flicks it up. The room remains dark.

'Hello, David? It's Pam.'

Her eyes slowly adjust to the darkness. When she can make out a desk against the wall, she shuffles over and turns the desk lamp on. The room is empty except for a bed and the desk. Removing the folder from her blouse, she sets it on the corner of the bed. Deciding to wait despite the odor, she sits down. Sitting there, glancing around the room, her eyes are drawn to a notepad lying near the center of the desk. Curious, knowing full well she is invading David's privacy, she reaches for the pad and begins to read.

'My god! What the heck?'

The notepad is a day-by-day record of Pam's movements—each page, a different day of the week.

Monday—
Leaves house at 6:45
Arrives at recruitment office 7:15
Lunch Cathedral Square
Leaves office 5:15
Home 5:45
Café Brûlé 7:30
Home 9:30

Tuesday—
Leaves home 6:55
Arrives at office 7:30
Lunch on steps
Leaves office 5:30
Stops at corner store
Home 6:30
Café Brûlé 7:10
Home 9:00

Pam flips to page three. She gasps in disbelief, her hand rising almost involuntarily to her mouth.

Pamela Walden
Daughter of Frank and Dorothy Walden
Age 40
Plain looking
Low self-esteem
Workaholic
Café Brûlé, Prior and Main
Window seat
Orange Pekoe Tea with honey

Best friend, Ethel McMillan
Knows too much
Easily seduced
Dispose of her

Pamela begins to whimper. Tears run down her cheeks. She stares blankly at the notepad, trying to comprehend what she just read.

No! This can't be. This, all this has been a lie? The coffee shop, the poetry, th-th-the sex? But why? Why would he do this to me? And how stupid am I? To believe someone like David, if that's his real name, could truly want me, love me? What a dope. Did he do all this just to get me to help him steal a file? Really? No. I don't believe it. I won't believe it. The dance, the love making. I felt something—a connection—it was real. There must be a reason. A logical explanation. I have to talk to David.

She pushes the notepad away from her and examines the desk more closely. The two larger side drawers are both empty when she checks. In the shallow center drawer above the leg hole she finds a worn brown men's wallet. Hesitating at first, she screws up her courage and thumbs through it: a small amount of Canadian currency, a driver's license and a laminated Winnipeg Free Press I.D. card with David's face on it for the. The name on both cards is Marcel Bélanger.

He even lied to me about his name! I am such a fool!

Pam looks nervously around the room. Her hand shaking, she wipes the tears from her face.

She is so upset that the foul odor is no longer tolerable; now it's overwhelming. She gags. The smell seems to be coming from the closet in the corner of the room. What appears to be a glistening pool of liquid has oozed from under the closet door and is drying on the floor.

She crosses the room and kneels to examine the thick translucent liquid. Dipping the end of her index finger, she raises it reluctantly to her nose. Immediately she vomits, adding to the noisome mess.

Trying to collect herself, she gets up. She reaches for the closet doorknob.

Please, Jesus in heaven, protect me from all evil and assure me that David, or Marcel, is safe. Dear Virgin Mother, give me the courage to face my enemies, and shield me with your eternal grace.

Terrified at what she may discover inside, but powerless to resist the urge, she opens the closet door.

Bodies—lots of bodies! Naked dead bodies—cadavers—men and women, all hanging from meat hooks, side by side. Pam's mind stops functioning. In shock, she is frozen in place, unable to move. She cannot process the horror before her. Their mouths are wide open, their purple tongues hang out, their vacant eyes stare down at her. Somehow their skin seems to be moving, trembling almost in some coordinated rhythm.

Pam slams the closet door closed, the only way to free herself from the mesmerizing sight. The door reverberates and bounces back open. One of the corpses rips from its meat hook and falls against Pam sending her backwards onto the bedroom floor. The body lands on top of her. Trapped by the cadaver, she vomits again, down the side of her face, over her neck and bodice. She lashes out wildly, punching and tugging at the dead body, desperately trying to get out from under. She manages to slide herself away, partly due to the slipperiness of her own vomit. With a final kick, she heaves the body backwards into the closet. The battered body bumps into the hanging corpses behind it. As she watches, frozen in fear, the dead bodies swing back and forth like a pendulum of an old grandfather clock. With each swing the hooks sink deeper and deeper into the rotten bodies until the skin begins to stretch. The hooks quickly tear through the decomposing flesh and bodies drop, one behind the other, like zombie dominoes. The first two hit the floor next to her, but the third lands directly across her legs. Trapped! She looks down at the bulky carcass staring up at her with hollowed glazed eyes. From somewhere deep inside herself, she finds the courage and strength to pull herself free.

A new sight makes her wretch, but all she has left are dry heaves. Her kick had split the bloated abdomen open, releasing a slurry of slithering maggots and fetid ooze. Pam, crying uncontrollably, stands up and backs away from the disgusting slimy heap. When her legs encounter the bed, she sits, drawing her feet up like a child afraid of the monsters under the bed. As she reaches to pull the blankets up around her, she feels something leathery and cool against her hip. She freezes. Against every instinct, she forces herself to look under the covers. The pale, blank-eyed corpse of her best friend, Ethel, stares up at her.

Jumping off the bed, Pam runs for the door. It opens before she gets to it and David steps into the room.

'What the hell, David? Why?'

David grasps Pam's delicate neck in his big hand. A smile broadens across his face as Pam draws her final breath, her question unanswered.

Matt & Jesse
1980

Frank sits down on the front steps, pulls a whiskey flask from his inside coat pocket and takes a heavy swig. From an outside pocket, he retrieves his smokes and a lighter, quickly lighting up with shaking hands.

'Shit. I can't believe you, Dad.'

'What?'

'Mom died of lung cancer. What more do you need to know?'

'Your mother gave up on life,' snaps Frank, taking another drink.

'Right. So what's your excuse?'

'Watch your mouth. Whoddaya think you're talkin' to?'

'A drunken coward, that's who!'

'Matt, don't. You know there's no point,' says Jesse, putting a hand on her friend's arm.

'No. He needs to hear it. Ever since mom died, you've done nothing but drink and hate. You've decided your life sucks and make no effort to try to improve things.'

'So what's it to you? You've got a roof over your head and food on your plate every day. D'you think it's easy bein' a single father?'

'Give me a break. Even a fuckin' dog gets food and shelter. And it's been a long time since you came even close to acting like a father, single or not.'

'Waddaya want from me, kid? You want a fuckin' hug? That what you want?'

'Fuck you! I want a father, goddamit! A father who cares for his son and has the courage to face life. A father who's got the balls to back someone when they ask for help. Not a coward who hides behind booze and excuses at the first sign of trouble.'

'I don't like the way you're talkin' to me, Matt. You know I loved your mother. She was the love of my life. She didn't have to leave me. She could've beat the cancer, but she gave up. She left me alone to raise you in this fuckin' shithole town. She broke my heart, she broke my spirit. Whiskey takes away my pain and helps me forget her.'

'So, why take it out on me? Wha' did I ever do to you?' implores Matt.

'Your eyes, your mouth, the way you talk—just like your mother. Every time I look at you, I see her. You remind me of the love, the joy, the adventure that filled my life back when your mom and me were together. We were so happy.

'I'm so sorry, son,' says Frank, eyes now beginning to tear up. 'You're right. It ain't fair to come down on you. It was never your fault.'

Matt stares at his dad, speechless in disbelief. Jesse pushes Matt towards his dad. 'Go on, Matt.'

Matt puts his hand on his father's shoulder. 'Thanks, Dad. Honestly, it's hard for me without her, too. For what it's worth, I forgive you.'

'It's worth more than I can tell you, son.'

Father and son flinch, leaping to their feet, as Kirkpatrick's limp body lands hard on the ground next to them. He lies moaning, his head and neck in a pool of blood soaking into the ground.

'Holy shit!' exclaims Frank. Stunned, unable to budge, he stands looking down at Kirkpatrick.

'Don't just stand there,' snaps Matt as he pushes past his dad and kneels next to the unconscious officer. Matt quickly takes off his jacket and pulls his t-shirt over his head. He tears it in half, folds the two into wide bandages that he presses firmly against Kirkpatrick's wounds.

'Is he alive,' asks Jesse.

'He has a bad gash on his head, a bruise and cut around his neck, but he's breathing. Hold these dressings snug, would you?' Jesse kneels next to Matt and puts pressure on the head wound. She stops short and lifts the covering to get a better look at the other wound.

'Just what I thought. This is no cut on his neck. It's a bite mark! A vampire bite, I bet.'

'Vampire?' mumbles Frank, staring down at the wounded officer.

'Dad, grab your rifle. We're going in.' Getting no response, he repeats, 'Dad, Dad! We need to go into the barracks and stop this guy before he gets to Donni.'

Again no reaction.

'Frank! Snap out of it,' shouts Jesse.

'Huh, what? No. No way. I'm not goin' in there after a vampire,' says Frank.

'Fine. Why does that not surprise me?'

'What? It's not that, son. It's just that someone should drive back into town and get help.'

'God damn it, Dad. We are the help.'

'I just thought it would be safer to...'

'Forget it! Take off your jacket and cover Tom before he goes into shock. Take over from Jesse and hold the bandages snug. And whatever you do, don't leave him. Understand?'

'Yeah, I got it,' answers Frank.

Matt puts his jacket back on and goes over to his backpack. Opening the main compartment, he pulls out a wooden stake. 'Jesse, I might need your help in there, but I understand if you say no.'

'I'm not going to pretend I'm not scared. But Donni needs us. Let's do this.'

'Okay, Haida girl. Let's go slay us a vampire,' answers Matt with a wink, trying to act a hell of a lot more self-assured than he feels. Matt walks towards the entrance.

'Wait, Matt. We should take the rifle,' suggests Jesse.

'Won't do us any good unless you happen to have a handful of wooden bullets in your jeans.'

'Right. 'Fraid not!'

'Wooden stake it is, then.'

Jesse follows Matt into building. Waiting for their eyes to adjust, they squint into the darkness for any sign of movement.

André

1980

André steps away from the podium and descends the stairs to the edge of the grandstand. He slips his gold medals over his head, grinning as he secures them in the front pocket of his backpack. He feels really good—first place in four of the seven lumberjack events. Sliding his treasured double-edged throwing ax through the side loop, he swings his pack over his broad shoulders and onto his back.

The competition was stiff this year with participants from as far east as New Brunswick, some even traveling up from Wyoming and Maine, south of the border. André had registered for most of the individual events, but he fell short of qualifying in competitions requiring finer balance and dexterity. André's main advantage is his incredible physical strength. The other lumberjacks are not in the same league. His natural strength gives him a decided advantage in power events, such as the Standing Block Chop and Underhand Chop events. With every mighty blow of his ax, wooden shrapnel explodes from the logs and sprays the crowd.

The Ax Throw is the event André is particularly proud of winning. The event requires more skill than strength, and although his chances were slim this year, hours spent practicing after school and on weekends paid off.

Leaving the grandstand, he slowly winds his way through the noisy crowd to the edge of the park. He sits down on a rust colored blanket of pine needles in the shelter of the tall cedars and even taller jack pines that border the exhibition grounds. He digs out an egg salad sandwich from his pack and contentedly enjoys his lunch in peace and quiet.

The solitude is broken by the low throaty rattle of a Raven perched on a branch above him. André looks up through the tangle of branches, but does not spot the bird. He shrugs his shoulders and returns to his meal. A dark streak in André's peripheral vision startles him, and his eyes track the movement into the thick underbrush of the trees. Peering deep into the dark web of willow branches, he tries to find trace of the bird. A rustling draws his attention. Expecting a raven, or maybe a grouse, he is surprised when his eyes pick out the shape of a boy. The boy's features become clear. André gasps, 'D-d-donni!'

André gets to his feet. 'Are you okay?'

The boy, now fully visible, stops. He stares at André for a moment, then turns and runs back into the forest.

'Wait! C-c-come back,' shouts André. Leaving his pack and lunch behind, he chases after the boy. 'W-w-where are you g-g-going? C-c-come back!'

André trips on a raised tree root. Barely able to stay on his feet, he crashes through the low-hanging branches like a bull moose in rut. Somehow he manages to keep up with Donni, but he is unable to close the gap. After a few minutes, André staggers out of the forest onto the beach. He drops to all fours on the wet sand, trying to catch his breath, all the while looking down the shoreline for the boy. Donni stands peacefully only a few meters away, looking down at André.

'D-d-donni. Everyone th-thinks your d-d-dead.'

Donni smiles and waves for André to get up and follow him.

'What? W-w-where're you taking me?' asks André as he stands, having regained his wind. Donni turns and begins to run along the beach towards the base of Look-Out Point.

'Donni, stop. C-c-come back. W-w-what is g-going on?' André stumbles after Donni to the end of the beach and stutters a swear in disgust as the boy, after waiting patiently for his big friend to catch up, cuts back into the trees. They jog along a beaten path that quickly changes into a steep climb. André, soaked with perspiration, manages to clamber and scramble up the path to the top of the ridge. Exhausted, he sits down on a moss-covered log and looks over his shoulder down at the cove below. He can't believe he just climbed the hill to Look-Out Point.

Wiping the pouring sweat from his forehead, he shakes his head in frustration. He looks at Donni standing by the road, as calm and rested as if he had just completed a leisurely stroll.

'D-d-donni, that's en-n-nough. You n-n-need to go home n-now,' pleads André. Donni shakes his head from side to side, points to the barracks across the street and runs off.

'Sh-shit,' stutters André again, even though his mom says it's a bad word, and he staggers after the boy. Donni crosses the road to the military site and quickly climbs over the gate. André, frustrated, unlatches the gate and swings it wide as Donni jogs down the road to the barracks. Following, André approaches the complex just in time to see the boy disappear around the corner of one of the buildings. As André comes around the building, he is startled by a black shape gliding past his head. By reflex he ducks, raising his hands in protection. When he looks up, a raven caws loudly from the top of a pine tree.

'André. What're you doing here?' asks Frank, surprised. Frank Taylor is seated on the ground next to the prone police chief.

'W-w-where's D-donni?' asks André.

'I think he might be in the building, but...'

André runs through the doorway and into the building before Frank can warn him. 'Hey! Wait! Don't go in there. Shit!'

Dawn

1980

'Look,' says Jesse, pointing towards the kitchen. A large flashlight on the floor dimly lights the corner of the room.

'Kirkpatrick's?'

'Prob'ly. Okay, stay close.'

The pair walk into the kitchen toward the flashlight, which goes out as Matt picks it up.

'Shit!'

He gives the bottom of the flashlight a tap. The light flickers, then emits a faint yellow light. 'I guess it'll do. Better than nothing.' He flashes the weak beam around the room.

'Where are you, you blood-sucking weasel. I know you're in here,' whispers Matt.

'Matt! There!' says Jesse, pointing at a small dark figure on the floor. Matt hurries over and flips the lifeless body on its back, lighting the boy's face with the flashlight.

'Donni! God, no!' cries Jesse. The boy's neck is all scabbed up and bloody from bites. 'Is he? Is he?'

'I'm sorry, Jess,' says Matt, looking up into Jesse's crying eyes.

'No, no. The poor little boy,' says Jesse, stepping backwards in disbelief. Her foot finding only empty air, Jesse screams as she disappears into the cellar.

'Jesse!' Matt chases down the cellar steps after her. 'Are you okay?'

'I don't know. I think so. I'm sore, though. I'm going to be really bruised in a few minutes,' says Jesse, lying flat on her back.

'Okay. Lie still. Don't move.'

'I think I'm okay, really. Just banged up my arm and leg pretty badly.'

'Thank God you didn't break your neck. That's quite the drop.'

Matt feels Jesse's head for cuts and bruises, and pats her body down for injuries.

'Hey, Whitey, watch where you put those hands,' says Jesse, sitting up. 'We're not on a date here!'

'Sorry,' answers Matt, blushing. 'I was just doing first aid.'

'Well, I'm okay. We can play doctor some other time.'

'Uh, I uh, sure—I guess,' mumbles Matt, embarrassed.

'What is this place?' asks Jesse.

"My guess is that the vampire kept Donni down here.'

'As a hostage?'

'No. I suspect as a host.'

'Host? Holy shit! Callaway, the librarian, was right. Celreau lives just around the corner. He must have kidnapped Donni and kept him locked up here in this cellar, using him as a host.'

'Yeah. That sure fits our theory, except Celreau is in custody at the police station. So obviously he didn't throw Kirkpatrick out the front door.'

Matt scans the room with the flashlight and spots a Kerosene lantern hanging from a rafter above a table. A box of matches rests on a table.

'A sec, let me get some light in here. Damn, it just doesn't add up—unless…'. He goes to the table, picks up the box and strikes a match. He lifts the glass to light the lantern, brightening the room with soft yellow light.

'Unless it wasn't Gabriel,' says a voice from the back of the room. Startled, Matt and Jesse look into the top corner of the room and see a figure hanging from the rafters. The vampire turns its head and looks backwards down at them.

'Dawn?' gasp the kids.

'Surprise!' says Dawn. 'I bet you never suspected the mayor's sweet daughter to be a vampire.'

'Actually, no, I'm not surprised. If anybody in town could fit the role of blood sucking vampire tramp, it'd be you,' answers Jesse.

'Who do you think you're talking to, you dirty little squaw?'

Anticipating trouble, Matt tightens his grip on the wooden stake.

'I'm talking to a sad little daddy's girl who spreads her legs for every desperate boy.'

Infuriated by Jesse's remarks, Dawn exposes her large bloody canines, leaps and lands immediately in front of Jesse. She slaps the native girl across the head, propelling her against the stone wall where she slumps unconscious.

'You Indian bitch. I am the Queen of Darkness! And you—you're nothing. Nothing more than my next meal.'

'Nooooo!' screams Matt. He raises the wooden stake and thrusts it at Dawn's chest. Dawn latches on to Matt's wrist, stopping the stake inches from her sternum.

'Stupid boy. Stupid, stupid boy,' chides Dawn. The vampire laughs and flicks the boy's arm, which emits a loud snap. Matt drops the stake, screaming in pain. His forearm, obviously broken, hangs at an odd angle.

'Awww. Does that hurt?' asks Dawn.

'Why are you doing this? Let me go. Please.' Matt begs between gritted teeth.

'Why? Well, I already had supper, and now I want a little fun. Would you like to have some fun with me?'

'Not if you were the last girl in Blood Cove.'

Dawn yanks Matt's arm, pulling him screaming in pain next to her.

'Matt, you know you want a piece of this.'

'No, thanks. Jesse is my girl.'

Dawn reaches down and grabs Matt's crotch. She leans over and whispers in his ear. 'Let me change your mind. You won't regret it.'

Matt pulls back and spits in Dawns face. 'Not in this lifetime, you skank!'

Dawn, angry now, wraps her hand around Matt's neck and squeezes. 'Look! We do this the easy way or the hard way—up to you.'

'What? You gonna rape me like you tried to do to André?' grunts Matt choking under her grasp.

'And here I thought you were brighter than that retard.'

'Fuck you!' snaps Matt. He drives his forehead hard into the vampire's nose. Dawn releases her grip on his arm dropping him backwards to the floor. Enraged by the assault, Dawn grimaces; her gums retract exposing her gleaming canines. Matt looks up in horror at the beast advancing towards him.

'I'm gonna rip you to pieces,' cries the vampire.

'Noooo!' shouts André as he hurls himself down from the top of the cellar stairs. Landing directly on Dawn, his heavy body slams her to the dirt floor hard. Matt scrambles backwards on all fours, grabs the wooden stake and slides to the back wall. He turns to find André with a choke hold on Dawn, squeezing her neck with his powerful arms.

'I hate you. Nobody hurts m-m-my friends!' the powerful giant stammers. Dawn stands, lifting André on her back still clinging to her neck.

'I will k-k-kill you, D-D-Dawn!' He reaches back to his pack for his ax with his free hand.

She reaches behind her head with one hand and grabs his jacket collar. 'I d-d-don't think so, you f-f-fucking retard!' imitates Dawn.

The vampire pulls his shirt upward and somersaults André over her head, slamming him on his back on the cellar floor. The big ax is knocked loose from his fist. Winded, André looks up with wide eyes at Dawn's foot descending to strike him directly in the face. His nose snaps and explodes in a spray of blood that covers his face and chest. Groaning in agony, he struggles to focus through the blood now draining into his eyes. Another quick blow from Dawn's shoe catches André square in the side of the head, fracturing his jaw. The excruciating pain overwhelms the big man and renders him unconscious.

'Push me down in the sand, eh? Guess this makes us even, retard!' Dawn looks over at Matt, evil twisting her grin. 'Now, where was I?'

Stepping over André, she advances on Matt, who stands against the wall, hand tightly gripping the cedar stake. He notices that Jesse, behind Dawn, has regain consciousness and is staring at him. With a slight head movement, he turns her eyes to the Kerosene lantern above the table. Rising slowly, quietly, she nods in understanding.

'Dawn, I changed my mind,' says Matt, stalling for time.

'Ha! Sorry. I'm no longer in the mood for having fun with you.'

'No, I mean I want much more than that.'

'More?'

'I mean, I want you to make me part of your world—the Underworld'

'What do you know of the Underworld?'

'I know that I want what you have. You are so powerful! And you'll be forever young, forever beautiful.'

'Too bad you didn't say that a minute ago, before you drove your head into my face.'

'I'm sorry. I was scared and I panicked.'

'It's too late for you and your lame excuses.'

'You're wrong, Dawn. I'm afraid it's too late for you!'

Jesse, now standing behind Dawn, brings the lantern crashing down on the vampire's head. Dawn's long hair and shirt get dowsed in pungent kerosene that ignites in a ball of flame.

'What the hell?' exclaims Dawn. Shaking her head violently, she pats at her hair, desperate to put out the flames.

Matt draws his good arm back behind his head, and with every ounce of strength he can muster, he drives the wooden stake deep into her chest. Dawn wraps her hands around the stake and screeches in pain. Her clothes are now totally engulfed in flames, the air reeking with the putrid odor of burning flesh. Still screaming, Dawn stumbles sideways and falls onto the mattress, twisting and turning in agony. The bed ignites. Flames and toxic black smoke rise to the ceiling.

'Jesse, wake André. We gotta get out of here now.'

Jesse shakes the big man's shoulders. André moans and grumbles, but doesn't come fully awake.

'Like this,' says Matt, squeezing André's cheek between his thumb and index finger. André sits up, yelping in pain.

'Where'd you learn that trick?' asks Dawn.

'Emergency First Aid course,' answers Matt with a wink.

'C'mon André. No time to lose.' André gets to his feet, and the threesome turn toward the stairs.

'Matt! Help!' screams Jesse.

The vampire's torched body is lying half off the bed, one charred hand tightly gripping Jesse's ankle. Before Matt has time to react, André's ax catapults past him to catch the vampire in the throat, slicing her flaming head clean off her shoulders.

'B-b-bullseye! Yes!' cheers André, pumping his fisted right arm above his head.

'Holy crap,' says Jesse. She pulls her leg free from the decapitated vampire's fist.

'Let's go. Run, run!' commands Matt. The three clamber up the stairs into the kitchen as tall flames and black toxic smoke climb the walls behind them. 'Stay low. This way, hurry!'

Jesse stops and kneels next to Donni's body. 'Matt. What about Donni?'

'No time. We've got to get out of here. Move!'

'We can't just leave him here to burn,' says Jesse, coughing and rubbing at her eyes.

'Donni is gone. We have to go!'

'No. I'm not leaving him here!' Jesse shouts through the heavy smoke.

'S-s-sorry,' says André. Bending, he lifts Jesse off the floor and cradles her in his powerful arms.

'Hey! No, don't,' cries Jesse, struggling against André's grip. They exit the building through the main door. André puts Jesse on her feet, and bruised and battered, the three move away from the building, where they are joined by Frank and Kirkpatrick. Standing clear, they stare in shock at the inferno that is engulfing the abandoned structure. The flames already lick the air high above the roof.

'Jesse, you okay?' asks Matt.

'Yeah. I'm just bummed about Donni. We shouldn't have left him in there.'

Matt steps over and hugs Jesse. 'I agree, but we just didn't have time.'

'Matt, how could we have been so wrong about Celreau? I was sure he was the vampire. We almost had an innocent man convicted.'

'Don't beat yourself up about it. I thought the same thing, and here it was our dearest Dawn all along. But hey, it's over now. How about you walk back to the Sergeant's Jeep and radio for help?' Jesse nods and heads down the trail to the main road as he turns to André.

'Come, let me take a look at your head. You may have a concussion.'

'Sergeant, please sit down,' suggests Matt. 'I'm pretty sure you do have a concussion.'

'I'm fine, young man. I'm just a bit dizzy.'

'And feeling nauseous, right?'

'Well, yes. How did you know?'

'Common symptoms of concussion. On top of that, the clear fluid running from your left ear is a definite indication that it's serious. Sit down, please, before you fall down.'

Kirkpatrick reaches for and feels the fluid running down his cheek.

'Dad, help him get comfortable.'

'Yes, sir. I mean, yes son,' answers Frank. Then sheepishly, 'Son?'

'Yes, Dad?'

'I, ah, I…well, I just wanted to tell you I'm sorry. It took a lot of balls for you to go into that building. More courage than I could ever muster. And the way you're taking care of the Sergeant and, well, everyone else. I am impressed.'

'I am just doing what I can to help.'

'No, no. Don't underestimate yourself, Matt. God knows I've spent most of your young life underestimating you. Damn it, I am proud of you and I intend to do my darnedest to appreciate you from now on.'

'Thanks, Dad. I know your life hasn't been a bowl of cherries either, but I know Mom would want us to carry on and be happy.'

'Your mother is the only woman I ever loved, you know. Why did she have to leave?'

'Mom's cancer was terminal, Dad. She didn't give up, she loved you just as much and didn't want the person she loved more than life itself to spend a year watching her deteriorate to skin and bones. Let her go, Dad. Mom needs to know that you forgive her so she can be at peace.'

'I forgive her, I do,' says Frank, holding back tears. 'I just miss her so much.'

Matt puts his arms around his father for the first time in what seems like years. They are hugging as the fire truck pulls up to the site.

Jesse

1980

Jesse climbs over the fence and runs to the patrol Jeep. Opening the door, she reaches in for the radio microphone.

'Corporal Fontaine, this is Jesse. Are you there? Hello? Hello? Anyone there?'

'Go ahead,' answers the Corporal.

'Send help quickly. We need an ambulance. The Sergeant is hurt—badly.'

'Okay, Jesse. I'll send an ambulance right away. What happened?' answers the Corporal.

'I can't talk right now, and you wouldn't believe me anyway. Just send the ambulance. Oh! And the place is on fire, so call the fire department, too. I gotta get back to Matt. He needs my help.'

She drops the handset and steps out of the car. She is startled by a silhouette leaning against the fence, darker black on black in the darkness, and she has to muffle a scream.

'Shit, you scared me. What do you want, Ne-kilst-lass? Or is it Uncle Bill tonight?'

'Well, and a Good Evening to you, too.'

'You promised to help us find Donni!'

'I did. You found the boy did you not?'

'Donni is dead! Thanks a lot.'

'We don't always get what we want in life, sweetheart, but sometimes we get what we need.'

'What the hell is that supposed to mean? I'm tired of you and your stupid riddles.'

'It means that Donni died so that many others could live.'

'It's not fair. He was just a little boy.'

'For the most part, neither life nor death is fair, but sometimes justice is served, and spiritual balance is restored. Prayer and a little outside help certainly don't hurt.'

'I don't understand.'

'The boy sacrificed his life so you could live, and you risked your life to kill the vampire.'

'You set us up!'

'You asked me for help. Remember?'

Jesse grimaces, disgusted. 'You never cared about Donni. Dawn was a threat to you and your netherworld, and you used us to do your dirty work. You bastard. I hate you!'

'I understand how you feel, Jesse, but what you did tonight was courageous, and I will always be grateful for your bravery. I will always protect my Haida people from the threat of evil, as I have from the beginning. But know that you are now in my favor. You may call me whenever you need help.'

Jesse turns away from the old trapper, towards the flashing lights and the blaring of the sirens of the emergency vehicles coming up the road. 'Thanks, but you'll understand if I pass.' Jesse, turns back to find herself alone. 'Huh? Where'd he go?'

Trottier
1980

'Hey, Kojack, you just drove past the station,' says Celreau from the back seat of the Jeep.

Fontaine ignores Celreau and continues down Main Street past the General store and the hospital. The police radio squawks and Jesse's somewhat distorted voice comes from the speaker.

'Corporal Fontaine, this is Jesse. Are you there? Hello? Hello? Anyone there?'

'Go ahead,' answers the Corporal.

'Send help quickly. We need an ambulance. The Sergeant is hurt—badly.'

'Okay, Jesse. I'll send an ambulance right away. What happened?' answers the Corporal.

'I can't talk right now, and you wouldn't believe me anyway. Just send the ambulance. Oh! And the place is on fire, so call the fire department, too. I gotta get back to Matt. He needs my help.'

The radio goes quiet, and the Corporal shows no signs of turning the Jeep around.

'Hey, Columbo! Where the hell you going? Didn't you hear? There's an emergency? Shouldn't you be going back up to the barracks to help Kirkpatrick?'

Fontaine steers the Jeep across Spirit River bridge, rolls through the stop sign and turns right towards the Kodiak Lumber Mill.'

Speeding through the vacant parking lot, the Jeep continues around the huge main mill and comes to a stop at the side entrance. A lone spotlight illuminates the empty lane. Fontaine gets out of the Jeep and opens the back door.

'Get out!' orders Fontaine.

'What? Here? Are we picking up wood scraps for the sweat lodge or something?

'Shut your hole and get out. Now!' shouts Fontaine pulling his revolver from its holster and pointing it directly at Celreau's head.

'Whoa! Easy. I'm out, already,' says Celreau, sliding his bum along the back seat and out of the Jeep.

Fontaine grabs Celreau by the jacket and pulls him to the side door of the mill. He points the revolver at the door padlock and fires. The shattered lock falls off the door. Swinging the door wide, Fontaine pulls Celreau inside. He leads Celreau through the darkness around several piles of neatly stacked plywood, around a pile of sawdust to a huge saw blade.

'Impressive!' says Celreau. 'You sure know your way around, and in total darkness yet. You must work here to get around the place without a hint of light.'

'Shut it!' commands Fontaine.

'Planning on putting in a couple or three hours overtime, Corporal? They start you off at minimum wage at the police station? I know times are tough but...'

'I said, shut-up, gypsy-pig-dog!' screams Fontaine, slapping Celreau across the face with his revolver. Celreau drops to the floor and stares back up to Fontaine, a look of total surprise on his face.

'Gypsy-pig-dog? Only one other fool ever called me that!'

'She loved me. She was my soul mate.'

'Pierre? Pierre Trottier?'

'She was my reason to carry on, my candle of light in this endless God-forsaken hell.'

'Have you been tracking me all these years? You're the one? And for what? Over a woman? Man, you must have one sad and sorry life.'

'Awrrrr!' growls Trottier, leaping through the air and landing feet-first on Celreau's chest. The vast chamber is filled with the sickening sound of ribs snapping like several giants cracking their knuckles. Celreau screams, the pain excruciating.

'You—you destroyed the only joy of my dreadful, cursed existence. You left me with nothing. Nothing but an eternity of misery. I swore I would find you and wreak my revenge. Oh, I came so close so many times. You are a shrewd one, my friend, but now—now you are mine.'

Already Celreau's fractured ribs have almost completely healed, flooding his torso with the ambrosia of relief.

'I told you then and tell you again—Tati didn't love either of us. She doesn't love anyone but herself. She's nothing but a heartless vampire tramp!'

Celreau abruptly rolls to his left, throwing the off-balance Trottier to the floor. With a quick flick of his powerful arms, he snaps the handcuffs like they're a child's toy. He reaches, grabbing Trottier by the ankle. Jumping to his feet, he lifts his enemy off the floor and windmills him above his head like a rag-doll. He releases his grip, catapulting Trottier through the darkness to strike and snap through a main building support beam. Part of the high ceiling collapses, burying Trottier in a jumble of heavy planks and trusses. Celreau waits for the dust to clear, then walks over to the rubble. Not seeing any movement nor any sign of Trottier in the pile of broken timber, he becomes suspicious.

Before he can act on his suspicion, the pile of debris explodes; boards and wood splinters fly in all directions. Once again, Celreau finds himself knocked to the floor.

Trottier stands, pointing down at Celreau.

'Imbecile. D'you think you can out-muscle me? Don't you understand? I am twice the vampire you'll ever be. I've been on this planet much too long to be defeated by a weak, pathetic Gypsy-rat like you.'

Springing to his feet, Gabriel backs away. Circling the five-foot-diameter mill saw behind him, he edges toward the end of a conveyor positioned in the middle of the huge chamber.

'If you are such a superior specimen, Pierre, why did your woman choose me over you?'

'You drugged Tati and placed a curse on her. You hypnotized her with one of your Gypsy spells,' answers Trottier, following Gabriel step for step around the saw.

'Pierre, Pierre, Pierre. Listen to yourself. Who is the pathetic one here? Who is the jilted lover?'

'Shut up! You deceived her into…'

'Sadly, the only person deceived, my ageless friend, was you. Deceived by a heartless wench who used you, then tossed you out like a dirty rag,' taunts Gabriel, continuing his retreat around a stack of plywood.

Trottier jumps up onto the plywood pile. 'Tati loved me. She would never have left me if it weren't for you.'

'Sooner or later, she'd have dumped your sorry ass for another clueless victim.'

Gabriel, now backed against the building wall, leaps straight up to land on his feet on a cross beam high above the mill floor.

'Never!' yells Trottier, looking up at Celreau.

'Hey, don't take it so hard. After all, she broke my heart and left me for a woman.'

'I'm not interested in your bullshit, Celreau. I swore I would find you and make you pay.'

Trottier climbs the mill wall like a spider on its web advancing to take its prey. 'You ran then as you run now—like the coward you are. You thought you could outsmart me, but I knew it was just a matter of time before I tracked you down.'

'Congratulations, you found me; but hey, guess what, Sherlock. That won't get Tati back.'

'No. No, I guess it won't, but today—today, I get my revenge. They say revenge is sweet, and this is going to be absolutely saccharine,' answers Trottier, stepping out onto the same beam only a few meters from Celreau.

'Listen, Trottier. I have no quarrel with you. You don't want this—I don't want this. I promise if you continue, it won't end well for you. Leave now and nobody gets hurt. And no one is the wiser.'

Trottier's facial expression changes; his brow expands, his pupils turn black and his fangs descend from his gums.

'May god damn you, then, Frenchman!' curses Celreau transforming himself as well.

The pair leap at each other, colliding in midair, fangs and claws exposed. They tumble through the air, biting and clawing at each other. Holding Trottier fast against his chest, Celreau hits the floor first, his skull snapping back and viciously rapping the angle iron brace securing the giant saw. Extreme pain lightnings through his body, momentarily stunning him. He is incapacitated only seconds as his skull fractures begin to heal, and soothing relief floods his being. He opens his eyes to find Trottier standing over him holding a fire-ax high over his shoulder, his crazed eyes staring at Celreau's exposed throat.

As the ax descends, Celreau shifts to the right, and the blade buries itself in the floor beam millimeters from Celreau's neck. In a continuous motion, he grabs Trottier by the throat and pulls him down face-to-face, as he plants a foot in the Frenchman's groin and catapults him into the air over his head. He leaps to his feet spinning to face his opponent in time to see Trottier's body bent backwards, almost double, against a four-by-four crossbeam near the ceiling. Trottier plummets to the floor, followed by an eight-foot length of the beam. Celreau gapes unbelieving as the beam descends like a spear, its jagged end piercing Trottier's chest and pinning him to the floor.

A loud 'CAW!' echoes from overhead, and Celreau looks up to see the Raven perched on the end of the broken beam looking down on Gabriel. Stretching its wings wide, it launches itself into the night through an open vent in the roof.

Celreau walks over to the electrical panel on the wall near the saw and slams the breaker arm up. The big saw blade screams to life and begins to spin with a high-pitched whine. He matter-of-factly approaches Trottier, pulls the timber from the vampire's chest cavity and tosses it aside. Wasting no time now that the 'stake' has been removed, he drags the limp body over to the saw. Laying the corpse on the conveyor head towards the saw, he manually pushes it through the blade. The splash guard prevents the fine mare's tail spray of blood from staining the walls and roof of the old Kodiak mill. The halves flop off either side of the conveyor, spilling entrails, organs, bone and tissue on the floor.

Vapor billows from the split body cavity, rising into the cool air. The disgusting stink of partially digested food, bile and shit assaults Gabriel's senses. He closes his eyes and takes a deep breath of the offensive odor. A smile of ecstasy crosses his face, as though he has just experienced the delicate bouquet of a fine wine. Opening his eyes, he breathes a gentle sigh, turns from the mutilated corpse and heads for the door.

'What a shame. All this over a damned woman!'

Outside, Celreau takes an old, partly overgrown trail to the bank of the Spirit River near where it enters the inlet. Through cupped hands, he raises a loud, eerie howl that carries for miles. After a few minutes, he repeats the howl. From a distance, barely audible, the howl is returned. Over the next few minutes, he exchanges howls with the pack of timber wolves, theirs growing stronger as they approach. Abruptly the pack break from the trees and come running along the gravel shore towards him. Snarling and growling, they surround him, pacing in excitement.

Celreau turns, the hungry pack close at his heels, and races back along the trail to the mill entrance. The wolves immediately catch the smell of blood, impatiently waiting as he opens the door. They tear past Celreau, giving themselves up to the feeding frenzy. Celreau watches as the crazed pack jumps up and over the stacked plywood, sniffs around the sawdust piles, finally tracking the scent to the fresh kill. In a tornado of grinding jaws and gnashing teeth, they tear indiscriminately at Trottier's fragmented remains.

Snarling and growling, a few of the wolves viciously tear his flesh from the bones while others rip organs from his abdomen, gobbling them down whole. The weaker of the pack, unable to safely approach the abdomen without being hurt by the alpha male, settle for devouring the entrails and lapping the bodily fluids from the mill floor, the splash guard and other bloodied machinery. Gaining courage, they soon reach for the less favored extremities, chewing at the corpse's nose, ears and toes. The tender morsels are quickly devoured and the brood attack the skeletal remains, dragging the bones past Celreau and out the door. They disappear into the woods scant minutes after their arrival, leaving no evidence of the evening's foul play.

Matt & Jesse
1980

Big Mama stands pensively at the kitchen counter and pours Carnation evaporated milk into her instant coffee. She measures a heaping spoonful of sugar into her cup and stirs the sweet mixture till it turns a caramel color. Jesse and Matt sit quietly at the kitchen table sipping hot chocolate. Matt is drinking with his left hand, his right arm encased in a cast from wrist to elbow and secured to his abdomen by a sling.

'Jesse told me your dad is getting better,' says Big Mama.

'I thought so, too, till he got home last night and downed half a forty-ouncer of whiskey before bed.'

'Well, you know, he won't break the habit overnight.'

'I guess not.'

'What is important, Matt, is that you break the cycle and stay clear of alcohol. You must make sure your children don't experience the lifestyle you endured with your father.'

'I wouldn't wish that shit on anyone. I don't plan on wasting my life on booze. Don't worry.'

'I believe you. I can only hope you are strong enough to resist the temptation. It's a terrible habit to break once you get caught in its grip.'

'Thanks, Big Mama. I won't let it happen. I promise.'

'I can't believe Donni is gone,' says Jesse. 'I wish I could wake up to find this has all just been a bad dream.'

The room goes quiet for a time. Eventually, Big Mama breaks the silence.

'I'm terribly sorry about Donni, dear, but at least you know he didn't suffer in the fire. If it's any consolation, remember—it's our belief that Donni's soul was transported by canoe to the Land of the Souls to await reincarnation.'

'I guess. I can't stop thinking about how scared Donni must have been with Dawn taking his blood like that,' answers Jesse, wiping a tear.

'The poor boy must've been terrified. Who would ever have suspected a vampire in Blood Cove? Dawn Brady, of all people.'

'She was no saint, but I never figured she was that evil,' adds Matt. 'She totally fooled me.'

'All the clues pointed to Mr. Celreau. Boy, were we wrong,' says Jesse, shaking her head.

'Are you sure about that?' asks Big Mama.

Jesse and Matt look at each other quizzically, then turn back to Big Mama.

'Huh? Yes, of course, Mom. Obviously, Dawn was the vampire. Why do you ask?'

'Two reasons, really. First, Dawn goes to school with you. You've seen her outdoors, fully exposed to the sun, almost every day for years? How could she be the vampire holding Donni captive these last couple of weeks?'

'Oh, man,' exclaims Matt as Jesse shouts, 'Holy crap, Mom. You're right.' The kids look at each other, bewilderment returning to their faces.

'Second,' continues Big Mama, 'a new RCMP constable arrived in town yesterday.'

'What's strange about that? Someone has to replace Kirkpatrick till he gets out of hospital and while he recuperates,' offers Matt.

'Of course, but the new constable's name is Fontaine. He claims he's the officer assigned here in response to the request for assistance Kirkpatrick submitted last week. Apparently he was delayed by another case in Fort St. John before being able to come help with Donni's case.'

'Huh? I don't get it? So who the heck is the guy already here?'

'The new Fontaine claims the man passing himself off as him is an impostor. No one has any idea where he came from or why he was here impersonating an RCMP corporal. But the strangest thing is that the impostor and Celreau have both gone missing. It's almost like they vanished into thin air.'

'What? Celreau and the first Fontaine are both gone?' questions Jesse.

'Yes. Last time they were seen together was getting into the Jeep at the barracks. They never arrived at the station.'

'What the heck? Could they have been working together?' suggests Jesse. 'And if they weren't, could one of them have killed the other, then fled?'

'I really don't know, guys, but I have my suspicions. The police Jeep was found abandoned at the mill, keys still in the ignition. And the interior of the mill had sustained some major structural damage, damage far beyond the physical capability of human beings.'

'What are you suggesting?' asks Matt.

Big Mama raises her eyebrows and shrugs her shoulders? 'I don't have all the pieces to the puzzle, but you said it yourself—all the clues lead to...'

Before she can finish, the doorbell chimes.

'Mom?' prompts Jesse.

'I'd better see who it is,' says Big Mama.

As she exits the kitchen, Matt asks Jesse, 'What do you think she meant by that?'

As Jesse shrugs her shoulders, Big Mama walks back into the kitchen holding an envelope. 'This is for you, Jesse. The courier said it was from the library.'

'Callaway,' they exclaim simultaneously.

'Callaway? Melville Callaway, the librarian?' asks Big Mama. 'What on earth would he be sending you by courier?'

'Shit! I forgot all about this, Matt,' says Jesse, taking the envelope from her mother.

'What are you waiting for? Open it, open it,' urges Matt.

Jesse rips the manila envelope open and out slides a letter and a smaller envelope. She flips the smaller envelope front to back looking for some indication of its contents or origins, but it is bare. She turns to the letter and begins to read.

'Okay. Enough with the suspense. What's this all about?' asks Big Mama.

'At first we figured Celreau was the vampire, so we did some checking into his past. None of it made sense. Way too many things didn't add up.'

'What do you mean?'

'Well, for example, we searched the library for info on Celreau's school records, but couldn't find any.'

'That's not unusual. Those records would not be available to the public from the library.'

'Right, so we told Mr. Callaway about Celreau's strange behavior, and he said he has been suspicious of our teacher. Something about the circumstances of Celreau's arrival and hiring just seemed weird to the librarian. He phoned an old friend who teaches at the University of Toronto to try to clear things up. Mr. Callaway said he would send the info over as soon as he received it. This is it, I'm sure.'

'It may just be some sort of clerical error or some such mix-up,' suggests Big Mama. 'These sorts of bureaucratic foul-ups happen more often than institutions like to admit.'

'This is strange,' says Jesse, looking at the letter from under a wrinkled brow. 'According to Callaway's friend, Dan Hathaway, the archive records indicate that Celreau was transferred from Laval University in Quebec. He goes on to say that he could not find any record of a Celreau registered at Laval, but he has included five photos of the history department, one for each of the last five years before Celreau arrived in Toronto.'

'They must be in the small envelope. Open it, Jesse.'

Slitting the sealed tab with a fingernail, she slides the old photos out of the envelope. Matt looks over her shoulder as she shuffles through them. Each has a caption listing the people depicted in the photograph.

'Hathaway is right. Celreau's name is not on any of these,' says Jesse.

'Wait a minute. Look! There! Fourth from the right in the third row. That's him. That's Celreau,' exclaims Matt, excitedly pointing at the picture. 'But his name is listed as Jean-Francois Fortier. What gives?'

'Holy crap, you're right! That is him! Look. He's in every shot and doesn't look any older from the first year to the last. How's that possible?'

'Jesse. He doesn't look a day younger than yesterday, either!'

Jesse is obviously puzzled and her gaze seems to turn inward as she begins to calculate. 'If he is twenty-eight today and spent seven years teaching in Toronto, and another five in Quebec, that means he would have joined the faculty at Laval at the age of...?'

'Sixteen,' states Matt, with a note of triumph. 'Not only that, he would have spent another six years getting his PHD, which means he'd have started graduate studies at the ripe old age of ten.'

'Okay, kids, this brings us back to our discussion before the package arrived. I've been as suspicious of Celreau as Mr. Callaway for quite some time. I didn't want to say anything until I was absolutely sure,' says Big Mama.

'Sure of what, Mom?' asks Jesse.

'The fact is, Celreau looks exactly the same today as he will next year and as he did possibly a hundred years ago or more. He doesn't age.'

'Are you saying we were right all along, Big Mama?' demands Matt.

'Yes. You got it right the first time. Think about it. Dawn could not become a vampire without being bitten and infected by another vampire. Celreau is your…'

'Vampire,' finish Matt and Jesse together.

Celreau
1980

The Greyhound pulls to the gravel shoulder of the road after passing Celreau. A loud squeal accompanies a blast of air brakes, and the bus draws to a stop a good twenty yards up the road. Gabriel jogs up to the door of the bus, which folds in half along its hinges and slides open with a bang.

'I almost drove by you, mister. I just caught your wave at the last second,' shouts the driver.

'I appreciate the effort. Sorry. I was late and couldn't make it to the depot on time,' explains Celreau.

'Well, it's your lucky day. I rarely stop along the road for passengers. It's actually against company policy, but seeing as technically we're not on the highway yet, and there's no traffic in sight at this time of night—what the heck. Climb aboard.'

'Thanks.'

'What happened to your shirt? You look like you just wrestled a bobcat,' asks the driver. 'You're not in any kind of trouble are you?'

'Ah, yeah! I mean, no, I'm not in trouble, and yeah, my shirt's a mess.

The boys gave me a farewell party at the pub and got a little carried away.'

'With friends like that, who needs enemies, eh?' says the driver chuckling.

'Yeah, exactly.'

'What's your destination?'

'Edmonton.'

'Not on this bus. I'll take you only as far as Prince George. You'll have to transfer at the bus depot there. Unit 54 will take you to Grande Prairie and on to Edmonton.'

'Okay, sounds great. Thanks'

'The fare to Prince George is twenty-five dollars.'

Celreau fumbles through his pockets and takes out a twenty and three two dollar bills. He hands the cash to the driver.

'It's okay. Keep the change. Buy yourself a coffee at the next rest stop.'

'The coffee's free for the drivers, but I'll enjoy a muffin. Thanks.'

'You're welcome. My pleasure. Least I can do. After all, you didn't have to stop, right?'

'No bags?' asks the driver.

'No. I left my belongings at the apartment in town. My wife's picking me up in Edmonton. I'll be heading back to Blood Cove in a couple of weeks.'

'I see. Well, take a seat and enjoy the ride.'

Celreau looks down the aisle at a busload of passengers, many of whom are peeking over and around seats, perturbed perhaps, trying to get a glimpse of the stranger who has delayed their journey. He lurches as the bus pulls back onto the asphalt.

A couple of seats at the back are vacant. The bus slows almost to a stop, then makes a quick right turn onto the highway. Celreau, braced this time, continues nonchalantly to the back. Dropping onto the seat, he slides over next to the window and opens the neck of his jacket. He slouches a little, sighs and leans to rest his forehead on the cool window.

He stares into the night. The shadows of power poles streaming by look like sentries posted to guard the Yellowhead Highway. His mind wonders, dream-like, to centuries past, to the only time in his life he experienced real joy, to the only person he has ever been able to truly trust and love without fault or conditions—Angela.

'Leaving without saying goodbye?' asks a nearby voice.

Jerked from his thoughts, Celreau looks at the old trapper sitting next to him and frowns.

'Where the hell did you come from?'

'I warned you about touching my people. Now you pay the price for not heeding my warning.'

'What are you talking about, you old fool?'

'Didn't we have an agreement? When you first arrived in the Cove, we agreed that you would not involve my people.'

'Ah. Ne-kilst-lass. You had me fooled for a minute. I've never seen you without feathers. Anyway, what do you want?'

'Time to pay the price.'

'What price? I got away Scot-free.'

'Did you, now?'

'Yes. It's over. Everybody believes the Brady girl was responsible for the Métis boy's death, and as a bonus, Kirkpatrick thinks she murdered the teacher, as well. The fire destroyed any evidence of my involvement, and I get to walk away unsuspected, to carry on another day.' A brief, humorless chuckle escapes Celreau's lips. 'You're such a fool.'

'D'you hear yourself, Gabriel?'

'Gabriel? Hey, how'd you…?'

'You're wrong, you old bloodsucker. Dead wrong, if you'll pardon the pun. You don't get to carry on another day. No, Gabriel. The truth is, you get to carry on for eternity.'

'So, your point is that I get to live forever? And this is a punishment how?'

'Don't you see, Gabriel? You're the fool.'

'How's that?'

'Only a fool would destroy the only thing in his life he ever loved. Now you are free to carry on for eternity. You get to spend eternity dealing with your memories of killing your first love, Angela'

'Why, you…keep Angela out of this!'

'Imagine! An eternity of guilt and shame for slaying the only woman you ever loved—literally sucking the lifeblood from her body. You won't ever, ever see your lovely Angela again. So I ask you, who is the fool?'

'It was an accident, and you know it! I never meant to hurt her. I just lost control. That doesn't make me a fool!'

'Bull shit! Make as many excuses as you want and deny the reality, but you are still a fool for killing Angela. Your lack of control rests solely on your shoulders. And more than that, you are an even bigger coward for running from the solution to your anguish.'

'I'm no coward. I'm not afraid of you. I stood up to you and beat you at your own game of tricks and riddles. I outwitted you, and now you're sore 'cause I won.'

'The battle with me is not the one you need to win, my misguided and cowardly friend. I'm not the one you fear or run from.'

'Yet another riddle, Yáahl, really?'

'No riddle here, Gabriel. Clearly you know what you fear the most; what you have been running from so many, many years.'

'No, I don't, but I'm sure you are going to tell me.'

'See? A coward! And, coward that you are, you refuse to face and admit your weaknesses, and put an end your pain and suffering.'

'I have no weakness. I am immortal.'

'You fool. That's exactly where you're wrong. Your eternal life has cursed you with an eternity of guilt and shame for the murder of your first love. What value lies in such a gift?'

'I told you it was an accident. It wasn't my fault. I…I lost control…I couldn't stop myself. It was an accident, damn you!'

'Accident? You sank your teeth into innocent young Angela, enjoyed every sweet drop of blood, then left her naked corpse behind to rot. Some accident. You wouldn't feel so guilty if you truly believed her death was an accident.'

'I didn't mean to…'

'Denial, excuses and centuries of whining and feeling sorry for yourself.'

'Shut-up! You don't know! You're not imprisoned by this bloody curse. I am! I have to suffer under the burden of those memories.'

'Again, the coward! You know damned well you can end your misery. All you need do is kill yourself.'

'I told you, I cannot die again. I am cursed to wander here for eternity. Don't you get it?'

'What I get is that you knew, the day you tied Petru to that tree and watched him burn, that sunlight is your salvation, but you don't have the balls, do you? You don't have the courage to do it. You're a coward, feeding on your own despair. Pathetic!'

'What do you want from me?' Gabriel turns in shame to look out the window.

'Oh, I don't want anything from you, Gabriel, but here's something I'm sure you want from me. Farewell and sweet memories.'

Gabriel is startled by a shadow flying past his window. He turns to see the seat beside him is empty. Angela's heart pendant rests gleaming on the worn cushion. Picking it up, he holds it tight to his chest. Ashamed and defeated, he curls into a ball and whimpers like a child.

Trottier

1980

Slightly overweight and disheveled, the burly man slouches back in his big chair. He peers over his half-lensed reading glasses across his desk at the nervous young man.

'So, why the sudden interest in the University of Seattle? Seems like a pretty drastic move, considering your previous positions.'

Visibly mustering his confidence, the applicant straightens his posture and leans forward. 'As I indicated on the application before you, Director Carlson, I suffer from a rare skin disease called Cutaneous Porphyria. The symptoms include burning blisters and swelling of the skin when exposed to the sun or any intense light. The long sunny days in Canada were beginning to take a toll on my health, making my time there intolerable. Seattle's overcast coastal weather is much more suitable. I would have the freedom to move around outdoors more often. My research into your institution revealed that U of S has an outstanding academic record and a reputation for accommodating handicapped and special-needs students and professors.'

'Well, you have done your homework. I can only imagine the difficulty of coping with such a restrictive affliction—we prefer not to use the term 'handicap'. Is there much pain associated with these symptoms?'

'Yes, The pain can be excruciating.'

'I can certainly understand why you might want to acquire a position on our teaching staff. The weather here for large parts of the year can be downright gloomy.'

'Gloomy suits me just fine, sir.'

'Well, I must say, young man, your academic credentials are remarkable.'

'Thank you, sir. I have been fortunate to study and work with the best.'

'Indeed! To have already taught at two prestigious Canadian campuses—Laval and the University of Toronto—at such a young age is also quite impressive. The enclosed reference letter from Dean Fortier certainly attests to the high regard in which your former superiors hold you.'

Glancing up from the letter, Carlson continues, 'As Director of Faculty, hiring new academic staff is solely at my discretion, and I have heard enough. I am quite thrilled to welcome you to the team, Dr. Trottier.'

'It's an honor, sir,' replies Celreau, 'but please call me Pierre.'

Raymond J. Belcourt

Raymond (R.J.) Belcourt was raised in Blezard Valley, a village nestled in the boreal region of northern Ontario. He spent his youth hunting, fishing and trapping around the Sudbury area. His great appreciation of the wilderness and his eye for landscape and natural form both have their origins in his many early adventures in the forest.

In the early 1980s he moved to western Canada to work on the oil rigs. After 40 years in the industry, He re-visited his artistic roots and developed skills as an amateur photographer, capturing unique perspectives of the prairies. Ray also enjoys writing short stories about past life experiences. He reunited with an old friend, Iggy Fay, who encouraged him to share his talents and passion with the public. Together they have published several short stories in magazines and also several books: *Haiga Moments, Artscapes/Pays-Arts Canada* and their latest, *Blood Cove–A Novel.*

Ray lives in Leduc, Alberta with his beautiful wife, Cami. He has four wonderful children, Jasmine, Devon, Rose and Luana.

Ignatius Fay, Ph.D.

Ignatius was born in Levack, a small mining town just northwest of Sudbury in northern Ontario. Born with lung, heart, digestive and immune system abnormalities, he developed several lung diseases in early childhood and has been chronically ill all his life.

He dropped out of university in his second year to buy a franchise in a local pizza chain, eventually owning three. At twenty-five, he realized that his first ambition was his true calling, and he returned to university. He was awarded his Ph.D. in Invertebrate Paleontology in 1983, at the age of 33. By that time he had been married for ten years and had two daughters. He became the first Invertebrate Paleontologist of the Royal Tyrrell Museum of Paleontology in Drumheller, Alberta during its design and building stage. By 1986, his health had deteriorated significantly; he had a lung removed and was told he'd never see the age of forty. And his marriage was over.

Ignatius is nothing if not determined. He dedicated his life to staying alive. At publication of this novel, he is sixty-nine. On twenty-four-hour oxygen therapy, he raised two happy and successful daughters, Kathryn and Danielle, taught himself computer graphics, and became a well-published and award-winning haiku/tanka poet.

Along the way, Ignatius reconnected with Ray Belcourt, whom he had given his first job as a teenager. Their friendship, always solid, has grown to be a mainstay in each of their lives. They have collaborated in a number of literary endeavors (see page 475), the latest of which you hold in your hands.

Ignatius still lives, alone, in Sudbury.

Previous Publications

R.J. Belcourt and I. Fay, co-authors
Blood Cove – A Novel (2019)

R.J. Belcourt and I. Fay, collaboration
Haiga Moments (2008)
Artscapes Canada Pays-Art (2012)

R.J. Belcourt, Author
I. Fay, Editor
Artscapes/Pays-Arts Canada feature
Our Canada Magazine, Dec/Jan 2019
The Raven
More of Our Canada Magazine, Dec/2019
Bear Bells
Canadian Stories Magazine, Dec/Jan 2019
Enough
Canadian Stories Magazine, June/July 2019
Fall From Grace
Montreal Writes Literary Magazine, Oct/2019

I. Fay, author
Points In Between (2011)
Farther Along The Route (2013)
Breccia (2012) (poetry, with Irene Golas)

CPSIA information can be obtained
at www.ICGtesting.com
Printed in the USA
LVHW022006240120
644726LV00012B/1308